Reviews

"The Rescues"

"*The Rescues* brings the series full circle, returning to Harmony Hills with a story that hums with quiet strength. Ripley Capilano's chance arrival at the ranch and her bond with a traumatized horse set the stage for one of the series' most emotionally nuanced romances. Her relationship with the guarded and steadfast Ty Stanton unfolds with slow-burning depth. Their journey from cautious strangers to soul-deep partners mirrors the horse's recovery—pain yielding to trust, and fear to faith." ~ **Prairies Book Review**

"*The Rescues* is a heartfelt exploration of love found through healing rather than perfection. As Ripley helps restore a traumatized horse's trust, she and Ty slowly confront their own fears and past wounds. Standridge's writing is immersive and compassionate, blending emotional growth and quiet romance into a cozy yet powerful story about learning to begin again." ~ **NewInBooks.com Review**

"For some years now, I've been looking for stories that have meaning, that are captivating but also offer a lesson. In *The Rescues,* I found everything I was looking for in a novel: a strong and determined protagonist, a gripping plot, and compelling characters...This is undoubtedly a story to fall in love with, to return to what we left forgotten, and to relive." **~ Amazon Review**

"I was captivated by this moving story from beginning to end...This book left me feeling good and gave me the knowledge that there is always hope for another chance and a better future." ~ **Amazon Review**

"This captivating story had me glued to every page. I found the use of a horse as both a connection and a mirror to be absolutely brilliant; it reflected exactly what the protagonists needed to face in their lives things they had been avoiding until that moment...It's a journey that helps you not only discover the true reasons behind your actions but also work through them to lighten the emotional load. I highly recommend this book to anyone looking for a story full of hope, where the great quest to find true strength and courage within oneself is at the heart of a beautiful narrative." ~ **Amazon Review**

"It left me feeling like I had actually been to Harmony Hills, breathing in hay, silence, and second chances. Seeing Ripley heal an injured horse while, almost without meaning to, letting Ty get close to her own emotional wounds, feels genuine, tender, and not at all forced. It's one of those romances where the process of learning to trust again is almost more enjoyable than the inevitable." ~ **Amazon Review**

"*The Rescues* is the perfect example that second opportunities appear anywhere and also that love changes everything. Jordan Standridge has penned a thought-provoking and tender story that touches themes such as love, courage, strength, and opportunities...It's a great novel with well-portrayed and complex characters that display a rollercoaster of emotions. So, if you're fond of love and touching stories, you should read this one." ~ **Amazon Review**

"The Secret"

"Standridge introduces Morgan O'Connell, a woman clawing her way out of grief to rebuild both her life and a sanctuary for others. Harmony Hills is more than a horse facility—it's the heart of Morgan's recovery. Standridge ties Morgan's emotional recovery to the daily work of restoring trust, both in herself and in others. Though the story's suspense heightens the stakes, it's Morgan's self-discovery and the authenticity of her connections that give it real depth." ~ **Prairies Book Review**

"Jordan has a gift for bringing characters to life. Her writing is passionate, vivid, and flawless in my eyes. I could imagine everything so clearly... The emotional depth felt real... Highly recommend!" ~ **ARC Reader/ Amazon Review**

"*The Secret* explores the inner lives of women who carry stories that signify strength and courage. These stories show how vulnerability and strength can go hand in hand, not as opposites, but as partners in growth. I found this book really amazing as it portrays women as emotionally raw, real, and deeply human. The characters were not flawless or unbreakable, but they continued to move forward and defy their challenging paths. The book was well-written in every single way. I loved how easy it was for me to connect to it and learn from the life lessons it instilled. An amazing read, as a whole!" ~ **Amazon Review**

"*The Secret* is a truly heartwarming story of strength, resilience, and second chances. Morgan O'Connell's journey after a personal tragedy is inspiring—she rebuilds her life from the ground up, transforming Harmony Hills Equestrian Center into one of the finest facilities in Arizona. What I particularly admired was how she navigated not only the business side of things but also the emotional healing required to move forward. Her friendship with Ty Stanton is lovely, and his support helps her take the brave step of opening her heart again. Enter Josh Wright, whose instant connection with Morgan adds a touch of romance. But, of course, Morgan has a secret—one that brings tension to the story. It's a beautiful tale of love, trust, and finding peace after hardship. A truly enjoyable read!" ~ **Amazon Review**

"[*The*] *Secret* was such an amazing book, it kept me in suspense from one chapter to the next. I am not an avid reader, but could not put the book down until I had it read. Such courage by the main character Morgan, that it would give anyone hope and courage to move on with your life. The love that grew between Morgan and Josh was so real and very uplifting...You will not be disappointed in buying and reading this book. I look forward to more books by this author." ~ **Amazon Review**

"This book [*The Secret*] is fire! The characters will draw you in, and make you feel like you're there. It is so good, I even read it in the bath tub! Must read!!!!" ~ **ARC Reader/ Amazon Review**

"Jordan is really great at making the reader attached to the characters. You can feel the soul behind them. She brought every character to life with the passion she's invoked! It's absolutely going to be a book I buy and re-read as a comfort.

"The humor has been amazing as well! I haven't laughed out loud reading a book in a long time. And I'm a stone, so to actually cry while reading it was amazing. This one book really was able to touch all of my emotions and made me tap into them as a reader. Reading certain chapters definitely had me on the edge of my seat. I feel such an attachment to the characters and I need more! I'm hooked!" ~ **ARC Reader**

"This [*The Secret*] was very good. It's like a Hallmark mystery movie." ~ **ARC Reader**

"Just finished *The Secret.* Loved it. Jordan writes so you can relate to the characters. You can feel their ups and downs. You felt what they were going through, and the courage they had to reinvent their lives and move on. The book completely held your interest so that you did not want to put it down but to keep reading to see what happened next. There was a surprise twist at the end that I didn't see coming. When reading the book, you actually feel what the characters feel. Can't wait for her next one. So far loving what I've read from her." ~ **Goodreads Review**

"The Witness"

"*The Witness* shifts gears into high-stakes suspense. Raina, whose act of selfless courage turns her into a target, is thrust into a nightmare of trauma and pursuit. What follows is an emotionally gripping narrative where action and tenderness coexist in perfect balance. The pacing remains taut, the stakes high, but Standridge never lets the heart of the story fade. Through Detective Channion Scott's devotion and his growing feelings for Raina, the novel becomes less about survival alone and more about endurance and human connection.

"Standridge's prose is vivid yet unpretentious, the dialogue authentic, and the pacing perfectly tuned...She brings both the ache of grief and the promise of healing to life with quiet emotional precision." ~ **Prairies Book Review**

"Raina is a vivid presence throughout *The Witness,* filled with urgency from the very first page. Author Jordan Standridge does a very good job of convincing the reader that this woman is the sort who would instinctively intervene to save someone's life. Her recovery from her injuries and developing relationship with Channion as he strives to protect her both emotionally and physically are compelling and authentic... The sense of danger as Raina slowly recovers her memories and the police close in on the criminals is convincing... *The Witness* is buoyed by its core character relationship. Channion and Raina's burgeoning romance set against the backdrop of danger is consistently interesting and engaging." ~ **IndieReader Review**

"HEA!!! Wow. A page turner for sure. Just about the time you think you know where the story is going, there is a twist and turn I was so not expecting. It's impossible to stop reading once you start." ~ **Amazon Review**

"I'm a huge fan. This book [*The Witness*] has incredible character development, making it easy to get attached to everyone. [Jordan's] attention to detail truly brings the story to life, immersing you in the world they've created. It's a fun journey to go on with the characters, and you can't help but feel invested in their adventures." ~ **ARC Reader**

"Fantastic book! Best book I have read all year. It has it all...courage, strength, laughter, romance, suspense, friends, and family." ~ **Amazon Review**

"This...was an amazing book. I got intrigued by all the characters and could easily relate to them. Once I started reading the book, I could not put it down. I would recommend this book as a great read." ~ **Amazon Review**

"Great mystery (police FBI). Best 'free book' ever!...Words to describe: RIVETING, PAGE TURNER, CLEAN, SUSPENSEFUL, GREAT CHARACTER DEVELOPMENT, WELL WRITTEN AND MORE! WILL BE READING MORE of this author's books, and they don't have to be free!" ~ **Goodreads Review**

"...This book keeps you in suspense. Lots of turns and twists with a few surprises thrown in. I loved this book even more than the first one..." ~ **Goodreads Review**

"Man, am I ever glad I read this book! I started this morning before going to work, was almost late to work because I didn't want to stop reading, came home from work and read non-stop until the book was finished. I connected with the characters. The descriptions in the book were so well written, I could visualize what was happening in my head."
~ Amazon Review

"I just finished Jordan's book, *The Witness.* Can't say enough. The main character starts her day going from just driving down the road to fighting for her life.

"The book is full of suspense from one page to the next. Just when I would go to put it down, something else would happen and I would have to keep reading to see what happened next. The book held [my] complete interest from beginning to end.

"The main character fights hard for her life, her loved ones, and for what she believes in. She never gives up, but holds on to her values along the way. Can't wait to see more from this author. Well done!!" **~ ARC Reader**

"The Women of Strength, Courage, and Hope" Series

"Standridge's heartfelt trilogy traces the intertwined journeys of three women overcoming loss and danger, each uncovering that the path to healing runs through connection as much as endurance.

"Rooted in the heart of Arizona, the stories feel authentic and alive. The expanse of the desert and the quiet pulse of ranch life anchor the emotional intensity of each story. Read together, the three novels form an emotionally cohesive trilogy that celebrates endurance, compassion, and second chances.

"Standridge's prose is vivid yet unpretentious, the dialogue authentic, and the pacing perfectly tuned to the rhythm of each story's emotional stakes. She brings the ache of grief and the promise of healing to life with quiet emotional precision. Harmony Hills feels real and lived in; a refuge where pain meets possibility and where the land itself seems to mirror the characters' longing for peace.

"Fans of Debbie Macomber's *Cedar Cove series* and Nicholas Sparks' *The Rescue* and *Safe Haven* will find much to admire. A page-turning, emotionally charged trilogy that blends suspense, romance, and redemption in equal measure." **~ Prairies Book Review**

"Jordan's work has genuinely inspired us. Each narrative resonates deeply, exploring profound themes of faith, resilience, and the transformative power of the human-animal bond. Her storytelling captures universal messages of hope and personal growth, making her work truly special.

"Jordan's work is captivating with its emotionally resonant themes and interconnected narratives. The layered storytelling not only keeps readers engaged but builds anticipation between books. Her stories on faith, resilience, and hope also make them ideal for book clubs and online discussions. She has a genuine, emotional storytelling that distinguishes her." ~ **ARC Reader**

Also by Jordan Standridge

The Women of Strength, Courage, and Hope Series

The Secret *

The Secret (Large Print)

The Witness *

The Rescues

*A *2025 Global Book Awards* Winner

The Rescues

Book Three

The Women of Strength, Courage, and Hope Series

Jordan Standridge

HAPPY TRAILS PRESS

The Rescues

ISBN: 978-1-967457-04-5 (KDP ebook)

ISBN: 978-1-967457-05-2 (KDP paperback)

ISBN: 978-1-967457-10-6 (non-KDP ebook)

ISBN: 978-1-967457-11-3 (non-KDP paperback)

www.JordanStandridge.com

Happy Trails Press

Cover Design by Damonza

Formatting Software: Atticus

To those who know animals are furry people who truly feel like we do. They experience sadness, fear, pain, and loneliness. They also exude love, loyalty, and compassion.

And those who know this also understand these furry people deserve those last three from everyone. Please spread the word to those who don't know.

Be their voice.

Chapter 1

Tuesday, July 7

THEY WERE FRYING EGGS on the sidewalk when she drove by. At least, that was her best guess when she saw the young kids squatting down, staring intently at them. She noticed all of the broken egg shells littering the sidewalk and smiled in amusement.

When she saw the little girl holding a yellow plastic spatula in one hand and a salt shaker in the other, she laughed. She hoped their parents had a sense of humor.

After running errands in town, she'd already decided to stop for lunch at one of her favorite watering holes, The Neon Moon. Seeing the eggs, though, tempted her to head to an IHOP or Waffle House instead. But since she was almost to her original destination, she decided to stay the course.

Cooking for one while her husband Josh was away wasn't all that appealing to her. Letting someone else do the cooking and cleanup definitely was. She figured she'd allow herself at least one freebie while he was away from home.

And this just so happened to be the one she chose.

When she turned into the parking lot of the Western-themed restaurant, she immediately noticed the large two-toned brown motorhome parked in the back of the large paved lot. Noting the tan car still hitched to it, she assumed the owners were inside enjoying the local offerings.

She appreciated the courtesy of the motorhome driver for parking out of the way—and for supporting a local business. She pulled into a spot near the door and put her truck in *park*. Since the Arizona sun was doing its best to melt metal—and fry eggs on sidewalks—she slid her windshield sunshade into place to block it. Rolling down her windows a little, she turned off her truck with a flick of her wrist.

The cool air hit her when she walked through the front door into the lobby. God bless the man who invented air conditioning! she thought. She snapped the carabiner hook that held her keys to her belt loop as she walked through the swinging doors that led into the afternoon dining area. She paused to remove her sunglasses and let her eyes adjust.

A waitress smiled and called out to her as she headed toward the kitchen with some dishes she'd just cleared from a table. "Hey there, girl! Sit where ya want. I'll be right with ya!"

"Will do, Jo!" she called back.

Glancing around, she felt a bit surprised when she didn't see any older people at any of the tables. She assumed the motorhome in the lot was being driven by an older couple enjoying their golden years in style. Or someone tired of expensive mortgage payments.

Looking to her left, she saw a middle-aged man in the corner booth reading on his phone, and a young couple sat at a two-top. Looking to her right, she saw three men laughing over something on one of their phones. Then she saw a lone woman who looked about her age. Sitting at a table by one of the wide windows that showcased the local scenery, the woman was dunking her French Dip in the little bowl of au jus. The window shade was partially pulled to tone down the bright sunlight over her table.

Remembering where she'd been, in particular the feed store and the vet clinic, she made a detour to the restroom. When she came out, she wandered over to the tall tables along the far wall, choosing one that was a respectable distance from the other woman. Sliding onto the stool, she waited for Jo to come back out. Glancing over, she saw the woman apparently texting somebody, and then her smile at their apparent reply.

Jo came back out, drying her hands on a towel and smiling at her as she walked over. "Hey, Morgan! Sorry about the lag time there. I was showing our new dishwasher how the Hobart worked. Where's your honey?"

"No worries. I'm not in any rush. Josh went camping with Ty and Damien. They left yesterday. Male bonding time," she replied, trying to keep a straight face. "If I'm not mistaken, my Fourth of July Extravaganza wore them out!" She shrugged her slender, muscled shoulders as she added, "It's the only thing I can think of that'd make them want to go camping in the hottest part of the year."

"Well, if they went up into the mountains more, it's bound to be cooler than down here. And it's always good to see *you!*" Jo rested her own foot on a stool rung and leaned on the tall back. "I stopped by that day, but you were so busy I don't know if you saw me. And I swear your event gets bigger and bigger every year! My family and I had an awesome time, by the way. My nephews from Nebraska hated to leave, so I have a feeling they'll want to come back next year."

Pleased, Morgan smiled. "I'm glad you all had fun. And I hope you gave me an amazing online review. They're so crucial in today's world." With a raised eyebrow, she warned, "And don't lie and say you did because you know I can log on right now and check."

Jo laughed before saying, "I *will* write an amazing review for you."

"I'll wait," Morgan deadpanned.

Jo chuckled. "I *will*... Cross my heart and hope to die and all that." She tucked the towel in her back pocket. "So, what're ya in the mood for today?"

"I'll do the blackened chicken sandwich combo. But I'll do a salad instead of the fries, with ranch, no croutons. And an iced tea. No, make that a Pepsi." Remembering she was trying to cut back on her only vice, she amended her order again. "Nope. Better make that the tea."

Twirling her pen in her fingers, the petite blonde grinned at Morgan's indecision. "Cutting back on the Pepsi again, I take it?"

"Trying to."

"Oh, just have one. Treat yourself."

"I'm a Pepsiholic. You should be supporting me in my decision, not encouraging me to fail."

"Sorry!" Jo laughed. "Make the tea half sweet, half unsweet?" At Morgan's nod, Jo said, "Coming right up." She went to the Point-of-Sale station the owner recently upgraded and put in the order. She poured the large iced tea and brought it over to her regular customer and friend. "It'll be a minute or two on the salad. They're being made now."

"Okay."

"Crackers?"

"Nope. Not this time around. Thanks though."

"No croutons. No crackers. No Pepsi. You're off your feed, girl. You sick?"

Morgan laughed and shook her head.

With a drawn-out, thoughtful "Hmmm," Jo gave her a doubtful look before she headed over to her other tables to check on her customers. As Jo chatted with the young couple, Morgan's attention returned to the woman who was now looking around at the Western décor as she sipped her drink. By its color, Morgan bet it was a Pepsi and sighed.

Noticing the lady who had just come in looking over at her now that the waitress had left, the other woman debated with herself for a split second as she set down her drink. Since the woman looked and sounded like a nice person, she decided to strike up a conversation. "Hi! I take it you're a local?" she asked with a friendly smile.

"Sure am!" Morgan replied with a smile of her own. "I take it you're not?"

"Nope. I'm traveling through and saw this place as I was driving by. It looked interesting so I thought I'd turn around to see if it was any good. I prefer to taste the local mom-and-pop type places rather than the chains, you know?"

"Absolutely. And trust me, the owner here appreciates it!" Morgan took a long sip of her tea before asking, "What do you think of it so far?"

"Service is great. Food is terrific. Atmosphere rocks!"

Morgan nodded. "Yeah, you got it all down. You should be here at night because *that's* when you really get to see the flavor of this place!

"We have a live band on weekends, karaoke on Thursdays, and pool tournaments on Wednesdays if enough people sign up, and they normally do. Oh, and line dancing lessons on Monday and Tuesday evenings, and sometimes in the afternoons on Fridays. Sunday is really the only down day here.

"And, of course, there are usually friendly people to chat with. But if you like to sing, come back in a couple of days if you're still here. I'm Morgan, by the way."

"Ripley. Nice to meet you, Morgan." She shook her head as she added, "And no, I don't like to sing. Not in public anyway. Sometimes, there are certain things one just shouldn't do. That's a huge one for me."

She turned in her chair to look around. Seeing the authentic pieces of various Western equipment hanging on the walls and from the ceiling, Ripley had a thoughtful look on her face. "You said you have dancing and a band? Here in the restaurant? That's different! Like a Mariachi band?"

Morgan leaned against the back of her stool to get more comfortable. "Oh, no... Actually, yes. But no."

Confused, Ripley asked, "What?"

Morgan sighed. "Can you tell I went to public schools growing up?"

Ripley laughed.

Grinning, Morgan clarified her answer. "Yes, here in this building but not in this restaurant part." Pointing, she said, "Over on the *other* side of that wall is another part of this building that has the bar and dance floor, and *that's* where the place comes alive. The band isn't Mariachi, but a local band that plays a bit of everything.

"Oh, I almost forgot to mention the gift shop!" Morgan pointed in the general direction. "They have the Elmers."

"The Elmers?"

"You need to go see him! He's with the Montana Silversmith stuff. Elmer is an adorable horse figurine. There's a filly, or mare, too... Ellie. Anyway, they're like collectibles and are absolutely precious!"

"Gotcha. I'd love to see them unless they're *too* cute because my RV lacks display space. But maybe as gifts? Maybe I'll check them out."

"You really should."

Ripley considered what Morgan had also said. "It's smart to have a bar, dance area, a full restaurant, *and* a gift shop. Handy too. If one area has a slow day, odds are the others will pick up the slack. And when all are going full swing, there's profit to be made!"

Morgan nodded. "Yep, and that's exactly what Kyle expects! This place has been around for decades, so it's a bit of a legend around these parts. It's family-friendly on this restaurant side, and then caters to adults on the other. There are lots of regulars, so we tend to spot newcomers pretty easily."

"That'd be me," Ripley said cheerfully.

They sat in a comfortable silence for a minute. Ripley really took notice of Morgan for the first time. The long, layered sun-bleached brown hair topped off a slim, fit body that showed defined muscles underneath the blue t-shirt. The dusty boots she had hooked over the rungs of the stool across from her looked worn and comfortable.

Ripley casually studied the woman, deciding she couldn't imagine the woman wearing anything but what she was. Her style seemed to be a part of her genetic make-up.

Morgan turned to face her fully, ready to ask the visitor a question. When she did, Ripley was struck by how captivating she was. She had these green eyes that seemed to lock onto a person's, making it hard to look away. How'd she miss seeing them when they introduced themselves? Morgan must've been in shadow for her to have missed seeing those eyes.

"Wow," she said quietly.

Her original question pushed aside, Morgan looked at her. "Wow what?"

"Your eyes... I mean, wow. I'm sure you get comments on them all the time, don't you?"

At that point, Jo walked up with Morgan's freshly-made salad with a side of ranch like she preferred. "Sorry for the delay, Morgan. They were apparently waiting for the tomatoes to ripen."

Morgan grinned as Jo turned to answer Ripley. "Hardly a day goes by without *someone* saying something about those eyes of hers. And yes, they're real. And this is her free of make-up too.

"Yep. Morgan here is known as our local Green-Eyed Beauty. People come from miles around just to look into her eyes. She'd have made a fantastic gypsy fortune teller. Still could."

Morgan laughed as she picked up the ranch dressing, using her fork to scoop it out before she responded to Jo's comment. "Is that so? Since *when* have people been coming around to stare into my eyes? I'm pretty sure I would've noticed."

Jo grinned. "They were discreet about it. They were worried you'd get uppity and vain if you knew. They like you as you are—sweet and humble, friendly to all." Jo gave her a couple more napkins as Morgan rolled her eyes.

Ripley laughed. "I think she'd be vain already if that was in her character. It apparently isn't."

Morgan shook her head but grinned. "Thank you. And as long as my man is happy, I am too."

Jo nodded. "Oh, your man is plenty happy. Josh is a lucky man, and he knows it. Of course, I'd have to say you're a lucky lady to have him. He's such a prize!"

Morgan readily agreed. "No argument there."

Intrigued, Ripley took a sip of her drink as she listened. "Are you guys like one of those perfect couples or something?"

Jo nodded enthusiastically. "Oh, yeah. Josh and Morgan are two peas in a pod. They go together like peanut butter and jelly. Maybe more like electricity and lightbulbs."

Morgan choked on her salad at that last comment, so Jo good-naturedly leaned over and whacked her back a few times. After she got done coughing, Jo asked playfully, "You good?"

Nodding, Morgan looked at her for a moment. "*Really*, Jo? 'Electricity and lightbulbs' is a new one," Morgan said when she could talk.

"Yes, ma'am. You two have this electricity between you. It's like this high-voltage current everyone can see or feel when you two are in close proximity to each other. Actually, when you even just *talk* about the other, you both just light up. It's the darndest thing!" Jo gestured to Ripley. "Look at her. Was she glowing like this *before* we began talking about her Josh?"

Ripley dutifully studied the woman. Looking at Morgan's face, it *did* seem to now glow like an old fluorescent lightbulb that was just warming up. There was now a certain softness to her smile as well as her facial features. Her body posture seemed to change as well.

Her own heart skipped a beat as her glance went from Morgan to the waitress. "Well, no, she wasn't. But now... Wow. That's so romantic! Oh... my... *gosh!* My heart just completely seized up in jealousy. How can you stand to be around them?" She looked back at Morgan, saying in awe, "You *are* glowing like a lightbulb!"

Blushing, Morgan just took another bite of her salad. She had to admit Jo was right. She and Josh *did* have electricity. The high-voltage kind, she thought with a secret smile.

Ripley leaned against her table, asking casually, "Does your Josh have a brother?"

Both Jo and Morgan laughed. Glancing at her occupied tables, Jo said, "Excuse me."

As Jo left to take care of one of her customers, Morgan replied, "No, just sisters. And his best friend is a great catch too—which his wife would tell you in a heartbeat." Morgan thought of Damien and Laura with fondness. "I'd have to say they're just like my husband and I are." She took another bite of her salad.

"Hmm. Must be something in the water around here. Maybe I really *should* look into staying for a while although I was already thinking about it. This just gives me more incentive!" Ripley joked.

Morgan grinned as she pointed her fork at Ripley. "Well, desert water is different than city water all right. You might wanna stick around. Maybe you could test out that theory if you're in the market."

"I'm not actively looking whatsoever, but never say never, right?"

Morgan finished her salad and was just pushing away the empty bowl when Jo plopped her blackened chicken sandwich down in front of her. "I threw in a few fries. No charge."

Jo walked over to Ripley's table, replacing her almost-empty drink with a fresh Pepsi. Ripley thanked her with a smile.

"Would you like dessert today?" Jo asked the visitor. "We have great desserts. Just ask Morgan here when her mouth isn't full."

With her mouth full of her chicken sandwich, Morgan just nodded in agreement. Her green eyes sparkled with humor.

"Were you a dentist in a past life, Jo?" Ripley asked as she shook her head. "I'm stuffed, but I'm sure you're right. Your portion sizes here are more than fair, and my meal was excellent. I'll be sure to give you guys a five-star review." She sighed. "Anyway, I should probably be heading out fairly soon. I still need to find a place to stay."

"Gotcha. Did you want a to-go cup of Pepsi?"

"Sure. And I can just dump this one into an empty cup."

"Comin' up." Jo went to the touchscreen computer and printed out her bill. She slipped it into the slim brown guest check presenter with a pen in case she wanted to pay with a card, then she put together a large cup and lid. As she laid the bill presenter and the cup down on the table, Jo asked, "Are you looking for a hotel? Bed and breakfast? Dude ranch?"

"A ranch would be great. That'd be a new experience, that's for sure. But I mean like an RV park or campground. I need somewhere I can park my RV that has connections for it. I haven't taken the time to look yet as I just got into town. Do you know of either that's clean, safe, and reasonably affordable?" Ripley slipped her credit card into the presenter and handed it back to Jo.

Morgan chewed as she listened. Recalling Ripley saying her RV had no display space made Morgan look at her again. With a surprised look on her face, she asked, "Does that motorhome out in the lot belong to *you?*"

"The tan and brown one? Yeah, that's my home. It saves me from taking chances on finding a clean and safe hotel with vacancies. It's generally convenient to travel in and way more fun. I travel quite a bit."

"It looks incredible. Where do you normally live, your home?" She took another bite of her sandwich.

"Excuse me again. I'll be back in a sec." Jo took the check presenter to the register to run her card.

"Home *is* my RV. In a nutshell, I guess you could say I'm homeless... Or at least houseless. No solid, permanent roots anywhere, I mean." At the surprised look again on Morgan's face, she explained, "Just think of me like a turtle. I take my home with me everywhere I go!"

"So, what then... You just live in parks or campgrounds?"

"More or less. It's hard to beat where I live sometimes. I've been on the circuit to travel the continental United States for the past few years or so mainly for work. And sometimes it's just for me because I want to, and I can.

"When I'm ready to move on, I just unplug my house, pack it all neatly away, hook up the car, and simply drive away. Footloose and fancy-free."

"It's *my* turn to say wow!" Morgan drank some tea as she mulled it over. "So how do you work? You said you traveled for work."

Ripley nodded. "Yes, I do. But I can work anywhere I want to. Because of what I do, my lifestyle is one of my choosing. It works well for me. As long as I have phone reception and hopefully internet access, I'm good to go. But I definitely work, and the hours are varied. I can, and do, take off whenever I want to though."

Jo, returning and putting the check presenter with her receipt copies on the table, asked, "What do you do that allows you to live in an RV and travel the country? That sounds like a plan!"

"I'm an independent distributor for a food science company that deals with natural supplements. I help people build their own businesses like mine. Others I just help to get better health results. Many times, it's both."

Opening the presenter, Ripley removed the receipts. She added a generous tip to the Merchant Copy and signed it before slipping it back in, hooking the pen in the loop. She slid her copies and her card back into her purse.

Morgan nodded. "Well, that sounds great. How long do you plan on sticking around?"

Ripley shrugged her shoulders. "I don't know. Sometimes I'll stay at a place for a month. Sometimes just a few days. There's really no rhyme or reason to it. When I've seen all I wanted to see, or done what I came to do, then I move on.

"I have distributors and customers all over the US, so most of my travel does include going to my people and seeing them. I spend my time doing meetings, sharing my story, and encouraging them to hang in there if they ever get down or frustrated. It can happen to the best of us and often does.

"Just because we have total freedom and control of our lives *doesn't* mean we didn't have to work hard for it."

Morgan motioned for Ripley to wait. "You asked about a place to stay? If you want an RV park, there's a few I know about in general. I don't know what they charge, or how good they are, but I can give you directions. Or, you can easily find them with a GPS. Those parks are pretty popular in this part of the country especially during the winter months."

"I'm sure they're packed then. It's actually one reason I planned on coming here later on in the year. And that'd be great, Morgan. Thanks."

A thought popped into Morgan's mind. She didn't want to rush into anything, so she took another bite of her sandwich, slowly chewed it as she thought it through.

Ripley patiently waited.

"You said you'd like the ranch idea?" Morgan drank some tea as she warmed to the idea she'd just had.

"Sure. Who wouldn't? Horses, cattle, dogs, and cats. I can add it to one of my adventures. I've visited a few ranches over the years but didn't stay at any of them. They seemed interesting, though, and I love country living."

Morgan nodded. "Well, if you want to, you could rent a spot out at my place. It's not an actual ranch but an equestrian center. I do have two dogs but no cattle. And the cat lives in my house."

"Really?"

"Sure. I wasn't just going to toss Freeway out on her own when Josh and I got married and he moved in. She's always been an inside cat. It's safer for her inside too. Coyotes and hawks, y'know."

Jo laughed as she set a fresh glass of tea down in front of her friend. "I think she meant about staying at your place, *not* that your cat lives in the house!"

Ripley laughed while Morgan just grinned, her green eyes sparkling with amusement. "I know, but I just wanted to be clear on that." She looked at Ripley again, a twinkle still in her eyes as she continued, "It's a large facility, and it's busy. Pretty much any-time-of-day-busy, but it's still quiet and peaceful compared to living in town.

"I have five spaces that can accommodate motorhomes and trailers. And where they are, it's quiet and fairly private even though you're technically out in the open.

"Since I hold horse shows out there fairly often, I've added them in over the years for those who have trailers with living quarters. Or for people who rent out stalls for their horses on long trips since my place is listed on the internet as a horse motel.

"You're more than welcome to take a look at it. I wouldn't charge you any more than a park would, I guess. Internet shouldn't be a problem if you can hook up to WiFi. I have internet in the barn offices, so if you have WiFi capabilities you should be fine. Our cell phones work great, so that shouldn't be a problem either.

"I just have a renter's form that you sign that releases me, my property and business from accidents and liability. There's no lease to abide by. You just leave when you're ready to because you pay in advance. You can stay for a day, a week, or a month or whatever. Well, unless you cause me issues."

Jo nodded. "If you want privacy, a different scene, and possible Western adventures, Morgan's place would be a great place to consider. She's as honest as the day is long. It's safe out there too."

Ripley nodded. "I think it sounds like a great idea! I'd like to check it out first. Is it available now?"

"Yeah, all spots are open. We just had a horse show a few weeks ago, and the Fourth of July event last weekend. It'll be a while before we have another show or anything. Follow me out, and take a look. If you don't want to stay there, it's no problem at all. I won't take offense. It's just an option for you to think about."

"Okay. Sure."

Ripley went to the restroom, and then wandered around the building as Morgan finished her meal. She went to the gift shop and saw the Elmers. She bought a few as gifts—assuming she could bear parting with them. They *were* too cute!

Since Ripley had assured her she was in no hurry so she didn't need to feel rushed, Morgan added a caramel sundae for dessert. Jo was busy cleaning tables, checking out her other customers, and taking orders from new ones while Morgan finished. When Morgan paid Jo and left her a tip, she added a note and a smiley face on the receipt about leaving a review for her horse business. She headed to the restroom again before leaving.

"Ripley... I'm ready to head back if you're ready?" Morgan called out.

With a nod, Ripley followed her outside into the dry summer heat and the bright sunshine. Both women slipped on their sunglasses immediately. Morgan pointed to her truck so Ripley knew what to follow. "Do you need to get gas or anything first?"

Ripley shook her head. "I filled up when I got to town, so I'm good to go."

"All righty then. Well, follow me, Ripley, and we'll see where this road takes you."

Chapter 2

MORGAN DROVE OUT INTO the desert and slightly into the mountains along the wide, paved highway to her place of business and residence. Harmony Hills Equestrian Center was her pride and joy, her purpose in life. She'd sacrificed everything she had to build it. It was now a well-known and respected business.

With her longtime best friend Ty Stanton at her side, she finally got it where she wanted it to be. She and Ty were extremely close, and she couldn't picture Harmony Hills without him.

Years before when she'd met Josh Wright, she was profoundly thankful he wasn't turned off by her having a man as her best friend. As it happened, Ty had met Josh before *she* did and had refused to let Josh near her. He guarded her until he was certain of the type of man Josh was, and she dearly loved Ty for doing that.

When Josh later learned the personal reasons *why* Ty was so protective of her, Josh respected him for watching out for her. Much to her relief, Ty and Josh had also become great friends.

There were times when Morgan would simply sit there, marveling at how blessed she was having two amazing men in her life. One was a dear, valued friend and the other her devoted, loving husband. She loved them both to pieces and would walk through the Valley of Death for either one of them—twice a day, every day.

Loyalty, trustworthiness, honesty, integrity, and a work ethic were something they all had in common. All that and a sense of humor were mandatory if you wanted to impress any of them. Not to mention a love of animals—especially horses.

All of her staff were loyal and great to have there. She was careful when she hired employees so there was less chance of issues arising. But she knew at some point, a couple might be leaving.

One of her instructors, Kat, had been offered a position in Iowa for a stable that was being built there and was still debating taking it. While Morgan supported her, she also wanted Kat to stay.

And Alexis... She had her sights set on loftier goals than cleaning horse stalls for a permanent vocation. Morgan would miss her the most since Alexis had been there since nearly the beginning.

Morgan was practically a foster parent to Alexis, who was now a young woman taking college courses. Ty often said he felt like her dad, so they joked they were Alexis' second set of parents while Josh was now her third dad. Alexis had first come there as a barn rat while in middle school, and now she was a big part of their makeshift family.

Nearing her place, Morgan activated her turn signal to give Ripley plenty of time to slow down for the turn into the driveway. Turning into the second entrance since Ripley had a large vehicle and was towing, Morgan led her to where the hook-ups were. She pulled to a stop and rolled down her window.

When Ripley stopped her RV, Morgan called out, "Leave your rig here, Ripley. Come in here, and I'll give you a tour."

Ripley nodded, shut off the engine and headed over to Morgan's truck. As she shut the truck's door, she said, "This place is awesome!"

"Thank you. I like to think so!" Morgan smiled in appreciation. "I'll drive you around so you can get the feel. People who stay back here generally use that second entrance we came in on and not the first one we passed with the overhead gate. Less traffic dust that way and more privacy. If you stay and are just driving your car, it doesn't really matter to me. But if you're in the RV or towing definitely use the second entrance."

Ripley nodded as Morgan drove slowly along the hard, sand-packed lane toward the barns.

"I require everyone to drive slowly for obvious reasons. You'll see my speed limit signs that say 'walk' or 'trot' to let you know what you can do. Cantering and galloping are only allowed on the highway!" She smiled when Ripley laughed. "If you speed, then you're endangering horses and people, so out you go."

She pointed to a large barn. "Up here is the barn for lessons and boarders. We have two indoor arenas as well as a few outdoor ones. All around are the paddocks and what we jokingly call the pastures. Not having grass out here like back East, we just make do with what we have. This barn is named Quail Run. Each barn is named after something I felt or saw that made me decide to buy this place.

"Customers and clients can come at almost any time they want to. I do have basic barn hours, and they can vary a little as the seasons change. In the summer months like now, customers can come out as early as six to beat the heat. Some of my workers come in closer to four-thirty to feed the trail horses, but don't worry because they're fairly quiet.

"I do close the barns by nine at night, year-round. I think the horses need some quiet time. I also have a security system in the barns I don't want people setting off at all hours. When it goes off by accident, Josh shoves me out of bed to take care of it. I've found out that I tend to bruise when I hit the floor!" Morgan joked as they drove by Quail Run.

Ripley smiled, picturing it in her mind. "I guess that means your famous electrical current gets disconnected?"

Morgan laughed. "Complete power failure!"

They both laughed. Driving slowly along, Morgan pointed out another building. "Red Rock is our feed barn. The doors to it are always closed in case we have a loose horse. It's also to keep out any wildlife like snakes, javelina, or coyotes."

"And to keep out the dust?" Ripley joked as a sudden swirl of air near them scattered dirt and dust every which way. Morgan chuckled and nodded as Ripley read the name of the pole building as they passed by.

It was so clean and organized here! It definitely made a favorable impression on Ripley to stay.

Driving through another parking lot and turning up a short lane, Morgan pointed. "This is where we hold horse shows and random events. It's also used as the horse motel. This barn is Grand View and is the largest overall due to the larger indoor riding arena, and of course, the shaded seating areas."

Morgan continued on to the last building. Although good-sized, it was the third largest building there. "This is where my main office is and also where the trail rides take place. It's called Sunset Ridge. Odds are if someone is looking for me, I'm up here.

"But I also give riding lessons, train some horses still now and then, go on the road for shows and clinics, and I have my own horse I love to ride. It's really a coin toss on where I'm at any given time, but try here first.

"If I'm at home, as in my house, I prefer not to be disturbed on my time off. We all respect each other's privacy here. Since we all work long hours, I insist on it. It's also just common courtesy. If you need something and I'm off, I'm sure anyone here can take care of it for you.

"I also detest drama. People who stir it up don't stay. My customers want to come out here to play with their horses, de-stress from their jobs or even family life, or to spend time *with* their family. They want to enjoy nature, fresh air, and fellow horse lovers. And they pay me a good sum to ensure they get it. I do my level best to honor that expectation, so gossip, drama, and such is not welcome... Ever."

Ripley nodded, saying, "I understand completely. That's one thing I love about living in my RV, and how I work. No drama! Is there anything worse? People who gossip and backstab others have always made me sick. People really need to mind their own business.

"And I agree, too, with your privacy. There has to be a time for us to recharge, to simply get away from work for a while."

Morgan nodded as she stopped the truck to wait for a middle-aged man heading toward them on a stocky black horse with two white socks to go by. The horse's ears were up, and he was looking right at them but was walking at a nice, forward gait.

"Nick's new horse here is still in training, so I'm going to wait until he passes us. He's just three. He's been learning fast, but he tends to look for things to spook at."

Morgan smiled at Nick as he rode by. She continued as they waited, "If I'm not here, next in line authoritative-wise is Ty. He's my longtime best friend and overall manager. He's kept in the loop on everything that goes on here so if I'm gone, he's it. I have Kat and Mel basically managing Quail Run, but Ty's over them too."

Seeing Nick get far enough away, she slowly drove the truck forward again.

"Josh also knows most everything. He has his own business and isn't here too often at the barns unless he's riding himself. Like you may have heard at the restaurant, both of them are camping. Our house is up there." Morgan pointed to a two-story house on a hill that was hard to actually see from there due to the natural foliage of various cactus species and trees.

Ripley nodded, her head trying to wrap around the scope of the property. Thinking about the property value of a place like this, she was wondering how someone of Morgan's age could afford it. She broached the subject casually. "So you own this place? It's yours?"

"Yes."

That's it? Ripley wondered to herself. A simple *yes?* What, did Morgan deal drugs or something? It wasn't any of her business, so she didn't ask further questions.

Heading back around to Ripley's home on wheels, Ripley noticed how friendly they all seemed as three riders waved and smiled as Morgan drove by them.

Morgan mentioned, "I'm always reminding people about wearing sunblock, drinking water, and preferably wearing a hat or helmet. The first two are stressed far more in the hotter months."

As she drove along, she saw her two German Shepherds come running across a paddock toward them. With a smile, she gestured. "Ah, there they are! The Darrells."

"The what?"

"My dogs. They're each named Darrell and are practically inseparable."

Morgan grinned at the two dogs trotting alongside the truck now. Their chocolate brown eyes were full of happiness at seeing their mom back home. She slowed down even more so they could keep up without overexerting themselves. "They're friendly, so you don't have to worry. Darrell G's the female, and Darrell B's the male... G and B for girl and boy, you see? We just call them Darrell, or The Darrells."

Ripley wondered about someone giving their pets the same name. As she thought about it, though, it did have a good dose of humor and common sense to it. She smiled as the dogs joyfully bounded alongside, giving out an occasional bark in their excitement.

Pulling to a stop beside the RV, Morgan turned off the engine and slid out her door. Ripley followed suit and stopped beside her as the two dogs vied for their mom's undivided attention. The Darrells noticed Ripley and immediately began nudging her for some more loving.

Ripley laughed in delight. "Oh, your dogs are gorgeous. Hey there, Darrell! Look at your doggie smiles!" She tried to pet both dogs at once, but their large, squirming bodies were making it difficult.

Morgan smiled as she watched Ripley try to pet them as they turned and twisted in their excitement at meeting a new person. "They're friendly, but they're still security dogs. They let us know if someone is prowling around, or if there's a wild animal or snake around. They're both snake-trained."

"Snake-trained?" Ripley asked, looking up. "What's that mean exactly?"

"It means they were sent to an expensive trainer on the other side of the mountain range over there"—she pointed in the general direction—"to be able to find, distract, or kill snakes.

"Personally, I don't mind them overall... even the venomous ones. They all have a part to play in the ecosystem, but I *also* have to keep my place reasonably safe." She added, "Josh has a healthy fear of them, so The Darrells are here for him too. I absolutely respect his fear of snakes. He's certainly not the only one around here who feels this way either."

Ripley replied, "Hard to blame him." She was still bent over, petting the dogs who were calming down some now. "How old are The Darrells?"

"They're around nine. Knowing Shepherds generally live ten to thirteen years, it saddens me to think they're nearing the tail end of their lives. They're siblings from the same litter, so it'll be doubly hard if they both go around the same time, you know?

"I love all of my animals like they're my kids, so I can't even think about not having them here. I've had these guys since they were puppies."

Ripley nodded as Morgan motioned for her to follow while The Darrells happily joined them. Walking down the line, Morgan said, "If you want to stay out here, I'd recommend picking this one at the end. It's farthest away from the barns so more privacy. And with you being at the far end, if I got a horse motel client they can park closer to Grand View and their horses."

Ripley looked around, gazing at the mountain views, the well-kept buildings and fences. She watched the horses in a nearby pasture lazily soaking up the sun while a couple more were cooling off underneath the shaded buildings, their tails occasionally swishing at the flies. Another horse, a young sorrel, trotted to the fence, whinnying to some horses being ridden nearby. It was so peaceful and quiet out here. She'd never get *this* in an RV park! Her thoughts were broken into when Morgan gave a little groan.

Morgan then exclaimed, "Oh... I hate it when horses don't whinny back! Murphy there is just trying to be friendly to those others, see? She's saying, 'Hi!' to them, but they don't even look at her. It's just so... rude. Poor little girl..."

Ripley laughed heartily. They listened as Murphy said 'Hi!' again in horse talk, but there was still no response from the others. Ripley looked at Morgan, who was still smiling as she watched and waited to see if they would. Ripley said, "Maybe they think they'll get in trouble talking to a stranger? Or not paying attention to their riders?"

Morgan laughed at her suggestions. "It's still rude!"

Both women watched as poor Murphy finally gave up and began slowly walking back toward her equine friends who were sunbathing. Her facial expression and slow walk made Morgan's heart hurt.

"Oh... She looks so *sad*, doesn't she? Poor girl!" Morgan said softly.

Ripley had to agree. "She *does!* Ouch. Man... I kinda feel like going over there to say hi to her myself!"

Nodding in agreement, Morgan watched until Murphy joined her pals.

Ripley looked around again. "How much would you charge me?" She squatted down on her heels so she could pet the two dogs again behind their ears more comfortably.

Morgan slid a glance her way. "To pet and console Murphy? Nothing at all. Kindness should always be free."

Ripley laughed as Morgan now grinned down at her.

Morgan finally got around to answering her. "Rent includes the space, water—try to use sparingly as water is a precious resource in the desert—electric, sewage, WiFi, pure country living, and privacy. You can also use the large dumpster up at Quail Run for your trash. Just be sure the lid is always down when you're done. There's a recycling bin there, too, if you want to help save the planet."

Morgan watched the woman pet her dogs while she continued, "My usual charge is forty bucks per day, and the standard week's deposit for those who know they'll stay a week or more that is fully refundable as long as you don't break anything, steal from me, or trash my place. And you get it all in writing. And I just ask for your ID and a contact in case of an emergency."

One of the dogs suddenly leaned against Ripley, and she had to catch her balance so she wouldn't topple over. She smiled at Darrell G, who was giving her the sweetest puppy dog eyes as she leaned on her, vying for more attention over her brother. Looking around, Ripley considered it. Only forty bucks a day. And people paid closer to three times that for a hotel with questionable cleanliness and noise issues! It was very tempting.

Morgan added, "You'll have to sign a renter's agreement and release papers, so if you get hurt or something, my property and business are completely protected. There are stipulations about trying to ride the horses, hosting loud parties, setting off fireworks, no bonfires, and that kind of thing.

"I don't mind if you drink alcohol in moderation, but no minors can. I won't put up with drunks either. Absolutely no drugs of any type are allowed at all. And if you smoke, it's not allowed *anywhere* near the barns, and you'd better be *sure* your butts are completely out and stored in a metal container. I better not see them on my property. Fires out here are beyond deadly."

Ripley nodded. "Sure. I can completely understand all of that. None of those are a problem for me. I don't smoke, do drugs, and rarely drink, so those are all clear."

Ripley looked around some more, making sure she wasn't making a rash decision. But no lease, being able to leave whenever she wanted to? An RV park or campground would probably charge about the same, if not more, especially if it was a fancy one with pools, a laundry facility, and a community center.

And where else could she get these views? There was plenty of space to go running, walking, or hiking too. And she was the only camper out here. It was really all just a breath of fresh air. And she was back with horses. She loved that perk the most.

Ripley stood up, hands on her slim hips. With a smile, she declared, "You got a deal, Morgan. We'll start with the rest of this month, and go from there."

With a wide smile, Morgan shook her hand. "Great! Welcome home, Ripley! Let's pop back up to Sunset Ridge to get you squared away."

Ripley got her purse from her RV, then climbed back into Morgan's truck. They drove back up to the office to complete the paperwork with The Darrells riding along in the bed of the truck, standing on old towels Morgan had in the back seat so they wouldn't burn their paws on the hot metal. Morgan introduced her to a few of her wranglers, Toby, Maya, and Drew, who were running the barn for her that day and taking out trail rides.

Afterwards, Morgan drove her to Quail Run and introduced Ripley to her two riding instructors, Kat and Mel, so they knew who she was. Ripley was impressed again at how friendly everyone she met was. They easily made her feel at home, and that was a feeling she didn't really recall getting anywhere else she'd been. At least not this quickly. She even met a couple of customers who were there getting ready for a lesson.

"I doubt I'm going to remember everyone's name," Ripley said as Morgan drove back to her RV. "I'm still working on the barns."

"Don't worry about it. Some of them won't remember yours, and you're only *one* person." Morgan smiled. "If you need anything, just head up to the office or ask anyone you see walking around. If they don't work here, they'll at least point you in the right direction of someone who does.

"And I'll give you my business card. If something should happen, or you need something, you can just call or text. But no calling in the middle of the night unless your place is on fire, rolling off a cliff or something, okay? Obviously if an emergency happens, call me!"

Ripley chuckled. "Yes, ma'am. Keep it within business hours. Understood."

Morgan watched as Ripley un-hooked her car before they discussed what'd be the best position to park the RV in. After moving it into position, Ripley activated the hydraulic jacks to keep it balanced and level. She opened one of the large storage compartments to get out the hoses and tubes she needed to hook up to the water and sewage lines.

Still watching, Morgan was impressed at how adept the woman was. Obviously, this was something she'd done many times as she had an efficient routine. Ripley hooked up the electric before they went inside to make sure everything was working properly.

Morgan had never been inside an RV before, and Ripley was more than happy to show her around. "Watch this," Ripley said as she flipped a switch. An entire section began sliding out, adding an impressive amount of space to the living area.

Morgan said in awe, "So *that's* how you people do that!"

After the living room was enlarged by one slide-out, Ripley motioned for Morgan to flip another switch. She did, grinning. "And there's your dining room! It totally doubles the width of this thing!"

"Yeah, so now I live in more of an odd-shaped rectangle than a narrow tube."

Ripley flipped a third switch, causing her bedroom to double in width. Morgan stood there, watching in wonder. She was also impressed with the many storage compartments. She couldn't believe there was even a small washer and dryer! And a kitchen that had every appliance a person needed.

As she was walking down the metal steps, Morgan said, "It's very roomy. And you have tons of storage space, don't you? You can carry everything you need. I never would've guessed there was that much to an RV. Josh and I might need to get us one of these toys someday!"

Ripley smiled. "They *are* nice. It's a huge pain if it ever needs work done, but for me, it's been fairly rare. Everything needs maintenance and repairs after all. I went a little more on this one to get that washer and dryer, and they've come in handy many times.

"This thing is horrible on gas, as you can imagine. However, it beats having to pack and unpack, find clean hotel rooms, and all that hassle. And I don't drive it daily, just when I'm going from one place to the next.

"And maybe best of all, since it can run off propane, electricity, has a large battery, and comes with a generator, I don't really worry if I run out of propane or a storm knocks out the power. I've got automatic backups."

Ripley walked around to the slide-outs, checking them over. "That should do it!" She wiped her hands on her shorts as she looked around, taking in the mountains. "Thank you so much for offering your place, Morgan. I'm so glad I decided to turn around and stop at The Neon Moon. If I hadn't, we'd never have met, and I wouldn't be here right now. It's my lucky day!"

"And *I* stopped there too." Morgan smiled. "I'm a firm believer in things happening for a reason, Ripley. Who knows where this might lead you? Maybe nowhere, but you're here now!" With a grin, Morgan got into her truck, saying, "Well, I need to get back up there. Gotta use all this horse wormer I bought. Here's my business card." She handed one to her. "If you need anything, just let me know.

"You can hike the trails whenever you want to. It'd be best if you let one of us know just in case something happened, okay? And when you get back so we don't worry. You can just text me, too, if you don't want to talk to anyone. Just for safety's sake, all right?

"If you're running, please slow down to a walk in case a horse feels like spooking. Watch out for snakes. They don't always rattle as a warning, day or night... And not all *do* rattle. And don't forget not all *are* venomous, but it pays to just *think* they are until you know for sure."

"Gotcha." Ripley automatically looked around, almost expecting one to suddenly appear. It'd been a while since she'd been in a desert environment for any length of time. Having to remember these all-too-real situations were reminding her of one more reason she loved to travel... away from the desert. But she also appreciated the desert life and scenery.

Morgan added, "Don't reach into dark areas without carefully looking first. Oh, and shake out any shoes you leave outside in case of spiders or scorpions. Tarantulas we don't really see much out here, unless maybe after a heavy rain. Frankly, if I were you, I wouldn't leave any shoes outside at all. And smaller snakes have been known to slither into boots before."

Ripley stood stock-still. "Seriously? Snakes *in* boots?" She shuddered at the thought. Then she asked, "Aren't The Darrells trained for bugs too? Like the scorpions and such?"

"They can't be everywhere at once." Morgan smiled. "I'm just giving you tips for living in the desert. They're also listed in those papers I gave you with your receipt. Coyotes generally won't bother you. The Darrells have them pretty much under control, so they don't really come too close to the barns. Plus, the horses can scare them off.

"Bobcats and lions are pretty much loners and don't want to be around you either. They really don't come down here but still, it pays to mention them." Tongue-in-cheek, Morgan counseled, "It's just good to pay attention to your surroundings."

Ripley's eyes were wide, and she audibly choked down her spit. "If this is your idea of saying, 'Welcome home, Rip. Enjoy your stay,' you really suck at it! You're making me a nervous wreck!"

Morgan laughed before she said, "You'll be just fine, Ripley. If you get scared tonight, it's okay to call or text me... even after midnight. I'll program your number into my phone so I'll know to answer it, okay? I do have the means to protect you.

"But seriously, I know the first night could be spooky out here for you. You can leave your windows open, but lock your door."

"You're mocking me, Morgan."

"Not at all. Just trying to say, 'Welcome home, Rip. Enjoy your stay!'" She grinned.

With a rueful smile, Ripley shooed her away. "Go to work, Morgan. I'll see you around. And thank you again."

"You're welcome." Morgan smiled as she reminded her to give The Neon Moon those five stars she said she would and drove back to her office.

Looking at the underside of the RV, Ripley wondered how would she know if a snake slithered up into the frame? Could one get *inside* her living quarters somehow? She needed to call a local RV dealership to inquire on how to *prevent* either from happening, or to have them reasonably try to reassure her neither *would*. And then what to do when it *did*.

Straightening her shoulders, she went to get some things from her storage compartments to get settled in. Before it got dark and the snakes came out.

Chapter 3

Sunday, July 12

Ripley stretched her arms high above her head, working out the kinks in her back and arms. She'd been working in one way or another since seven that morning. It figures all her calls that day came from the East Coast. She yawned and bent over to touch the floor to stretch out her stiff back. It felt so nice, she thought about just staying that way.

It was her fault she was tired though. She'd found a book while in town yesterday she'd last read when way younger and got sucked into it. She had to force herself to put it down around one that morning. Louis L'Amour books were one of her favorites to read. One thing she couldn't resist was a good book!

Ripley walked stiffly to her compact kitchen. She was pondering what to make for a snack when she heard her name being called. Looking out her window, she saw one of the wranglers riding a gray horse. It looked like a half-Arabian to her.

She slowly opened her door so the horse wouldn't spook. "Hey, Maya. That's a nice ride you've got there. He's a cutie!"

"That he is! This is Doolittle." Smiling, Maya patted the horse's sleek neck. "Morgan asked me to pop down here to see if you'd like to come up to her house tonight. It's our game night. We play board games, cards, maybe basketball. Or sometimes we'll just watch a movie. Maybe games and a movie. Whatever feels good at the time. It's potluck. Do you want to join us?"

Ripley was petting Doolittle as she listened. It felt great petting and smelling a horse again! "It sounds like fun. I probably need to get out of this thing for a while anyway. What time?"

"We usually start around seven. It's very casual. Most of us wear shorts. It's just us having fun and eating. If you don't have anything on hand to bring, no worries. There's always extra food."

Glancing at her watch, Ripley saw it was after three already. Where had her day gone? "Well, I have a couple more calls for work this evening. I might be late, but I can be there by eight or maybe a little after. Would it still be worth my coming up there?"

"Sure! We'll still be rollin' right along then. We could be there at least another two hours."

"Okay. I'll try to come up as soon as I can, all right?"

"Cool beans. You can use the lighted path up to the house. Walk up to Sunset Ridge, and you'll see it." She gathered the reins before she turned Doolittle away. "We'll see ya then!"

"Tell Morgan thanks for the invite. And thanks for coming down."

"You're welcome." Maya nudged Doolittle into a slow canter.

"You're speeding, Maya!" Ripley called out, smiling.

Laughing, Maya waved back to her as the gelding carried her away.

Morgan was setting out the toppings for her taco soup that was simmering in the crockpot as she spoke with her husband on the phone. He'd called to see if she was okay with them camping an extra day.

"I think we can handle it. Did you check with Ryan? He might need you back."

Josh answered, "No. I figured if you said no, there was no point in calling him."

"You called your wife before your foreman?" Morgan teased.

"I figured it'd be in my best interest to."

"You were right." She smiled, both at her husband's joking and at her friends walking across her patio. "Oh! I should tell you that I rented out a camper space to a woman. She has a large RV and a little car. If you guys come in late, you might like to know that. She's at the number five space."

"Is she a horse motel guest?" he asked.

"No. She travels for her work and was looking for a place to park her RV for a while. I met her at The Neon Moon over lunch. She seemed nice when Jo and I were talking with her, so I made her an offer she couldn't refuse.

"I actually haven't seen that much of her. She came up for a ride the other day, though, and had a great time. She's pretty friendly, mature, and has a fun sense of humor."

"Okay. How long's she staying?"

"I have no clue. She doesn't either. She just moves on when she feels like it, I guess. I like her so far, so I invited her up here for game night. I thought it'd be rude to have a party and leave her all alone down there. She doesn't know too many people here... Well, that I know about."

Josh replied, "All right. If we come in late, we'll use the front entrance so we don't disturb her. I wouldn't want to spook her if she's down there on her own."

"She is. Let Ty know about her being here too."

"Sure."

"Well, I'll leave you men to your camping then. We're all good here. Laura and I can survive one more night or two without our men. Although, Sasha might be wanting her daddy," she said, referring to Damien's wife and their young daughter.

Josh asked, "Absence makes the heart grow fonder, right?"

She laughed when she heard Ty and Damien razzing him in the background. "Well, that remains to be seen. You'd better go before they lose all respect for you, honey!" She heard him laugh good-naturedly. "I love you, Josh."

"I love you too. See you when I get home."

When she walked into her living room, Toby, Maya, Drew, and Bo—her wranglers—were setting out the board games on the folding tables. Her instructors, Kat and Mel, were walking in the front door with Laura Hinton right behind them. Alexis was just pulling in.

"Hey there, Laura! I just got off the phone with Josh. They might not be back until either tomorrow night or the next morning now. Did you know that yet?" Morgan asked.

Laura nodded. "Yeah. Damien called me as I was leaving, so I was just getting ready to say the same thing to you! I think they were hoping we'd beg a little more for them to hurry home." She wiggled her eyebrows.

Everybody in the room laughed as they began filing into the kitchen for the food and drinks. Glancing at the clock, Morgan saw it was seven. She hoped Ripley could make it as she didn't want someone to feel alone on her property. She knew what it felt like to be all alone, so she went out of her way to include people whenever she could.

They were split into groups playing checkers, Monopoly, and Uno when the doorbell rang. Gently shoving Freeway, Josh's orange tabby cat, from her lap, Morgan scooted back her chair and stood up. She took her Uno cards with her to the door, not trusting Toby and Maya to not look at her hand. Opening the door, Morgan smiled in greeting.

Ripley smiled back. "I wasn't sure which door to go to, so I took a chance."

"Any one will do. I'm married to a talented contractor so they all work. Come on in!" Morgan gestured for her to enter.

The sounds of music and laughter were as warm a welcome as her smile, Ripley thought.

Looking at the item her guest was holding out for her, Morgan grinned. "Fig Newtons! Those are going to go fast... Just watch!" So saying, Morgan grabbed the package, tore it open and popped one in her mouth.

Ripley smiled as she shut the door and followed her hostess into the living room, her flashlight swinging from her hand. She stopped as she took in the Spanish architecture and the complementing Western décor. "Wow, you've got a great place! It's gorgeous in here, and it feels so cozy."

"Thank you." Morgan motioned for Ripley to follow her.

After greeting the others, Ripley followed her hostess into a modern, spacious kitchen. Seeing all the windows, she exclaimed, "The views from up here must be incredible!" She walked over to a side door and looked through the clean window panes. She saw the patio lit up by little recessed lights. There was even a fire pit in the corner. "Geez, Morgan... I'd *never* want to leave the house if I lived here!"

Morgan grabbed a reusable plastic plate and held it out to her. "Oh, trust me. It *is* hard for me to leave it for long. I *love* my house!

"When we got married, Josh being a contractor was just a bonus. He's added on a few things over time. Now I wonder how I ever lived without them. He's spoiled me rotten... Just like he should!" She grinned at Ripley's chuckle. "The gazebo was his wedding present to me. If you like the patio, wait until I show you the gazebo sometime. It's peaceful and calming especially when—"

"Morgan! We're waiting on you to play your hand!" Toby called good-naturedly from the other room, interrupting her. "Or are you forfeiting?"

"Hold your horses!" Morgan called out, making Ripley laugh. Turning back to her guest, Morgan said, "Please excuse me while I go kick his butt!" She gestured to the counter. "Take all you want, Ripley. Drinks are in the fridge. Just bring it all in there with us, okay?"

Feeling welcome, Ripley nodded.

After filling her plate with finger food and getting a bowl of the taco soup that smelled so inviting it made her mouth water, she took a root beer from the fridge. After sticking a spoon in the bowl, she grabbed a few napkins. Balancing her plate and bowl with her drink, she wandered back into the living room. She sat down and watched a blonde woman she hadn't met yet and Mel playing checkers. She ate while she watched Mel contemplate her move.

The unknown pretty blonde woman reached out her hand. Ripley shook it as the blonde said, "Hi! I'm Laura. My husband Damien would normally be here, but he's out camping with Josh and Ty." When the cat jumped up on the couch beside the new guest, Laura grinned. "And this is Freeway. She's got personality galore so don't let her con you into feeding her human food!"

Ripley nodded. "Understood."

She smiled as Freeway stepped up on her leg, sniffing the edge of her plate. Ripley raised it up out of the way a bit and the cat, apparently knowing that meant *no*, instead sat down beside her. And just stared. Her green eyes never wavered like she was trying to hypnotize the new person into feeding her. Ripley pet her instead.

After a minute, she asked, "So is Ty's wife here too? It seems like all the wives are here while the men are out."

Groaning in dismay, Laura shook her head as she watched a grinning Mel jump several of her black checkers. "Dang it, Mel. I was hoping you wouldn't see that!" Answering Ripley's question, Laura said, "Ty isn't married. But I figure if my Damien ever leaves me, I'd take pity on Ty and swoop him right up though!"

Morgan heard her and laughed. "Get in line, Laura."

Grinning, Laura joked, "You had your chance, Morgan. Too late. He's fair game for me... But only if something happened to my Damien."

"I didn't mean *me,*" Morgan replied, shaking her head.

Another woman—Ripley couldn't remember her name—added, "You'd better get in line now then. Be prepared to wait as it's getting longer every day!"

The guys all rolled their eyes and shook their heads.

Ripley took a sip of her drink, watching Laura make her move against Mel's red checkers before she asked, "So Ty's Morgan's manager and a friend to you all?"

Laura replied, "Yep. Ty's a super person in general. He really is. As far as I know, we all like him, and he likes us. Right, Morgan?"

Morgan glanced over. "You put me on the spot, Laura. Now I *have* to answer yes. Luckily, it's true. But he's also my best friend—Right after Josh, of course."

From the Monopoly table, Kat said, "Ty's been here from almost the beginning like Alexis here. And he really is an all-around good guy. He's not hard on the eyes either. Oh... And when he speaks in Spanish?" She patted her heart and fluttered her eyes, smiling.

Toby and Drew glanced at each other while Bo said plaintively, "Hey! You're making it sound like we're just chopped liver over here. What about *us?*"

Toby and Drew added their grunts for male solidarity.

Maya reached over to rub her boyfriend Toby's shoulder. "Don't be jealous. You know we all think highly of you boys too!"

Toby frowned. "*Boys?*"

Maya shook her head. "You know what I mean."

"Say what you mean, and mean what you say, darlin'!"

With a smile, Maya ran her hand over his hair. "You're not chopped liver to *me.*"

Toby smiled back at her. "I better not be!"

Morgan smiled as she remembered while she'd been out of town a few years ago, Toby had asked Ty if it was okay for him and Maya to date. They didn't see any rule against it in Morgan's employee handbook. Ty later joked to Morgan that he'd felt like Maya's dad giving permission to Toby. He'd told them to keep it professional at work and no drama if they didn't work out. Morgan still remembered she'd just been happy someone had actually read her handbook.

Now Toby and Maya appeared to be a sweet, loving couple. And that made Morgan happy too.

Morgan's thoughts were broken into when she heard Ripley ask her, "Your best friend is a man? And your husband doesn't mind?"

Morgan had certainly heard those questions before. "Yes, Ty is. And no, Josh doesn't mind. Ty and I go back years. We built this place together and lived to tell about it. Experiences like that tend to either break people or bind them together. We bonded." She laid down a Draw Four card and called out, "*Uno!* Red." She smugly watched as Toby had to draw the four cards, thus adding to his hand.

Turning back to Ripley, Morgan continued, "Josh was well aware we were pals first and very tight. As a matter of fact, Ty met and knew Josh before *I* did. Besides, Josh doesn't have anything to be jealous about, and he knows that."

Maya slapped down a Draw Four card of her own, forcing Morgan to now draw cards. "Yellow. *That's* what you get for messing with my guy!" Maya teased her boss. Looking at Toby, she said, "See, babe? I got your back!"

"You do. That's just one of the many reasons I love ya!" Toby grinned when Morgan glanced at him, shaking her head but smiling.

Mel said, "If Ty ever *does* find who he's looking for, she's just going to have to understand Morgan's part of the package. Personally, the way I see it is he picked *me,* so why be jealous? Or even feel insecure about his best friend being a woman? After all, he *chose* me, right?"

Moving her checker on the board, Mel continued, "Anyway, Ty, Josh, and Damien are all tight and went camping again. I can't believe they left all the work to the women." She held her smile, knowing the guys were going to object to her choice of words. It wasn't long in coming.

Drew objected immediately. "What the...? Excuse me, but there *are* three men in this room, y'know. And Ty is not a god, *girls!*"

Mel refused to recant her statement. Instead, she said cheerfully, "Y'all are just jealous."

Drew threw some popcorn at her. "No, we aren't."

She grinned at him before picking up the popcorn before Freeway found it. "All right. You guys rock as well. We really do like all the men here. But the place *is* owned and run by a woman, who just happens to rock all on her own!"

Morgan grinned at her. "Your raise will be on your next check, Mel."

Smiling at their banter, Ripley asked Laura, "So Damien's your husband. Does that mean he works here too?"

Laura shook her head, took a drink of her beverage before answering. "No. Damien owns a computer business, and I run a travel agency. He and Josh are childhood friends, more like brothers. After we ended up out here in Arizona, Josh followed later on and began his construction business here."

Thinking for a moment, Laura made her next move on the checker board. "And then when Josh and Morgan got together, we got to know Ty and these crazy barn people." They all smiled at her. "And since the stars and planets were aligned, we all became friends."

Morgan smiled at Ripley. "Well, it's also important to note that Ty's *other* best friend, and for even longer than myself, is his male cousin, Channion. I'm just his best friend out here."

As she moved her silver car on the Monopoly board, Alexis said, "He's quality, and quality knows quality."

Bo pointed out, "He likes us too. So you know what *that* means, don't you?"

Alexis laughed. "Sadly, no one's perfect. Not even our Ty."

Bo got up, put her in a headlock and lightly squeezed, making her laugh again before he made his way into the kitchen. They soon heard him call out, "Hey! We got Fig Newtons in here!" He walked back into the living room, dropping off Fig Newtons at each table. "Eat 'em before Morgan makes us give 'em to the horses!"

Knowing he was teasing her, Morgan chuckled.

Changing the subject, Laura said to Ripley, "Damien and I have a little girl, Sasha. She's two and with the babysitter tonight. Normally we bring her out here, but tonight I thought it nice to just get in a little break and have some adult time."

Maya said, "Nothing wrong with getting a little break, Laura. Moms everywhere need one from time to time. You deserve a little rec time for yourself."

"Yeah, I know. And I'm getting better at feeling less guilty for leaving her home now. Thankfully, the neighbor lady is trustworthy, and Sasha took to her right away. She doesn't cry anymore when I leave. *I* might, but she doesn't!"

Drew teased her, "So you left your little girl with the neighbor so you can come here to play kids games without her?"

Her brows furrowed and her lips pursed together, Laura looked stumped for a moment as that question settled in her mind. She soon laughed. "I never thought of it like that! I guess that's *exactly* what I did. She'll be forever traumatized if she ever finds out!"

Everyone laughed.

Fully entertained, Ripley asked, "What about Damien? Does he cry when he leaves his little girl?"

Laura chuckled. "Sasha has her daddy wrapped around her finger, but he's still really good at not letting her get away with things. She knows temper tantrums aren't allowed no matter who she's with. But no, Damien handles leaving her better than I do.

"And you know, it's the sweetest thing in the world when she sees his car pull into the driveway. She's right there at the door, dancing in place until he walks in and swoops her up. It melts our hearts every time! I've even got it on video. Someday when she hates us, we'll play it back to her."

They all laughed at her again.

Laura smiled, her eyes sparkling. "And heaven forbid we try to tuck her into bed without reading a story to her first. Damien loves that time of night with her, so he generally has the book picked out in advance, ready to go. I've got that on video too. He's such a fantastic dad!"

"He is, and you're a wonderful mom," Morgan said. Turning to Ripley, she ordered, "You... Get over here. We need to even out this game since Maya won that one. You can leave your dishes there for now."

As she expertly shuffled the deck as Ripley sat down at the table, Morgan explained, "Josh and I are Sasha's honorary aunt and uncle so she spends time out here with us fairly often. And Sasha loves to ride Ivy."

Laura confided, "And that's the *other* reason why I left her with the sitter tonight. She wouldn't be able to ride Ivy *or* see her Uncle Josh. I sure didn't want to disappoint her by batting zero... *Not* that she wouldn't have been happy to see her Aunt Morgan!"

Morgan took a Fig Newton from her plate and gave her friend the side-eye. "Nice save, Mom. And just in time too." She was just about to say more when she heard her cellphone ringing in the kitchen where she'd left it earlier to charge.

Getting up, she went to answer it.

Chapter 4

"HELLO?" MORGAN LISTENED TO the voice on the other end. "Yes, it is. Can I help you?" She listened, saying, "*Oh no!* Where is it exactly?"

Grabbing the pad of paper and pen beside her, she wrote as fast as she could. She repeated back what she wrote down. "Yes, I'll get there as soon as I can! How many total do you think?" Another pause. "At least two large trailers then? Maybe three? All right. Give me about forty-five minutes to get there. We'll try to be quick, but you know how the roads are with trailers. We should be able to get through on the highway exit before there, right? Is it clear?" At the answer, she replied, "Okay... We'll leave right away. Wait! Give me your number or who to call on scene in case I need it."

After repeating the numbers she was given by the dispatcher, Morgan hung up the phone. She called out loudly, "*Guys!* We have an emergency and need to go!" Everyone looked up when she came out of the kitchen. "We have to go now... Thank God you're all here already. That's a *huge* stroke of luck!"

Laura gasped and asked in fear, "It's not Damien or one of the guys, is it?"

"No, Laura. Thank goodness! But there's a big wreck on the interstate north of here. One of the semis was carrying horses. They need transportation and board for them. The vets aren't able to do it at their places. It sounds like some are injured pretty badly. Two vets are on their way to the scene now. We need to go get the horses, and bring them back here."

They all got up, rushing to put on their shoes and boots. Morgan was slipping on her boots as she calmly called out orders. "Drew, Alexis, Kat, and Mel... I want you four to stay here to set up the temp stalls in Grand View. If you need help, call Rory and Kim. Hopefully they can make it out. Put up water buckets but don't fill them up. We can deal with that later.

"They said we're looking at maybe sixteen to twenty horses. I'm not sure if that includes any that may need to be put down at the scene though. You'll need to work quickly. Try to put up enough stalls for sixteen, just in case. I know that's a lot in very little time, but we already have a few that are up. We'll call you and let you know once we're there.

"Laura? Can you stay for just a little while and help out?"

"Yeah, I can stay another couple of hours." Laura began going around the room, turning off the music and some lights. She went to the kitchen, locked the patio door. No time to worry about the food, she unceremoniously shoved the fruit, meat, and cheese snacks into the fridge to keep them cold. She checked the crockpot. Since it was pretty much empty, she put the lid back on it and unplugged it.

As Laura went to the kitchen, Morgan instructed the others. "Bo, Toby, and Maya... We're taking both the long stock trailers with the dually trucks and the shorter stock trailer with mine. Toby and Maya, you take one long, and I'll take the other. Bo, are you comfortable with the shorter trailer in my truck?" At his nod, she turned and looked at her renter. Morgan asked, "Ripley, are you willing to go with me? We could probably use an extra hand."

Ripley nodded. "You bet. Whatever you need me for!"

"Thanks. If any of us leaving need to use the bathroom, we'd better go now!"

Maya ran down the hall while Morgan grabbed three sets of keys, tossed a set each to Toby and Bo. She described to them where the wreck was while they waited for Maya. Once she ran back into the room, Toby headed to the bathroom. When he was back, Bo then Ripley went. Morgan ran upstairs to use her master bathroom to save time. She ran back downstairs, grabbed her purse, phone, and keys, then herded everyone out the door. She left on the porch light, set her alarm, and locked the door behind her.

Ripley followed Morgan to her truck as almost everyone automatically jumped into the bed for a faster ride to the barns while Laura and Alexis got into their own cars to follow. Although they watched the humans rushing, The Darrells weren't overly bothered and followed along at their own pace.

Morgan dropped Drew, Kat, and Mel at Grand View before heading to the duallies and trailers. Morgan hitched up to the shorter gooseneck while Toby and Bo hitched up the others. After checking the breakaway box, Morgan got back in the truck to test the trailer lights with Ripley calling out they were all working. Ripley checked the tires as she removed the tire chocks and tossed them in the back of the truck just in case they needed them later. She went over and helped Bo get hitched up, checking the trailer lights and pulling the chocks as Maya did the same for Toby.

Morgan and Bo switched vehicles so she'd drive the second dually and the longer trailer. She knew Bo wasn't as experienced with the longer trailers, so it was better they switch. She trusted him but still erred on the side of caution. He didn't mind at all.

Morgan called over to Toby, "You have enough fuel? Bo and I should be okay."

He called back, "We should. I'm at about half a tank... A little over."

"Same here. Hopefully we'll all have enough!"

Thinking ahead, Morgan stopped at Sunset Ridge. She and Ripley jumped out to grab halters and lead ropes. Their arms full, they hurried back to their truck.

"OH... MAN... THIS IS a *mess!* These people are going to be stuck here for *hours!*" Morgan slowed down as they neared the end of the backed-up traffic on the interstate. It was just a long line of red taillights leading off into the night. The sight of taillights at night like this always reminded her of a very long, red mechanical serpent.

She'd tried to get ahead of most of it by taking another highway and coming down the off-ramp closest to the wreck. Unfortunately, there were still miles to go. She stopped on the exit ramp behind a line of cars, unable to go any farther, and studied the situation.

Looking at Ripley, she said, "We're going to have to go on the shoulder on this side and hope we fit. I don't have that much room to swing out here to turn... These cars are in my way... Crap. I hope the trailers don't hit anyone!"

Carefully, Morgan steered her rig onto the right shoulder and saw in the mirror Toby following her with Bo following behind him. She turned on her hazard lights, the blinking lights hopefully a warning to others.

After driving on the shoulder about two miles, she saw a pickup truck up ahead pull onto the shoulder to block them from going by. "Oh, that piece of..." she yelled. "He thinks he's all about keeping people from passing him and cutting into line..." She honked her horn and flashed her lights, but the guy refused to give way.

Ripley, adrenaline and blood pumping, said, "I'll take care of it!"

She jumped out of the truck, running to the blocking truck driver's side and began pounding on the window and door. Morgan heard Ripley yelling at the driver to get out of their way. As it was, the cars behind the guy pulled up so there was nowhere for him to go but into the desert to get out of their way. Ripley kept yelling at him and made him do it.

As Morgan pulled forward, Ripley jumped back in, slamming the door. "I can't stand people like him! Telling *me* what jerks we were for trying to get ahead of everyone else. And such horrid, foul language he used to a woman... What a *prick!* Even if we *were* just trying to get ahead, seeing horse trailers should signal we aren't normal idiots. Jerks, my ass. Who's in the desert *now*, mister? And I bet *you're* gonna try to get in line ahead of where you just were too. Friggin' hypocrite!"

Morgan had to smile at Ripley ranting in her righteous fury. They drove by the guy now in the desert sand, Morgan blaring her horn out of frustration and a little spite. After a moment, Morgan glanced at her passenger and blandly inquired, "Feel better?"

Ripley glanced at her. "No. And I think I dented his door with my fist. If I didn't, it sure feels like it. If I did, hopefully he won't notice until it's too late so he can't call you."

"Thanks for the heads up," Morgan replied dryly. When her phone rang, she just handed it to Ripley to answer. "I don't have my phone set up for Bluetooth in this truck."

Ripley nodded and answered the phone. "Hello? No, I'm Ripley. Morgan's unable to answer at the moment, but she's right beside me driving."

Morgan glanced at her. "Who is it?"

"It's a policeman waiting for us at the wreck site. He's asking where we are."

"Tell him coming from the south about three miles out, on the right shoulder."

Ripley relayed the message, and then said, "Okay. An escort would be nice. People are trying to block us from driving on the shoulder to get to you. I already had to get out once so we could get by." A pause. "Yes, it would. Thank you!"

She hung up the phone. "They're sending a car back to meet us to escort us in."

Morgan grinned. "You're pretty handy to have along, Miss Capilano. Glad I brought ya!"

Ripley grinned back, saying modestly, "I try."

Chuckling despite the circumstances, Morgan drove on. They soon spotted a squad car heading toward them with its blinding, colored lights swirling in the dark of night. They watched him turn around in the desert, and then he led them back toward the wreck.

WHEN THEY GOT TO the wreck, they were shocked at what they saw. Bright lights were swirling on all of the emergency vehicles which was just more stress to the trapped and injured horses, but they had no other choice. Thankfully, the emergency vehicles closest to the semi just had on their colored lights, but they weren't swirling. Morgan saw some temporary lights being set up in the flat desert ground beside the road. They saw a semi on its side, another one jack-knifed and six other cars behind them. It was fairly obvious by the damaged cars they'd been tailgating each other.

Trying to push the cars in front of them to speed even more like the impatient idiots they were... Chain reactions, people! Morgan thought.

Policemen and other First Responders wearing yellow and orange hi-vis vests were everywhere. Their legs and arms glowed as the lights reflected off their safety-striped coats as they moved. The news van was parked out of the way as the cameraman prepped the equipment.

Morgan slowed, wondering where she was supposed to go. She had to keep close to the trailer the horses were in, she figured. Was there spilled gas or diesel over there? she wondered.

An officer ran up to her, flagging her down. "Morgan! I'm so glad you're here!"

"*Matt!* Good to know you're on scene. Where do you want us?"

Deputy Matt Harvey often worked security at her horse shows at the Center since his daughter rode there. Having a familiar face on the scene was a relief to Morgan.

Matt pointed to a spot to their right. "As best you can, get in there. It's the flattest, hardest spot we have here. You shouldn't get stuck in soft sand there. Plus, it's fairly close to the horses. The vets have put down three so far. They were at the back of the trailer. Another couple died before they even got here. It's sickening, really sickening. They just got that one off the trailer..." His voice trailed off as he pointed to where some men were kneeling by a horse on its side.

Morgan nodded, tears instantly misting her eyes. She blinked them away quickly. No time for tears, she scolded herself. She could cry later. And she knew she would.

Chapter 5

His heart wasn't made for such sadness, he thought. Veterinarian Shamis was kneeling on the ground, shaking his head. One more gone.

He stood up when Morgan and Ripley neared him. "Morgan, I'm so glad you could get here. We've got a lot of work to do. We've lost six now. This one here is the latest. It was more humane to put her soul to rest..." He shook his head, genuine sorrow etched on his face.

Morgan personally knew how much he hated to put down a horse, that it was always the last resort for him. "I'm sure you did the right thing. You showed her compassion and mercy. At least she's not suffering anymore, Doc," Morgan said softly, rubbing his shoulder in consolation. "We hate that more. So much more."

"I know." The tall vet ran his weathered, calloused hand through his hair.

The second vet walked over. "Morgan." Dr. Sanders, looking more somber and solemn than she'd ever seen him, nodded to them. "Let's see what we can do here. The First Responders have helped us get some of them out already. We've looked them over but not too deeply. Can we have you look at the others, see who's in the worst condition? Or help in getting the others out?"

"Whatever you need." Turning to Bo, Toby, and Maya, she said, "Let's go."

Ripley said, "I can help, Morgan. I know horses. Let me help somehow."

"Of course! You're with me, remember?"

They followed the two vets to where some officers and firemen were watching over some horses, holding on to makeshift lead ropes, some made from their own belts or their emergency paracord bracelets.

Ripley gasped. "What? No halters?"

An officer heard her. He replied, "No, ma'am. This trailer was probably heading toward Mexico to the slaughterhouse. And halters and lead ropes aren't needed for a place like that."

Ripley nodded before she, Bo, and Maya ran back to the truck to get the ones she and Morgan had brought along. Thank goodness Morgan had thought about that before they'd left, Ripley thought. Not knowing the situation, it was better to be prepared, she'd said.

They quickly came back. Slowly and carefully, they eased halters with their attached lead ropes onto the skittish and scared horses. Ripley, Bo, and Maya softly crooned to them in hopes of settling their nerves and gaining a little of their trust. Morgan and Toby were now with the vets. Bo took a few halters to them as they waited for more to get unloaded. He immediately returned to Maya and Ripley to help hold the horses they had.

A couple of firefighters called out they'd just freed another horse so Dr. Shamis and Toby ran over to them. Dr. Shamis gently slipped a halter on the terrified horse. After a quick check of its body and legs, he gently tugged on the lead rope to see if it could walk. It could, but the poor horse was favoring his front left leg. Dr. Shamis motioned to Dr. Sanders, who was an expert in equine legs, to have a look at it for a second opinion.

After checking the leg, Dr. Sanders said, "Toby, I don't think his leg is broken. It could be a bowed tendon. I can't say for certain just yet. Just give him all the time he needs to walk over there. I wish we could get the trailers over here closer, but we just can't."

Nodding, Toby led the trembling horse toward the others. He spoke softly to the horse, stopping when the horse needed to rest. He softly encouraged him, trying to reassure him he was going to be fine now. He hoped he wasn't lying.

As Ripley stood there, she did a head count. They had nine horses so far, including this latest one that Toby was walking over.

Bo was now holding a few of the horses so the First Responders could return to do their jobs. A couple of them were putting their own belts back on, having used them as makeshift lead ropes.

Maya took the lead rope from Toby, quickly looking over the horse in the glow from the portable lights. Its poor body and legs were trembling. Her heart broke as she tried to soothe and comfort the horse. She noticed its eyes were wide-eyed as it shook.

Ripley did the same to the horses she was holding. All of them were shaking too. She felt her heart shatter at their fear and pain. She was amazed they were more or less standing there. She'd expected them to be trying to get away, rearing, and biting in fear. She assumed they were in shock.

Looking one horse in its eyes, her next thought was the saddest one. There was no hope, strength, or love coming from these eyes. They were just filled with defeat in the hopeless situation they were forced into through no fault of their own.

Seeing this made tears rush into her own eyes. She ran her hand gently down the nearest horse's face. She spoke softly to it, trying to tell it everything would be all right now. But would it? What could she do to help these glorious horses? These innocents?

Toby led another horse to Ripley. As she reached for the lead rope, he said, "Her wounds will need stitched up, but she can at least walk. Her eye looks really bad, but it's so hard to tell in this darkness."

Toby told them there was one more horse they were trying to get out. It was apparently a fighter and was thrashing in the trailer where it had fallen. Maya's eyes filled with tears. It was a terrified, beautiful animal fighting for its life, not knowing if the people surrounding it were friends or foe.

What Toby didn't tell them was Morgan was in there with it. She was trying to use her horse magic, as Ty called it, to calm it down. They heard the calls from the cops and firefighters to each other, could barely make out the many men over there trying to assist in any way they could.

Ripley had to ask the question no one else had yet. "What do they plan on doing with the dead horses? Are we supposed to take them back too? Or are the vets going to take care of them?"

Toby shrugged his shoulders. "We'll probably need our three for these guys. It makes my gut churn thinking they were just packed in like sardines. I'm going to have really bad dreams about this." He blew out a long breath. "My guess is we take the live ones back to the Center. Either we come back for the dead ones, or maybe they'll have a livestock truck come get them."

Maya nodded. "Yeah. They'll need a winch to get them up into..." Her voice broke on a sob.

"Sweetheart, stop. Don't picture that. You won't get it out of your head if you do." Toby quickly hugged her and placed a kiss on her forehead. "It's not the night we had planned, is it? We can do it another time, but I'm sure glad we're here to help these horses."

Maya nodded, wiped her nose with her hand. "I know. Me too."

Deputy Harvey came over to them. "Morgan said she's working on getting this last one out so—"

Interrupting him, Maya cried out, "What? Morgan's in there with *that* one?" They all heard the commotion coming from the steel trailer. That's all everyone heard—the terrified squeals and kicks as the hooves hit metal. "Get her out of there, Matt!"

He placed his hand on her shoulder. "Give Morgan some credit, Maya. She knows what she's doing. She's the best person *to* have in there."

"I know, but..."

He nodded, understanding her worry. "She said to begin loading up the horses to get them back to the Center. Start with Toby's trailer. She said to leave room in hers for this last one."

They all nodded. With a couple of officers helping, they began slowly leading the shell-shocked horses toward the trailers. People were watching from their cars, many hanging out the windows taking pictures with their phones. Officers and volunteer emergency responders were there, too, keeping everyone in their vehicles. They were still not letting traffic move, not until the horses were secured and a detour set up.

Oddly enough, not a single person there for the horses ever asked about the drivers or passengers of the semis or the cars. Focused on their duty, their minds and hearts did not waver from the traumatized animals that couldn't ask for help but so obviously needed it.

They painstakingly began loading up the horses. Quite a few were understandingly refusing to go into another metal cage on wheels. It was just a big black hole or scary tunnel to them. A portable death trap.

Thankfully, Ripley was able to handle them with little fuss. Having an endless supply of patience and a calming voice, she was the one who led them up and into the trailer. Once in, she handed the rope to Toby so he could tie it with a safety release knot. He talked to the horse, trying to keep it calm until another one was brought in. It was a dangerous job he had. They tried to get him out of there as quickly as they could, knowing they also couldn't rush.

Bo and Maya held the remaining horses as Toby and Ripley loaded them. They put six horses into Toby's trailer before shutting the back door, latching it securely.

Toby asked, "Morgan's *still* in there?" At Maya's nod, he said, "Let's get these others in her trailer then. We'll use Bo's as a last resort... Or for the dead ones if we need to."

They loaded the remaining horses into Morgan's trailer, closing the door while they waited for this last one. The kicks and squeals from the horse Morgan was with had stopped, and the heavy silence was almost eerie.

Maya whispered, "I'm not sure if this quiet is good or bad..."

Ripley just nodded, her eyes not leaving the trailer as they all waited for Morgan to walk out of its black, gaping shadow. "Do we need to call the Center to let them know how many are coming?"

Maya nodded. "Good idea... I don't think anyone else has yet... I'll do that now." She pulled out her phone to call Kat.

Finally, they saw Morgan cautiously step outside the metal semi, leading a tall horse. The horse picked his way as carefully as she did, their feet slipping and sliding on the metal underneath the blankets the cops had put down to cover the sharp edges. Morgan kept talking calmly to the horse, letting him take his time. She saw the huge gash down his chest and torn flesh even in the shadows cast by the portable lights.

When both woman and horse stopped on the firm, sandy desert ground, the vets calmly walked over to see the damage. The gaping chest wound made Morgan's heart stop. Flesh and skin just hung down, baring muscle and tendons. The horse laid back his ears at the vets, but he was in too much pain, or shock, to carry through with any real threats he made at them. His entire body was shaking like he had chills, his legs splayed out for balance. It was a wonder his legs could even hold him up. Morgan felt it was only through his sheer will he was on his feet at all.

The vets quickly checked the horse over. They decided they couldn't really do much in the way of surgery or stitching there, so they made the tough decision to let it stay as it was. They needed to safely rush the horse to the Center as quickly as they could, and do it there. The two vets already had a mental triage assessment going. He'd probably be the first to be taken care of. Next would be the mare with the bad eye, and the gelding with that sore front leg.

Ripley joined Morgan so they both slowly led the wobbly horse to her trailer. Being the last one on meant he'd be the first to get off. As expected, he was not willing to get right back into another metal death trap. It took both vets, Toby, and a cop to literally force the horse into the trailer, quickly shutting the tailgate behind him so he couldn't scoot back out. Morgan already had the end of his rope pulled through the slats of the trailer and deftly tied him from the outside. Ripley stood beside her, ready to offer assistance.

His panicked, pained squeals rang out in the desert air. The rolling whites of his terrified eyes stood out as he tried to thrust his head through the slats of the trailer, desperately seeking his freedom. Ripley could barely stand the pain tearing through her at his distress. She wiped the tears from her face as she watched him struggle to get out. His terror and desperation now also had the effect of making the other horses react to him.

Morgan's own eyes filled up with big tears. Blinking them away, she said, "These poor things! They're absolutely terrified. We need to *go!*"

Dr. Sanders said to Morgan and Toby, "Let's get moving! You'll have an escort to your place. Just drive carefully especially on turns and curves. Watch how you speed up and slow down so no one falls. Just try to coast as much as you can. We'll meet you there as soon as we can leave here. They've suffered more than enough, and we need to doctor them as quickly as we can. A livestock truck will be coming out for the ones that didn't make it. They may have been the luckier ones, sad to say."

Everyone there understood.

"Go to Grand View, the show barn. That's where we're keeping them," Morgan told the vets.

Dr. Shamis nodded. "We'll be right behind you."

Morgan and Ripley rushed to their truck as Toby and Maya rushed to theirs. Bo got into his truck, personally thankful he didn't have the responsibility to haul any back because he was driving alone. Deputy Matt Harvey waved to them to signal he'd lead while another officer was to follow them.

Releasing the emergency brake, Morgan began to inch forward, hoping to make a wide turn around the wreck site as none of the horses were steady on their feet. Every time they went over a bump in the ground, she winced. She saw Ripley wipe tears from her eyes as she drove. "Hang in there... Hang in there," she heard Ripley say softly as if the horses could hear her.

Matt Harvey waited in his squad car for Morgan and Toby to come around while he mentally planned the best route back to the Center. When he saw Bo behind Toby, he drove forward to give them more space. Once they all straightened out and reached him, he led them onto the interstate. They'd have to go farther north to reach an exit ramp in order to turn around to head back south. Glancing in his side mirror, he saw his fellow officer following them.

His heart heavy, he cleared the way to Harmony Hills.

Chapter 6

THEY COULD HEAR THEIR own heartbeats thudding in their heads. As Morgan and Ripley followed the squad car, its lights on but siren off unless needed, they talked little. Morgan was attuned to any sounds coming from the trailer. Ripley, also listening intently, was too nervous to distract her. Morgan kept her eyes forward on Matt's squad car while Ripley mainly kept hers looking in her side mirror.

Halfway back to the Center, Morgan's phone rang. Recognizing the ringtone, she just handed it to Ripley to answer it for her. "It's my husband."

"Hello, Josh?" Ripley paused to listen. "No, she's driving right now. She wanted me to answer for her... We're rushing back to your place with some hurt horses... No, no... She's fine. She's not hurt or anything. I promise she's fine..." She paused again as she listened to Josh. "Hang on, please." Turning to Morgan, she said, "He wants to know why you aren't using the truck's Bluetooth, and why I'm on your phone. What do I tell him?"

"Tell him all of it," Morgan replied. "I just don't want to be distracted here."

"Okay." Ripley held the phone to her ear again. "Josh? I'm Ripley. Morgan said to tell you what's happened. She doesn't want to be distracted right now because she's driving. We're following Deputy Matt... Yes, Matt Harvey... He's escorting us back to Harmony Hills.

"We were called out to an emergency on the interstate north of town. A couple semis and some cars wrecked. One of the semis was full of horses heading toward probably Mexico. We think to a slaughterhouse.

"Some horses were put down on site, and a couple others were already dead before we got there. We have eleven live ones that we're taking to your place. Some are in really bad shape. Two vets are following us back... Sanders and Shamis, I think?" She paused as she listened to Morgan's husband, hearing the concern in his voice. "Um, I'm not sure. They just called and asked Morgan to get them."

Morgan glanced at her as Ripley listened. "Yeah, Morgan had some stay behind to put up the stalls in Grand View. Toby and Maya are in the second trailer with horses following us right now. Bo has the third trailer, but his is empty. We have a police escort in front of us and another behind in case something happens." She paused again. "I don't know... Let me ask her."

Ripley looked at Morgan, who was trying to stay close to the deputy's car. "He wants to know if you want him and the guys to come back now?"

Morgan thought about it for a moment. "It'd be really nice to have them, but it's probably not necessary for them to come back early. We've got it covered. We can make it through another night and day without them. Tell them to stay where they are if they want to."

Ripley relayed the message, and then listened to him talking. Answering him, she said, "Of course, and I'll let her know." She listened some more before saying, "Sure." Another pause before she asked, "Really? All right... I will." She smiled before replying, "You're welcome. And yeah, we will." She hung up and looked in her mirror to study the side of the horse trailer for a moment. After a long sigh, Ripley relayed his messages. "He said he loves you and to take care until he gets home.

"He also said he's going to wring your neck for saying they could stay put. I'm not sure I was supposed to tell you that last part. He said I was, but I'm not sure if he was serious."

Morgan found her first smile in hours. "He was. Looks like you'll be meeting my husband earlier than you thought you would. He'll be here by tomorrow morning with Ty and Damien in tow. Not that they'd stay behind, mind you. Besides that, they all went in his truck."

"But you just told him to stay there as planned."

"Josh and I are a team, like Ty and I are. We all are actually, and we never leave the other hanging. They're packing up their tents and throwing dirt on their little sacred bonfire right now. Unless they've been drinking, they'll head right on out. None of us *ever* drive if we've been drinking more than is responsible to do so."

Ripley studied her for a moment in the dark. The dashboard lights added a glow to the black of the truck's cab, along with the red, white, and blue flashes coming from the squad car in front of them. "If that's the case, then why did you tell me to tell him to stay there?"

Morgan smiled at her. "Because I'm terribly stubborn at times. Truth is, we *do* have it covered. But it's *also* truth it'd be fabulous to have the men here to help out. Josh and Ty know me well enough to know this."

She paused to look in her mirror before she continued, "So they'll be the wonderful men that they are, pack up, and rush home to be there to support me just like I would for them. Besides, there's no way they'd be able to enjoy their last, extra day off knowing I'm swamped with an emergency at home. That phone call effectively killed that in one fell swoop, I'm sorry to say. I simply gave them the option to make the choice to return home seem like theirs."

Ripley nodded slowly. "Okay... You're sneaky. I'm going to remember that about you."

Morgan looked again in her side mirror a moment before she said, "Well, look at it this way. If they come racing back home in a time of emergency, they'll be seen as heroes. Men charging in on their white steeds, right?" Ripley nodded. "Okay, well, I just gave them the opening they needed to do so.

"Men love to be needed, Rip, especially by independent women like me. In fact, I dare say they *need* to be needed especially by independent women. And in all honesty, I absolutely love knowing I have a man like that. A man all to myself who can ride that white steed to come back home to me and not fall off even when it's bucking and kicking."

Ripley looked out the window, thinking about it. How would it be having a reliable man like that around? "Well, hell," she muttered.

Morgan glanced at her. "What?"

"You've got me flat-out jealous. I want one for myself too. And I don't even care what color of steed he's riding as long as he has one!"

Morgan gave a quick smile before she turned her full attention back to the task at hand. She appreciated the cars that moved over for them as they flew down the interstate. When they finally arrived at Harmony Hills safely, it was a relief. Morgan had Ripley call Kat to let them know their ETA in case Maya hadn't yet. Deputy Harvey turned off his flashing lights when he got close to the Center, not wanting to spook the horses that lived there. Morgan appreciated his thinking ahead as she turned into the second gate.

Pulling up to Grand View, Morgan carefully swung around and backed all the way in. Mel guided her in, getting as close to the stalls as they could. She then did the same for Toby. Bo parked his trailer in the lot where he got it from, then ran to the barn to help out. Once both trailers were in, Morgan had Bo and Kat close the large doors to keep the building secure in case a horse got loose and tried to flee in panic. As the doors were being closed and latched, she checked over all the stalls, making sure they were secure.

It wasn't that Morgan didn't trust her staff, but she wanted the responsibility to end with her. If something were to happen, it was *her* name that would get dragged through the mud because it was *her* business.

Morgan approved of them setting up most of the stalls near the walls for more support. The sturdy temporary stalls were set up facing each other in parallel lines. "I thought having an aisle between the two rows would help with working with the horses as needed, and so they could see each other," Kat explained as Morgan checked them. "I wasn't sure what we needed."

"This will work just fine, I'm sure. You all did a great job."

Walking with them, Alexis said, "We didn't need Rory or Kim. We kind of figured we'd get it done about the time they arrived anyway. We didn't want you to think they refused to come in or anything. We just didn't call them. And Laura left just before you called the last time."

Morgan smiled. "Thanks, Alexis. You all did just what I needed you to."

Once the building was secure, Morgan began with Toby's trailer instead of her own. Figuring the last horse put on would be a handful, they decided to unload the other trailer first while they were all calm as could be expected. As they carefully unloaded the frightened horses, she was able to see more of what they were dealing with now. She assigned a horse to each stall. The two officers stood to the side, out of their way but ready to help if they were needed. Matt let their dispatcher know what was going on.

The two vets arrived about fifteen minutes later. Once the vets arrived, the officers left. Morgan had just finished unloading the last horse from her trailer when they saw the two men walk through the people door at the end of the building. Once the last horse was secure in a stall, Drew opened up the large door so Toby and Bo could drive out the trailers and let the vets drive their trucks inside. Once they did, he closed the door again.

The first horse they went to was the last horse they'd loaded up at the wreck site. Morgan had put him in a stall on the far end, hoping he could feel secure there. Since he was still able to see other horses, he also knew he wasn't alone. He looked to be in shock and in obvious pain like the others.

Finally tranquilizing the horse as it wanted to fight them, the two vets competently cleaned and sewed up the sorrel's ripped-open chest, leaving a tiny drainage hole. They worked on the other deep gashes on his body, checked over his cut-up legs, and gave him antibiotics and painkillers. The horse fought them the whole time even with a mild sedative. By the time they were done, he looked completely worn out.

So did the two vets, and he was only the first horse they'd been to. They left him alone in his stall to recover in peace. Once the vets were done, Mel filled his water bucket half-full. They worried about when the last time was any of them had been given food and water. Having them colic was the last thing any of them needed to have happen now.

As the vets went to work on the others, Ripley took over the horse's care. She carefully removed the halter from his head while speaking to him softly and gently stroking his neck. She found it nearly impossible to leave his side. "Sleep, my darling. We'll take care of you. You just rest now, little man. You're safe here," Ripley whispered. She noticed his ears would flicker when she spoke to him.

When Ripley finally closed the stall door, his head was drooping down. She watched over him until his skinned nose was almost touching the straw Mel and Kat had chosen over the sawdust for bedding. With a quiet sigh, she finally walked away.

Down the line they went, each vet working on a horse to get to them all as quickly as they could. On the worst ones, they conferred with each other. With the assistance of some of the staff, they were able to move along efficiently. There were some badly cut legs and sides from the metal of the trailer, or from the slicing cut of another horse's hooves seeking traction as the trailer was hit, and then toppled over.

The mare with the bad eye looked in worse shape now that they could see her better under the lights. She had more injuries than they'd been able to see in the dark too. The vets discussed their options with Morgan, not wanting to put her down unless necessary. Wanting to give her a fighting chance, they stitched her up and did their absolute best to make her comfortable. It was a delicate balance between doing everything one could and playing God.

It was almost two in the morning when the vets took their leave, looking as exhausted as the eleven horses. Morgan had Alexis make them some fresh coffee in her office so they had something to keep them awake on their drives home. Alexis poured the hot coffee into the biggest capped mugs she could find. As they were leaving, Dr. Shamis promised to come back out the next day sometime to check on them.

Finally, Morgan closed down the barn. The horses were exhausted and drugged. They also had some water and grass hay in case they woke up before they were expected to. Morgan didn't feel the need to stay out there since they'd be right back out to begin their usual work day in less than five hours. Ripley could see Morgan was fighting that decision of not staying out there just in case. But she decided the horses would just be sleeping in the short term, and they all needed to catch up on any sleep they could get themselves.

Once everyone was outside, Morgan offered her place to her staff. "I've got the two spare rooms so that makes three beds, plus the couch. I've got pillows and a sleeping bag for the floor too... Unless Josh took both of them."

With no hesitation at all, Alexis said, "I'll take the couch!"

Toby and Maya took her up on her offer of one room while Bo and Drew took the other one. Kat would crash at Mel's as she didn't live too far away.

Morgan nodded. "Okay. Let's hit the hay. Kat and Mel, please drive safely. I'll loan those of you who are staying over some clothes so we can wash what you're wearing now. We've got sweat, blood, and dirt all over us. And Ripley, thank you for helping out. It was very much appreciated. Thank you *all*, seriously. You're the best crew I could have. Overtime pay for you all, of course.

"We'll have to wait to see what's to happen to these guys. They're not ours, and I don't know exactly what's to become of them." But she had a good idea, and she simply couldn't deal with that right now.

Ripley said goodnight to them all and headed back to her RV with a flashlight from the barn Morgan loaned her since she'd left hers in the house earlier. The Darrells trotted along beside Ripley like they knew she wasn't too keen on walking down there alone. She grinned when they simply sat down beside her RV door like they knew that's where she had to be to go in, or out of, the vehicle. She trusted them to have scared away all the possible snakes.

Bending over, Ripley pet both of them vigorously. She thanked them for escorting her, unlocked her door and went inside.

After she took a shower and put on some pajamas, Ripley sat on her little couch to let her mind clear before she went to bed herself. She was so tired she could hardly think straight. But the horses in the barn, all alone, tormented her. She just couldn't leave them there all alone like they were abandoned.

Tears streamed down her face as she remembered their fear, both at the wreck site and in the barn. Her face raw from wiping it clean, she made her decision.

She changed clothes, slipped on her shoes, thought twice about snakes and switched them for a pair of cowboy boots. Guided by the flashlight and the moonlight, she made her way back to the barn. Knowing Morgan had left the alarm off—worried it'd get set off by accident and terrify the injured horses—she slipped inside. Using the flashlight to find the light switches, she turned on a couple of them.

Peeking inside the stalls as she walked down the row, Ripley's heart ached. Some were just flat out on their sides on the soft straw, not bothering to get up as she looked in. She figured it was exhaustion and drugs that allowed them to be in such a defenseless position. As a prey animal, horses didn't tend to do that for long even when they felt safe.

One horse didn't even open his eyes or acknowledge her presence at all. Her own heart anxiously pumping, she stood there long enough to make sure the horse hadn't died. Once she saw his side moving, she felt a wave of relief wash through her.

She dutifully stopped at each stall, letting her conscience see each horse was fine. A few were still on their feet, a hind leg cocked, sleeping. Some blinked their sedated eyes at her, and then simply went back to resting. The poor mare didn't even acknowledge her presence.

When Ripley got to the last stall that housed the last horse Morgan had walked off the semi, he was waiting for her. Watching her look at him, it was like he was thinking to himself about whether or not to make the effort to walk over. After a minute of listening to her talking softly to him, the tall horse gingerly made his way closer, his ears moving back and forth as he listened to her.

After what seemed an eternity to her, he pushed his nose through the bars and blew his warm breath on her. She blew back, gently brushing her index finger down his skinned nose as she did so. She spoke softly again to the horse, letting him know she was a friend.

She peeked inside the stall through the bars, studied his chest that was all stitched up. It made her own chest hurt just looking at his. All the horses had nicks and scrapes while some also had deep cuts. The other ones with stitches weren't as bad as this horse though... with the exception of the mare. Many of them had swollen legs, but the antibiotics, wraps, and medications should heal those in time. Would any of them founder? Some horses founder due to stress, and they'd all been in a whole lot of it just tonight, she thought. Having that painful hoof condition was a real concern.

But medication and drugs couldn't heal what was really wrong with them. No drug could fix a horse's spirit, his zest for life. No kind of drug could infuse an animal with hope again. These poor horses looked so defeated.

But this horse seemed different. Even as tired as she was, Ripley felt something else from this battered horse. From his brown eyes, he truly seemed to be asking for her help. There was this mysterious sense of presence about him that she connected to, so she stood there and talked to him through the bars. He seemed to be listening to her, soaking in every whispered word.

Hearing a noise behind her, her heart leapt into her throat. Quickly turning her head, she realized it was The Darrells coming down the aisle toward her. They nuzzled her hands when they reached her side.

"You guys *scared* me!" She bent down to pet them, calming her racing heart. Did she leave the door open? She'd better make sure it was closed all the way when she left. She swore she'd closed it though. Maybe there was a doggie door somewhere? But she couldn't see Morgan having one simply for the wildlife she was trying to keep out. Of course, the doors were usually open anyway.

After Ripley realized she was barely able to keep her eyes open, she decided she really needed to go to bed. She kept yawning too—but that may have been because the two dogs did it first. When she turned around to leave, the horse began banging his foot on the door. She rushed back, and he stopped. He thrust his nose through the bars at her.

"I'm *exhausted*, little man. I'll see you later, okay? I promise I'll come back. You've had a much rougher day than me, so if I'm tired, then you must be too."

Again she tried to leave, and again the horse banged his hoof against the door. "*Shh!* Sweetie, you're waking up the others! They need their sleep too!"

Four more times Ripley tried to leave, but the horse refused to let her leave his sight. The Darrells simply sat there, watching her with those all-knowing brown eyes of theirs. Why did those two dogs seem more intelligent than they should be? she wondered as she studied them with tired, blurry eyes. They just stared back at her, neither moving a muscle.

"Well, hell." Hands on her hips, she said softly to the dogs, "I guess I'm staying here, huh?"

They immediately wagged their tails while their bright eyes looked at her like she'd answered the million-dollar question correctly.

She remembered seeing a blanket by the door and hurried to get it, hearing the horse banging the door again the whole time she was out of his sight. Making sure the human door was securely closed, she quickly headed back to the horse still banging on his door. Seeing a plastic lawn chair, she grabbed it too. Carrying the two items down the aisle to the horse's stall, she set them down. The second he saw her, he stopped making such a racket. His ears were up, and his tired, pain-filled eyes followed her every movement. It made her heart break.

Walking over to him, she whispered, "I can't *believe* I'm doing this for you!" But she smiled at him, stroked his nose a few more times before she kissed it.

She'd forgotten the lights and hurried to turn them off, deciding to leave on just one. The horse banged on his door until she got back. Shaking her head, she sank down in the chair in relief and pulled the blanket over her bare legs. The Darrells lay down beside her, let out dual sighs and closed their eyes. As she sat there, she could see the big horse in the shadows intently watching her like he was making sure she wasn't going to leave him again.

"Go to sleep, little man," she whispered to him. "I won't leave you. I'll stay here. Promise."

His ears flicked forwards and backwards a couple of times. She watched in the peaceful silence as his eyelids began to droop down, then his head.

A few minutes later, she was out cold herself.

Chapter 7

THE THREE WISE MEN arrived at the stable early that morning. The sun was just peeping up over the mountains, casting deep shadows over parts of the valley floor while softly highlighting the rest. After haphazardly packing up their campsite and making sure their fire was completely out, then driving the rest of the night after being up since early the morning before, all three men were exhausted. They could only imagine what the others back home were feeling like.

After coming through the main gate, Josh stopped at the barn lot where Damien and Ty had left their vehicles. After they transferred their belongings into their own cars, they stood there a moment, looking around, noticing how quiet it was. They noted the workers' cars and trucks in the lots, but there was no sign of anyone anywhere. Even The Darrells weren't around. The place seemed eerily deserted.

Damien stretched and groaned. "You guys are the real horsemen here. You okay if I go home, or did you want me to stay for a while? I will if you want me to."

Josh shook his head. "We've got it, but thanks for the offer. Go on home to your family. Maybe they missed you," he teased.

"Doubtful," Ty joked before assuring a grinning Damien. "Between us and the staff, we should be fine."

"Okay, well... Call if you need me," Damien said as he got in his car and soon drove away.

Josh intended to stop at the house before going to the barns. He figured Morgan would be up soon, if not already.

"You want to come up to the house?" he asked Ty. "Get something to eat? Use the bathroom or anything?" He stretched his arms and back, a bit stiff after the ride in the truck after the long day of hiking, boating, and fishing the day before.

"Nah, I'm good." Ty yawned as he stretched his own muscles. "But I might come up to talk to our girl if she's not down before I leave. I'll go from there."

Josh nodded, knowing Ty would always think of Morgan as his girl too. Josh truly didn't mind. After all, Ty and Morgan were best friends long before he showed up. His trust in them both was solid. Since yawns are contagious, he yawned himself before turning away.

"Don't you want to see the horses?" Ty asked, a bit surprised.

"Yeah, I do. But I'd rather see Morgan first. Unlike you, I have my priorities in order." Josh's voice was deadpan level. Even though his eyes darted to the large barn, he didn't miss Ty's quick grin at his dig. "She could be down here already, but my guess is she's in bed. I'll check there first."

"In bed, huh? Well, I guess I could go with you then... Get my priorities straightened out."

Finding the energy to laugh at Ty about wore Josh out. His voice full of humor, he said, "Unless you're a woman, you're not allowed to change your mind that fast!"

Ty smiled. "I guess I'm going to the barn then." He was curious to see what shape these horses were in. He'd noticed all the doors at Grand View were closed which was unusual. "But I still might stop by in a bit to get the lay of the land."

"Sure." Josh headed toward the house on the hill, hoping he wouldn't trip and fall flat on his face. Tired as he was, he wasn't sure he'd be able to get back up. He decided if he fell, he might just take a dirt nap wherever it was he landed. He suddenly realized he was walking instead of driving his own truck up to his own house. Shaking his head, he turned around and walked back to his truck. Feeling like a complete idiot, he got in and started it up.

The fact that Ty didn't even say anything to him about it could only mean he was as dead tired as Josh was and didn't even notice. That was huge to Josh's mind as Ty was always sharp. He slowly drove his truck toward the house as Ty headed to the barn.

Walking around to the people door on the end nearest him, Ty entered the quiet building. He heard nothing as he hung his sunglasses over the edge of his t-shirt at his throat. He saw a single light section on and figured someone must be in the building, so he made his way over there. He turned the corner and came to a stop at the sight before him.

There was a person stretched out in the arena sand on top of what looked like an old horse blanket at the opposite end of the rows of the temporary stalls. There was a plastic chair at their feet. The Darrells were snuggled up beside them, one of them with their head across the person's back. The dog picked up his head as he saw the familiar figure walking toward him, his eyes bright and welcoming.

Ty grinned at the two dogs that were now slowly thumping their tails in the sand. However, neither dog got up for attention like they normally did. Maybe they were just as tired, he thought with some humor. He walked over to see the horses.

The few horses that were barely awake ignored him as he walked by them, peeking in to see their condition. He shook his head, his heart hurting when he saw them and their injuries. One mare had a nasty eye wound that made his empty stomach turn a bit.

Although The Darrells recognized Ty, neither was in any particular hurry to leave their comfortable spot beside the sleeping person. They did, however, wag their tails faster in excitement as he got closer to them. Darrell G cocked her head to one side as she watched him approach.

Ty realized it was a woman sleeping on the worn-out blanket. He assumed it'd be Morgan keeping watch, but as he got closer, he noticed this woman's hair was much darker and wavy. Morgan's hair wasn't that dark due to the sun bleaching it and was straight most of the time. The Darrells finally got up and greeted him as they normally did with little jumps and bumps of their noses, showing their happiness at seeing him. Ty obligingly bent over to pet them, rubbing their ears and scratching their necks.

When he approached the last stall, the tall sorrel horse in it suddenly charged. Having ice in his veins, Ty barely even flinched. This horse flared his nostrils, snorted, and banged his hoof repeatedly against the door, ears flat back, while his teeth raked the bars. Both dogs had jumped back a bit, now watching warily as the horse banged on the door again. Ty simply stood where he was, letting the horse know he wasn't a threat to him. Ty looked over what he could see of him, reading animal body language like some people read a book.

The horse's eyes were not friendly in the least. The bared teeth and ears flat back were further testament to this horse not being receptive to humans... if the charging hadn't been warning enough.

As the horse banged on the door again with his front hoof, Ty spoke quietly to him. "It's okay, big fella. I'm not gonna hurt ya."

Bang, bang, bang.

Ty stepped forward slowly, chanced a better look inside the stall. He now saw the stitches in the horse's wide chest and more stitches in his side. When the horse snaked his neck at him, Ty saw long stitches in his cheek as the horse rolled his eyes and bared his teeth while biting at the vertical bars. Ty also saw the four swollen legs. All from the wrecked trailer, he assumed.

His voice whisper soft against the horse's snorts, Ty spoke to him, "Aw, I bet all that hurts, doesn't it? And you're scared too. You don't know what to do to defend yourself locked in here. It's gonna be okay."

Ty stood his ground as the horse lunged once again at him. Deciding to give the poor horse some respect and space, Ty backed up a step before turning to look at the woman sleeping there. How could she sleep through that racket? he wondered.

As he looked down at her, he had to admit he was more than a little curious. Who was she?

Her arms were under her head like a pillow. Ty couldn't see her face since it was turned away and covered by some of her long, thick, black, and wavy hair. The rest hung over her shoulder, some in the sand. Sleeping on her stomach, her long legs lay on top of the dingy blanket until the blanket stopped, then the rest of her legs, capped off in cowboy boots, lay in the sand of the arena. Her tan shorts and green tank top showed her entire body was nicely toned and in good shape. She wasn't a stick figure of a woman but not overweight by any means either. She just looked healthy.

Ty figured she didn't spend much time in the sun as her skin was more white than deeply tanned. That was refreshing as he really wasn't into women who spent time trying to look like leather, risking skin cancer just to try to look sexy in a bikini or shorts. This woman had just enough of a light tan that said she spent some time outdoors but didn't waste her time sunbathing. She'd look younger when she was older because she apparently took care of herself in that regard. No leathery look for her, Ty mused.

It took less than a few seconds for him to study her and arrive at his conclusions. The Darrells had once again stretched out beside the woman, both looking happy and protective of her.

When the sorrel horse again banged against the stall, Ripley turned her head, dragging her hair out of her face. She'd heard the horse banging on the stall a couple of minutes before, of course, but she was trying to figure out *why*. Since he'd been so quiet, it seemed very odd he'd be making so much noise all of a sudden. She sluggishly wondered if she'd heard a voice but figured she'd just been imagining things. She'd missed feeling the warmth and comfort of the dogs beside her when they got up and left her. She was content again when she'd felt them come back and had smiled inside.

But now, curiosity made her open her eyes. Once her hair was out of her way, she saw she wasn't alone. Seeing the man towering over her, Ripley gasped in surprise. Now she understood the sorrel was warning her of an intruder. The man looking down at her grinned.

Scrambling, she sat up while The Darrells quickly scooted out of her way. She then simply leaned on her elbows for support, her head spinning from lack of sleep. She closed her eyes until the head rush went away. The Darrells nudged her with their wet noses, and she automatically began petting them. Opening her eyes once her head cleared, she looked at the man again. Her thoughts scattered in a thousand directions when her mind finally focused on the man standing over her.

Bang. Bang. Crash.

Ripley's gaze quickly went to the horse across from her. She hurriedly gestured at the man still grinning at her. "Move! He can't see me." Her throat was scratchy and dry.

Although Ty heard her, he still asked, "What?"

She cleared her throat and tried again, louder. "He can't see me. If he can't see me, he bangs on the door. You're in his way." She motioned again for him to move aside.

Ty studied her for a moment. For a woman who'd just slept in sand, and who knows what else, she looked awfully good. Or perhaps he was so tired himself, he was hallucinating. The Darrells watched him with their intelligent eyes like they knew what he was thinking.

Bang. Bang. Crash. Teeth scraping down the wall.

It then sounded like he'd landed a solid kick. Ripley quickly looked over to see if a board had been busted loose. She didn't see one but thought she'd better check.

Hearing the very agitated horse behind him, Ty took her suggestion to heart. He took a step closer to her but also to the side, so the horse could clearly see her. Neither was sure what caused it, but the horse didn't like that any better. He snorted and lunged again, blocked by the wall and bars of the temporary stall. Ty was glad it was secure as he had no doubt this horse would charge and attack on purpose. Most horses didn't do that, but he suspected this horse was driven to his present state of mind through no fault of his own. It wasn't his fault he ended up this way.

His behavior was now unsettling some of the other horses. Both of them saw a couple startle at every bang the sorrel inflicted on his own stall. A few others snorted.

"I thought you said he'd stop if he could see you," Ty commented.

Ripley studied the horse for a moment. "Well, he did before..." The horse wasn't looking at her though. Those brown eyes were locked on the man. A sudden thought hit her. "He doesn't like *you*."

"He doesn't know me," Ty countered.

"It doesn't seem to make a difference to him! Move down the aisle, and let's see what he does." At the man's doubtful look, she gestured for him to move farther away, pleading, "It's early. Humor me. He's going to hurt himself if he doesn't stop!" When he still hadn't moved, she added firmly, "*Move!*"

At her more forceful tone, Ty nodded and did as she asked. Sure enough, as soon as the horse couldn't see him, he began to quiet down. It took a couple of minutes, but he slowly calmed down even more. Still sitting on the ground, Ripley nodded to herself before motioning to the man to come back within the horse's line of sight.

Bang. Bang. Bang. Lunge at the door with teeth bared.

"Son of a..." Ty said, his soft voice trailing off. "You're *right!*" He quickly backed up as he didn't want to stress out the injured horse anymore.

Saying nothing, Ripley sighed. Thinking it through as best as she could in her present state of mind, she studied the horse. Transferring her gaze from the horse to the man, she commented, "He was quiet as a lamb until a few minutes ago." After a thought struck her, she asked, "Did he begin this as soon as he *saw* you?"

He simply nodded. Out of respect for the horse, Ty stayed out of the horse's view and kept quiet. The horse had calmed down somewhat, but the look in his eyes told Ripley he knew the man was still there.

Reasoning her thoughts out loud, she said, "Don't take it personally. My guess at this point is it's going to be *all* men. He's probably been abused by men, not women." She slowly got up, stretched, whimpered in pain. "*Ouch!* I'm not going to be able to move for a *week!*"

Ripley practically hobbled over to the horse, unafraid. He immediately thrust his nose through the bars like he was making sure she was all right with a man around. Blowing gently into his nose, she stroked it with her hand. His nostrils still flaring from his agitation, the horse blew gently back at her. She noticed the horse had broken out into a sweat. She talked softly to the horse before preparing to walk away. Her heart was in her eyes when she turned to look at Ty. Her eyes were now full of sorrow.

Intending to leave, Ripley took a few steps toward the man who was intently watching her. She also wanted to check on the other horses before she returned to her RV for some much-needed rest. Not to mention another shower.

Bang. Bang.

She immediately stopped and returned to the horse. The banging ceased.

"I guess you can see now why I slept in the barn. If he can't see me, he bangs the door. He would've kept up all these other sick horses and probably injured himself even more. He still might be drugged up enough to not know to stop from pain."

With a quiet tone in the hopes of not disturbing the horse again, Ty asked, "So you slept in here all night to keep him company?"

"Yeah, but it wasn't all night. I came in around three-thirty? I'm not sure..." Her head felt light. She yawned, and then glanced at her watch. "Oh... I haven't slept but a couple of hours..." She blew out a breath as she leaned against the stall wall for a moment. "I have to admit I'm about ready to fall over. I'm sure the others around here feel the same way!" She suddenly realized no one else was around except this man she didn't even know.

She earned Ty's respect at that moment. Not many people would be sensitive to an animal like that. Or been able to form an incredible attachment to them so quickly. But she had. And not only that, she stayed in a barn, sleeping in sand on an old, dingy horse blanket so the injured horses could rest. And because she didn't want a poor, traumatized horse to be scared and alone.

"Thank you," he said softly.

"For what?" she asked, leaning her head back against the stall bars. She felt the sorrel's warm breath blowing beside her head. Automatically, she raised her hand to the bars and felt him nudge it.

He still spoke softly, hoping he wouldn't set the horse off again. "For having a caring, loving heart. You stayed for him just so he knew he wasn't alone. So he knew he was safe and protected here. That's a lot more than a lot of people would've done. He needed you, and you were there for him. An animal rarely forgets kindnesses given to him. It looks like this one here needs as much as he can get."

A slight flush crept up her face at his sincere words. She looked over at him. "Oh, well... Morgan would've done the same had she known. They were all basically drugged up when we left them earlier so they were fine. I came back a little bit later to just make sure they were all right. He did this when I tried to leave. It's not like I could just leave him..."

"Exactly." Again, the soft voice and the kind eyes latched onto her.

She mentally shook herself back to reality. After a moment of staring at him, she finally asked, "Who are you anyway? Are you Josh?"

"No. He's up at the house checking on Morgan."

For some odd reason, knowing he wasn't Josh made her happy. "Okay, now I know who you *aren't*..." A thought hit her. "Oh, hang on... Are you *Ty?*" she asked in surprise.

"Yeah. You know me?"

"Ha. Only by the glowing references given to me by all the females I've met so far. My goodness. You have *quite* the fan club!" She grinned at him in pure amusement.

His broad smile was charming as he replied modestly, "They're a little biased, I think."

Ripley's raised eyebrow told him she didn't think so. He reminded her of someone, but she couldn't put her finger on who it was. She guessed he was around six feet tall. His obviously fit body was capped with either dark brown or black hair—she wasn't sure in the light—and topped off with those sharp but gentle brown eyes. Eyes that were accented with those sexy laugh lines that came out when he smiled. And that voice... He had a great voice.

Holy cow. She could see why the females last night were fighting over him. The man so far deserved having his own fan club, at least as looks go. But she wasn't that shallow.

"Since you know who I am apparently... Who are *you?*" Ty asked her with a raised eyebrow of his own, interrupting her thoughts.

"Ripley Capilano. I'm renting a camper space over here for a while." She took a step toward him, offering her hand but stopped at the *bang! bang!* behind her. She dropped her hand, sighed. "I've got a jealous and protective guy over here, don't I?"

Ty stepped forward instead but was mindful to remain out of the horse's sight as he offered his own hand. Out of respect for the horse, his voice was still quiet when he answered her. "Well, he doesn't own you unless you allow it. It's nice to meet you, Ripley Capilano."

She shook his hand, immediately liking the simple firmness of his handshake. It was neither a limp, wet noodle nor was it accompanied with a deliberate squeeze in an attempt to impress. Ripley took another step back. Petting the horse's nose but directing her question to Ty, she asked seriously, "So, how do you propose I get out of here?"

Chapter 8

Ripley came to a quick conclusion about Ty: He obviously hadn't been paying enough attention, otherwise he never would've said what he did.

"Just follow me," Ty said quietly, motioning to her.

When Ripley shook her head, he nodded back. She shook her head again, harder. Ty smiled and nodded again. After a moment, she sighed and cast a glance at the horse watching her. Ripley took only a few steps, but that's all it took. If the sorrel horse couldn't see her, he threw a fit. She stopped, torn in indecision. She gave a *What do I do now?* look at the tall man who was again gazing intently at the stall.

She stated the obvious in a concerned voice, "I can't leave him."

Ty looked back at her as he contemplated the situation. "The mind is a very powerful thing, Ripley. It has invisible ties that are sometimes nearly impossible to break when they latch onto something. You and the sorrel there apparently have a strong connection going on, but even cables have some give to them. He's going to have to let you go. You can't live in here forever."

"I know that, but—"

"Come on... He'll adjust. Trust me." Ty waited patiently for her to decide.

She still hesitated. "But what if he hurts himself trying to get out? He's already in so much pain... Maybe I could add some padding to the walls first?"

"We might do that later. If he does hurt himself, we'll help fix him right back up. If he doesn't, then it's a big first step for him."

"You make it sound so logical and easy. It isn't to him."

"It *is* logical. But no, it isn't easy for any of us." He waited.

Taking a breath, she joined Ty to follow him out, turning back once in hesitation at the consistent banging. Ty motioned for her to keep walking and guided her through the door, shutting it after The Darrells trotted out behind them. She turned to fully face the outside light and had an immediate reaction.

"*Oh my gosh!* It's already bright out!" she shrieked, covering her eyes like she'd just witnessed a nuclear blast. She practically doubled over to shield her face, then groaned in pain at her still-stiff body protesting that movement.

Laughing at the woman's reaction to the admittedly bright early sunlight, Ty put on his own sunglasses. Grinning, he led her by her arm to his truck, now full of a week's worth of camping gear. She still kept one hand across her eyes to shield them from the blinding sun. Reaching into the backseat, he grabbed his ball cap and pulled it over her head, tugging down the bill.

"There. That'll help. I'd loan you my spare sunglasses, but I'm not sure where they are." He grinned at her as she still refused to lower her hand. He gently tugged on it.

She tentatively lowered the hand that was shielding her eyes, letting them adjust to the brightness of morning. Her automatic blinking finally slowed down, but she still squinted a little.

He motioned for her to follow him, which she did without realizing it for a moment. She suddenly stopped in confusion. "Hey, where are you taking me anyway?"

"To the house."

"Why?"

"Because I'm hungry, and you probably are too. There's free food up there."

She pointed to her RV. "I have my own food, and it's down there."

With a straight face, Ty said, "Oh. So, you're inviting me to your place to have breakfast then? Okay. Thank you." He began walking down the lane that led to her RV.

Watching him casually walk off, she laughed. "Ty! Come back here. I don't know you well enough to have you over for breakfast. Let's go raid Morgan's fridge!"

"I thought so." Turning around, Ty walked back to her, smiling.

Ripley glanced at him as they made their way to the path leading toward the house. "You know, almost everyone stayed at her house last night as it was so late. They may not even be up yet."

"That's okay, but they should be up by now. There's work to be done and lots of it. The horses need fed before the rides go out. But if they're still sleeping, I can cook. Do you?"

"Not in someone else's kitchen when they don't even know I'm there! People have been shot for less!"

He chuckled. "It's all good. She won't mind. Anyway, Josh is up."

"Oh, I get to meet Josh too. Looking like this?" Ripley groaned.

"Well, you didn't mind meeting me looking like that."

"I didn't have much of a choice!" She barely paused before blurting out, "And what's wrong with the way I look?"

He laughed heartily at the tone of her voice. "Nothing at all. You look really nice in the morning sunshine, Miss Capilano."

With a snort, she replied, "I see the sun burned *your* retinas too!" At his laughter, she couldn't help but smile as she followed him.

Before they even got to the front door, Josh opened it. He stepped outside, closing the door softly behind him, smiling at Ty. "Ha! I *knew* it. You *do* want breakfast!" He glanced at the woman trailing along behind his friend. "Who's this?"

Ty flashed a smile at him, then answered with a level tone, "Oh, some waif I found sleeping in the barn. Says her name is Ripley."

Josh smiled at her, thought for a split second. "RV Ripley? Welcome to Harmony Hills... Wait... What? You were sleeping in the barn? Why? We charge way more for sleeping in the barn than renting out camper spots, you know. I'll have to let my wife know about this."

Ripley looked up at Ty and said dryly, "Thanks for ratting me out."

He grinned. "I'll cover ya." Looking back at Josh, he explained, "Seems like one of the rescues fell in love with her. She can't leave his line of sight without his trying to tear down the stall. We might have to make other arrangements for him soon. If he keeps it up, he *will* bust through it. Or hurt himself even more trying.

"Anyway, she stayed outside his stall all night to keep the place quiet and him company until I rescued her."

Josh looked at her, saw her slight blush. "Seriously? You slept in the barn for a horse?"

In her embarrassment, she absentmindedly removed the ball cap Ty had plunked on her head. She ended up squinting her eyes against the brightening sky before she realized what she did and immediately put the cap back on.

"Yeah. I was worried he'd keep the others up too. And he'd probably end up hurting himself even more, and he just survived an awful wreck... The poor thing likes me. And I just couldn't bear the thought of leaving him... well, *all* of them... alone. He's been alone long enough, I'd say. He might still be hurting himself even now trying to get out... I can't hear from up here though..."

Her obvious worry about that wasn't lost on either man as she turned to look back at the barn.

"I can see why he fell in love with you. We'll take care of him soon." Impressed with her heart and genuine concern, Josh held out his hand. "I'm Josh, Morgan's husband. It's nice to meet you, Ripley. Morgan told me on the phone about you. And you were the one I spoke with last night, right?"

"Yes. The one and the same. One Ripley is more than enough, I'm sure." She smiled as she shook his hand. Like Ty's, it was firm and confident.

Josh smiled back at the attractive, but disheveled, woman standing there. "Why don't you two come in? Morgan left me a note on the two main doors we use letting me know the house is full and to be quiet. I guess I've lost my mystery!" He grinned broadly, humor lighting his eyes. "No one else is up yet, but once we start cooking, they will be. Alexis is out cold on the couch, so try not to disturb her." He sent a meaningful look at Ty, who grinned mischievously.

Josh opened the door, leading them inside with a stealth-like quality Ripley found funny. She tried to not laugh at his exaggerated steps to remain quiet as they walked by Alexis. She was on her back, one arm flung over her head and the arm of the couch, the other was hanging over the side. Her legs were wrapped up in the blankets with Freeway sleeping in a little ball at her feet. Alexis was obviously out like a broken light.

Glancing at her, Ty chuckled. Softly, Ripley noticed.

They heard movement upstairs, a signal that Morgan was up and getting ready.

They made their way into the kitchen, still not cleaned up from the night before.

For some reason, Ripley felt a little obligated to apologize for the mess. She whispered, "We were playing games when the call came in last night. We just ran out the door."

Josh shrugged. "It's only dishes. It sounds like a crazy twist of fate that had you all here when that call came in, so a mess is nothing. Besides, this happens every game night." He opened the dishwasher and began putting in the dirty plastic dishes he'd already gathered as he spoke quietly. "Why don't you two have a seat at the bar?"

Ty pulled out a tall chair for Ripley before sitting down beside her. They watched as Josh filled the dishwasher competently and rolled in the racks, added the detergent, shut the door, and turned it on. Ty yawned, causing the other two in the room to follow suit. Josh turned to the crockpot, tossing out the liner bag Morgan cooked the taco soup in, wiped out the ceramic pot and the outside of the appliance before washing the lid.

Ripley, feeling punch-drunk since she was so tired, smiled. "Morgan told me you don't have a brother. That's a shame."

"Why?" Josh asked, now hand-drying the glass lid.

"Any man sweet enough to do the dishes and clean the kitchen for his exhausted wife without being told to is a keeper. And you've obviously done it before as you're efficient at doing it. Plus, you have to be tired yourself, I imagine, so that just makes you incredibly sweet." She shrugged and grinned at him. "I figured a brother could learn from you, and if so, he'd be a keeper too. Theoretically."

Ty nudged her with his elbow, saying, "I do my own dishes. Does that count?"

"Oh, so *you* have a brother?" she asked, humor in her eyes.

He laughed softly at her. "Neither one of us have a brother. Just sisters. You're out of luck there, Ripley. And I really hate to disappoint you so early in the morning!"

Josh put away the crockpot and wiped down the counters as they quietly talked. With a mental ability to judge how long it took his wife to get ready, Josh began pulling out breakfast food. Ripley soon heard Morgan's feet and their rhythmic pattern coming down the stairs. When she came around the corner, Morgan immediately saw her husband.

"*You're home!*" Morgan's face lit up like a beacon in a lighthouse. She quickly gave Josh a tight hug and a long, smacking kiss before she went over and hugged her best friend, kissing his unshaven cheek. Both men smiled at her happiness at seeing them home.

"Hey, darlin'!" Ty kissed her cheek in return.

With a mock frown, Josh shook the cheese slicer at him saying sternly, "Ty, didn't I say something to you before about you kissing my wife?"

Ty grinned unrepentantly. "Yep. More than once. But she kissed me first."

Morgan also grinned, obviously not worried at all as her hand rested on Ty's shoulder. Josh held back his own grin as he shook the cheese slicer now at her. "Sweetheart, didn't I talk to you about—"

"Yep. More than once. But it would've been rude of me to not welcome him home too! We don't allow rudeness in our house, do we?"

"Do you have to kiss him though?"

"Only on the cheek, sweetheart... Wherever it is!" Morgan patted the short, dark beard her friend now sported like her husband did after almost a week of camping.

Josh sighed. "I suppose that's okay." But Ripley could easily tell he wasn't upset in the least. Teasing his wife, he pointed out, "You didn't kiss Ripley here. That seems rude. Why didn't you kiss her?"

"I don't know her all that well. Plus, *she* didn't just get home." Morgan smiled as she walked back over to Josh and put her arm around his waist. Looking at their guest, Morgan greeted her, "Morning, Ripley!"

Amused at their banter, Ripley returned her greeting. She removed Ty's cap from her head, hooking it on the back of her chair.

The other thing Ripley had noticed was how Josh's face lit up the same way as his wife's did when she'd walked into their kitchen. Sure, Morgan was gorgeous, but it was far more than that. He was genuinely happy to see her. They didn't hesitate at all to take the other into their arms in front of people either.

Taking a look at Morgan's husband as he sliced cheese for the eggs, Ripley assessed him. He was also tall like Ty—she guessed around six feet easy—with dark brown hair and a scruffy beard like Ty had. His build and the tanned muscles she could see around his old blue t-shirt and his black shorts spoke of manual labor, probably from his construction business and working with horses. He definitely came across as an outdoors man, not a city dweller who worked in a cubicle.

Despite all his bulk and muscle, she also sensed a gentle, soft side to the man. All because of how he greeted and looked at his wife and naturally did household duties for her. He obviously shared doing the housework with her on a regular basis.

That waitress hit the nail right on the head, Ripley thought to herself. They *did* go together like electricity and lightbulbs. How more absolutely refreshing and adorable could they be?

Seeing Ripley transfer her gaze from her husband back to her, Morgan smiled broadly. She looked from her husband to her best friend then back to her guest with a knowing look. Giving her a wink, Morgan and Ripley then shared a grin. Yes, Morgan knew her two men. They came home immediately just as she'd expected they would.

Impressive, Ripley thought, and romantic and just plain sweet. She felt an unexpected, quick stab of envy. And it was sharp.

Morgan's eyes were on Ripley, now assessing her. "Rip, did you know you have hay, or maybe it's straw, in your hair?" She peered closer. "Did you just get up?"

Ripley shot an accusing look at both men. "I'll be right back."

Both men chuckled as she quickly scooted off her chair. Morgan followed her to the guest bathroom down the hall.

Ripley gasped when she saw herself in the mirror. "Oh no! I met those two guys looking like *this?*" She was dismayed at what she looked like. Her hair did indeed have hay in it. Absentmindedly, she wondered if she smelled. "And neither said a *thing...*" Ripley wailed quietly. "There went a good first impression, huh? I'm so embarrassed, Morgan!"

Morgan smiled at her, said reassuringly, "Don't give it a second thought. Seriously. My guys are always polite, no matter what. Out of curiosity, though, how'd you get hay in your hair? And what *is* that on your face?"

"Leave me alone for a moment. If I don't die of embarrassment in here, I'll come out and tell you."

Morgan grinned at her before softly shutting the door and returning to the kitchen.

When Ripley returned, her hair was more orderly and all the hay and sand she could find were gone. Her hair was wet at the roots from when she splashed soap and water over her face as she scrubbed it clean. She tossed another reprimanding look at the two men as she walked back into the kitchen. They just grinned at her as she took her seat next to Ty again.

Morgan was leaning against Josh, her arm wrapped around his waist as she listened to the two men talk. Josh had his long arm draped over her shoulders, holding her close to his side.

Glancing at the clock, Morgan grabbed her phone and called Rory. She asked him and Kim to feed the horses at Sunset Ridge so they had time to eat before being pulled for the day's rides. She knew Rory and Kim were at the barns since they didn't come to game night and always worked the early shift. She told him briefly about what had happened, letting him know they'd all be down once they were up and fed themselves. She told him to leave the horses in Grand View alone for right now. "Are Mel and Kat here yet?"

"Yeah. They got here a bit ago," he replied. "You want to talk to them?"

"No, that's fine. Just tell them we'll be down fairly soon."

"Will do."

"Thank goodness we didn't have any early morning rides," Morgan said after she hung up. "We'll still need to get the gang up soon so they have time to get ready." As she spoke, Morgan got a large bowl for the eggs while Josh placed the silverware and plates needed on the counter. The kitchen smelled now of the brewing coffee.

Morgan commented as she cracked eggs into the bowl, "Considering how early it is, Ripley, I figured you'd be sound asleep in your place. How on earth did you end up here at this time of day? I mean, you're welcome here and all..."

Ripley looked at Ty. "You didn't tell her how we met?"

"Nope."

Ripley explained to Morgan, "I'm awake because your best friend here woke me up. The guy who's in love with me didn't appreciate it any more than I did. The two of us were sleeping quite soundly until this guy showed up. It was pretty rude," she said with a straight face.

Ty laughed and Josh grinned at her, appreciating her humor.

Before adding taco sauce to the eggs, Morgan looked from one to another. "Okay, what am I missing here?"

Ripley shrugged her shoulders. "Well, after we all went back to our places last night, or rather, this morning, I couldn't shake the guilty feeling I had leaving those poor horses all alone. So, I went back down to see them just one more time. When I got to the big sorrel on the end, the one you had to go in after at the wreck site, he—"

Josh interrupted, looking at his wife, "What was that? You—"

Morgan interrupted him, "Later, sweetheart. I want to hear Ripley's story." She kissed his cheek before saying to Ripley with a sweet smile, "Go on, please."

"As I was saying,"—Ripley grinned pointedly at Josh—"the horse at the end wouldn't let me out of his sight. Every time I tried to leave, he threw a fit. I honestly thought he'd tear down the stall or really hurt himself more. Every time I went back, he quieted right down. Over and over, I tried to leave.

"Finally, I decided to just sleep there so we all could get some rest. I started out in a chair, but it was more comfortable on the sand so I could stretch out.

"Anyway, he was sound asleep like me until *this* guy came in and woke us all up. The sorrel wanted to bust through his stall when he saw Ty there!"

Ty nodded in agreement, noticed the coffee was done brewing, and then simply got up to pour himself some. "Coffee anyone?"

Josh nodded, but Morgan and Ripley both shook their heads.

Ty added to the story as he poured coffee for himself and Josh. "She's not exaggerating. I walked down the aisle looking at the horses and all's fine. I saw this person sleeping in the sand on an old blanket with The Darrells tucked in right beside her. At first, I thought it was you, Morg.

"Anyway, the second I got to him, the sorrel went crazy. We're talking ballistic crazy here. He repeatedly attacked the door." He pointed a serious look at both Josh and Morgan. "That's a dangerous horse down there. Don't turn your back on him."

"He woke me up," Ripley stated again with a straight face.

Morgan and Josh chuckled.

Ty shook his head, holding back his smile. "No, I didn't. *He* did!"

Ripley smiled, knowing she had to give him that.

Ty continued as he sat beside her again, "She figured out a couple of things immediately. One is, he has to have Ripley here in his line of sight or he throws a fit. I sure hope he's calmed down by now.

"Secondly, he apparently hates men. We need to test out that theory to be sure so we know how to handle him. He tries to tear down the stall when I'm near it, but he's quiet as can be with Ripley here."

Teasing him, Ripley replied, "Perhaps it's just because he's a male. Maybe if he were a female, it would've been way different. You do seem to make *quite* the impression on the females around here from what I can tell!"

Morgan and Josh laughed. As he chopped fresh tomatoes, his brown eyes sparkling, Josh said, "I've noticed that same thing. I guess he's all that's left around here since I got married. Now all the women have learned to settle for less!"

Morgan snorted when she laughed good-naturedly at her husband's comment.

Fighting to hold back his smile, Ty shook his head. Looking dejected, he said, "It's too early in the morning for me to take such abuse."

But Morgan was intrigued now about this horse. She got a Pepsi from the fridge, and seeing how Ripley was eyeing it, slid it to her and got another one. Josh grinned at them. Another morning Pepsi drinker had taken up residence on the property.

Morgan asked, "So we have a man-eater on property then?"

Ripley nodded her thanks before saying, "Yeah. I think he was horribly abused by men. He doesn't trust them... or *can't*. There's a big difference there. However, I think there *was* a woman in his past at some point that truly loved him by the way he responded to me so readily."

Ripley took a long drink, anticipating the kick the caffeine would hopefully give her soon. "But the instant he saw Ty, he tried to break through his stall. Ty had to move down the aisle before the sorrel would—*could*—calm down. I'd say he's been abused and often and not just traumatized by last night."

Listening, Josh sipped his coffee as Morgan got the bread to make toast.

Ty nodded his agreement. "I think she knows her horses well, Morg. How was he with other people last night?"

"Well, he didn't like the idea of immediately getting back on a trailer after almost dying in another one. It took four men to get him on it. We just chalked it up to trauma and being afraid, and rightly so," Morgan replied as she put bread into the toaster, slid down the handle. "And having two vets, both males, poke and put a needle through your skin after all that isn't going to help either."

She paused for a moment, thinking. "But you know what? The guys at the scene *did* have to ask me to go into the trailer to get him out. It was tricky to go up to a stuck, thrashing horse in the dark in a semi on its side. But now that we're talking about this, perhaps he was really fighting *them* and not just the whole terror he was experiencing."

Josh stopped sipping his coffee as he stared at his wife. He raised his eyebrows while Ty gave her nearly the same look.

She knew what they were thinking. "Yes, I knew what I was doing. I got him out, didn't I? Now he's here.

"But if Ripley *is* right, let's keep you men away as much as we can. Let's just see if we can keep him calm and stress-free. All of them, for that matter. He's not the only one in sorry shape."

Ripley watched them begin breakfast again. After a moment, she asked, "Shouldn't we wake everyone up first? Wouldn't they prefer to eat the food while it's hot?"

Ty shook his head. "No! They're little badgers if we try to wake them up before they're ready to on their own. We learned our lesson years ago. We found if we just make them food, the smell puts them in a happy place. They come in with smiles of appreciation instead of snarls of ungratefulness for waking them up."

Morgan and Josh laughed.

Josh backed him up, saying, "Badgers is an accurate term too. Aggressive little buggers Morgan hired on. Thankfully, we really like them so we can overlook this quirk they all seem to share!"

Morgan retorted, "I'm more thankful we're quick learners. It took us a bit of time as we don't normally have situations where we all wake up at the same place in the morning, you know? We figured it out when we had a dangerous storm a couple of years back. I ordered everyone to stay here where it was safe."

Morgan put bacon in the microwave, set the timer, and pushed the *Start* button while Josh scraped the chopped tomatoes and green peppers into the eggs. She smiled, humor radiating from her green eyes. "It was like discovering penicillin. It was purely an accident that we figured out how to get them all awake and happy."

Josh and Ty chuckled at her comparison.

Sure enough, as more food was prepared and the smell filled the house, they heard stirrings. As the food was being cooked, Ty went down the hall to the bathroom to clean up himself before eating.

The four of them sat at the bar and ate in peace, waiting patiently for the others to begin wandering into the kitchen. Alexis came in first, wearing one of Morgan's nightshirts. Looking like a pretty zombie, she shuffled more than walked into the kitchen as Freeway scampered across the kitchen in front of her to her own food bowl.

Josh glanced at Alexis, gauging her level of wakefulness before greeting her. "Good morning, Alexis. Would you like some—"

"Please. Coffee would be great!" She walked right past Josh and got a mug from the cabinet. She poured herself her own coffee, blowing on it first, still half-asleep as she drank some.

Ty gently nudged Ripley with his elbow, put his finger to his lips in a silent gesture to remain quiet and grinned. Not being able to miss the humor in the situation, Ripley grinned back. Josh and Morgan just kept their distance and ignored Alexis until she woke up on her own.

Bo came in next, his hair looking worse than Ripley's had. She couldn't help but smile as he made his way over, grabbed the mug from Alexis' hand and took a big sip. Alexis whacked him over his head with her open hand, taking her mug back when he reached up to rub away the sting.

The original four held back their laughter and simply continued to eat. Drew finally showed up, looking like he'd jumped in the shower first. His hair was wet as he padded barefoot into the room. "Mornin' all. Oh, coffee! Fantastic. Mind if I get a mug, Morgan?"

"Nope, go ahead. Laundry is done if you want to get your clothes. It's all on the dryer. What would you three like to eat?"

Alexis, beginning to wake up now that she had coffee running through her veins, sighed. "How accommodating are you feeling?"

"Fair to middlin' right now. Why?" Morgan took a drink of her Pepsi. So much for cutting back, she suddenly thought. She forgot she was.

Alexis asked, "French toast? It's okay if not."

"Sure, it's easy enough to do. I think we have enough eggs." She chewed and swallowed her toast before venturing an indirect order to Bo. "How about you go wake up Toby and Maya?"

"No way! Do you think I'm stupid?" he replied as he poured some coffee into the mug Drew handed him.

"Chicken," Drew chided him.

"So what?" Bo looked over the rim of his own mug before asking, "How come *you're* not knocking on their door?"

Drew replied, "Boss lady asked *you*."

Alexis smiled, leaning against the counter. "I think Ty should do it."

"Hush, girl. I'm eating, and I don't want to get indigestion." Ty took another bite of his scrambled eggs before he shook his fork at her.

"Oh, I'll do it," Ripley volunteered. Everyone gaped at her, their looks a warning. "If Morgan can walk into a twisted piece of metal to save a terrified horse in the black of night, I can surely withstand a couple of people being woken up in the morning light."

Josh immediately pointed down the hallway. "They're down there."

"The woman's got guts," Ty said with appreciation as she slid off her chair.

They watched her as she confidently left the kitchen. Ripley headed toward the only closed door, assuming it was theirs. She'd die of embarrassment if she did what she was planning on doing to a closet full of coats.

Gently knocking on the door to make sure it was their bedroom, she waited. No response. She knocked harder, listening for any sounds from the other side. She finally heard movement. Before she opened the door, the thought came to her that they were a young dating couple and that meant they could like morning sex. She hesitated, and figuring—hoping—they'd be too worn out to even *think* about it this early, she took the plunge.

Opening the door, she peeked inside. They were asleep, so that was a good start.

Quietly closing the door, she walked toward the bed.

Chapter 9

In no time at all, Ripley returned in one piece without a scratch on her. She walked back into the kitchen just as Alexis was being handed her French toast and eggs from Morgan. They all looked at her expectantly, but she didn't say a word as she sat back down beside Ty.

Josh handed the bottle of syrup to Alexis as she headed to the table before he leaned down and scooped up Freeway. Immediately, Ripley could hear Freeway purring in contentment from where she was sitting. Freeway, looking undoubtedly happy about having her dad home, kneaded his arm with her front paws as he scratched her cheek.

Barely a minute later, Toby and Maya padded in on bare feet looking fairly refreshed and more or less awake. They smiled as they looked at Ripley.

"Okay, what gives!" Ty exclaimed. "How did she get you two up without a war on her hands?"

"Sorry, darlin'!" Ripley answered instead, shaking her head sadly. "It's a secret that's been passed down for generations in my family. They have both been sworn to secrecy. I don't know if you're trustworthy enough to know family secrets."

Josh piped up, "I am!"

Ripley chuckled and shook her head.

Maya walked over to get some much-needed coffee, just to find the pot empty. "Hey! What's this?" she cried.

Morgan shrugged. "We thought you'd like it fresh and piping hot. We were just waiting for you to join us."

Toby asked, "Didn't we just do that?"

Morgan laughed and immediately began a fresh pot. Knowing they both liked creamer in their coffee, she took the milk from the fridge and handed it to Maya before she returned to the stove to make them eggs. After putting Freeway down and washing his hands, Josh put more bread in the toaster.

Alexis, Bo, and Drew sat at the table, eating their eggs, bacon, and French toast and drinking their coffee. Bo soon got up and said he was going to take a shower. Morgan nodded as he made his way to the laundry room to get his clothes. He walked back out of the kitchen, nodding when Alexis told him to be quick and save some hot water.

Morgan scooped the eggs onto plates for Toby and Maya just as the coffee finished. While Toby was handed their plates, Maya got their coffee. Sitting down at the table, Toby poured milk into their mugs. No one said a word for a while. Except for the sound of most everyone eating, the silence was almost deafening.

Ty looked at Ripley again, but her look gave nothing away. She did wink at him, though, a corner of her mouth tilting up in a grin. He shook his head as he turned back to his coffee.

It wasn't long before Bo came back in. He refilled his mug with coffee as Alexis asked, "Did you save me some hot water?"

"I tried to."

"Thanks." Alexis got up and put her dishes in the sink before heading to the laundry room. She walked back out with folded clothes in her arms.

When it seemed like everyone was awake and fed, Ripley did ask of the latest arrivals to the kitchen, "So, you two... I could be wrong, but is there something you guys wanted to share with the rest of your friends here? I had the feeling you wanted to say something to them last night."

Toby and Maya looked over at her, their faces showing their surprise. They looked at each other next, questioning looks on their own faces. Toby's then split into a grin. "Why *not* now?"

Maya smiled back at him and announced cheerfully, "Well, Toby has *finally* asked me to marry him, and I said yes before he could take the words back!"

Ripley joined in the cheers of congratulations. After the cheers wound down, they all prepared to head down to the barns to get to work. They'd have to hurry since they all had slept in, taken showers, and lingered over breakfast. Josh shooed them out of the kitchen, his eyes on the clock.

When Alexis came in from taking her quick shower, she was told of their engagement. She hugged her two friends, nearly jumping up and down in her own excitement. She couldn't stop smiling as she put on her shoes, asking them questions they didn't have all the answers to yet.

Toby and Maya got their clean clothes from the dryer and hurried to their room to change. As her workers were leaving, Morgan told them to answer the barn phone as the four of them were going to the rescues first. Maya nodded, saying she'd take it.

Morgan reminded them the halters and lead ropes were in one of the trucks. Since they'd left a set at each of the rescued horses stalls, they needed to get more. "We'll need to keep those there for those guys. We can borrow some from Quail Run. Actually, just get some new ones from the back room," Morgan told them.

Ty was gathering the trash while Josh tossed all the loaned clothes and towels into the washing machine. Ripley had volunteered to help, but Morgan told her to sit as she washed their dishes by hand so they didn't have to wait on the dishwasher to finish the current load.

Watching quietly from the bar, Ripley suddenly realized Morgan must have stayed up just long enough that morning for her workers' clothes to be washed. She assumed Toby and Maya took their showers before going to sleep earlier while Morgan most likely did the same. And Morgan, probably after tossing all their clothes into the dryer, crashed into her own bed upstairs. And yet was the first one awake just a few hours later.

Considering them all as she sipped her second Pepsi, Ripley felt another stab of envy. This group of people was tight. Although they all worked together, they also spent time together even when they were off. They joked and conversed with each other in friendly and fun terms. They weren't just co-workers, or even just a team. They weren't just friends. They seemed more like family in the best sense of the word. They were pals.

As the four of them walked down to the barn, Ripley carried the trash bag. She got a free breakfast, she reminded them, so the least she could do is take out the trash. Morgan smiled and graciously accepted her offer.

Ripley glanced at her watch as they walked. She intended to take another shower and nap before her calls began later, but she'd readily agreed to go with them to see the rescues when Morgan had asked her to. Since the sorrel had apparently bonded with her, it might be best to have her there. It was as impossible to say no to Morgan as it would be to the horse, but the thought never occurred to Ripley to say it to either.

Glancing at Ripley as they walked down the path, Ty asked her, "So how'd you know they were engaged before any of us did? Or at least that they wanted to tell us something?"

Ripley thought for a moment. "I picked up on it last night at the wreck. It was just something Toby had said to her and her reaction. It got me thinking when I saw them this morning. I felt my hunch was correct, so I thought I'd ask.

"I had no clue what it could be though. They could be having a baby, or moving, or buying a house for all I knew. And if it turned out I was wrong, then I'd just be wrong."

"First the horse, and now Toby and Maya. Interesting gifts you have there, Miss Capilano."

Ripley made a stop at the dumpster first, then joined them at the door so they could all walk in together. They walked down the aisle slowly, eyeing each horse through the bars of the stalls. Ripley answered a question Morgan posed to her at one of the stalls. As soon as Ripley began speaking, they heard the sorrel begin softly banging on his door.

Ty said incredulously, "He didn't bang on his door until he heard *your* voice, Ripley. He recognized it!"

"Well, I *have* been told it's quite sexy," she teased.

They chuckled as Ripley walked the rest of the way down, stopping in front of the sorrel. He immediately stopped banging on the door.

After turning the ball cap around backwards so she could lean forward to the bars, she blew softly into his nose, running a finger down it as she spoke to him. She loved the velvety softness of horse noses. She kissed it before saying softly, "You missed me, did you? Sorry I had to leave you there for a while, but I'm back. See? And it's all right. You didn't hurt yourself anymore, did you?"

His brown eyes bored into hers, practically pleading with her not to leave him alone again. The earnest look in those eyes just tore her heart to pieces. She blinked back the tears that suddenly welled up in her own. She blew into his nose again and smiled inside when he blew back. "That's my boy," she whispered.

After a moment, Morgan joined her and waited to see what the sorrel would do. He tossed his head in the air but didn't charge the door or even snort. He looked at Morgan but made no further moves against her. Morgan softly spoke to him as Ripley had done. Responding to her, he blew a soft breath toward her so Morgan blew back. He shook his head, and then tossed it up and down before his gaze settled back on Ripley.

Did he remember Morgan being the one who rescued him from the trailer? Did he recognize her scent? Would he bond with Morgan the same way he did with Ripley? Or was there just something about Ripley he sensed? Was it because Ripley was with him when all was quieter and safer? Or did she remind him of whoever had loved him before?

Ripley said, "Good so far. Now for the test... I seriously *hate* to do this to him!"

Both women stepped back to let Josh walk in front of the stall. Almost immediately, the tall horse charged the door, teeth bared, and ears back. Josh stood his ground, being a lifelong horseman himself.

He shook his head sadly, talking softly to the horse raking his teeth up and down the bars. "Shh, big guy. It's okay. We're not going to hurt you..." He kept talking to the horse even as the horse tried to rip out the bars with his teeth.

"That's enough, honey." Morgan shook her head, looked at Ripley. "So far, your theory's correct. Let's try just us again."

Josh had already moved back up the aisle to join Ty. The women walked up to the agitated horse, talking calmly, and the sorrel began to wind down. His eyes rolled white, and his eyebrows expressed worry and uncertainty. He already had a thin sheen of sweat on his coat. That quickly, he'd worked himself into a frenzy. This was not a good sign, but he calmed down as the two women stayed with him.

Although they all hated to do it, Josh motioned for Ty to go next. Same thing happened. In order to not stress out the horse anymore, Ty immediately moved back out of sight. He never said a word.

Quickly, Ripley walked up again to calm down the horse. "It's okay... I'm here. Men weren't nice to you at all, were they? Any of them? But you've a lady in your past who loved you, don't you?"

Her eyes filled with tears again, just picturing a gentle woman being separated from the horse she loved and vice versa. Did she die? Was she forced to sell him? What happened?

"You poor thing. You can trust *these* guys, okay? They won't hurt you. We're all here to help you."

She talked softly to the horse, not really remembering the three people near her now. All her attention was on the tall sorrel horse with the blonde mane and tail and the lonely brown eyes. She stroked his face and his nose, blew into it. He always blew back.

Morgan listened and watched as her mind raced with thoughts. Ripley had caught onto this horse's spirit remarkably quickly, and *she* had something about her that the horse immediately latched onto. She patiently waited for Ripley to walk away. The banging began immediately. When Ripley returned to him, he stopped and thrust his nose between the bars. They could see his nostrils flaring, searching for her scent, looking for *her.*

Looking at the three people watching her, sorrow on her face, Ripley said softly, "And *that's* how I ended up sleeping in the barn."

The three watching her all understood.

When she walked away to leave again, the banging started right back up. This time, Morgan walked over to him. He stopped but didn't treat her quite the same as Ripley. He lifted his foot and swung it but stopped just short of hitting the door. He tossed his head, his blonde mane rising and falling with the motions of his long neck.

"Well, at least we know we just need a woman around," Josh said quietly. "I think Ripley's right on. *Men* abused this horse terribly, and he knows one by scent, by sight, alone. I hate to think what his life must've been like. Only God knows what he's gone through. It must've been horrific to make him this bad by sight alone. It's almost unbelievable!"

Being able to hear his soft voice from the sorrel's stall, Morgan nodded in complete agreement. She watched the horse's ears flick back and forth as he heard Josh's voice too. "And if he'd been passed from one person to another to another, probably all men, who didn't understand his past, he'd just get worse treatment.

"It's no wonder he was on his way to Mexico. No one understood him or took the time to. He was most likely sold at an auction for body weight alone. Being tall and muscular, he'd fetch a good price from the slaughterhouse. Assuming he kept all that weight on him throughout the ordeal anyway."

Ty added quietly, "What I notice, too, is *how* he's reacting to us. He's not so much shaking in his shoes in paralyzing fear. In fact, it's the opposite. It's rather an attack action, like he's going on the offensive to protect Ripley. He acts like a guard dog, doesn't he? I find that very interesting."

He paused, thinking. "I wonder if he'd been turned into a rodeo bronc at some point? Some of those horses get soured really fast and don't recover. This is just a guess, obviously."

Josh nodded, also speaking quietly, "Well, it could be the answer... Or part of it. Those contractors want the biggest, meanest bronc they can find to draw in the crowds and money. The cowboys need them to score the highest points.

"And neither could care what it takes to make the horse *get* that way. It's not always about just wearing a bucking strap. Horses aren't born mean. Not all contractors are that way, of course, as some contractors and true cowboys want it humane and fair... If you can still call it that."

Morgan agreed. "Yeah, I've seen them come and go through the auctions. In all honesty, I think it's more humane to put those horses down than to let them suffer any more at the hands of unscrupulous humans. Give them blessed peace." She looked at the sorrel again, wondering if he'd lived through one or more of those types of people. He'd had *some* type of person beating and abusing him for sure. People like that made her sick.

Ty offered another perspective, saying, "When I was a teenager, I worked at a show horse stable for a while. They had this young gelding, not more than three years old. He was barn sour to a degree I've never seen before or since. He, like the others, was confined to a stall and only let out to run for like an hour a day.

"It broke him. He became very mean-spirited, a charger when you opened his door. No one could turn their back on him because he'd take a chunk out of anyone who did. Only the owner and the manager were allowed to handle him. It made me sick to see him like that. And he was so young!

"I soon left that place, but I've never forgotten the deep guilt I had for not just letting him free before I left." He *still* felt guilty thinking about that poor horse. Some memories just don't die.

Josh asked, "You think he's just barn sour? And men by association with it?"

Ty replied, "I bet it has something to do with it. If he was confined, beaten, abused, starved, maybe all of it, wouldn't you?"

Ripley asked, "What will happen to these horses, Morgan?"

"I imagine they're the property of the owner of the rig that was transporting them, or maybe whoever paid them for transport. Either way, these horses aren't mine. If someone comes here to take them away, I have no legal leg to stand on. As long as I get paid, they can take them."

"That's not right!" Ripley said, incensed.

Josh said, "That's not something the law can do much about. They'd have some authority in an abuse case, but this is something else. It could be said that they were abused *before* but not necessarily *by* the people taking them to Mexico. For all we know, they could've been taking these horses somewhere nice to live out a peaceful life. We can only assume they were headed for an actual slaughterhouse."

Ripley's mind raced with possible solutions. She asked, "Can you buy them?"

Josh replied, "It'd take a bit to do it. Then there'd be the vet and hoof care, homes to find, feed, and maybe training until then." He sighed. "It'd take quite a bit to do it. My family has done horse rescues since I was a boy, so I know it's not cheap to do. They aren't like cats or dogs. It's not impossible, but we can't afford to save every horse we see. I wish we could! The entire Center would be filled to capacity, and then some, in less than a week."

Ripley suggested, "What if you kept them to use here at the Center? With the exception of this guy, all the others seem friendly enough. After they healed, could you see about keeping them here? They could earn their keep if you were able to use them for riding, couldn't they?"

Morgan nodded. "Technically, yes. I have about all I need right now, but I'd do whatever I could to make it happen if it saved them. Normally I prefer to find out what the *horse* likes to do, not what *I* want it to do. But at least they'd be safe and loved here.

"There's always the possibility that someone retires or dies. I strive to take excellent care of my horses, and I keep them until they die naturally, or I have to put them down for the sake of mercy and compassion.

"Adding eleven to the mix is actually more expensive than one would think. Especially here in Arizona where food for them is so expensive. It's not like we're in Kentucky or somewhere with a large grass pasture we could just turn them loose in. Out here it's just sand."

"How about doing a fundraiser?" Ripley suggested hopefully. "Something to defray costs?"

Morgan considered. "It'd have to be big. It'd also be probably only a one-time shot. We could raise money to feed them or pay the vet bills for a while, but what happens after that? They'd make news *now* but a few months from now? They'd be old news and forgotten." Morgan gazed at the bay horse housed next to the sorrel that had walked to the edge of the stall to sniff her hand. She ran her hand down the dark brown head.

The four adults looked from one horse to another, each one silently wondering what the horses' fate was going to be. Could they be saved and find homes, or would they simply resume their trip to the slaughterhouse?

Ripley broke the silence when she said, "Well, I hate to go, but I need to. I have to work, but if you need me here for this guy, come get me. I'll do whatever I can. I should be at my place all day."

Morgan nodded. "Thank you so much for all you've already done, Ripley. For going with me last night, staying with this guy this morning, and being here now. You've been a great help!"

"Anytime. And thank you again for the breakfast." She ran her hand down the sorrel's nose as she said, "Okay, kiddo... I need to go. You're safe here... All right? Be good. I'll come back later to check on you... Promise." She kissed his nose and turned to leave.

Josh said, "Thanks for both your help and for your insight on this horse."

"You're welcome." As she was leaving, she grabbed the chair and blanket to put them back, but Morgan gestured for her to leave them. Seeing the borrowed flashlight, she handed it to Morgan. As Ripley began to walk away again, she realized she was still wearing Ty's baseball cap. "I'll get your hat back to you in a bit, Ty, if that's okay?"

"No rush. That one's just my old smelly fishing hat," he joked.

"Oh, thank God! I thought that was *me!*" Ripley joked back.

They all laughed until they heard the dreaded reaction of the sorrel. *Bang! Bang!*

Ripley shook her head, her eyes instantly sad, as she left the lonely horse yet again.

Morgan told Ty to go home since it was still his vacation time. He nodded after she insisted she was going to handle it all without him anyway since he wasn't even supposed to be home yet. As he left, she and Josh stayed behind for a moment, talking about the situation.

When she finally headed toward Sunset Ridge, Josh headed up to the house. He smiled when he saw Ty drive away in his truck per Morgan's orders, but then turn into the lane heading toward the house.

Ty was waiting on the front steps for Josh when he rounded the corner of the house. "If it's all the same to you, I'll rest up here until the vet comes. She needs the help as I know she's going to be busy in Sunset Ridge later. I snuck a peek at the reservation book while she was talking with you. And I originally *was* supposed to be back to work by now."

Josh nodded as they walked through the front door. "Since that's the case, *you* should be down there right now. Why aren't you?" He grinned when Ty shoved him. "But I'm sure she'll really appreciate our help. She'll call me when Doc gets here."

As Ty closed the door, Josh glanced back at him. "And why didn't you just wait to give me a ride up here if you knew you were staying? Why'd you make me walk?"

Shamelessly, Ty grinned. "I noticed you began to walk up here earlier this morning instead of driving your truck. I just thought you wanted the exercise."

Josh laughed. "Here I thought you missed seeing that! I should've known better." He shook his head, but he was still smiling. "Which bed did you want to crash on? I can get sheets for yours. Or did you just want the couch?"

In the past before Josh came along, Ty stayed there when Morgan was out of town so someone was always on property in case of emergencies. She'd designated one of the spare rooms as his years before. After she and Josh got married, he still tended to stay over since he and Josh were friends, and Josh's hours weren't regular with his own construction business.

Ty sighed. "Whichever one is closest."

MORGAN HEADED BACK TO her office just as she saw customers pulling in for their scheduled trail rides. She finally got a minute and called Rory and Kim via the handheld radios, asking them to come up to Sunset Ridge when they could. When they did, she gave them instructions about the rescues. She stressed for Rory to stay away from the sorrel as he had an issue with men.

With the addition of the eleven new horses, and in what medical condition they were really in she had no idea, Morgan got to work creating a file for them. The best she could do was to keep them in quarantine in the show barn until they were told what to do with them by the authorities.

She wished she could just let them all outside, but at least they could open up the barn doors now and let in fresh air. She worried about them getting stiff being kept in the stalls, but she knew it was safer for them to be in one right now. When Dr. Shamis came out, she'd ask about hand-walking them for exercise.

She'd also have to remember to keep anything in connection with them separated until it all got sterilized in case of a contagious horse disease. They hadn't noticed anything obvious like Strangles, but there were other contagious diseases that couldn't be seen with the naked eye.

Morgan prayed she hadn't made a mistake bringing them here to her home, knowing in her heart she'd do it all again.

Chapter 10

THE MEN WERE AT their wits end. Ty and the vet stood outside in the shade, trying to figure out how to do an assessment on the sorrel gelding.

"Are you sure?" Dr. Shamis asked.

Ty said, "It's the only thing I can think of. I hate to ask her, but she did offer. If we don't want to drug or twitch him, she's the best option I can think of."

The experienced and kindhearted vet scratched his chin. "Well, it's your place. If she's the best option, go get her!"

Ty glanced down at the motorhome. He hadn't seen or heard anything from Ripley since she left the barn over six hours earlier. He hated to wake her up if she was sleeping, or bother her if she was working. He wasn't sure what she did but knew she did it from there. "Well, it won't hurt to ask her anyway."

Dr. Shamis sat down on a picnic table with a bottle of water to wait. According to those working there, the sorrel had bonded with this Ripley lady. Hopefully she could get the horse to allow men around him to do an assessment. If not, they'd have to resort to somehow either drugging him or twitching him—which none of them wanted to do at all.

The horse had already attacked the vet, Ty, and Josh. All three men were concerned the horse would not only seriously injure them, but himself even more. They preferred to not do any drugs so they could get true and accurate test results. And twitching him in any way would only reinforce his mistrust and hatred of men.

No, they needed to go about it from a softer approach. They at least needed to *try*. They owed this horse that much.

Barring the circumstances, all three men agreed horses like this—dangerous, attacking ones—were best to be humanely put down. His only saving grace at this point was women.

The horse was practically a lamb with a woman, Dr. Shamis was told. Unfortunately, the world isn't comprised of just women. Dangerous animals just sometimes needed to be put down humanely—for everyone's safety. They all just hated to do it, especially since the horse responded to women. There was a chance, a glimmer of hope, for this horse in that.

Dr. Shamis sighed again as he wondered what in the world made the horse this antagonistic toward men. He took another drink as he watched Ty make his way toward the large motorhome.

When The Darrells spotted Ty from Quail Run, they trotted over to him. When they led him toward the motorhome parked in the middle of seemingly nowhere, Ty smiled. Funny how they just assumed in their own dog way he was heading to Ripley's and nowhere else. How did they know he wasn't just out for a walk?

He was hoping for a sign like music playing so he knew she was awake or maybe just not busy. No such luck. Walking around the motorhome, he stopped in surprise. She'd raised the large awning for shade and put down an equally large rectangle of fake, green grass. She'd weighed it down in the corners with concrete blocks. With her lawn chair and table, it was inviting and cozy.

The Darrells stopped at her door, looking at him expectantly. Darrell B sat down to wait, lightly panting in the heat. Darrell G stood there, her tail wagging so hard her entire body moved. Her eyes danced with excitement as she impatiently waited for Ty to get Ripley out to play.

Listening for any sounds, Ty still didn't hear anything coming from within. Hesitating, he decided since he was here, he might as well do it. With a last look at the dogs and a sigh, he knocked on her door.

Ripley pulled the pillow over her head. She had her nature sounds playing softly in her stereo to help her fall asleep more easily. She'd learned long ago if it was too quiet, she couldn't sleep at all.

When she first heard the faint knocking, she wasn't sure if she was dreaming... or was in a nightmare. She sat up groggily on the side of her bed. Running her hands through her hair, she waited until her brain caught up with the rest of her body.

There it was again. Someone *was* knocking on her door. With a groan, she got up and made her way to the door, checking herself in her bathroom mirror as she passed through.

Ripley slapped herself on the cheeks a couple of times to wake up—not missing the irony since just a minute ago she was desperately trying to fall asleep.

Looking through the window in her door, she frowned. A man she figured was Ty was standing there with his back to the door. She saw The Darrells sitting at his feet, their tails wagging as they looked up at her door in anticipation.

When she opened it, Darrell G immediately barked in greeting, making her smile. "Hey back, Darrell!" Looking at Ty, she asked, "Did you want your smelly fish hat back that badly?"

When he turned around to face her, she was fairly sure her heart stopped. The man cleaned up extremely well. Gone was the camping beard, and in its place was a clean-shaven, handsome face. She was never one for facial hair on a man, but she'd actually thought him attractive with it. But he was even better without it. She had to force herself to relax to get a grip on her errant thoughts.

With an appreciative smile at her humor, Ty shook his head. "Nope. I honestly forgot you had it." He paused before asking, "Did I wake you? Or were you working?"

"No, I got my morning calls done and... Well, yeah, I was just trying to go to sleep for a nap. I have some more calls in a few hours to do. Do you need something?"

"I'm sorry to bother you, Ripley. Man, I bet you're bushed. But, well... The vet's here, and we've been trying to work with Cappy. But he won't, or just can't, settle down. We've got all the other horses done and saved him for last. We were wondering if you'd be willing to come up to see if he'd calm down if you were there."

He looked up at her apologetically. Dang it, she was trying to get in some sleep and he woke her up... again!

"Cappy? Who's that?"

"The big sorrel who hates men."

"How'd you find out his name?" she asked, surprised.

He grinned. "We didn't. We named him after you a little while ago. It's short for Capilano... Cappy. It's just for now. We needed to call him something."

"Cappy, huh? Not *Rattler* since you never know when he might strike?"

He shook his head and chuckled.

She asked, "Do I get a reduced rate of rent for that namesake honor?"

"You'd have to check with Morgan on that since that's her business, not mine. But we *did* make you breakfast this morning! That has to count for something, right?"

"Wow! That *was* this morning, wasn't it?" Her voice was filled with wonder. "It feels like a *week* ago!"

He nodded. "I know what you mean. We all do."

Looking at him standing below her, a thought came to her suddenly. "Hey, aren't you supposed to be off today?"

"I rested up at the house. Josh and I hung out up there until the vet arrived. Friends never leave friends hanging," Ty answered solemnly. "Morgan needed help so here I am. Josh went into town to get lunch for everyone, so I thought I'd come get you while we waited for him to get back. The family who runs the food truck that's normally here is on vacation for a month, so we had to go to town for lunch. We already ate the leftover food from game night."

Leaning against the door frame, Ripley analyzed what he'd said. These people stuck together like super glue. Teamwork just didn't seem to be the right description for them. They didn't just talk the talk, but walked the walk.

Ty waited, wondering what was going through her mind as she had a thoughtful look on her face. "Ripley? Can you come up?"

Breaking out of her thoughts, she looked back down at the man who'd asked for her help. "Of course. Have a seat there, and give me a couple of minutes, all right?"

"Sure."

She closed her door and went back into her bathroom to brush and pull back her hair into a ponytail, her wavy layered bangs framing her face. As she put on her socks and shoes in the living room, she wondered what they expected her to do. Whatever she could, she assumed. She picked up Ty's hat as she passed her table. As she walked out the door, she quickly reached over to grab her sunglasses, slipping them on.

Ty stood up when he saw her door opening. He couldn't help but notice her long legs and nice body as she came out the door and down the steps. He thought the ponytail and sunglasses added to her charm.

"Thanks for the loan of your hat," she said as she held it out to him.

"You're welcome." He took it and waited while she made sure her door was latched.

He looked around her outdoor space again. "I like your set-up here. It's very homey, isn't it?"

"I do what I can. And yes, it is."

"The fake grass is a nice touch. Do you carry it with you everywhere you travel?"

She looked down at it and smiled. "No. I actually bought it just a few days ago. It serves three purposes at this time. One is to catch dirt from my shoes. Two, it's to make a nice place to sit and enjoy the spectacular views and peacefulness out here. But the *real* motivation was because I figured I could see a brown snake on it. It'd stand out more on a bright green background. It's just an added safety measure to relieve my mind since Morgan got me paranoid my first day here!"

Ty smiled while certainly respecting her worry. He commented, "Well, that'd work for a Western Diamondback rattlesnake because they're brown, like you said. But the Mojave rattlesnake isn't. It's more green... and more aggressive."

Ripley's heart skipped a beat hearing that news. Hotly, she replied, "Well, that sucker isn't as green as I am! I drive a hybrid... A *Prius*, dang it!"

Ty laughed heartily at her retort and spunky attitude. He signaled to the dogs to follow them as they began walking. He chuckled as they walked, thinking again about her reply. He looked at her, his smile flashing. "You have a great sense of humor!"

"Who's joking?" she said with a straight face.

His laugh caused her to start laughing. She figured they were both punch-drunk tired.

Ripley again deadpanned, "So you've now joined the ranks of males banging on doors to keep me from sleeping. How does that make you feel?"

Ty laughed again. "It seemed like a sure-fire way to get your undivided attention."

She smiled. "Well, you weren't wrong."

As they followed the dogs back toward the barn, she glanced at him. "Did you get any sleep yourself?"

"A little. You?"

"Not really. I got in about an hour or so when my phone started ringing. Then I got stuck on the phone for longer than I expected. Actually, I'd just laid down when you knocked."

"Oh, Ripley, I'm sorry. Why don't you go back—"

"No worries. You just stopped me from suffocating myself with my pillow." She smiled at him when he glanced over at her, grinning. "Besides, friends don't leave friends hanging."

"I didn't say that to twist your arm."

"I know. But it's a good way to live one's life. Maybe more people should think like that."

They walked a few more steps before he asked, "Does this mean we're friends?"

With a deliberately neutral tone, she answered, "No. Not really, anyway. But we all have to start somewhere, don't we? This is as good a place as any other I've been to start a friendship."

He saw the grin she was holding back, and he smiled. "Amen to that."

Chapter 11

Ripley met Dr. Shamis again, shaking his hand when he met them at the barn door. After talking for a while, they decided to see if she could work her magic with the horse. She headed toward the end of the row where she saw the vet supplies put aside, safely out of the way.

She stopped at Cappy's stall and looked inside. She smiled when he immediately made his way from the far back of the stall straight toward her, albeit on sore legs. "Hey, my darling. I've been told you've been terrorizing these guys who are just trying to help you. Is that true?"

She blew on his nose when he poked it through the bars. She noticed the sheen of sweat on his body. She instinctively knew he'd broken out in that sweat when the men were trying to work with him. She wondered if it burned in his wounds like it would for a human.

"I heard they named you after me. Cappy is a cute name for you," she said as she stroked his face through the bars, gaining his trust and letting him calm down some more.

Down the aisle, Ty and the vet could see the muzzle poke through the bars. Ty whispered, "See what I mean? That horse trusts her for whatever reason. She's our best bet here, I think."

Wordlessly, the vet nodded as Ripley grabbed the halter that had a lead rope already attached to it. She unlatched the door, slowly opening it. Her heartbeat sped up a bit, but she kept her voice calm and steady as she slid the door open a little more. Cappy seemed accepting and was relaxed with her entering his space.

Making sure the latch was pushed back and out of the way in case she had to leap out the door in a hurry, Ripley took a step inside. The last thing she needed to do was gouge open her side on a metal latch that was sticking out.

Talking to the horse, she let him sniff the halter and lead rope. Slowly, she ran her hands down his neck before gently rubbing the halter and rope against him. He tossed his head when her hand neared it. His skin twitched, but he didn't object, didn't try to bite, or run her over like he did the men. With her, he kept all four feet on the ground and his mouth closed. Ripley leaned against the horse gently, letting him get used to her being so close.

She let him sniff the halter and rope again at his own pace. He blew on it, snorted a bit but was calm. Smoothly and with little fuss, Ripley slid his nose through the opening of the halter, and competently, quickly, slipped the end of the strap through the buckle and slipped the tiny metal bar into a hole. There. She had him. His skin twitched nervously, but he stood still.

Letting him adjust to the situation, Ripley continued to pet and praise him. As she gave him time to relax, she realized he was taller than she remembered now that she was right next to him.

Talking louder for the men to hear her, she finally called out, "I've got the halter and lead on him. He's calm. Twitchy skin, white eyes a bit, but he's standing for me. Do you want me to lead him out, or do you want to come in here?"

Dr. Shamis looked at Ty, whispered, "Incredible!" He shook his head in wonder. "Inside the stall in case he tries to get away?"

Ty thought for a moment, answered softly, "He might think we're cornering him. And there's not a lot of room in there for all of us. It might get too dangerous. I myself prefer more room to move in.

"We could bring him out into the aisle. But if he gets loose, he's got a lot of barn to be loose in. He might knock down the round pen Josh and I put up in here earlier if he got into one of his moods. We want neutral territory. I'd like him to think of his stall as a sanctuary, somewhere safe."

Dr. Shamis nodded. "The aisle then, close to his stall?"

Ty nodded back in agreement before calling out, "Ripley?"

The sorrel's ears flicked back and forth, his tail swished, and he shivered. Ripley talked to him first before answering Ty. "Yeah. We're good. He shivers when he hears your voice, Ty. He knows you're here."

"Okay... We'll go slow here."

Cappy's skin quivered again. Ripley smoothed her hand over his neck and shoulder, both already beginning to get a shade darker with nervous sweat. "Cappy, my boy, you're going to have to trust us, okay? I know it's really scary for you because you've had it bad somewhere else. But this place is a good place. It's a safe place for you, all right?"

She called out to the men, "He's beginning to break into a sweat, so he knows something's going on. Stay out of sight just in case."

"Okay," Ty replied.

Sliding the door open wider, and then all the way, Ripley stepped out, letting Cappy set the pace. She was afraid he'd run her over in his haste to find freedom, but he surprised her. He didn't.

His poor legs were swollen and probably felt as wobbly as her own. She tried to control her apprehension as she walked him down the aisle a little bit. He slowly walked alongside her, turning his head to look at the other horses as they passed by them. She stopped to let him sniff noses with a bay gelding. Ripley noticed they got along fine. Maybe they were buddies from a holding pen?

She called out to the men, "We're in the aisle about two stalls away from his. He's being friendly with the little bay here. It might help having him distracted by a friendly horse. Why don't you come out, and see what happens? I've got him."

Ty replied calmly, "You be careful, Ripley. He's charged us three times already today. Try to hang onto him, but don't put yourself at risk. *Don't* let that rope get wrapped around your fingers or hand!

"If he charges, either hang onto him until I get to you, or let him go. With any luck, he won't run us down. We'll figure out a way to catch him sooner or later." Ty waited for her reply before they stepped into the horse's line of sight. She was quiet. "I mean it, Ripley."

"I hear ya." She continued to pet the sorrel, letting him look around his new surroundings.

Cappy saw the two men immediately, of course. His ears laid flat back in his threat toward them, but he didn't charge.

Ripley, ready to spring away if he got overly violent, just continued to pet and talk to him. Her plan was to not let him go as she refused to let the horse think bad behavior resulted in freedom, no matter how much *he* believed it. It was imperative that Cappy learned some new behaviors, and she was committed to helping him begin. It could be his only chance at a new life, or even life itself.

He raised his front leg like he was preparing to strike out with it before he began to sidestep nervously. But he didn't charge or rear up to a terrifying height over her. Ripley stood to his side so if he did, she wouldn't be run over or struck by a powerful hoof. She continued to pet and talk to him like this was the most normal thing in the world. And for most horses, it would be. But for an abused horse, *normal* was a relative thing.

As Ty and the vet approached them, both were ready to either spring out of the way or rush in to help Ripley. Their eyes on Cappy, they walked closer to him. Cappy snaked his head, snapped his teeth at them, pawed his front leg in the sand, but then suddenly stopped.

Dr. Shamis assumed it was because it hurt to do it. The vet saw the sweat already breaking out on the horse's neck. His ears were still laid back, but Ripley never stopped touching him, talking to him, letting him know the men were friends. At the very least, friendly.

The horse's skin quivered like he was ridding it of biting flies. The sweat on his neck had turned his reddish-brown coat to almost black. In agitation, his tail swished a few times. They all saw the whites in his eyes as he waited to see what would happen to him.

Ripley saw that worried eyebrow look he had. The poor horse was just waiting for the other shoe to drop and to react to it the exact second it did. She just kept petting him, soothingly reassuring him he was safe.

His ears were still laid back as the two men came closer, but that was all he was doing now. The two men came even closer, both aware the large horse could run them down in an instant. Instead, the horse moved closer to Ripley in what looked like an attempt to protect her from them.

But, amazingly, he stood.

Reaching Cappy and Ripley first, Ty took a calming breath and held out his hand, a piece of apple in it. He was hoping the horse just took a bite of the apple and not his flesh. After a while, he saw the horse's soft muzzle tentatively reach out, sniff his hand before he suddenly yanked it back. He snaked his head, snapped his teeth, laid back his ears again. Ty called his bluff and stood still. He tried to not look Cappy in his eyes but just watched his body language.

Ripley's heartbeat sped up, but she continued talking to the horse, running her hand down his wet neck and shoulder. When Cappy backed up, she followed. He charged forward a couple of steps before attempting a half-hearted rear. Ripley reprimanded him gently but firmly, letting him know that wasn't allowed.

Ty stood still, not moving but ready to. He oozed confidence and gentleness toward the horse, letting Cappy feel in control and not be threatened.

After a few minutes of a stalemate between man and horse, Cappy gave in with Ripley's encouragement. He tentatively reached out his neck and nose, his lips trying to roll the apple off Ty's flat hand without having to actually touch Ty. Patiently, Ty just waited.

The apple finally rolled enough for the sorrel to grab it—gently—before he quickly backed up the aisle in retreat. Ripley again allowed him the freedom to feel safe by doing what he wanted to do. If he wanted to back up all the way to New Mexico, she'd let him.

They all heard him crunching the apple and smiled.

The bay gelding in the stall could now smell the sweet apple scent and stuck his nose through the bars for some. Slowly, not turning his back completely, Ty put out his hand. He felt Dr. Shamis put another piece of apple in his palm. Ty reached out again, this time letting the bay have it.

All the while, Cappy watched from down the aisle. His ears flicked, his skin shivered, and his tail swished as his eyes intently watched every movement Ty made.

Ripley watched also, still coaxing Cappy to relax. She'd noticed the fine sheen of sweat covering his neck was working its way over his body now. It broke her heart to see the horse in such distress at the mere sight of a man.

Ty got more apple, offering it to the sorrel again. It took a few minutes, but Cappy took a chance. Ever so slowly, step by tiny step, he approached Ty on his own. Ripley simply walked beside him, stopping when he stopped, walking when he walked. Long, long minutes later, Cappy stopped about three feet in front of Ty. All three humans were ready to explode with the victory. Cappy was learning to trust—one step at a time.

After a few more moments, Cappy took another few small, tentative steps toward the man. After another long pause, he reached out his long neck and sleek head. Stretching as far as he could without moving forward another step, Cappy took the piece of apple from Ty's outstretched hand again. Ripley praised the horse over and over with voice and touch.

Without taking his eyes off the horse, Ty said quietly, "I hate to ruin this. Maybe we could leave him be to end all of this on a high note."

In a normal volume, Ripley answered him, "We could, but when's the vet going to be able to come back out? I may not be available then, if needed. What all do you need to do, Doc?"

Dr. Shamis stepped beside Ty, both men waiting for the possible charge. Cappy was eyeing them, but Ripley had him in her spell. He stomped his front leg, then stopped. Dr. Shamis noticed he then picked it up slightly off the ground. His suspicions were confirmed that it hurt when he did that. Tendon, maybe? Bruised hoof? It could even be his shoulder.

Dr. Shamis quietly answered her, "Blood tests, respiratory, check for dehydration, and I wanted to check his legs more closely. There's something wrong with the one he's using as his weapon and threat. He's not putting it down all the way. It could be tendon, hoof, or shoulder. I may need an X-ray of the bones.

"I'd also like to give him more antibiotics and painkiller as well as take a look at his chest up close. I think his sides and face look fine from what I can see from here. I'm more concerned about his chest."

Ripley nodded before saying cheerfully, "Okay then! You're not asking for much at all, are you?" The men smiled at her. After a few moments, she asked thoughtfully, "What if I did the tests for you?"

Dr. Shamis shook his head. "Can you draw blood *and* hold him?"

"Why didn't you just get blood from them last night?"

"Neither one of us did. I think our focus was on the immediate crisis and getting them taken care of as quickly as possible to alleviate their pain. In hindsight, yes, we should've thought of that."

Ripley nodded. "That's all true. Obviously, none of *us* did either. It's not anyone's fault unless it's everyone's fault."

Ty asked, "What if Doc walked around behind you, Rip? Where Cappy can't really see him? Could you cover his eyes so he can't see behind him so Doc can get to you? He could get blood from his neck if you moved toward me a couple of feet. He could pop a shot of antibiotics in him too."

She nodded. "Let's see how he lets me handle him first. You know, we could blindfold him if nothing else works. Or a pair of blinders could work, if you have a pair. But we'll try this way first." Looking at the vet, she asked, "For dehydration, would a skin pinch or a gum test work for you?"

"Sure. Can you get him to open his mouth?"

With a wide grin, she answered, "Sure! He tends to do that every time one of you gets close. Who wants to step forward?"

Both men grinned back at her, but neither volunteered.

Ripley moved to hold up the sorrel's head which he didn't much care for her touching. She finally was able to lift his upper lip and pushed her thumb against his top gum. The white spot turned pink in good time. She did it again, having to hold on to Cappy's head a little more firmly this time.

"He's not dehydrated. Gums have good color too. And, hey... He's not that old, guys. His teeth tell me he's probably around six or so. I think I'm reading the Galvayne's Groove right. And the angle of his teeth is still more vertical rather than elongated and pushed out. He's in his prime. He's just a young whippersnapper!" She kissed Cappy's velvety-soft muzzle and smiled.

Highly impressed, Ty asked, "How do you know so much about horses, Ripley? You're a god-send!"

"I read a lot of horse books as a kid."

The men laughed at her. Cappy's ears flicked forward at the sound.

Ty held out another piece of apple, waited to see what the horse would do. After another long impasse, Cappy finally took it. Ty gave another piece to the little bay who was still trying to get his nose through the bars for more himself. The other horses had also caught the scent of apple and more than one was trying to get some too. Some of them were now nickering and shoving their muzzles through the bars of their stalls.

All three people realized Cappy was probably being a bit more inclined to eat the apple from Ty's hand simply so no other horse could have it. If greed was his motivation, they'd take what they could get for now.

Dr. Shamis said, "Let me get around behind her, Ty. When I motion to you, distract him with the apple pieces. Just keep them coming until I'm done!"

"Hang on while I cut up a bunch." Ty used his pocketknife to slice five apples into chunks so he'd have a fair supply of them ready, dropping them in a small bucket he could hang off his arm to have them close by. "That hopefully should be enough. If he eats all of these, he'll probably get a tummy ache. We don't want him to colic so you'd better work fast, Doc!"

Ripley turned Cappy's head away and covered his eyes as the vet walked around them, coming up behind her, mindful of a possible kick. He'd already prepared a needle to draw blood, and another with the antibiotics. He had a third prepped with a pain medication.

Silently, he motioned for Ty to give Cappy some apple. He'd try to stick Cappy at the same time so he didn't notice it. Ripley got prepared since no one knew how the horse would react to the inevitable prick.

"Wait," Dr. Shamis said almost under his breath so Cappy hopefully wouldn't hear him. "Let me pull up some of his skin first..."

Ripley moved out of his way a little more. She glanced at Ty, who held out his hand with a chunk of apple on it. Ty was ready to jump out of the way if Cappy bolted at the feel of the needle prick.

When Cappy reached out for the apple, Dr. Shamis quickly inserted the needle, drew blood. Ty held out more apple to keep the horse distracted while Ripley continued to pet him. The horse never reacted to the needle as he munched away on apple pieces. Ty held out more as soon as the horse took the previous piece.

Dr. Shamis removed the needle, deftly put the cap on it and slipped it in his pocket. He then quickly gave the horse a shot of antibiotics. Cappy flinched a little as Ty kept feeding him apple pieces and Ripley pet him. Finally, the pain med shot was done too. Ripley praised Cappy, over and over. They all let out a breath of relief and smiled.

While he was there, the vet took a closer look at Cappy's legs. The back two just looked stocked up, probably from inflammation from stress from the wreck. Cautiously, he felt the hooves for heat before running his hands along the hock, and then down the lower section of his legs. Cappy gave a weak kick before he lowered his leg again. Doc finished his inspection before straightening up again. The front ones most likely bore the brunt of the impact, so he was more concerned about those two.

He took a chance, sidled up beside Ripley to get a little closer, running his hand on the horse's neck and shoulder beside hers. She led the vet's hand down the horse's leg without the horse seeming to be any wiser a man was touching his body too. The vet had to take a chance of touching the horse on his own since she couldn't reach too far down without putting herself in a bad position should Cappy jump or startle.

Dr. Shamis ran his knowledgeable hands around the knee, cannon bone, felt the tendons in the back. When he felt the hoof and coronet band just above the hoof, he frowned. He then repeated his action. Ripley watched him with one eye. "Do you think he's foundering, Doc? Are his hooves hot?"

Not wanting the horse to know he was there, he just nodded.

Ripley walked around the front of the horse and covered his eyes again to distract him so Shamis could walk around his back end to get to the other side. There was no way for her to walk behind the horse with him so they had to take the chance of doing it this way. Ty held out more apple bits.

The vet competently checked the other front leg, again following Ripley's hand as the horse didn't appear to notice the differences in touch. He put his stethoscope to the horse, listening. Cappy's skin quivered, and he side-stepped a few paces. Ripley and the vet followed him until he stopped.

When the vet was done inspecting the stitches and being satisfied with them, he motioned to Ripley by crossing his arms over his chest, then pointed to the front hooves.

Since *she* could talk, she confirmed, "You want to take X-rays of his front hooves or legs?"

Doc nodded. Holding up a finger and motioning for her to cover Cappy's eyes again, she understood. She blocked Cappy's view of the vet so he could get his X-ray unit set up behind Cappy. He quickly did so and carefully got back behind Ripley.

He bent down, lining up the square film and the machine. Efficiently, he got shots of both legs and was even able to pick up his front legs enough to slide a piece underneath his hooves. Ty just kept handing out the apple chunks, giving the bay one now and then too. Hoping they all took correctly, Dr. Shamis slowly stood up with his portable machine and backed away into a safe zone.

Ty smiled at Ripley. "We owe you *big* for this!"

"Normally, you would. But for this fella? No charge!" She grinned at Ty as she pet the horse again. "Doc, do you think his chest is all right?"

"Yeah. And I think those stitches will hold. I didn't see any infection earlier, but it's hard to tell when he's charging you. From here, it looks fine, and what I could sorta see when I was checking his legs. I didn't want to risk poking at him.

"Can you check him since you're closer? Any oozing pus? Tears in stitches? Abnormal swelling? Smell of infection?"

She looked, tried to be thorough. She lightly touched his chest, feeling for too much heat. "Um, I don't think so. Whoa, Cappy boy... I bet you're sore, aren't you? I understand..." Cappy backed up a few paces. She patiently followed until he stopped. "I think he's getting tired of me."

Ty nodded. "Let's end this now while he's happy."

The vet agreed.

When Ripley began to turn Cappy, Ty said, "Actually, hang on a few more minutes, okay? Let me clean his stall while he's out. Josh and I have been cleaning out the others as we worked on them. Can you move him over here so I can get the wheelbarrow by him without him hammering me?"

"Probably." She smiled at his grin. She tugged on Cappy's lead to get him to move up and over. The little bay horse followed Cappy, so he was thankfully distracted.

Ty carefully went by him and quickly cleaned his stall. It took only one small load to clean it out since the horse hadn't really eaten or drank too much yet. Ty shook out some fresh straw from the stack Kim had placed at the end of the aisle earlier. He checked the water bucket, satisfied when he noticed Cappy had been drinking some.

He also walked around the stall, looking for damaged boards. Surprised, he only saw one board that he'd kicked hard enough to damage. They'd have to get him out again later and fix it, but it was okay for now. He didn't see any nails, screws, broken wood, or metal stripping that could cause Cappy more injuries from his earlier pawing or kicks.

Satisfied, he walked around Cappy again, who was now happily sniffing another horse's nose. Ripley just let him do his thing. When he was safely out of the way, Ty nodded that he was done.

Ripley turned the horse around at his own speed and took her time leading him into his stall, again turning him around so he was facing out. Praising the sorrel, she partially closed the door before removing the halter, careful to not scrape it against his facial wounds. Backing out, she closed the door then latched it shut. When she joined the two men in the middle of the aisle, she smiled when they heard the familiar *bang, bang.*

"Okay... So he's not *completely* sick of me yet." She went back to his stall to keep him quiet.

Ty said, "I'll see if Josh and I can rig up a padded bag or something, screw it into the door there. But then it'll be in the way when we need to open the door... Maybe hang something down on the inside, and tie to the bars so we can remove it? We'll see. There's one board I saw that we'll need to fix later. It's fine for now though. We may need your help in getting him out to fix it unless Morgan can do it."

Ripley looked at the horse. "Hear that, Cappy? The doctors here think you need a padded room! That's just awful. You need to prove them wrong!"

They all smiled when Cappy blew a huff of air through his nostrils at that moment like he was disagreeing with them. The men then headed toward Dr. Shamis' supplies organizer at the end of the aisle so he could add the blood sample to it. He recorded the information he needed, added a few extra notes. After he was done, Ty helped the tired vet carry it all to his vehicle parked just inside the barn door. The vet wrote out some notes and the bill for Ty to give to Morgan.

While she waited, Ripley found the last two remaining apples. Using her fingernails, she broke off chunks and fed the other horses a small piece as she felt bad only two horses got any. Two apples were hardly enough for nine horses, but she managed it. She looked in the bucket and saw some apple leftovers, so she went around and handed out the last of those chunks too. Since Cappy could see or hear her, he behaved himself. But the second she left the barn with the men, they all heard the *bang! bang!* coming from his stall.

Dr. Shamis smiled at her. "Thanks, Ripley. That horse trusts you with his life, you know. And Ty, let Morgan know I'll get these lab tests run as quickly as I can so we know if any of these horses are contagious to any others. I don't think so, but it'll definitely pay to be sure.

"Even if we had the papers required to be at an auction, it doesn't mean they're real or current. There are a lot of shady people out there. There's too much at stake here, so I'll try to get the lab to put a rush on them."

He handed Ty the coffee mug from that morning. "This is Morgan's. Alexis made Dr. Sanders and I fresh coffee before we left earlier. It was very much appreciated."

"Thanks, Doc." Ty tapped the side of the truck as the vet pulled away. He tapped the mug against his leg as he thought through the situation. He turned to Ripley, standing a few feet away from him.

"He's right. Cappy *does* trust you. It was a chance we took with you. I can't tell you how much we all appreciate your willingness to help. I'm beyond glad you're here. If you weren't, we would've had to resort to drugging him or something else. Neither one of us wanted to twitch him. He would've just fought us more if we did."

Ripley nodded. "I'm so glad I *could* help. Who knew I'd be needed like this when Morgan and I ran into each other last week?"

"Life's little twists are always interesting and timely." He paused. "Are you hungry? If you're not too tired, I'm sure Josh has the salad and pizza up at Sunset Ridge by now. Want a slice or two?"

"Sure, why not? Maybe I can take a slice or two back down with me as payment for saving your butt."

He grinned at her teasing tone. "I think I can talk Morgan into that. If not, I think I have enough weight around here to make it happen on my own." He led her toward the trail-riding barn. Seeing Toby and Maya eating at a picnic table in the shade, he joked, "I hope the lovebirds there left some for us!"

Morgan was just hanging up the phone when they walked in. "Hey, Ripley! Josh told me you were working your magic with Cappy. He peeked in the door down there but didn't want to distract you all." She looked them over. "You're both still in one piece. How'd it go?"

Ty leaned against the counter, setting the mug on it. "Marvelously. She charmed the poor thing until he was eating out of *my* hand, let the vet check his legs, take X-rays, take blood, *and* give two shots. I told her she could take a couple of pizza slices back with her as payment."

"Cappy let you do all of that?" At their nods, Morgan said, "Take a whole pie if you want to, Ripley. Thank you so much!"

"You're welcome. Glad I could help out." She looked behind Morgan, asking, "Is that my flashlight?"

Morgan handed it to her, saying, "Yep. Josh found it earlier when he was cleaning. He brought it down to get it back to you. Are you guys hungry?"

Ty nodded. "I could eat something. Anything left?"

"Yeah. I think Josh was trying to build up my reward points on my credit card," Morgan joked as she led them into another room in the barn, holding open a screen door.

"You told me it was better to have too much than too little," Josh replied to her comment. He grinned at his wife as she walked over to him.

"I did. We'll have enough for dinner tonight, breakfast, and lunch tomorrow!" Pointing to the sink, she said, "Wash your hands in the sink there, and grab some lunch, you two!"

After washing their hands, Ty motioned for Ripley to go first. Taking a plastic fork from the box, Ripley sat down in a chair to eat her salad. Morgan handed her an ice-cold Pepsi from the fridge, smiling back when Ripley grinned at her in pure gratefulness. Sitting by the wide open doors in the tack room, they ate their lunch, talked, and watched a ride come in. Eating pizza, Ripley watched in true interest as Bo and Drew worked.

After a while, Ripley glanced at her watch. "Well, thanks again for the food. That's three meals in a row now! But I've got to get back to my place as I should have some calls coming in soon, and I'll need to be on my laptop for them. But you be sure and get me if you need help with Cappy anytime, okay? And as selfish as it sounds right now, I'd still like to try to get in some of the sleep Ty keeps denying me."

They laughed when Josh said, "Shame on you, Ty. Have you apologized yet to the lady?" To Ripley, he added, "We'll try to keep him away from you for a while."

"I'd appreciate that," Ripley joked as she slipped her sunglasses on. She smiled when Morgan handed her a box that had a full cheese pizza in it. "Aw, thanks!"

Morgan replied, "It's the least we can do. Thank *you,* Ripley."

Ty walked Ripley out, offering her a ride back to her RV. She gratefully accepted the lift and climbed in the front seat of his truck. She waved to Toby and Maya as he backed up.

"You guys sure are fascinating to be around," she said as he drove slowly toward her place.

"You're not too bad yourself. One of these days, I'll have to make it up to you for not letting you sleep every time you need it. But for now, I'll give you time to catch up on your sleep. Then we'll go from there."

Looking at him for a quiet but somehow momentous second, she asked, "Are you asking me out?"

With a chuckle, he replied, "If I was, I obviously did it all wrong if you had to ask." With a grin at her laugh, he answered, "And nope. Not yet. Just letting you know I will... If you're still around."

Her heart beat faster as even through her sunglasses, their eyes locked for a brief moment. With a slight nod, she said, "Well, okay then."

When he stopped at her RV, she fumbled for the door handle, finally getting the door open. Was she that addled that she forgot how to open a door? She slid to the ground, praying her legs would hold her up.

Just before she closed the door, he grinned at her. "Hey, Ripley... You want these?"

She reached for the pizza and the flashlight he held out to her. Still a bit dazed from his declaration, she said, "Thanks. See ya later, Ty. And thanks again for the lift."

She walked to her RV door and, balancing her flashlight and pizza carefully in one hand, opened it and felt the blast of cool air rushing across her body. Glancing back before she walked inside, she saw Ty still watching her from the truck.

With a smile aimed right at her, he tipped his cowboy hat at her and drove away.

Chapter 12

Mid-August

Five weeks later, the eleven rescued horses were still being boarded at Harmony Hills. So far, the only person paying for their care was Morgan. She had yet to receive a dime to pay for their feed, vet care, or board.

According to Dr. Shamis, the test results that he'd put a rush on confirmed all were healthy enough to be at the Center and posed no health risk to the other horses on the property.

Once he'd notified her, Morgan slowly began integrating the rescues into the pens and pastures to socialize with each other. She wasn't going to make the poor horses just live in stalls until their fate was decided. They needed, and deserved, to be just a horse so fresh air, sunshine, room to run and roll, and being with other horses was what they got.

Making a schedule as the horses healed, Morgan, Ty, Josh, Kat, and Mel began to work with the rescues. They'd gone down to get Ripley a number of times, and she helped out with Cappy every time they asked. The gelding simply became another horse when she was there.

She'd been able to get him to let them water down his legs, then his entire body without trying to run them all over. He shivered when they checked the stitches in his chest and his sides, but with Ripley reassuring him, Cappy stood still. His X-rays came back fine to everyone's relief. They kept up with the medications Dr. Shamis gave them, and Cappy's body responded.

Dr. Shamis came out again to check on them all and especially the mare's eye. She was healing from all of her other wounds as well. The gelding with the bad front leg was also healing slowly but surely. The vet gave the credit of the rescues' healing success directly to Morgan and her staff.

With his past apparently a violent one, Cappy was a project all on his own. They'd found if they paired him with the little bay stabled a few stalls away, he was fairly easy to catch when they let him out to stretch his legs to be a happy horse again. The first few times—before they figured out the bay gelding could be used—they'd had to go down to get Ripley to catch him.

They didn't want to stress him out while he was still recuperating. While his legs were healing, they were careful of his running in panic, sliding to a stop, spinning around, and taking off again. They also didn't trust the horse to not run through, or even jump, a fence.

Cappy still threatened Ty and Josh but not as badly as before. There were always at least two people around when they worked with him in case he attacked them. He was also allowing them to groom him without rearing and kicking at them anymore... But only when Ripley was there. He'd behave with Morgan, but he behaved better with Ripley. But, as they all said, he was getting better. It was simply one day at a time.

Cappy's mental health was just as important as his physical, so Morgan wanted him to just learn to be a horse again. Finding out he liked the bay helped immensely as the bay gelding was easy to work with. Morgan put them together to let Cappy unwind and relax, hoping he could maybe work it all out in his mind that he was in a safe place. She even switched the bay with the horse beside Cappy so he'd have a friend next to him he could see through the wood slats. Mentor horses could work wonders, she knew.

Good-naturedly, Ripley smiled every time they knocked on her door. She'd slip on her shoes and sunglasses and follow them up to the barns. Sometimes she'd be talking on her phone doing a business call as she walked along. They'd had to wait a few times until she hung up, but they didn't mind.

It never occurred to Morgan, Josh, or Ty to not swallow any pride or ego when they had to go get Ripley. Their sole focus and purpose was to rehabilitate the sorrel so if he wanted Ripley, then he got her. They *did* wonder what they'd do when Ripley left, but they hoped to have made enough progress by then for that not to be an issue. All they could do was hope.

Morgan warned both men that Ripley could leave any time she wanted to. She herself hadn't expected Ripley to stay this long. It'd been almost seven weeks now, but Ripley hadn't uttered a word about leaving.

Ty had found that besides apples, carrots, and Fig Newtons, Cappy liked peppermints. Within one minute of giving one to the sorrel, he found out so did many of the other horses.

In true Ty character, on his day off he went down to the wholesale price club and bought a huge bag of peppermint candy. He stored the bag of treats in a bucket with a lock-on lid near the rescues. Morgan offered to reimburse him, but he declined her offer, telling her she could buy the next bag since it appeared the horses would be staying a while.

Morgan had a huge heart for the rescues and was trying to figure out a way to keep them all. If she couldn't, she wasn't sure what would happen to them. And every time it occurred to her that they all could be taken away from her and still sent to the slaughterhouse, her heart would once again get torn in two. She and Josh had discussed every avenue they could think of, even calling Josh's mom since Annabelle had done horse rescues for decades in Kentucky.

Morgan knew she could swing the cost of buying the horses. They were worth it because no amount was too high to ease her burden of guilt. She figured they'd sell fairly inexpensively—unless the owner realized how badly they wanted to keep them. Then he'd jack up the prices, she was sure.

But the fact was, the horses simply weren't for sale because of the custody battle and the ongoing legalities from the wreck. She got updates when Deputy Matt Harvey came out to do check-ups on them with a Humane Society member, a man named Dell Shannon.

For court purposes, Morgan recorded every dime spent on the eleven from practically every seed and kernel of grain to every stalk of hay to every bit of straw and sawdust. She had files for supplies from halters, fly spray, and fly masks, for vet care, labor spent for her workers to take care of them, training time to be able to assess them individually, to her increased water and electric bills.

She also charged mightily for the nighttime emergency run with three trailers, employee labor, and mileage—not to mention them all working until the wee hours of the next morning with the vets. She also included boarding fees, and one day when she got ticked off thinking about how the horses were just pawns, she even charged for the peppermints and bags of apples.

Always impressed with her attention to detail, neither Ty nor Josh were surprised with her records pertaining to the horses. She also took lots of photos and videos of them as evidence. She wanted all her ducks in a row should she be subpoenaed for court.

She was fully intending to get all of her money back that she was being forced to shell out. She didn't mind at all about taking care of them, but she was a businesswoman and expenses *were* expenses. And eleven horses being thrust onto her made for *large* expenses. She was already into many thousands of dollars just for the basics.

And Morgan fully intended on being reimbursed one way or another.

In the meantime, Ripley helped with Cappy the most when Ty or Josh wanted to work with him. Now and then, they had Toby, Bo, or Drew hang out just for another man to be around to see how Cappy would react.

It was slow progress, but none of them wanted to rush the horse into trusting men again. Quite frankly, they couldn't have anyway. They knew for an abused animal to trust again, it was not an issue that could be forced, nor was it going to happen overnight. It may not even happen at all.

If she wasn't helping with Cappy, Ripley was working. And the little time she had when she wasn't doing either, she was taking walks for the fresh air and sunshine. Now and then when she went out, she'd stop for a while to visit with the staff. And she always texted Morgan when she left and returned for safety as requested. She'd also done a second trail ride, and she'd made it to a couple more of Morgan's game nights, enjoying the camaraderie and company of these people she'd met by chance.

In an unexpected twist for her, the one person that had captured her attention was Ty Stanton.

Since that first day when he'd dropped her off after helping the vet with Cappy, telling her he was going to ask her out, she couldn't stop wondering about him. She couldn't ask him about it because wouldn't that make her seem anxious, needy, or desperate? She wasn't either of those... But she *was* getting interested. They also didn't really spend much time together actually alone. When they *had* been together, they were each focused on Cappy and not getting hurt by him.

As the weeks passed by, Ripley couldn't tell if she was relieved or disappointed in this turn of events. She really didn't trust men any more than Cappy. She'd realized that one day when they were working with him. She figured they both had legitimate reasons. But Ty was different than other men she'd known, she admitted to herself.

Had he just been joking with her, or was he setting her up? Was it a game? He simply didn't come across as a player especially considering who his friends were. None of them came across as accepting of players.

Did he say that to make her look forward to a date that she never knew for sure would happen? Or did he simply change his mind, knowing that at some point she'd leave? Or did he say that to plant the seed just to make her think of him, to build anticipation? If so, he was a clever man because it was working like a charm.

Tomorrow morning she was heading to a work conference in Phoenix. As she was setting out clothes and packing her suitcase for the next week, the thought came to her that she really should let someone know she'd be gone. Would they want to know that? Maybe just in case something happened with her RV, or if they wanted her to help with Cappy? Of course they would.

Since it was too late at night to contact Morgan (being outside of those business hours), she decided to stop at the office in the morning when she left. Excited to see her own friends again, she was leaving early to pick one up at the airport, but there was a good chance someone would be at Sunset Ridge when she stopped. If not, a note would suffice.

After checking to make sure her door was locked, Ripley returned to her bedroom. She turned on the nature sounds in her CD player before flipping off her bedside light. As the ocean waves rolled in with a crash and then peacefully receded from the shore while the seagulls called out to each other, Ripley lay in her comfortable bed, staring at the dark ceiling, waiting for sleep to claim her.

Some nights when she didn't turn on her CD player, she could hear coyotes yipping in the desert. She never knew how far away they were though. With the clear, desert air, she knew sounds could carry quite a distance—she'd read that in a book.

A few times, she'd slipped outside in her nightshirt, wearing her boots just in case and carefully checking the area with her large flashlight for snakes and anything else that might make her jump out of her skin. She'd sat in her lawn chair just listening to the night sounds. The breeze that blew during the day generally died down at night just as the sun set, but it was normally at least a bit cooler out. And the night she did that under the bright, full moon and the twinkling stars, she suddenly wished she wasn't sitting there alone.

There were times she adored living alone and being single. But there were other times when the loneliness caught up with her, making her again question the hours she worked, and the lifestyle she'd chosen years ago. She never thought she'd be forty and still single. But now she was forty-four.

And still no house to call her own, no husband to welcome her home, no kids to brag about or despair over. She'd never really wanted kids, so that part of her musings never really bothered her. But not having a house of her own or a man all to herself to grow old with sometimes pushed her a little bit toward depression.

There was more to life than work, she knew. And she'd made it a point to live on her terms, more often than not working long hours but also able to take off whenever she wanted to. Overall, she liked her life.

She had some great friends—in and out of her business. Her family was about as dysfunctional as anybody else's, she figured, but they got along. And she was a very successful business owner. She just never let people outside her business know *how* successful. She'd learned a long time ago when people knew you were rich, you never knew who to really trust. Were they being nice to you because they genuinely liked you, or were they faking it because they hoped to get access to your money?

Her lifestyle was of her choosing. She could pick up and leave anytime she wanted to. She'd experienced many great places, met interesting people, seen gorgeous views. She was debt-free, had money set aside for emergencies and retirement just in case something unforeseen happened to her business. She never relied on others' experiences to lay all her faith for her own path on just one, so diversity was key with her finances.

In essence, Ripley Capilano hedged her bets. She had more than one bank account, and they were in different banks—again cushioning against the chance of some unforeseen situation arising. She'd seen it happen to others, so she did what she could to make sure it didn't happen to her.

She invested some of her money in a wide variety of options—from a Roth and a traditional IRA, more mutual funds, Certificates of Deposit, online savings, and real estate. She also paid quarterly taxes so she didn't get hit all at once. And she had cash money set aside that wasn't in a bank, in case she just needed hard, physical cash. She was still considering gold or silver but hadn't yet bought either. That diversity was all part of her financial stability and security, her personal freedom.

And she did quite a bit with her favored charitable organizations, from the military to animals to protecting the environment. And that didn't count her side organization and business some trusted family members handled for her.

She'd worked very hard and put in endless hours for years to get to where she was. It wasn't all about the money although that was the main reason she began her business. She enjoyed helping people. She just preferred helping animals more. They couldn't speak for themselves and were completely reliant on a human's whim. People could help themselves if they really wanted to.

But the one thing really missing was that special someone to share it all with. How could she know who she could trust with her heart? Her money?

She'd been let down by men too many times to count. Dating to her took far too much effort to determine if what she was told by some guy was truth, exaggeration, or just flat-out lies. She was *so* sick of liars!

Did any man alive truly respect women anymore? What happened to men being classy? Most of them couldn't even wear their pants pulled up all the way. Jeans and shorts had a *waist* measurement for a reason. It wasn't a mid-thigh or knee measurement on the tag, was it? "Pull them up, and keep them up!" she wanted to yell at them.

Over time, she'd basically lost interest in dating men at all. She liked them, sure, and missed their company at times, but she just couldn't seem to find one she could truly trust. Many of her better friends were men, but they were all plutonic relationships. And she couldn't say she trusted them all.

She only wanted *one* man. Not two or three or ten. Just one. Was that really asking for too much? Apparently, the answer was a resounding *yes.*

She'd always been very selective in who she dated. She had to be. She wasn't an easy woman by any stretch of the imagination either. And with her current lifestyle of just picking up and moving on when she was ready to, it didn't give her a lot of opportunities to meet men she might become interested in if she'd just stayed longer... or permanently.

On the other hand, her lifestyle put her in front of a lot of men. But still no one who caught her interest in the least. And truth be told, she hadn't met *any* that made her even consider settling down.

Until now.

For whatever reason, Ty Stanton had captured her attention, and she couldn't understand why. Maybe it was because his best friend was a woman—an intelligent, fun, successful one at that. Morgan wouldn't have a male best friend if he wasn't of a high quality, would she? Morgan seemed trustworthy, so wouldn't that mean Ty would be too? The fact that his best friend was a woman like Morgan quite simply intrigued her. *And* the fact Josh didn't mind.

Maybe it was because Ty was more than just a little attractive. He still reminded her of someone that she couldn't pin down. Ripley admitted to herself she could be happily content to just stare at him day and night. Some people were just nice to look at, she thought with a smile.

And his sense of humor was a little warped and dry like hers. To her, a sense of humor was mandatory in *any* type of relationship. Not that she was actually *in* one with Mr. Stanton, mind you. It was just the principle. She *needed* someone who could make her laugh and that she could make laugh too.

Looks would fade over time, so they had to have something else attractive between them. Humor was a top choice. Humor could make a simple day brighter or an event more memorable. And humor could even help them get through tough times together.

How could she forget his smile? It could make her heart speed up and her brain functions slow down when he aimed that smile of his right at her. His smile had a very high potency factor.

Ty was also confident, masculine, fit, and loved the outdoor life. He wouldn't be caught dead getting his nails done, and he didn't use vulgar language. He somehow looked clean even when he was coated in dust and horse slobber. He came across as reliable and mature. There was also this aura of power and authority about him that he didn't exploit.

And as tough as she sensed he could be, she'd also seen his nurturing, gentler side when she'd heard him talking to Alexis like he was her dad, or at least a respected father figure or mentor. The way he played with The Darrells and Freeway made her smile. Of course, she'd seen how incredibly patient he was with Cappy. And when Cappy responded to him, how his face lit up in genuine pleasure.

He sincerely enjoyed working with horses, and he loved his life here. She always thought one could tell a lot about a person by how they treated animals. Ty was an animal lover and very much against abusing them. This told her a whole lot about his character. And this knowledge carried a whole lot of weight with her.

Ripley also recalled how Morgan had predicted her guys would come home to support her. And they did. How he'd dropped everything along with Josh and Damien—who she'd yet to meet—to rush home in the wee hours of the morning to support his best friend when she needed it. And he'd stayed all day long to care for the horses and to help out his friends.

And as tough as he was, he was still able to swallow that manly pride and come down to ask her for help with a horse. They could've drugged or twitched Cappy that first day, but she knew that was the absolute last thing they'd wanted to do. He'd have rather walked down and asked for help from a woman than perpetuate semi-violent acts on an abused, traumatized horse. This told her Ty had some humility.

Afterwards, he'd thought of her. Making sure she had lunch with them, and then giving her a ride back to her RV knowing she was tired to her very bones. And she knew he was probably just as worn out. And hadn't he somehow managed to get her breakfast that first morning too? He was smooth in his ways of handling people, she realized now that she was thinking about it.

That he had the love and respect of everyone she'd met so far showed her he knew about building and maintaining relationships. That he understood the irreplaceable value of real friendship and of loyalty spoke volumes about his character.

And his work ethic was comparable to her own. He wasn't lazy or a dictator. She'd seen him work alongside the other staff members, just like she'd seen Morgan do, more than once. Doing that was most likely one of the reasons he and Morgan had the respect of the staff. They both pitched in and didn't just delegate orders.

He had to have *some* flaws because everyone did. She just couldn't figure out what they could be or how bad.

It was almost intimidating to her that she'd met someone who actually met her high personal standards. She wondered what Ty thought of her... *if* he even did. And if so, would she measure up to whatever high standards she was sure *he* had? Surely there was a good reason a man like him was still single.

Ripley finally faded off to sleep with thoughts of Ty Stanton still drifting through her mind.

Chapter 13

THE MORNING SUN WAS sneaking over the top of the mountain range, highlighting the tops of ridges, cliffs, and tall saguaros while simultaneously throwing the lower valleys and washes into dark shadow. The sheer rocks near the summits of the mountains were shining white, reflecting the brightening of the desert sun. Birds were chirping, welcoming a new day. Lizards scurried in their rounds of hunting insects, wary of becoming breakfast themselves. A gila monster hid in the shade of a bush.

Amidst all of this, Ripley finished loading her car, locked up her home, and slowly drove up the lane to the office. Not seeing any cars there yet, she parked her own. Since she'd run into Alexis the other day and was told Morgan was working at a clinic in New Mexico, Ripley decided to leave a note for Ty on the office door since he was in charge when Morgan was away.

Turning off her car and opening her door for fresh air, she grabbed her notebook and was writing out a message when she heard moving tires crunching the hard sand and gravel of the lot. Looking up, she saw Ty drive in and park. She heard country music playing through the open window before he shut off the engine. Noticing her, he made his way over.

Putting down her notebook, she got out of her own car as he ambled over in that easy way he had of walking. "Good morning, Ty!" Just seeing him made her morning feel brighter. It honestly did.

"Good morning, Ripley. You're up awfully early, aren't you?" Glancing in her car as he neared it, he saw the suitcases and bags in the back seat. He said, dismay all over his face, "Are you leaving me already? Give me another chance!"

Deadpanning, she replied, "I'm sorry, darlin'. While waiting for you another guy whisked me off my feet. I'm not getting any younger, you know. I have to take what I can get!"

He shook his head. "Never settle for less than what you deserve, Ripley. Tell that other guy to shove off. He's not for you!"

She laughed. He stood beside her, enjoying just looking at her and listening to her laugh. It was attractive. *She* was attractive... on more than one level. He'd been watching her over the past month, more than she knew. She'd unknowingly captured his attention, and that was hard to do.

He looked over at the horses walking toward the fence nearest them for a moment. In a forlorn tone, he asked, "You're still going to leave me, though, aren't you?"

With a smothered grin, she laid her hand on his shoulder and patted it in a friendly manner. "Just for a few days, but I'll be back." At his playful look of disbelief, she said, "I *have* to come back to get my home, don't I?"

At his mollified look, she explained, "There's a business conference up in Phoenix I need to go to. I should be back in about five days, maybe six if I stay up there to sightsee or something. Odds are, I will.

"That's why I'm here. I decided I should tell you guys I'd be gone in case you needed me for Cappy. I was going to leave a note for you on the office door when you pulled up. Alexis told me Morgan was in New Mexico."

"You could've called."

"I only have Morgan's number, and it's too early." She smiled in remembrance of her first meeting with Morgan. "She specifically told me to not call her outside of office hours unless my place was rolling off a cliff. She seemed fairly serious."

Ty chuckled. "She does guard her time off, which she should." With a twinkle in his eyes, he asked, "Where's your phone?"

Removing it from the case attached to her belt, she automatically handed it to him, belatedly asking, "Why?"

He took it, opened it up and began typing. Ripley leaned closer to him, smelling what she thought was Dial soap. Yeah, the man even *smelled* good. She watched as he put in his phone number as a new contact.

With a thoughtful tone, she said, "Bold. Confident." She waited a beat. "Presumptuous."

His mouth turned up in a little grin as he handed back her phone. "I just sent myself a text so I now have your number. That's called hopeful."

She felt her heart squeeze tightly for a split second. She couldn't help but smile in appreciation. The man had some charm all right. "I'll see what I can do about not dashing your hopes."

"I'd appreciate that." He gave her that smile again before commenting, "So you're going to Phoenix all by yourself. Ever been there before?" Casually, he leaned back against the side of her car in no hurry at all to start his day.

"Just on business. And I won't be all by myself."

"Sugar, you're already dashing my hopes!"

She chuckled before she replied, "It's all plutonic, Sugar. Business is business."

Ty smiled. "Well, if it's *just* business." He looked over at the horses watching them, some nickering a welcome while others stared intently at him, hoping their combined stares could make him get moving and feed them. "Where will you be staying?"

"Stalking me?"

"Not my style." He shot a glance at her before his attention was caught by The Darrells trotting down from the house. Josh was obviously up and moving about the house. "My woman never wonders where I am because I'm right there with her."

"I prefer your style over the other—unless that means you're controlling. Then I don't like either." She didn't break eye contact although it was hard not to. She felt herself getting warm from the heat in his gaze.

They heard a car pull up, and both looked over to see that Bo had arrived.

Ripley was the first to speak as they watched Bo get his things from his dusty car. "Well, here we are again in the early morning hours at the barn, alone, before anyone else arrives. We're gonna have to stop meeting like this, Ty. People are gonna talk!"

He grinned, his gaze studying her for a moment. "That's all right with me if it's all right with you. I don't mind."

Bo walked toward them, his faded blue lunch cooler gripped in one hand, a mug of coffee in his other. "Hey there, Ty, Ripley. What're you two doing up here so early?"

With a sigh, she said quietly, "See? He's already wondering." Ty just grinned again. Turning back to Bo, she replied, "I stopped to let you guys know I was going to Phoenix for a few days for work. Just in case you needed me for Cappy, or my place catches on fire or something like that."

Bo admonished her with a shake of his head. "Don't jinx us, woman! *Fire* is a bad word around here! Ever hear of Old Tucson?"

Ripley nodded. "The movie set place? Sure. What about it?"

Bo explained, “It burned to the ground some years back. All of it. Lickety-split.”

“Oh.” She paused before saying, “Sorry. Um... Okay... I was letting you know I’d be in Phoenix for a few days in case my place rolled off a cliff.”

Ty and Bo grinned at her, both chuckling.

“Okay, I’m glad you both like me losing my home from a cliff fall over a hypothetical fire!”

Both men smiled again.

With a shrug of his wide shoulders, Ty said, “It’s a hypothetical cliff.” He shot her a glance, saying casually, “But if something *should* happen to your place, I have plenty of room at my house, Ripley. You could just stay with me until something else came along. You’re welcome to stay as long as you’d like.”

Sure enough, Bo looked from one to the other. Ripley could see the wheels begin turning in his head and the speculation spark like an unwatched fire in his brown eyes as he took a careful sip of his hot coffee.

She didn’t dare look at Ty. She knew he said that on purpose. After a moment of heavy silence, she said, “Thanks for the offer. It’s very generous of you.” She pushed away from her car as she continued, “Well, on that note, I’d better get moving.

“Oh, I put my chair and table inside and lowered my awning in case a storm pops up. My grass should be weighed down enough unless it gets really windy. If you could please keep an eye on my place, it’d be appreciated.”

“Will do, Ripley. Like it was my own,” Ty said, opening her car door. She shot him an exasperated look, but Ty could see the humor lurking in her eyes. “Be safe up there, and let me know if you need me for anything. You’ve got my number, right?” he added, holding back his smile.

“You’re incorrigible!” she muttered as she slid inside. She started her car as he shut the door, sending a charming smile her way as it clicked shut. Ripley fastened her seatbelt before she waved to them and drove away.

She didn’t smile until she was sure he couldn’t see her anymore.

Chapter 14

Saturday, August 22

Her business conference over now, Ripley really wanted to explore the area. But the lack of sleep the past four days was foremost on her mind. She could feel the tiredness creeping up on her as she walked along the sunny and blistering hot sidewalk.

She adjusted her sunglasses as she looked around, feeling the heat rolling up in waves from the pavement. It was like walking in an oven. Just thinking of walking in that heat made her change her mind.

She needed to be rested first for both safety and more enjoyment. A nap in air conditioning before dinner was more inviting than exploring in triple-digit heat anyway. She continued toward her hotel's entrance, neatly trimmed with glaring white rocks, muted native bushes, and shaded by desert palm trees.

When she walked into the spacious, air-conditioned lobby, she automatically glanced over at the people sitting in the plush chairs to see if she knew any of them. When one of them caught sight of her and smiled, she stopped dead in her tracks. Slowly removing her sunglasses, she wondered if the heat had fried her brain and had her hallucinating. She hoped her pounding heart wasn't loud enough for everyone there to hear.

After a moment of direct eye contact, she called out to him, "Well, either you're stalking me, or I'm suddenly homeless, and you drew the short straw to tell me."

Appreciating her humor and quick wit, Ty grinned at her and stood up. He said goodbye to the couple he'd been talking to and walked toward her. "Hello, Ripley!"

He knew he'd surprised her. Fact is, he'd surprised himself. Knowing he was taking a chance of looking like a fool, he'd taken off work once Morgan returned and driven to Phoenix. He knew the name of her hotel because she'd finally texted it to him when he'd repeatedly texted her asking for it. They'd texted each other a few more times since then. He'd taken that as a good sign.

As he neared her, he said, "Your home is as good as when you left it. No fire. No cliff."

"Good to hear." She looked at him for a moment. "I honestly don't know what I'm supposed to say or do right now," she said softly when he stopped beside her. Ripley couldn't move from her spot in the middle of the lobby.

"That's all right. It's really good to see you, Ripley. I almost didn't recognize you dressed up like you are. You look great. Would you like me to carry your bag for you?"

"No, thanks. I've got it."

Heading toward the elevators, he asked, "How was your conference?"

The older couple sitting in the chairs was watching her with a twinkle in their eyes. She was well-known in her company so if they were in her business, they probably had an idea of who she was. She smiled at them, bidding them a good afternoon as she joined Ty at the elevator. He'd already hit the *up* button.

Ripley studied him, wondering why he was there. She figured she just needed to ask him to be sure. Would he come up there just for her? She simply couldn't believe he'd do that.

As they waited alone for the elevator, she answered, "It went very well although it's usually hectic. I have dinner plans tonight with some friends before they leave in the morning so we can just relax and catch up. Our conferences are very much like a big family reunion. I always look forward to them."

"Yeah? My family has a huge reunion every summer back in Illinois. It's the highlight of my year so I try to not miss it." The elevator dinged, the doors opened, and Ty waited for her to enter first. "Coming?"

She stepped inside. When he followed her, she saw him punch in a floor number. She leaned over, punched in another one. The doors closed softly in front of them.

"Okay, what's going on here, Ty? Why are you here?"

"I came to show you Phoenix. It's much more fun with someone who knows it."

"I know people here who know it."

"Those are business people, Sugar. You work a lot, so I decided to give you a break. It's just for a day or so, with no work involved. We're just two friends sightseeing. Besides, it's safer this way."

When the door opened on the floor he'd selected for himself, he made no move to get out.

She looked at him. "Aren't you getting out?"

He looked out the doors, then down at her. "Why? It's not my floor."

"But you..."

"Sure. I figured I'd either get lucky and hit your floor number, or you'd punch it in yourself. Which you did, by the way." He grinned.

The doors shut with a quiet *swoosh*. She held back her own grin as the elevator went up to the floor she'd selected. When the doors opened again with the familiar double *ding*, she made no move to get out.

Ty glanced at her, waiting. "Aren't you going to get out?"

"No."

"Why not?"

With a wide grin, she said, "It's not my floor."

He tilted his head, contemplating her. "This place has a lot of floors, Ripley. You don't seem like a ground floor girl. Are we going to ride up to each and every one until you tell me which one is yours?"

The doors slid silently closed again. Neither made a move, each silently testing and waiting the other out. Ty just raised an eyebrow at her.

She fought to hold in her grin. "No, I'm not a ground floor girl," she finally replied to his comment. They stood in the elevator quietly another few, humming seconds before she admitted, "Okay, fine. I *am* on this floor. Dang it."

She pushed the button to open the doors before it moved to another floor. She stepped out, waited for Ty to join her. "Since you're not stalking me, it's safe for me to let you know which floor I'm on, right?"

The doors closed with the quiet, soft rush of air. They stood there looking at each other for a moment before he said seriously, "I've never stalked a friend. You're safer with me than without me, Rip. Believe me on that."

"How do I know that's the truth?"

"Call Morgan for a background check on me. I'm positive she'll give me a glowing reference. Any of the females there would," he said, humor in his eyes.

She grinned, shook her head. "Seriously, Ty. Why are you here, in my hotel?"

He waited for a couple with their toddler to exit the other elevator beside them before he answered her. "I'd like to take you out on a date. And I figured it'd be easier on both of us if we had our first one in neutral territory with no prying eyes or eavesdropping ears.

"I'm known everywhere back home so this seemed like a perfect opportunity. You were already here, had your own place to stay, and Morgan owed me time off."

Stunned, she just stood there. "Seriously? You came all this way just to ask me out on a date?"

"Not just ask you, but hopefully to take you." Ty watched her a moment then rephrased it. "Would you go out on a date with me, Ripley?"

Her heart pounded in her chest while she thought about it. She couldn't decide if this was a little scary or insanely romantic. She'd never picked up a scary vibe around him before. Knowing the people he associated with, surely he couldn't be a serial killer kind of guy, right? But aren't they the most normal guys around? But his voice... How could she resist him asking her so politely in that voice?

It was probably a perfect serial-killer voice, she thought ruefully.

"Well, the thing is, I already have plans to go to dinner with some friends tonight. It's just a casual but nice place... Nothing too fancy. We're meeting at six."

She waited a beat, listening to her gut instincts and said, "Since I've met your friends, maybe you could meet some of mine. Why don't you come along? If you think you'd feel comfortable with a bunch of strangers on our first official date, I mean. And since it's a dinner with *my* friends, and I just asked you to join us, it's my treat. *This* time."

He smiled at her. "I'd love to. And for you, there's safety in numbers. No pressure, just a relaxed night out with friends. Thank you for asking me. And if you'll remember, I told you so."

"Told me what?"

"Told you you'd be happy I came up here to visit you."

"You never told me that!"

"I meant to. Besides, I just did."

Chapter 15

Ty looked down the long hallway, already knowing the answer. "And I know you're not on this floor either. I can't believe you're on the ground floor, Ripley!"

Surprised, she asked, "How in the world do you know that?"

He could explain how he knew in detail from her body language but figured that might scare her. Could he say it was because of her tells? She hadn't made a single move to remove her room key from her purse since they got in the elevator. But she *did* have her hand on her purse when she'd walked into the lobby like she was about to reach into it. He'd caught that, but he just didn't believe she'd be a ground floor girl.

She'd also not automatically hit her floor when she'd walked into the elevator. Everybody did it immediately, but she'd hesitated. She was too smart to be on the ground floor—he'd assumed anyway.

He finally replied, "Power of deduction."

"That's... I don't know what to say." She stared at him with a mixture of confusion and amazement on her face.

"I don't either. How could've I thought you not a ground floor girl?" He sounded more than a little surprised like he was rarely, if ever, wrong in his conclusions.

"I guess because I'm a woman not a girl." She hid her smile as she pushed the *down* arrow for the elevator.

Ty smiled at her reply.

As they waited for the car to make its way back to their floor, she admitted, "I'm not *normally* on the ground floor. I've always considered anything *not* ground level to be safer. But I had asked for one this trip for business reasons."

Ty nodded. It actually let him know he wasn't losing his instincts. He felt she was a woman who knew basic safety and was self-aware. Of course, in a nice hotel like this with the rooms being accessed from the inside hallways and not outside from a sidewalk, it was a little safer. It'd make sense to relax one's guard.

The doors finally opened again with the familiar *ding* and the soft movement of air, and they both walked inside. Oddly, it was once again empty. Ty hit the ground floor button.

She looked at him as they felt the elevator smoothly and silently glide down. "Can I trust you to know which room I'm in too?"

"Sure." He grinned at her, wiggling his eyebrows.

Sternly, she said, "Don't get ahead of yourself, cowboy."

When they stepped out of the elevator, Ripley took hold of Ty's arm to lead him away before the couple he'd been talking to spotted them. She'd feel like an idiot if the couple saw them getting off the elevator like they forgot which floor was theirs.

As they walked down the long, carpeted hallway, she removed the key to her room. Ty shot her a glance as he walked beside her. She'd also made a move to her purse earlier. There was her tell.

She stopped at her door, sliding in the key card. As she opened it, she gestured for him to go inside first. She flipped on the lights as the door closed, locking it out of habit.

"Have a seat." Dropping her heavy bag on a chair, she plopped down in one herself, easing her feet out of her high heels. She sighed in true relief at giving her feet freedom, wiggling her toes.

"Are you going to wear those when we go out for dinner?" he asked, sitting down across from her and getting comfortable.

"Not if I can help it. Why?"

"They're sexy on you. I like them." Not saying a word, Ripley just looked at him. Nonplussed, he continued, "If you don't wear them tonight, that's fine. I'll just have to take you out somewhere nice that requires them. I guess that'd be the next time we go out when I'm supposed to pay. And you look very professional and quite attractive in that business suit by the way. It becomes you, Ripley."

Her face felt flushed at his compliments. She never really fell for flattery from guys, but he sounded sincere. "Thank you."

"You're welcome." He leaned forward, his elbows propped on his knees. "Where are you taking me tonight anyway?"

When she named the restaurant, he smiled. "Good choice and hard to argue with it. I'm glad you're taking me somewhere nice. It makes our first date that much more memorable, don't you think?"

His grin made her laugh. With a deep, long sigh, she shook her head, grinned back at him. "I can be totally honest with you, right?"

"I never want anything *but* total honesty, ever. I deplore lies. I don't play games with people, especially not with friends. I shoot straight from the hip, and I think you do too. It's something I very much value in a person."

Nodding, she said, "Good to know. I don't hang around with liars or players myself. It's a solid ground rule I have."

"Something else we have in common then."

"Apparently."

"Should we get married now, or do you want to wait a little longer?"

Laughing, she shook her head. "As tempting as it is, let's wait."

"That's probably for the best," Ty teased back. He waited in the silence, listening to the air conditioner kick on. Finally, he prompted her, "You asked if you could be totally honest with me, right? What did you want to be honest about?"

Trying in vain to focus her thoughts, Ripley sighed and answered, "I forgot."

Ty laughed as he leaned back in his chair while she tried to remember.

She stared toward the window for a moment. "Oh! I can't believe you have me rattled like this. And I can't believe I just *said* that to you!" He grinned but didn't make fun of her this time. She blew out a breath before saying, "I just meant to say that I don't see how our first date could ever be anything *but* memorable considering how it's started out. I've never had one quite like this before in my life."

"So how am I doing?"

"Grand, actually. I can't see how you could top it!" she said, smiling at him. "Have you ever done this with any other woman? And be sure to remember our recent discussion about telling the truth!"

Ty smiled at her, appreciation showing in his dark eyes. "No, I can honestly say this is a new one for me too. I've never ditched work and driven for hours to meet a woman who didn't know I was even coming just on the off-chance she'd go out with me.

"It did occur to me I could get shot down by you. If so, I'd have to crawl back home in total humiliation. But I thought it was worth the risk.

"And with no one knowing about it except you and I, well, that made it a little easier. But it makes it more fun being unscripted like this, don't you think? We can just bumble along together and see what happens. There are no expectations, no disappointments, since we're making it up as we go."

"Agreed." Ripley eyed him for a moment before getting up her nerve. "Okay. Question."

"Shoot." He looked completely relaxed in the comfortable chair. He stretched out his long legs while he waited for her to begin questioning him.

"You said you've never stalked a friend. Truth?"

"Of course. Why would I?"

"Logical answer." She paused before asking, "Have you stalked non-friends?"

"Lots. It was just never in a romantic way."

He answered it so smoothly, she didn't know how to respond. "Really?" She paused. "You know what? Don't answer that."

"Okay."

She eyed him again, pulled her feet up into the chair, getting comfy herself. "Does Morgan know you're here? With me?"

"No."

"Why not?" She couldn't hide the surprise in her voice.

"Why would she? Didn't I just say no one would know about this except us? I certainly don't ask her for permission on who I date. I mean, we're best friends and talk about a lot but not about everything. We might get around to it, eventually. Most likely, actually. But we do have our own lives. She's my friend, not my warden or my mom."

"I just assumed you would've told her."

"You know what they say about assuming."

"Yeah, okay. What about Josh?"

Shaking his head, he replied, "No. Just me. Not even my mommy knows."

She smiled at him, knowing he was making fun of her now.

"Okay, Ripley. Question for you. Why are you wondering if anyone knows I'm here?"

"Well, a couple of reasons come to mind. Like, is this a bet that guys do? Get the girl kind of thing. If you think this is some sort of a one-night thing or... or... a bootie call, I'll tell you right off, it's not. I hate to think that as I expect way more from you. You just don't seem the type. On the other hand, I don't really know you all that well."

He tilted his head before saying, "Well, that's what dating's all about—getting to learn about someone new. And I'm glad to hear that you'll stand up for yourself. And, no, I've never been a part of something as distasteful as those immature, hurtful, and disrespectful games. I don't toy with a person's emotions. My parents raised me differently than most, I guess.

"And I have sisters—Mavis, Vanessa, and Vivienne—that I watched out for from those same types of guys, so I'd hope I wasn't one myself." Ty paused before he added, "I came just for you with no ulterior motive other than I want to get to know you."

"Okay," Ripley said after a moment. He didn't seem to be playing her, but how could she know for sure? Thoughts went through her mind as she looked at him.

Ty waited. When she didn't continue, he did it for her. "Would you like to call or text someone close to you so they know who you're with? That way, if you should end up murdered, missing, or forced into the illegal sex trade, they know who to look for first?"

"You're good, you know that?" Fact was, that thought *had* crossed her mind. It wasn't that she believed it, but she was fairly sure none of the murdered, the missing, or the sex slaves had thought that either. "No, I think I can trust you to not do any of those things. And we've been seen together already by people in this hotel. Besides, the parking lot, lobby, and hallways all have cameras."

"Are you sure they're plugged in and recording though?"

"Geez, Ty! Are you *trying* to freak me out here?"

"Nope, just curious." He paused, evaluating her, seeing how her mind worked. "So do you know if they are?"

"Do you know if they're not?" she retorted. When he shook his head, a smile forming on his face, Ripley nodded and said firmly, "Okay then. You'd better behave yourself."

Ty couldn't help but be taken in by her.

They sat in silence for a moment, each in their own thoughts. Both could feel the sizzle and tension building in the room. Both were just ignoring it as best they could.

Ripley abruptly stood up, telling him, "If you need the bathroom, it's that door over there. Make yourself comfortable. Turn on the TV if you'd like."

She took in his nice black jeans and the collared beige polo shirt he wore. Even his boots were cleaned, she noticed. The fact he cleaned his boots for her touched her more than she cared to admit. Obviously, he had more than one pair of boots. But still, it was all in the details. It showed he took care of his appearance. That in turn showed not only self-respect but respect for *her*. To a woman, or to a man, things like that *mattered*. Details always mattered.

"What you're wearing is absolutely fine, but I'm going to change clothes. I'd prefer something comfier and more relaxed for my friends."

"Need any help?" he asked, innocently.

She saw the sparkle in his eyes and answered nonchalantly, "Nope. I keep a personal butler in my bedroom to see to my needs." As she walked toward her bedroom, she added, "He's probably considered missing or murdered somewhere. If they only knew what he *really* did for me."

She heard his laughter as she shut—and locked—the bedroom door. Undressing and choosing casual clothes with care because Ty was there, she took her time. When she was satisfied, she unlocked the door and stepped out. He'd moved to the couch, looking quite comfortable. She saw his boots neatly lined up beside it. He'd turned on the TV and had the volume turned to a respectable level.

She glanced at the sports show as she headed to the bathroom. When she came back out, her hair was brushed, make-up retouched. She was feeling more settled. Not fully, just more so.

"Out of curiosity, where are *you* staying tonight? I assume you're staying the night?"

She walked by him, wondering how he could look so calm. She hoped she looked and sounded calmer than she felt. Her insides were churning. Had any guy ever had such a powerful effect on her before? She couldn't think of a single one. Maybe it was because he'd been in her mind for weeks... Since he'd said he was planning on asking her out, but then never did so. Until now.

"Of course. I can't show you Phoenix in only a few hours." He looked at her before adding, "I'll find a room somewhere. I arrived shortly before you walked in the lobby. I had to make sure you didn't shoot me down first before looking for a place. No need to waste my money, you know."

"You do realize it's a Saturday night, right? Rates will be pretty high because of the convention and many of us are still here. They do love to jack up their rates for special events."

Ty leaned back, getting more comfortable. "Don't they, though? It's atrocious, but I'll manage. I'm not exactly poor, Ripley."

"But will there be an available room?" she wondered.

Unconcerned, he shrugged a shoulder. "There's bound to be at least one somewhere. There's always the lobby. Or even my truck. Mine comes with a long bed in the back. It's sweet of you to be concerned about me and my sleeping arrangements."

Not knowing if he was serious or not, she just studied him. He smiled at her. That smile that made her heart flip over. She picked up her pair of heels to take them to her bedroom.

"C'mon now, Ripley... Don't dash my hopes so soon!" he complained. "Couldn't you wear them just for me? They'd look great with your outfit."

"Sorry, honey. Not tonight."

Ty sadly shook his head, but he had a sparkle in his eyes. Sounding resigned, he said, "The first 'not tonight' of our relationship. It came much sooner than I expected."

Ripley burst into laughter. She was still laughing as she left the room, the heels dangling from her fingers. When she returned to the seating area, she sat down across from him.

Suddenly remembering her manners as an impromptu hostess, she asked, "Would you like something to snack on or a drink? I have munchies in the drawer over here, and some drinks in the fridge. After last night's meeting in here, I'm not really sure what I have left. I just told people to help themselves."

"Sure. What do you think you have to drink?"

Nothing strong enough for me right now, she thought to herself. To him, she said, "Let me check."

She walked over, opened the little fridge door, looking inside but not really seeing anything. Her emotions were running rampant, and she was trying to get them under control. She closed her eyes for a moment, taking a deep breath. Opening them, she was just about to call out she had water, a 7Up, Ginger Ale, and Pepsi when she felt the air stir behind her.

Almost silently, Ty came up behind her, sending her nerves scattering. Her hair stood on end when he leaned down close beside her. His warm breath close to her face, he said softly, "Do you feel it, Ripley?"

She answered just as quietly, "Feel what?" She kept her gaze in front of her, staring blindly into the little fridge.

"That intense, invisible pull between us. It's strong enough to make the air practically quiver. You do, don't you?"

"Yeah." Her heart was pounding in her chest again. It actually took effort to control her breathing. She forced herself to turn her head to look at him and felt the pull between them get even stronger.

When he leaned in, giving her a moment to stop him, she didn't. Couldn't. And when he closed his mouth gently over hers, she felt the air in her lungs just evaporate. She closed her eyes as she felt him lean in more, and her hand rested against his cheek on its own accord.

Adjusting her position to face him fully, she almost shyly returned his kiss. She felt his strong hands gently frame her face before sliding back into her hair. He adjusted his position as he kissed her more passionately even as he still managed to keep it tender and sweet. Her hands wrapped around his neck as she felt something inside of her just bloom.

She had to pull back, struggling to get air back into her lungs once she had. Ty still held her head tenderly in his hands, but he let her pull back. He took in air himself. When she looked up, met his eyes again, the force of their attraction hit them both. There was more than just a sizzle between them now. Both were pulling in air, both feeling almost dizzy from the lack of it. She dropped her hands to his hips.

Leaning forward, he placed a single kiss on her forehead. The gesture was so sweet and tender, and so unexpected, tears almost sprung into her eyes. She closed her eyes to keep them at bay. What's *wrong* with me? she asked herself. It's not like that was my first kiss! But why did it feel like it? Had it really been that long? Or was it because it was *Ty?*

Whispering, Ty asked, "Sugar, you all right?"

The simple gentleness that poured from his voice so close to her made her open her eyes and look into his. "I'm sorry, Ty. I can't believe I'm... I wasn't expecting any of this... I wasn't looking to be in any type of relationship with anyone at all."

She took a deep breath. She was a public speaker who couldn't talk sense right now. She fought for her usual control over her emotions. She felt his hands leave her face and immediately missed their warmth. Gazing into his brown eyes, she saw the emotion in them.

Softly, she admitted, "You just overwhelm me, Ty. I'm not used to a guy like you. It's been a really long time for me to be with a guy even on a date, and you're so unlike any others I've known." She took another deep breath before saying, "It's all good. Really, it is. And if I'm not embarrassing you, I'm for sure embarrassing myself."

She felt the heat of her blush infusing her face, making her even more embarrassed. She was too old to be blushing, wasn't she?

She offered a small smile, shrugging her shoulders as a form of apology for practically falling apart with one, simple kiss. Except there was nothing simple about it. And they both knew it. If they couldn't be honest about that, there was no hope for them.

He gave her a tender smile, his warm gaze taking in her every feature. "There's no need to be embarrassed, Ripley. And I didn't mean to ambush you like this... like that. I really didn't. I feel I should maybe apologize for that. I'm sorry if I moved too fast there. I don't want to push you or scare you... It just kind of needed to happen, if that makes any sense."

She nodded. Oddly, she knew exactly what he meant. "Well, this wasn't expected at all... But on the other hand, at least we got that initial wondering out of the way." She ran her hand through her hair because she suddenly didn't know what else to do.

Ty smiled to himself. If she ran her hand through her hair like that again, he'd be forced to kiss her again. He watched the dark, soft strands slide down into place on the sides of her face.

Ty tried to re-focus on their conversation. "We did. But I still want to apologize. And since we're being honest, I have to admit you fairly overwhelm me too. There's just something unique about you. Something that snagged me from the start. I've given you... *us*... space to see if the attraction would go away, but I feel it only got stronger. Am I wrong? Just tell me if I am."

"No, I think you're right. I wasn't looking for anything whatsoever myself. You also caught my attention, but it happened over time. Maybe Cupid shot us both with one arrow. You got hit first, then I got hit with the ricochet!"

He chuckled, leaned forward to place another kiss on her forehead. He was still smiling when he pulled back. "I love your wit and sense of humor, Ripley. It's refreshing to meet someone else who has them. It's attractive." He gently kicked the open fridge door shut, a drink all but forgotten.

"Your best friend has them." *Why* had she felt compelled to mention Morgan at a time like this?

He looked at her before answering. "Yes, Morgan does. And I love hers too. They're a couple of many things I love about her. She'll always be special and very close to me, Ripley."

Because he had to know, he had to ask. "Is Morgan and I being close like we are a problem for you? Will it be a problem for us? Our friendship is strong and not likely to ever change. But we're just friends, always have been."

He ran a hand through his own hair, unsure of what he'd feel, or do, if her answer wasn't what he hoped.

It suddenly occurred to him he'd never once really cared if any of his ex-girlfriends minded his close relationship with Morgan. He knew they weren't for him; therefore, it didn't become an issue or even a concern.

But he knew in his gut that Ripley Capilano was different. He didn't know why or how, but his instincts were fairly screaming at him to pay attention to her. He'd learned long ago to never ignore his instincts. They'd saved his life more than once.

After thinking a moment, she had to be honest. "I don't know. I can't lie and say it doesn't bother me a *little* bit, or make me wonder about the two of you. How you could be so in tune with each other? What makes your friendship so special?

"But it also seems to me she loves Josh with all her heart. And she seems to love you just as much, just differently. It's just... different for me."

"She does love Josh, to her very soul. He loves her the same. Our relationship isn't a problem for Josh. It never was." Ty had to say it, not defensively but just as weight to the fact his and Morgan's friendship is acceptable to another very close to them both.

She looked at him as she thought how best to reply. "I'm not Josh. I have my own feelings. But I understand what you're saying. It's just new to *me*, Ty. This all is. And I can't rush into something like this. I mean, I don't even know how long I'll be here in Arizona! I travel. I live in an RV. I don't normally even return to an area I've been in because there are so many other places I have to go to.

"What kind of relationship could we build if we're not even together? I mean, if that's what you're thinking... I mean..." She trailed off before she made a fool of herself. She sat down on the couch, moving the throw pillow out of the way when he joined her.

"Do you *have* to travel all the time? If so, we can cross that bridge when we get closer to it, Ripley. Many relationships are made between people who travel or are apart more often than not. It just takes more work, more trust. I can honestly say I've never once been unfaithful to anyone, if that's a worry you have.

"We're just starting out here. If we both compromise, we can build something special between us. I know it." His voice sounded firm with conviction.

Ripley said, "You seem so certain."

He replied, "We should at least give it a try, right? An honest attempt? Let's just start out slowly here. Why rush into anything? Let's just get to know each other better. That's why I'm here. Let's begin as friends because we have to be friends first.

"We've been around each other for almost two months so there's already a little foundation of friendship to build on, to use as a springboard. We know there *is* something between us as we both just confirmed it in the best possible way."

She had to smile at that, as did he. Yes, that kiss was something.

Trying to keep them from moving too fast, Ripley fought to remain grounded. They hadn't even gone on a real date yet, they'd already kissed, and now they were talking about a relationship? Her heart was beating quickly, urging her to run with the feelings coursing through her. But as usual, she made herself think with her brain and not her heart. He was right that they needed a friendship first.

But she still asked, "Where do you see us going? We could just fizzle out in no time flat. We're jumping into this kind of fast, don't you think? We could simply drift apart. What then?"

Ty sighed. "No one can predict where a relationship will go, Ripley. And we're not blindly rushing into anything. We met almost two months ago, not a few minutes ago. We *could* just drift apart, that's true. It happens. You could even be gone from the Center by then, and we'd simply end it. We just have to ride the wave together.

"I can guarantee we'll have ups and downs, and maybe even a crash or two. I hope not, but it's always a possibility in *any* relationship. We just need to remember we're dealing with another's feelings and emotions. Mutual respect can go a long way.

"We need to always remember to be honest with each other, keep private things between us, air out arguments and disagreements with each other. I don't care for people who air out their dirty laundry with friends or family... and most especially on social media. I'm not on it, and I don't *ever* want to be.

"That *would* be a problem for me if you're the type of person who uses social media as your personal, daily diary. Are you?"

She shook her head. "No. My communications are mostly by phone or in-person. Sometimes with texts or emails. I don't have a burning desire for that social media chaos myself, so I'm not on any of it. From people I know who *are* on it, I also don't trust the so-called security or privacy features on any of it."

Ty looked relieved because he was. "That's great to hear. Airing out laundry to others is always one-sided. And it forces people they mutually know to take sides. It destroys everything—trust, friendships, lives in general.

"At the same time, I understand how sometimes we all need a sounding board. I guess there's just a balance. But I keep private details to myself, and I'd like it if you could do the same.

"If we decide later on to go our separate ways, then that's what we do. I won't bash your name because I'd prefer to remain friends, or at least on friendly terms. I haven't made enemies of any of my ex-girlfriends, at least not that I know about. No, they all didn't end nicely, but they also weren't hateful. It's fact that sometimes things simply don't work out.

"There's no rule anywhere that says people who break up, go their own ways for whatever reason, have to be enemies. So many people just fall from love into hate, and it's stupid and immature. And I get that hurt plays a big role there, so people lash out. But either we work, or we don't. In the scheme of things, it really is that simple. You can't manufacture feelings, manipulate endings. Or shouldn't anyway.

"Can we agree and promise if we *do* go our own ways that we keep it mature and peaceful? To try and remain friends if we should happen to run into the other sometime by chance?"

Ripley considered. "I promise I'll try my best. Sometimes that's easier said than done. The one who *gets* hurt and disappointed can't always be nice back. That's reality."

She took a breath before forcing herself to admit to him, "I'm very rusty at relationships except for business ones. I just don't know if I'm even built for a personal one. Maybe it's just that I haven't dated the right kind of guy. Maybe I was still growing and learning. All of that is probably true.

"I'm bound to really grate on your nerves and patience. Can you just be patient with me? It's been years since I've dated anyone even semi-seriously. Dating is such a chore and so stressful, it's usually not even worth it. It's going to take me time to wrap my head around this, around you. Even in a casual sense of seeing you.

"And I'll have to adjust to having someone in my life. I've been quite content to be on my own, completely free. Over the years, I've become more independent. It doesn't mean I want to *stay* that way though. I've never wanted to be solo my entire life. But here I am.

"And I have to warn you now that you'll probably bug *me* at times, especially if I begin to feel smothered or hampered. And I don't like someone telling me what to do. I *am* very independent, Ty. Can you handle that?"

Ty respected her because he could tell she was nervous telling him how she felt. He had to admit he felt a little jittery himself, for more than one reason. It makes a person vulnerable to hurt and disappointment when they admit their feelings. But it also opens many doors to more positive aspects.

Maybe laying ground rules and basic expectations now would give them a better chance of building something between them. He remembered how Josh and Morgan had seemed to lay down their own when they'd first begun dating. It gave them a sense of security and reduced pressure. They'd never really told him what all of their personal rules were, but he'd noticed they had some. And look how far they've come, and how happy they still were after all of these years.

Ty finally answered, "First off, I prefer independent women. I'm *not* a man who can tolerate a woman clinging to me for her security, her self-worth, for constant attention, status, whatever. And I for sure don't report my every move to anyone, so I'm warning you about that now. I'm talking about anything beyond common courtesy or out of necessity.

"I just want to clear the air on this right now, Ripley. If you're insecure or a control nut who wants to know my location, what I'm doing, who I'm with, at any given time, I can tell you it's best I go now.

"I'm independent and private myself. And I'd also like to point out that independent people who are balanced can make strong relationships. Although it doesn't sound like it'd be an issue with you, I need to be clear on this right now before we go any further."

She shook her head, confirming his impression of her. But he still let out a small sigh of relief when she said, "I'd say we're in agreement on things so far. As you said, common courtesy is different. Like if we have a date and one of us is running late, we let the other know and not just leave the other hanging, waiting, getting upset or hurt. As opposed to I'm out with friends, and you constantly keep texting or calling me, asking where I am, who with, what we're doing, when I'll be back, or vice versa."

"Exactly," Ty said.

Remembering a conversation he'd had with Josh years ago, he decided to continue to emulate what his friends did as it had seemed to work. If Ripley was anywhere near as cautious as Morgan had been—and he felt she was, but for other reasons—he felt it couldn't hurt.

"How about this? We remember we both just have to compromise and always be honest. We also need ground rules that we both agree to abide by. Rules or boundaries that we can add, delete, or tweak as we go. We can put those together later, like we're talking about now. No cursing the other, no shouting matches, no gossiping, no insane drama. Or anything else deemed illegal or immoral."

Ripley replied, teasing, "Illegal or immoral? Does this mean I can't keep that butler that someone thinks has been murdered or is missing?"

Ty grinned. "Correct. You must let him go immediately, and leave him free for eternity."

She smiled. "Fine. He was getting on my nerves anyway!" But getting serious again, she said, "And one more thing I need to be honest about. It *could* be a deal breaker. If it is, then at least we know it now. But I need to get this out of the way."

She took a breath, gathering courage to say it to his face. "I'm not an easy woman, Ty. Don't be expecting, or planning for, me to hop into bed with you and have sex because that's not the way I operate. I swore that off a long time ago because men tend to just use a woman for sex. I'm tired of being used and discarded by anyone for any reason. I get that it works both ways... I'm just saying from *my* side, it's not going to happen.

"Once sex happens, the relationship suddenly tends to revolve *only* around that. I don't want that type of shallow expectation or relationship in my life at all. If I'm with someone, I want to be more than his sexual object. I'm my own person, with my own brain, and not a sex machine... And definitely not a breeding factory. I don't want it, and I don't need it. Can you handle that?"

His answer wasn't what she was expecting.

It surprised her when he said, "Good to know, Ripley." At her doubtful look, he insisted, "I mean it. If you were easy, I wouldn't want you like I do. Easy women tend to not care about or respect themselves enough. At least not enough to say no, and then to stand up for themselves. Most women don't have boundaries for themselves or aren't strong enough to enforce them. You have them, and I think you're strong enough to stand up for yourself. You are right now.

"It's actually a relief on my end, too, because I feel the same way. How many relationships do we personally know about that began with them having sex right off the bat that actually lasted? Are those relationships meaningful? What else holds those two people together? There's also the whole pregnancy scare, the diseases, all of it.

"When did adults, especially younger ones, decide to just ignore common sense, any morals, and just jump into sexual relations with someone who is basically a complete stranger? I guess it's been that way since the beginning of time in some ways, but it just seems way more prevalent now.

"They don't realize having sex with a new person means they're basically having sex with everyone *else* that person has been with. If it was previously unprotected sex, and again now... That's a major concern.

"It has a domino effect they can't hope to stop quickly without sometimes serious damages and consequences. Why aren't parents teaching their kids how to stand up for themselves, to say no, to have boundaries anymore? Probably because their own parents didn't do it for them, so they didn't do it for themselves. It's not a snowball, but more like an avalanche that's nearly impossible to stop.

"And outside of us, it's how I want my own sisters, cousins, friends to be, and hope to God they are, or were before they got married or whatever. I realize I'm definitely in the male minority here, but I feel as you do. Sex complicates things. It always changes things especially if that's the first thing that happens between people.

"I want more than a casual fling, a one-night stand. We *need* strong women out there to be role models for these younger women and girls who don't know what's right or which side is up. It's far more detrimental to the female than the male. I'm talking about the emotional depth as well as the possibility of an unwanted pregnancy.

"A woman gets pregnant and literally *every* single thing in her body and entire life changes. Even her career and friendships are affected. It's absolutely incredible. But if a *man* gets a woman pregnant, he can literally just walk away. Not a single thing changes in his actual body or his life. It's the most lopsided thing I can think of.

"And if I didn't have sisters, close family, and friends who got pregnant and heard, and saw, all of these things happening, I can't say that I would've thought about it all that much on my end. But I *did* see or hear about it, so I *have* thought about it.

"So in a nutshell... Yes, Ripley, I *can* handle that. And I respect you big time for it." He added with a smile, "It doesn't mean I won't be *thinking* about it though."

She laughed, impulsively hugged him close. She felt him squeeze her back before she pulled away and got comfortable on the couch again. Relief flooded through her at his calm acceptance of her declaration.

If a man couldn't, or refused to, respect her most personal issues, her own body and beliefs, then *how* could they possibly respect her at all? It's simple. They don't.

No one needed people in their lives who didn't respect them and their personal beliefs, no matter what they were. Most especially when their beliefs were in regards to their own body, their own person, their own feelings.

If a man shuns a woman for being her own person, why should she even be with him? Nothing else in her life was going to be positive being with a man like that! If a woman *was* with someone like that, she needed to move on. Immediately.

Looking him in the eyes, she said, "Thank you, Ty." Another thought suddenly hit her like a sledgehammer. "It's crazy I'm even thanking you... I shouldn't *need* to! A man should just accept what a woman says or feels. He certainly expects—even demands—a woman to accept what *he* says after all. A woman shouldn't feel the need to thank a man like she needs his damn permission to feel what she feels in anything!

"As a woman, I wouldn't thank *you* in the same way. Why should she... Should I?" She was now highly irritated at the way she'd automatically thanked a man for respecting her own body—even when he agreed with her! Why were women conditioned to doing that? she inwardly fumed.

Ty admitted she was right. It hadn't really occurred to him to see it that way. He definitely didn't need—or even expect—her thanks, but her subsequent thoughts made him think about it.

He said, "You're right. I love how your mind works. I love that you actually *use* it! Most women don't even notice things like that. Or men, to be honest.

"It's just society, Sugar. And I don't agree with it any more than you do. Women have been seen as less for centuries, and it's been wrong for centuries. Both sexes seem to just accept it... Until a woman with a mind of her own, courage, and strength brings it to the attention of others. Like you just did. There's a big difference between a woman being a ball-buster and a woman who insists on having equal rights."

Ripley looked at Ty for a long, long moment. "You have no idea how much that means to me to know you respect me in that regard. Or to any woman, really. If and when I ever change my mind on this other matter, I'll let you know."

Ty gave her a shocked look that made her smile. "*What?* What makes you think *I'm* easy and will just roll over because *you* changed *your* mind? Haven't you been *listening* to me?"

Trying to contain her smile, she apologized. "See? I'm rusty here, remember? My apologies for assuming you were like every guy I've ever known or heard about. I will do my best to curb that reaction and thought process and applying it to you."

Mollified, he said, "Apology accepted." With a smile, he slowly leaned forward and kissed her, both of them lingering over it. Her arms wrapped around his neck, and he took the kiss a little deeper, feeling her respond.

When he pulled back, he said, "But just in case, why don't you make sure my number is one of the speed dials on your phone?"

Chapter 16

Hours later, Ripley happily let Ty drive them to the restaurant to make it feel more like a date than a dinner party he was joining at the last minute.

She'd already texted her friends that she was bringing along a friend. She'd also phoned the restaurant to add a seat for Ty so he'd feel welcomed and accepted from the start. It'd be the opposite if he were just standing there, waiting for an extra place setting to be prepared for him. Plus, it was respectful to the restaurant employees who were probably already short-staffed.

Ty had heard her on the phone, and her thoughtfulness impressed him. When she'd walked out of her bedroom with her phone still in her hand, he'd pulled her into his arms and tenderly kissed her. "Thank you. Calling ahead was very sweet and considerate of you."

Getting her breath back, she could only nod. "It was common courtesy," she'd finally managed to say.

When Ripley and Ty walked through the restaurant's double doors with their pristine, shining glass panes trimmed with dark wood, a friend of hers caught her attention. "Ripley! We're over here!"

Looking up at Ty, she asked, "Are you ready for this? They're super people, but I have a feeling they might grill you a little."

Smiling, he reached for her hand, squeezed it. "What better place to be grilled in than a nice restaurant like this one?" She chuckled at his humor and wit as he said, "I have a feeling they're going to grill you just as much, but most likely when I'm not around. Let's make it easy for them, shall we?"

Ripley grinned. "I'm not sure why I asked if you were ready when I'm not sure I am!"

They walked to the long table together, Ty still holding her hand. All eyes were on them. Reaching the table, Ripley took a deep breath and made the introductions, trying to ignore the speculative looks being tossed—no, more like *thrown*—her way. She already felt the bruises.

"Ty, this is Lydia, Zahra, Andy, Ron, Eric, Jennifer, and my best friend, Julia. Everyone, this is Ty Stanton. I'm sure we're now tonight's entertainment."

Seven pairs of curious eyes in smiling faces watched as Ty held out her chair and helped her in before sitting down himself beside her. He didn't waste any time. As soon as he sat down, Ty said with a smile, "Ripley tells me you're all in business together. She also said you're wonderful people who she's proud to call her friends.

"I always find it interesting to meet someone's friends more than their family. Who the people they choose as friends says a lot more about that person as a whole, don't you think? Thank you all for letting me join you this evening so I could check you out and indirectly learn more about Ripley here!"

Ron laughed at how this man already turned the tables on them. "We'll check *each other* out, I think! Okay... Phones off?" He looked at Ty, asking, "Did she explain our rule when we eat out? No phones?"

Ty nodded. "Personally, I think it's a great idea. More people should do it. Mine's off!"

Turning his attention to Ripley, Ron inquired, "Have you been keeping a secret from your friends, Ripley? Why is it that we're meeting him now, *just* before we all go home? Or do I really need to ask if this is a case of deliberate timing?"

Julia smiled. "Really, Ron! I'd say she wanted to keep him all to herself. I can understand that!" She winked at Ripley and Ty before picking up her menu.

Ripley sat there, shaking her head and smiling as everyone made a comment. Ty just rested his arm around the back of her chair, listening to her friends and learning more about each one as they talked.

After they wound down, Ripley explained, "He's not a secret. He just arrived this afternoon. Ty doesn't live here in Phoenix but knowing I was here, he came to show me the sights." She paused before adding, "And when you begin to grill us, I want you to be *nice* about it, okay?"

She sent them all a warning look, but she was also grinning. Her friends could be amusing, so she wasn't overly worried about being grilled to a crisp.

With a grin and no hesitation, Andy said, "Okay, I'll start off here." He had a friendly demeanor that naturally set people at ease. "Ty, just for conversation starters and since the subject has already been broached, what do you do?"

Before Ty could answer, Zahra broke in, "No, wait... Let us guess, okay? Me first."

"He's not a parlor game, Zahra!" Ripley said, amused. She looked at Ty, who smiled back at her, letting her know he didn't mind at all.

Zahra flashed a grin and said, "Quiet, please... I'm thinking." She studied Ty for a second before announcing, "Construction. You have an outdoorsy, handsy feel to you."

Shaking his head, Ron said, "He looks too intelligent for that, Zahra." He paused to look Ty over as Ty calmly buttered his roll. "Maybe the outdoors part could be true, but I'd say a businessman. Calm, professional demeanor, manners, not ruffled in a group of strangers..."

Lydia suggested, "Well, with his opening statement, I suggest a psychologist of some sort." She smiled at Ripley. "*Not* that I think our Ripley here needs mental help."

Andy shook his head. "No, I got it... I think he's a golf pro. He's too tan to be stuck behind a desk all day long. Golf is huge around here. Are you a golfer, Ty? Like a professional one, or maybe an instructor?"

Eric immediately nixed that suggestion by shaking his head. "No way, Andy! Ripley doesn't like golf. She practically detests it, so it doesn't fit how they'd meet and have enough in common. He looks rugged, and he's tanned. My guess is he works on a ranch. *That* would be more up Ripley's alley. Am I right?"

Jennifer broke in with her opinion. "If it was something he *did* that had to catch her attention, it'd be related to animals for sure. Maybe a veterinarian?"

Julia nodded her head at Jennifer's comments, pointing her butter knife in her direction. "Ah, yes! Jennifer, I think you're on to something there." She smiled at Ripley and Ty before she took a bite of her roll.

Ty was truly entertained by how her friends asked him the questions, but then answered them amongst themselves.

When they all finally looked at him expectantly, Ty replied seriously, "Some great career options for me have been presented with substantial and valid points. All of you are wrong though. I'm just a lowly tour guide. I actually just give mountain and scenic tours to visitors, generally for tourists."

Ripley had to admit he wasn't lying. He was just leaving out a lot.

Her friends quietly sat there, not in disappointment but just thinking it over.

Eric finally asked, with some envy in his tone, "Really? You do tours in the mountains? That sounds like a blast! Is it on a dude ranch kind of place?"

He was apparently fixated on ranches, Ty thought to himself with amusement.

Jennifer looked at Ripley. "Is this one of your many adventures to do, Ripley? Was this like on an ATV?" She turned to Julia before Ripley even tried to reply. "Remember when we wanted to go skydiving? But they were booked, so we couldn't because we had to leave too soon?"

Julia nodded, chewing her roll, her speculative eyes resting on Ripley.

Thoughtfully, Ron said, "A tour guide. Hmm... Yes. I can see that. He's outdoors and around strangers all the time, so he's not shy. This makes sense. He'd have to be mature and responsible to do this too. But I don't think on an ATV, Jen. Ripley works to *protect* the environment, and those noisy things aren't known for doing that. Unless it's a strict trail..."

As Ty simply listened, his mind was practically recording everyone's comments and body language cues. He had purposely chosen to say a low-level job, one that he knew wouldn't put his earnings anywhere near Ripley's, or her friends, if his guesses were correct. He was simply testing her friends' characters.

He admitted to himself he was mildly surprised he hadn't caught one inkling of condescending looks, disappointment, or anything negative. In fact, her friends did the opposite. They seemed genuinely accepting of his status. Was that to support Ripley, or were they that accepting of people in general? he wondered. No pretentions, no smirks, no apparent judgments.

Having seen what he did from her friends, giving himself more indirect insight to Ripley, Ty decided to come clean. "Well, there's a little more to it." He grinned before he commented, "One of my best friends owns a successful construction business out here. I'll be sure to let him know I look too intelligent to be in his line of work, and see what he says!"

Now Ripley laughed, knowing Josh would wonder what that meant about himself. She added, "And handsy!"

Looking at Eric, Ty replied, "You were the closest, Eric. I *do* give tours, but I really help manage an equestrian center."

Julia smiled broadly. "Perfect, absolutely *perfect!* Oh, a real cowboy from Arizona is eating with us? Ripley, girl, you're just so full of surprises!"

But Ty shook his head as he replied, "No, Julia. I'm a horseman. There are no cattle at the Center. We deal only with horses."

Julia leaned forward, her eyes lit with curiosity and excitement. "A horseman? Even better. Are you like the guy in *The Man from Snowy River?*"

Ripley laughed. She just couldn't help it. "Jules..."

Amused, Ty smiled. "Sugar, it's all good." Looking at them all before resting his gaze on the spunky Julia, he said, "Minus us *not* being in Australia and *not* having any cattle? Maybe, but it's still a stretch, Julia.

"We *do* train horses there. We also board them, give riding lessons, take all sorts of tourists out on trail rides in the mountains, host horse shows and other events, offer a horse motel, and lately, emergency services for rescued horses." Feeling Ripley's gaze on him, he turned to her. "Did I leave out anything?"

"Nope, I think you got it all in. You obviously would know more about it than I would."

He smiled at her as he bit into the warm roll he held in his hand.

Gauging the two of them, Julia now asked casually, "Horse rescues? That's a very noble thing to do. God's creatures are in dire need of help more often than not from us humans. Does he..." She sent a knowing look at her friend, and Ripley slightly shook her head.

Julia nodded before moving on, saying, "A horseman. I like it." She closely looked Ty over again, measuring him up in her mind as she nodded to herself. Looking again at Ripley, she stated, "Yes. That completely fits."

"Your own horses, Jules? Rein 'em in there..." Grinning, Ripley quietly stopped her best friend from jumping the gun over her and Ty's brand-new relationship.

Her other friends laughed at her reply to Julia.

Julia laughed herself and leaned back in her chair. Taking a sip of her water, she looked at her longtime friend with a twinkle in her eyes. Grinning, she replied, "Yes, ma'am. I'm tying them up at the hitching rail as we speak."

Everyone laughed.

Thinking a moment about Julia's comments, Ty tilted his head. He asked, "How does what fit? And do I... what?"

Julia grabbed another roll from the basket, ripping it open as she said, "Goodness. These rolls are the best, aren't they? My husband Cory would die for the recipe! He's a chef, Ty. A quite talented one when he wants to be. It's a shame he couldn't make this trip." She studied the roll like she'd be able to figure out how it was made just by looking at it.

With a little shrug, Julia got around to answering Ty's questions. "Ripley's a big-time supporter of animals. She has a special interest for horses and wildlife especially. You being an animal person, so to speak, complements her own interests. Relationships must have some common ground and interests in order to not only get started but to build."

Ripley agreed. That was one thing she'd already put into the plus column for him. Her other friends nodded in agreement.

The waitress finally came by to take their orders. "My name is Zoey, and I'll be your server this evening. I'm sorry it took me a bit of time to get to you all. We're just a little short-staffed right now, but it's a temporary situation."

Zahra said, "Oh, did you hear that? Another woman whose name begins with a Z! This is a wonderful omen, y'all." Speaking to the waitress, she added, "It's no problem at all, Zoey. We're not in any hurry, so we'll hopefully be a nice, stress-free table for you. But to make a liar out of what I just said, we'll all be on separate tabs."

Ripley interrupted, saying, "I told Ty it was my treat tonight, so Zoey, this guy will be on my tab, okay? And *just* him!" The waitress smiled and nodded as her friends laughed. "And we'll order last as I have no clue what I want yet! Something not *grilled*..."

Her friends caught her dig at them and laughed.

As Zoey went into their specials, Ripley listened with one ear as she began to peruse the menu. She hadn't even looked at it yet since she'd sat down with Ty. They both looked over their menus, discussing it between them.

Watching the two of them closely, Jennifer could see the sparks between her friend and the man sitting beside her. She didn't miss the smile Ripley sent him. And this man sent the same smile back. The man certainly wasn't hard on the eyes, she thought to herself.

After Zoey left, Jennifer announced, "My turn now! How did you two meet? Ripley, I thought you were just going to travel through Arizona on the way to Texas? I didn't realize you'd planned to stop and spend a length of time here."

"That was the plan, Jenny. But this one day, I stopped for lunch at this local restaurant that showed some cute Western charm. And by pure chance, I met a woman there. When I was getting ready to leave, I mentioned I was looking for an RV park or campground. She then simply invited me out to her place where she could take in RVs.

"And it happened to be a place called Harmony Hills Equestrian Center. It's a serious horse facility. It's a phenomenal place. A little while later I met Ty who, as you now know, helps run it." She smiled at him, knowing she was leaving out the juicy and dramatic details of their first meeting, the rescued horses, bonding with Cappy, and the rest of the gang.

"Anyway, we'd run into each other fairly often, and we became friends of a sort. All the people there are great. I mean, they really are. The other day, I stopped at the office to let them know I'd be here for a business conference in case they needed me for something.

"Ty was there, and he more or less offered to come up and show me around since I wasn't from the area. He said it was seen better with someone who knew it. And that it was safer than going it alone which is also true."

Ty smiled inside, enjoying how she summed up their entire situation of meeting. She added just enough detail, but then left out so much more. He had to admit, she impressed him.

"What about Texas?" Julia inquired.

"I'll get there sooner or later. I'm not on a strict time table there, Julia. I've also been working there locally."

Ty looked at her, placing his arm on the back of her chair again. "What's in Texas?"

"Just more people I told I'd be there at some point. Normally, my visits are planned so they can prepare, let their people know. But with the Texans, I never said exactly when.

"One of the perks of doing what I do is I do *what* I want, *when* I want to do it. I wanted to just take some time off from work, simply cruise around for a while. That's how I ended up at The Neon Moon that day when I met Morgan. But I plan to get to Texas in the next month or so. Again, I'm on my own schedule with that... to an extent. We'll see."

Ron asked, "How long have you two been dating? I assume you are?"

After consulting his watch, Ty answered him with a straight face, "We're going on about four hours now, right? Maybe five?"

"Sounds about right," Ripley answered. Her eyes were full of laughter.

Her friends just looked at them both, wondering if they were joking. They all knew Ripley's sense of humor could be witty, dry, or deadpanned at the drop of a hat.

Skeptically, Ron asked, "Four *hours?*"

"Maybe five." Ripley reached over and grabbed Ty's left arm. Twisting it gently so she could see his watch, she nodded. "Officially, yeah." As she let his arm go and leaned back in her own chair, Ty grinned at her. Her eyes were full of laughter when they looked up into his own.

Her friends laughed.

To Ripley's great joy, Zoey arrived just then with their drinks. A little bit of alcohol was a welcome addition at this point, she thought, amused at herself.

As their dinner progressed, Ty held his own with her friends. He casually asked specific questions of her friends, learning more about them than they'd have ever guessed. And Ripley was right. Her friends *did* seem to be super, genuine people. They had an easy way of getting along, mixing business with pleasure, stories, jokes, and laughter.

Ty asked about their business, and how it all worked. Eric admonished Ripley for never even mentioning the business to her boyfriend. She shrugged her shoulder. Truth was, it was actually nice being with someone that had *nothing* to do with her business. Everyone needed a break from what they did for a living even if they enjoyed doing it.

Besides that, once he got introduced to the business, he'd find out sooner or later how much money she made. She simply did not want that to be known—at least not yet. She needed to know he cared for *her*, not her money.

Money just had a way of changing people's perceptions, and she didn't want Ty's colored toward her. It was a more than reasonable bet she earned substantially more than he did. Some men simply couldn't handle the knowledge that a woman—*his* woman especially—earned more than he did.

She didn't know Ty well enough yet to even gauge how he might react. At this point in their new relationship, it also wasn't any of his business. She didn't need to know how much *he* earned, so why should he know how much *she* did?

Since her friends knew her firm stance and beliefs in regard to her financial situation, they all discreetly skirted the issue of her personal earnings. Eric and Ron told Ty how much they earned but not to brag. It was just in general terms to show the *potential*. Ty seemed accepting of their six-figure earnings but not overwhelmingly impressed. He just took it in stride like they were talking about the weather.

It surprised Ripley as most people seemed *quite* impressed with their lucrative earnings. But not Ty. She looked at Julia and noticed her satisfied smile at Ty's bland reaction.

As they ate and socialized over the next couple of hours, Ripley decided Ty Stanton had made a very favorable impression on her friends. She never doubted he wouldn't.

Chapter 17

Content, Ripley sat in the front seat as Ty drove through the city. It was almost ten o'clock, and the streets were still busy.

Thankful he was there doing all the driving, she soaked in the sights around her. The radio played country songs in the background, and the air conditioning kept them cool in the late August heat. They made small talk as the truck cruised down the streets and highways.

It suddenly occurred to Ripley there were less buildings and lights. Looking over at Ty, she asked, "Are we lost?"

Ty smiled. "Not at all. I just thought you might want to see something that you can't see during the day."

As he kept driving into the mountains, slowing around hairpin curves, Ripley finally said, "Ty, I don't know where you're taking me, but you don't have to take me so far!"

Laughing heartily, he reached over and took hold of her hand. "You're safe with me, Ripley. I'm not taking you anywhere you won't like once we get there. I promise."

When he finally came to a stop, he turned to her and said, "Close your eyes. Don't peek. I mean it. You'll ruin it if you peek."

Obediently, and trustingly, Ripley closed her eyes, covering them with her hand just in case they opened on their own accord. She felt the truck move forward again as he drove slowly. When it stopped again a few minutes later, he reminded her to keep her eyes shut so she nodded. Her heart beat faster and her ears strained to hear at the unknown.

She heard Ty's door open and close, then heard her door open and felt the fresh air touch her skin. Ty's hand reached for hers, guiding her out of the truck. He walked with her a little way, making sure she wasn't peeking, helping her to not trip as best he could using his bright flashlight to look for trip hazards and snakes.

Turning off the flashlight, he waited for his own eyes to adjust before he instructed, "Okay, Sugar. Open your eyes. Tell me what you think."

Removing her hand and letting her eyes adjust, Ripley gasped. "Oh, Ty! That's... It's gorgeous! All those lights... It's like a maze!" She stared down at the bustling city of Phoenix at night. High up on the mountainside, she could see the entire valley, miles wide and miles long.

Ty moved behind her, holding her close to his warm body. She leaned against him, her arms resting on top of his that were around her waist.

Together, they just watched the tiny moving lights navigate around the stationary ones. The only sounds they could hear were of the slight breeze blowing around them, or an occasional coyote yipping far away. The moon was bright enough to light up some of the cacti and trees around them, but otherwise, it was pitch dark. They both soaked in the quiet, the solitude, the peacefulness.

Leaning her head back, Ripley saw a plane probably heading to Sky Harbor Airport gliding silently over them. Only its blinking lights showed its location in the vast black sky. The shining stars seemed so big, so close, she felt like she could simply reach out and grab one, or maybe even scoop up a handful. What would a star even feel like?

Ty nuzzled her cheek, placing a soft kiss on it. He felt her shiver, and he tightened his hold.

Loving the feeling she had being in his arms, Ripley closed her eyes for a while, wanting to remember this feeling. She opened her eyes and looked up at the timeless stars again. When she got dizzy from staring so long, she transferred her gaze back down to watch Phoenix at night. The contrasts between sparkling, stationary stars to the perpetual movement of modern man were many. Ripley preferred the stars.

"This is incredible, Ty. It really is! We're stuck in-between two worlds, aren't we? Below is civilization, noise, restrictions, and technology. Above is emptiness, freedom, peaceful quiet, and limitless possibilities. And we're right here in the middle, able to experience both. This is beautiful. What a perfect night!" She sounded breathless in her happiness.

He kissed the top of her head before he softly asked, "So you like my surprise?"

"All of them so far!"

He led her back to the truck using the flashlight again, then told her to wait. Reaching into the back seat, he grabbed two blankets and a mini cooler. He led her around to the bed of the truck and lowered the tailgate. He helped her up before handing her the blankets and slid the cooler inside.

After jumping into the truck bed himself, Ty folded and laid down one thick blanket for cushioning before motioning for her to sit down on it. She did, sliding the cooler closer by her side before scooting backward. He propped the second blanket against the hard metal of the cab and had her lean back against it. He then sat down beside her, both stretching out their long legs and getting comfortable.

When Ripley suddenly laughed, Ty asked her what was so funny. Not even bothering to hide her smile, she shook her head. "I just realized where I was sitting!" She laughed again. At his questioning look, she said, "Our first date, and I'm already sharing your bed. Even though it's a truck bed, it's still a bed!"

He laughed. "Don't worry, Sugar. I'll still respect you in the morning!"

Ripley laughed and said, with a thread of seriousness in her voice, "As long as I do myself, we're fine."

He reached over to open the cooler, pulling out two ice-cold small cans of Pepsi. He handed her one, the cold water dripping onto her hand. "I know you prefer Pepsi over Coke. I also brought water."

Ripley's heart flipped over. He'd planned ahead, confident she'd go out with him. She could've resented his confidence, even bristled at it, but instead she found it to be appealing and a definite positive attribute. Plus, it was romantic, pure and simple. She'd never considered herself one for the traditional trappings of romance, but this moment had her questioning herself.

She looked into his eyes, where the only light that shone in them came from the moon. "You are the best first date I've ever had. I could never forget this date. Never in a thousand years." Going with instinct, she leaned up and kissed him. "Thank you, Ty."

"You're welcome, Ripley." Her face in the moonlight was too much to resist. Leaning down, he captured her mouth with his. Angling his head, he slanted his mouth over hers, hearing her quiet moan as she responded to his touch. Mindful of not rushing, Ty pulled back. After a moment, he asked, "So, best first date ever for us both?"

"Without a doubt. You're doing a marvelous job!"

Ripley smiled before they popped the seal on their drinks. The sharp crack and hiss of the cans being opened sounded unusually loud in the silence of the dark mountain.

Alone on the secluded mountainside, they sat there in the bed of his truck, just talking and learning more about the other while the world went on far below them. They could hear coyotes in the desert not far from them, the occasional hoot of an owl. Now and then, the silhouette of a bat would appear in front of them, disturbing for a split second their view of the city below them.

Nestled against his side, Ripley finally asked, "All right. How many other women have you brought up here, Ty?"

"Do you want a rough estimate or an exact figure?"

She gasped and stared at him.

He laughed at her instant reaction before he admitted, "None. Just you."

"I don't believe that. Are you teasing me? I know you promised to not lie to me!"

"I *do* mean it. You're the only one who didn't freak out halfway out here, and let me drive the entire way!"

Laughing heartily, she imagined it. "If that's the whole truth, then I'm glad. It's ours now. I hope I ruined it for anyone else you might want to bring up here if we don't work out."

Her blunt comment made him laugh. Well, he'd told her to be honest, hadn't he?

After a while, she wondered, "Those other women who freaked out on you... You must've known them longer and better than you know me. I wonder why they didn't trust you like I do?"

"Maybe longer but not necessarily better. Time doesn't always make the difference. Some people can date for years and not really know the other. And then there are people who know the other in a few weeks or months. Either it clicks, or it doesn't, Sugar.

"Look at us. We've only known each other about two months, but I know more about you than you'd think. That's why I chanced looking like a fool and driving up here, hoping you wouldn't shoot me down."

She nodded. "I can only imagine the courage, and the nerve, it took for you to do that. I have to admit, I'd be too insecure, too vulnerable to even leave the Center to chase after some guy and do all this. Doing a grand gesture like this to someone I barely knew would do me in!"

Ty smiled, appreciating her honesty and her opening up. "We're all vulnerable when it comes to relationships, Sugar. None of us want to get hurt, but life isn't lived without some hurt, some bumps and bruises. I simply choose with care to try to limit the damages done."

After a sliver of silence, she said quietly, "I don't ever want to hurt you, Ty. I feel like I will though. I feel like I need to apologize to you for whatever I may do in the future. It's a sure bet I probably will. But I just want you to know, I didn't mean to." She squeezed his hand in hers. "If I ever do, just don't hate me."

He studied her face in the moonlight. "You're sounding pessimistic, and that's not the Ripley I know. Relax, Sugar. Let's just see what comes along. No use in worrying about what could be or could happen. Let's just move along at a slow pace. Let things fall into place as they need to."

She nodded. Changing the subject, she asked, "How'd you ever find this place anyway?"

"I got lost."

She laughed. "No... Seriously. Tell me."

Ty chuckled. "I just did. *That's* what happened. I got lost. I remembered a place I saw once in a Visitors Guide or something, and I wondered if I could find it on my own. Somehow, I ended up here. It seemed like a cool spot, so I remembered it instead." His voice had a thread of humor in it.

She asked, "Did you ever find the other place?"

"No."

They both laughed at his blunt answer.

They stayed up on the bluff for a couple of hours. They talked and laughed all without the pressures or expectations from others who knew them. When they both kept yawning, they decided they'd better head back to the hotel.

On the way back to civilization, they made a detour to an all-night travel stop to use the bathroom and fill the truck up with gas. Ripley bought a small carton of milk and some donuts. She had a feeling they weren't getting up in time for the free continental breakfast the hotel served every morning. She realized she was already assuming Ty would be in her room, or at least still with her. She took a minute to think about that as she stared blindly at the over-priced bananas.

Later as they neared the hotel, Ripley offered, "Okay. I don't want you to jump to conclusions here but since you don't have a room to stay in, just stay in mine. It'd be stupid to hunt for a room, pay an outrageous amount just so you can sleep for a few hours before you had to check out."

Ty smiled. "Well, I guess it beats sleeping in the truck. I promise I won't jump to conclusions. I guess you mean I'm not on your speed dial yet?"

She smiled. "Yeah, that's exactly what I mean. Can you handle that?"

"It might kill me... But yeah, I can handle it," he teased. After a short pause, he said, "But seriously, we're on the same page." He pulled into the hotel's parking lot and parked in the back row, backing in. "I can take the couch," he offered to ease her mind and worries as he turned off his truck.

"Well, *I'm* sure not!" she retorted, making him laugh. "It pulls out into a bed, if you want that option."

Once they got to her room, she put out the *Do Not Disturb* sign and put the milk in the mini fridge while he headed to the bathroom with his duffle bag to shower. When she heard the bathroom door open, she grabbed her clothes to take her own.

When she caught a look at Ty, she stopped and stared like a deer caught in the headlights. He wore only a pair of black shorts and socks. Her gaze took in his muscular torso and arms. Every bit of him was tanned and defined. She could tell his forearms were a bit darker than the rest of his torso, probably because of working in short sleeves. His damp, tousled, towel-dried hair invited her to run her hands through it to straighten it out. Or tousle it even more. Her gaze traveled down to his muscular thighs and calves. She'd bet even his toes were defined.

Well, hell. The guys at game night were wrong. He *was* a god. A chiseled one at that, she thought as her heart raced in her chest.

Ty dropped his duffle bag on the floor beside the couch. Walking to her, he wrapped her up in a tight embrace, pressing a chaste kiss to her cheek. His ego was close to bursting at her reaction at seeing his body. Every man—and woman—wanted to be desired. He wasn't any different than any other man. Her hot gaze was about to send him back in for a cold shower though.

"Is my number on speed dial yet, Sugar?" he teased her, whispering in her ear.

"No." Smiling, she pulled away. Resisting another look, she headed straight for the bathroom.

He was laughing softly as she shut and locked the door.

She took her time in the shower, enjoying a full-sized one for a change. She finally got out, worried she'd fall asleep in it, fall down, and drown because she plugged the drain. Ripley hated to use the hair dryer this late out of respect for others who may be next door, but she figured she had the right to use it too.

When she came out, it was dark except for the nightlight the hotel had supplied in one outlet and the light from the table lamp beside Ty. She made her way to her bedroom, dumping her clothes in a pile by her suitcase. She was wiped out and was looking forward to sleep, but she walked back out as he was obviously waiting for her.

Ty decided it was easier to just sleep on the couch rather than pulling it out. Finding the spare pillows and a couple of sheets and blankets in the nook by the door, he'd made his temporary bed. He'd slipped on a t-shirt in case the sheets or blankets were scratchy—or not as clean as he hoped—and got settled. He hated wearing socks after showers and to bed, but he wasn't about to walk in any hotel room barefoot. He was casually looking through a Visitor's Guide when she came over to him.

His gaze ran over her body, the shirt and shorts leaving little to his imagination. He was a healthy male, and it didn't take much to get his juices flowing. But he'd also been raised to respect women. He'd never take one who wasn't ready or willing, especially *this* woman. That also wasn't what he was looking for. He was looking for more... So much more.

Deadpanning, she asked, "Still trying to find that lost spot in the mountains?"

Putting down the Visitor's Guide, Ty looked up at her and she saw the amusement in his eyes. He remarked, "I was wondering if you fell asleep in there and drowned. I was about ready to check on you!"

Ripley laughed. "I nearly did. It's wonderful to take a long, hot shower without banging my elbows against the walls or running out of the hot."

Nodding, Ty said, "Go to bed before you fall asleep standing up, Sugar. I'm not being blamed for you not getting sleep this time!" They both smiled. "Do we need to set an alarm? I have my phone charging over there. Do you need to check out tomorrow?"

"One, you *are* to blame for me missing my pre-dinner nap. But I won't hold it against you because you made it worth it." She grinned at his dismayed expression. "And two, I'm paid up for what's left of today, since it's after midnight, and check out is tomorrow."

He reached for her hand, gently tugging her down beside him. She came willingly, resting her hand in his. He looked at her for a moment before he leaned forward to kiss her. She didn't resist at all. Her hands were cupping his face when they pulled apart.

"Goodnight, Sugar. Don't worry about me being here. I was raised to be a gentleman so you don't need to lose any sleep over that. And don't worry about sleeping in if you want to just because I'm here."

Nodding, Ripley stood up and said softly, "Thank you, Ty. I had a stellar night."

She saw the light beside him turn off once she reached her room. She quietly shut her door. She didn't lock it, trusting in her instincts he was, in fact, a gentleman.

Chapter 18

Wednesday, August 26

She had great aim but she still missed him, Ripley thought to herself with a smile. A lot. There was no way she could deny that fact or even would.

On Wednesday morning after her work call was finally over, Ripley gathered her courage and headed up to Sunset Ridge to see Ty. They'd talked on the phone and texted numerous times since arriving back home late Monday night after their adventures in Phoenix. He'd been able to stay with her both Sunday and Monday, telling Morgan he'd work on his day off to make up for it. Morgan had no problem with it. She didn't even ask why he wanted another day off. Ripley decided she was the coolest boss in the world.

Walking through the office door, the only person she saw inside was Morgan. Smiling at her, Ripley greeted her warmly. "I haven't seen you since you got back from the clinic. How'd it go?"

"Hey, Ripley! Have a seat. We just had a ride leave so I have some down time here." Morgan swiveled in her chair. "The clinic went great. I go there a few times a year since they aren't terribly far away. I got back late Friday night, but I'd talked to Ty on the phone beforehand. He let me know you'd be gone for a few days. Did your conference turn out well?"

"Better than expected! It was also wonderful to see my friends in person again. But it's so nice to be back home. I think I'm turning into a homebody the older I get! But you know what? I missed this place too. I hadn't realized how much it'd been growing on me. It's so nice just being here, isn't it?"

Morgan was pleased. "Thank you! And I know that feeling very well. There's never been a time I've been away that I wasn't excited to be back home." She paused before asking, "Are you just checking in on me, or did you need something? You're not leaving, are you?"

Ripley sat down on a stool before answering. "No, I'm not leaving. I just needed a break for a while and thought I'd take a walk as I need some fresh air to clear my head. Since I was up here, I thought I'd check in with Ty to see if he was planning on working with Cappy anytime soon. Do you know where he is?"

Ty had warned her Morgan would know they were dating if they didn't watch it. Neither were worried about her knowing, but it made it more interesting to see how long they could go before she found out.

Morgan's ears picked up on the too-casual tone in Ripley's voice. Interest flickered in her green eyes as she studied Ripley. "He's out fixing part of the trail where Maya mentioned there was some wash out."

"Oh. Do you know when he might get back?"

"Are you in a hurry to work with Cappy?" Or to see my best friend? Morgan held back her smile, idly wondering if there was something going on between her best friend and this woman. A little brewing romance in her barn? she pondered, intrigued by the possibility.

"No, I was just wondering. It's been about a week now since I've helped anyone work with him, so I was just curious. I had some free time later, so I figured to let Ty know in case he had some himself. If not, no worries. I just thought I'd offer my help if it was needed."

"Hang on a sec. I'll radio him." Morgan picked up the two-way radio sitting upright on her desk. "Ty? Come in, Ty."

Ripley's heart began to beat faster, wondering what she was supposed to do or say to get out of the office. Ty's previous warning may have been an understatement of Morgan's abilities! For some reason, she felt Morgan was suspicious suddenly. She did her best to stay calm. She'd been careful and nonchalant in her words... Hadn't she?

Ty's voice came over the radio after a moment. "What do you need, Morgan?"

"Switch to channel five." Morgan switched over herself, waiting for his voice to come back over. Channel five was the channel they used when it wasn't necessarily a business matter.

"You there?" Ty's voice came over.

Morgan answered cheerfully, "Yep."

"What do you need? I'm not done here. You're interrupting my work mojo."

"I have your girlfriend in my office. She wants to know when you're coming back." Morgan grinned broadly at Ripley, whose face went beet red.

"*Morgan!*" Ripley hissed at her.

Ty was quiet for a moment before asking, "Which girlfriend are you referring to?"

Morgan laughed. "How many are you up to now? Did you add someone I don't know about yet?"

"You know I don't keep track of them anymore. Give me a hint so I can try to give you an accurate total."

Morgan's eyes were full of humor as she watched Ripley closely. Ripley was looking down at her lap, shaking her head. Her face was now just a little pink, Morgan noticed.

Morgan radioed back, "What was your last total? Let me see if I can figure it out for myself."

Her hands hidden from Morgan's view behind the counter, Ripley was silently texting Ty. She was hoping he had his phone on him like he normally did. *With her. She's fishing. Help.*

She turned off the ringer so it would only vibrate if he happened to text her back.

"Hang on a second," they heard Ty say.

Relief and hope flooded through Ripley. She hoped his comment meant he had his phone on him and saw her text. She shook her head at Morgan, asking in bewilderment, "What are you up to? I can't believe you *said* that to him! Is something going on I should know about?"

Grinning, Morgan said, "I'm not up to anything. Are you?"

"No!"

Ripley's phone buzzed silently in her hand. She looked down, read Ty's reply: *What did you do?! I told you to stay away from her! Stay calm. I'll handle.*

Ty's voice came back over the radio, sounding calm. "Morgan, I'm back. Just a friend needing help. What would they do without me? I'll see them later today. Where were we?"

Ripley looked down again, hoping Morgan didn't see the humor shining from her eyes. She knew Ty's comments over the radio were aimed right at her. It was hard to contain her laughter.

Morgan watched Ripley but couldn't tell for sure by her reaction if there was something between her and Ty. She finally answered Ty's question, "I was letting you know you have someone waiting for you in the office. She wants to know when you'll be back."

"A 'she,' huh? Who is it this time? It's not that girl from yesterday's ride, is it? The redhead who—"

Morgan's contagious laughter cut him off. "Nah. I sent her on her way. You owe me for that one, by the way!" She released the button on the radio, thinking. Maybe she was wrong thinking there was something between these two. Ty wasn't giving her a hint he knew who or what she was talking about.

His voice came over the radio when she didn't speak again. "Hey, I'm trying to work here. My boss gets testy when her workers are goofing off on the radio," he teased her.

Morgan smiled. "Fine. When are you coming in, do you think?"

"Oh... About half an hour or so. Are you busy in there for the rest of the day?"

Morgan answered, "Nothing I can't handle. Why? You want some more time off?"

"No. But as I was working here, I was thinking we need to work with Cappy. Toby told me earlier we haven't done anything with Cappy since before last week. If you don't need me, I could see how he's responding to men today when I get back. If you're too busy on rides, we can do it another time."

"We?" Morgan asked, latching onto that one word like a hawk catches a mouse in its talons.

Smiling to himself, Ty replied, "Yes, *we.* We don't want to work alone with him yet. Whoever's available."

Morgan said cheerfully, "My vote's on Ripley. I'll see if she's available and can meet you down there. Get back to work. Out."

Smiling, Morgan switched back over to channel two, set the radio on her desk. Leaning back, she said casually, "I guess I should've asked you if that works with your schedule."

Ripley shrugged. "Well, I wasn't planning on it that soon, but it shouldn't be a problem. I was going to go for a long walk, but I still have half an hour or so, right?" She thought for a moment. "I'll be sure to stop by Cappy's stall in case Ty goes down there before I'm back. Otherwise, I'll be at my place. That work?"

At Morgan's nod and smile, Ripley slid off the stool, barely restraining herself from running out the door in panic escape mode. "Maybe I'll see you again later. Glad you're back. You must be growing on me!"

Morgan grinned as Ripley's phone buzzed silently again. She glanced down, read from Ty: *Get away from her. NOW!*

Clearing the screen and hiding her smile, Ripley made her escape as casually as she could.

Chapter 19

"OKAY, RIPLEY. LET'S SEE how he responds with just me." Ty's soft voice carried to her as he motioned for them to trade places in the round pen.

Cappy eyed the man warily. Thankfully, he no longer attacked men or broke out into nervous sweats when he simply saw them. They were making progress with the horse slowly but surely.

Ty watched the horse eyeing him as he headed toward the center of the large round pen inside the barn. It was like Cappy was working it all out, realizing not all men were mean and violent. His large, intelligent eyes stayed on the man walking toward him. He swished his long tail at a fly as he waited to see what the man wanted. To Ty, he looked relaxed and open to communication. He couldn't have asked for anything better.

"He's behaving but still be careful," Ripley said as they passed each other. She closed the gate behind her, latching it loosely in case she needed back in quickly to protect Ty.

Ty was now in the center. Cappy still stood by the far metal panel, glancing at her as she stood outside the pen before transferring his brown-eyed gaze back on the man now alone with him.

Standing still, Ty waited for Cappy to adjust to the idea of it being just the two of them. Not wanting him to stand still too long—movement was always better—he used the long lunge whip to get Cappy moving forward at a calm walk. Ty slowly lifted it, positioning it behind Cappy to indicate which direction he wanted him to go. No whip cracks, no yelling, just a simple raising of a training aid.

Cappy looked at the long whip again and then the man like he was thinking it all through.

"Walk," Ty softly but firmly coached the horse. His right hand shook the long whip behind Cappy, who just looked at it for a moment.

With a tentative step at first, Cappy walked along the railing, his ears flickering back and forth, paying attention to Ty. That's what they wanted. When he tried to stop, Ty gently encouraged him to move forward again by voice alone. "Walk, Cappy. Walk."

Cappy shook his head like he was talking back, making Ty grin, but it was probably just a fly annoying him. Ty again raised the training aid to his waist, held it out behind the horse's hindquarters. He verbally repeated the command.

The horse walked forward again. "Good boy, Cappy! Good boy! Walk..." Ty continued to talk to the horse. After a few rounds to let him relax, he said, "Whoa." Ty smiled when the horse immediately stopped. "Good boy, whoa." He waited a few beats, saying again, "Walk. Walk on."

Cappy did.

Ripley smiled but kept quiet.

After a minute, Ty's soft voice instructed, "Trot. Trot, Cappy." He used the aid to encourage him again. Cappy broke into a trot, no longer the mixture of walking, trotting, and crazed stop-and-go, crash, turn again, cantering he used to do.

Around and around Ty had Cappy go, seeing him relax some more as his neck and head lowered a bit and his back began rounding out. Once he saw Cappy moving freely, his ears flickering as a cue he was waiting for the next command, Ty asked him to walk again. Cappy trotted on.

Ty repeated, "Walk. Walk." Cappy did, turning his head to look at Ty like he was making sure he did it right.

Smiling, Ty praised the sorrel. "Good boy! Walk."

Getting him to trot again, Ty then asked him to canter. He about pumped his fists in victory when the horse transitioned into an easy canter and not the frantic galloping and stopping he used to do. Staying focused on the horse, knowing he couldn't quite fully trust him yet, Ty let him go around and around the pen. He watched for the signs of Cappy relaxing again. When he did, he let him continue on. He needed the exercise, Ty figured.

He then commanded, "Whoa! Whoa, Cappy!" The horse slid to a stop. And stood still, his sides heaving lightly. He turned his graceful neck to look at Ty again.

"Good boy! You're a smart boy, aren't you? Good boy, Cappy!" Ty lowered his arms before motioning for the horse to turn toward him. When Cappy obeyed the hand gestures, Ty praised him again.

He then reversed direction and went through it all again, mixing up the commands to make sure the horse was actually listening to him and not getting conditioned to a routine of commands.

Ripley smiled broadly as she watched the horse go around and around, following the commands Ty asked for. She stayed stock still so she wouldn't distract the horse although what she really wanted to do was clap while jumping in excitement. She could feel her own heartbeat pumping in her contained excitement and couldn't even imagine how Ty felt.

Finally, Ty had the gelding stop. He made the horse stand still, not moving a hoof until Ty asked him to move again. The next time, Ty had him stand still longer. He pushed the length of time out as long as he dared, reading the gelding's body language as a gauge.

Then Ty asked him to canter again. He smiled at Ripley when they made brief eye contact as the horse cantered calmly by her. Returning his focus to the horse, he let him canter another minute.

Ty called out to her, "Hey, Ripley. Let's try to distract him now. Start walking around, make noise, jump, whatever. See what he does."

She banged the metal clasps on a halter on the metal rails, then ran in the opposite direction Cappy was. She jumped up and down, clapping her hands. She even did some Jumping Jacks. Not getting much of a response, she gently threw the lead rope at the horse as he trotted by her.

Cappy glanced her way now and then, probably wondering what in the world the human was doing. But he continued going around and around, listening to Ty's cues for different gaits. Amazingly, he never truly spooked once. A couple of twitches and hesitations, but no real reactions to her bizarre movements and noise.

Both Ty and Ripley were more than a little surprised. They each expected the horse to do *something*. Either Cappy was just not impressed with her antics, or he was simply trusting them to not hurt him.

When Ty felt he was at a good stopping point, he lowered his arms, asking the horse to stop. "Whoa, Cappy. Whoa. Good boy."

Slowly but confidently, Ty asked the horse to walk toward him. This was the tricky part with Cappy. Previously, he'd threatened to charge and sometimes *would* do a small one. But little by little, his trust in men was evolving. At least trust in *this* man.

When Cappy walked four steps in, Ty asked him to stop. "Whoa. Good boy! Good boy, whoa."

The reddish-brown ears perked forward when they heard the sound of peppermint candy being unwrapped in Ty's fingers. "Whoa! Whoa, Cappy," Ty commanded firmly as the horse wanted to break out of the stop, one front leg stepping forward.

At the tone of Ty's voice, the horse stopped. After a slight pause, he slid his leg back with a reluctant look on his face.

Ty laughed at Cappy's expression. "There you go, big fella. You're doing great. Whoa." Ty walked the last two steps to reach him, giving the horse the candy as a reward. He stroked the warm neck as the horse happily chewed.

As the horse crunched another piece, Ty again ran his hands down the warm neck and shoulder. Then his hands cruised over Cappy's back, rump, sides, and belly. Ty put a little pressure in his hands as he feared a light touch might tickle the horse and cause an unwanted reaction, breaking down the progress they'd made. Other than a skin twitch, Cappy allowed the man to touch him.

Another victory! Cappy wasn't trying to reach around and bite him, his skin was no longer shivering at a man's touch, nor was he trying to cow-kick him anymore. Ty turned his head, raising his eyebrows and smiling at Ripley, who nodded and grinned back silently in acknowledgement.

The transformation in the horse was remarkable. With patience and skill, and Ripley's undeniable calming influence on the horse, Ty was now able to run his own hands freely around the tall horse. Cappy would even allow Ty and Josh to pick up his feet without kicking or striking anymore. They still couldn't fully trust the horse, but he was making tremendous strides.

Ending the session on a positive note, Ty picked up the lead rope Ripley had thrown earlier at Cappy. Ty clipped it to his halter, always watchful for any warning sign he might need to get out of the way, and led the horse to the gate. When Ty nodded to her, Ripley swung it open.

Ty led the horse out and back to his stall with Ripley following safely behind. They were slowly weaning Cappy away from his need to see her at all times.

Having trained him to stand in the cross-ties, Cappy seemed happily content to stand in the aisle as Ty curried his coat, being careful where the stitches had been, before smoothing it with a soft bristle brush. Ripley combed out his mane and tail, adding some conditioner to the dry, coarse hair. Both checked his injuries from the crash, noting with enormous relief he was healing well just like the others.

She then misted fly spray over his body. Cappy no longer shied away at the squirting noise of the bottle nor the fine mist as it landed on his coat. When she was done, Ty picked all four hooves clean. While he did that, Ripley cleaned out Cappy's stall, checking his water bucket on her way out.

Both of them just talked about mundane, everyday topics as they worked together while the radio played pop music in the background. Walking by, Alexis smiled when she saw how happy the horse looked. She stopped to pet Cappy as she talked with Ty and Ripley for a few minutes. She smiled when the horse gently bumped her with his nose, looking either for treats or a scratching post. She kissed his nose before she left for the other barn.

When they were finished grooming Cappy, Ty led him back to his stall. After Ty removed the halter, he gave Cappy another peppermint and more praise.

Standing in the doorway of the stall, Ripley was barely able to contain her excitement. Her eyes bright, she exclaimed, "He *did* it, Ty! You've made wonderful progress with him! Can you *believe* he's the same horse?"

Smiling, Ty stepped out of the stall. "It's hard to, but thanks to you he's learning to trust again. He's calmer when he knows you're around, but he's slowly transferring that trust to me now as well as to Josh. Little by little here, with no rushing, he's making progress. I'm sure he'll be at ease with us men soon enough. He's intelligent, so he's figuring this all out. He's coming along great!"

Ripley pet Cappy's head as he stuck it outside the open stall door, sniffing her hands with the hope more peppermint candy would magically appear. Looking at him, Ripley said, "I'm out, fella. We don't want you to get too spoiled."

She ran his ears through her fingers, loving the silky feel of them. "I can't get over how gorgeous Cappy is. His conformation is nearly perfect. He had to have been a show horse or something at some point in his life, don't you think? He shows good, strong bloodlines. He's not a backyard breeder's horse, you know? Now that he's cleaned up and healing, I just can't see how he ended up on a truck bound for Mexico. Well, minus the man-hating thing. Where did his path go so wrong?"

Ty nodded as he gave a candy to the bay horse next to Cappy. "I know. It seems to me a whole lot of wrongs have been done to that horse in particular." He shut and latched the door after Ripley gently shoved the large horse back out of the way.

Ripley, knowing the routine, went to the candy bucket and grabbed a handful of mints. She walked over to Ty, handing him some. They both went down the line, feeding the treats to the rescued horses. The sound of crinkling wrappers was all they heard until the sounds of teeth breaking hard candy began.

Ripley was smiling inside. She loved helping the horses and seeing their eyes fill up again with hope, trust, and love. Gone was the despair she'd seen even in the dark of night when she'd held them on the side of the interstate. The only haunting thought she had now was although they were hopefully saving these horses, there were still others being shipped that they knew nothing about whatsoever.

That night seemed like forever ago to her. It didn't even feel real anymore.

"They smell good, don't they?" Ty grinned at her when she came to get the wrappers from him to throw away.

"Better than some men I've met!" Ripley grinned at him as she walked toward the little trash can.

He was about to comment when Morgan walked down the aisle. She called out, "Hey, you two. That was fantastic! It's hard to believe that's the same horse."

Her eyes taking in both of them, Morgan watched their body language. Her gut was telling her something *might* be going on, and she was too curious to wait any longer. She'd been silently watching them the last fifteen minutes, but so far she couldn't see anything out of the ordinary between them.

Ty nodded. "Dr. Shamis will never believe it! Cappy's definitely coming along like the others. I think just working with them, grooming them, letting them be themselves is the best medicine.

"But I think pretty soon we do need to see how they are about loading and unloading in a trailer like we were talking about earlier. The few you told me about may need us to work with them. Anything they need help with, we need to know now while we have the time.

"And I'd like to have us begin riding them to see what they're made of. Cappy should be ready to go under saddle soon. We'll probably find out if he was a rodeo bronc when we do that!" Both women grinned at him. "Ripley and I have line-driven him only once with just his halter on, but I think you said Josh was doing it with you around?"

Morgan nodded. "We've done it twice. He did fine."

"Okay. Well, if you two are in agreement, I say let's put a saddle on him next time and see what happens. If he's okay with it, we'll begin line-driving him around the place with it on. I still wouldn't turn my back on him, but at least he's not trying to kill men on sight anymore."

"That's always a good sign!" Morgan agreed with a cheerful grin. She pet the Haflinger gelding she was standing next to, opening the door for more access to him. "And I agree with your assessment, Ty. I think riding and trailering them will be beneficial.

"I'll have Kat and Mel schedule these in on their regular riding schedules but leave Cappy to us. We'll start trailering them soon too. I don't want to overwhelm them, but I want to give them the chance to know it's safe. I haven't heard from Matt or Dell lately, so I have no idea what's going on with their case."

She closed the stall door and began walking by the other horses, mentally assessing them. Although looking at the horses, she was speaking to Ty and Ripley when she said, "You two work well together. We're going to miss you when you leave, Ripley."

Ty's glance shot over to Ripley, wondering if she was leaving why she didn't inform *him.* Her glance shot over to him too. She saw the look in his eyes, a bit of confusion, questioning, and of possible hurt.

She hurried to answer Morgan, thereby reassuring Ty that she had no plans to leave in the near future. "Did my rent check bounce, or are you kicking me out, Morgan? I wasn't planning on leaving anytime soon. Do you need the RV space?"

"Not at all. I like your company, and you've been such a tremendous help with these horses especially Cappy. Plus, the extra money I'm getting from you is helping to pay for feeding these guys." Morgan smiled at Ripley as she walked over to her. "I just meant, in general, you leaving sometime. I didn't mean to hint or imply I wanted you gone. Sorry about that!"

"You know I'm very glad to help out. I enjoy it." Ripley smiled back. It had crossed her mind once or twice that the rent she was paying Morgan was probably being used to help buy the feed for the rescues. Or help pay that vet bill, which she knew couldn't have been cheap.

Ty walked over to join them. "Life's little surprises come from nowhere, don't they? Just think, if you two hadn't met that day, most of this would've turned out quite differently.

"We should all go out sometime, don't you think, Morg? Somewhere other than game nights? Since she's here, we should show her the area. Grab Damien, Laura, Josh, and show her the town sometime."

Transferring his gaze to Ripley, he added, "That's only if you're interested, Ripley. Maybe you know someone else you'd rather take you around. Someone else you might know from your work?"

Morgan glanced from one to the other, but she still wasn't picking up on anything solid. But it *did* sound like Ty was maybe thinking about dating Ripley—at least in an informal group setting. Or it could just be he wanted to show her the local scene. They *were* becoming friends after all.

Recognizing his little dig at her, Ripley simply replied, "That sounds like fun. I've been working more often than not since I got here. I've driven around a bit, but I haven't really stopped to be a tourist or anything. It's probably nicer to go around with someone who knows the area. Someone *not* related to work would be good."

Ripley smiled at him, knowing they were secretly referring to their Phoenix conversation again.

Morgan nodded. "Yeah, that'd be fun to do. We should do it! Is there any place you want to see while you're here, Rip?"

Ripley thought about it. "A few places have caught my attention. Hey, what about going back to where we met sometime? You said the nights were the best times to be there."

"Yeah, pretty much any night is. When do you think you'll have time off?"

Thinking of her schedule, Ripley answered, "Next Thursday should be good. I'm booked up all this week and have a meeting to do on Friday night. I might not be back in time on Saturday to go out. My nights are popular times for many people. But I can just not schedule anything for next Thursday. Do you think Laura's sitter for Sasha can do Thursday?"

Ty asked, "You know Laura and Sasha?"

Turning to him, she replied, "I met Laura that night we got these horses. She mentioned Sasha was at the sitter's, a neighbor lady that Sasha took to right away."

"Good memory you have there."

"I try." She smiled, modestly shrugging her shoulder.

Morgan watched them, noticing they were quite at ease with each other. She felt there was a bit of a spark there too. She really did like Ripley, so maybe it was just her sort of wishing they could maybe get together. She didn't like Ty being alone like he was.

"Well," Morgan said, "I'll check with Josh. He's been swamped lately so if he can take off early, I'm sure he'd love to have some downtime with us. I'll have him ask Damien and Laura. Or I can, I guess.

"If they can't do it on Thursday, there's always the following weekend if you're free. And Ty's off right now on Thursdays, so you two are free at least." Her green-eyed gaze went from one to the other again.

Ty nodded, laughing inside at his best friend. Oh yes. She was fishing all right! "Well, I guess I could show her around if no one else is available—if she doesn't mind." Turning to Ripley, he said, "We'll see what we can put together and get back with you. Or just head up to the office to check in."

Ripley looked directly at Morgan. With a wry smile, she said, "Yeah, right. I'll be sure to do *that!*"

"What? You have a problem coming up to my office all of a sudden?" Morgan laughed heartily as she waved and turned to leave. "I'll see you guys later!"

As Morgan left to return to Sunset Ridge, Ty and Ripley put away the tack and grooming supplies they'd used with Cappy. They waited to make sure Morgan had indeed left the building, and they were alone. Ty suddenly grabbed Ripley's hand, pulling her into the stall that was lined high with straw bales to block anyone's view inside.

Both were smiling when their lips met and clung. Wrapping her arms around his neck, Ripley enthusiastically kissed him back. She'd been waiting to kiss him again, to be back in his arms like this. Getting to do it secretly in a barn in broad daylight added some excitement to it.

Ty finally pulled back. Speaking softly he said, "I missed you, Rip. Even though I knew you were just right down the lane there, I missed you. It's been hard to stay away, but I know you have work to do. And it'd be odd if I just left the barn to head to your place for no reason."

She nodded and replied just as quietly, "I have to admit, I was really missing you! I'm still working all of this out in my head, but I am. And it's hard to stay away from you too. I just had to take a chance and headed up earlier today to see you. I got your pal instead. My lucky day!" she added dryly.

He chuckled. Running his hands over her braided hair, he asked, "What did you say that got her suspicious anyway?"

"Nothing. I swear!"

"You said *something*, Sugar, that got her attention. I warned you about her!" Ty placed a soft kiss on her hair. Smiling, he rubbed her back.

Her heart always skipped a beat when he kissed her like that. And his strong hands rubbing her back felt wonderful.

Trying to keep focused on their conversation, she answered, "I told her I was out for a walk. Then I decided to stop by the office to see if you were going to work with Cappy since it'd been a week or so. Since you weren't in the office, I asked if she knew where you were."

Ty listened, thinking, picturing it in his mind. "It was your voice and body language then. *Something* gave you away just a tiny bit. She's *definitely* fishing as she just isn't sure. That's why she came down here, you know."

He kissed her again, both lingering over it. When he pulled away, he said, "She'll find out sooner or later. Frankly, this is fun. Let's see how long we can go. You game?"

"I thought you said you didn't play games with people?" Ripley asked.

"It's *Morgan*." He stated flatly, causing Ripley to laugh softly. "That's the difference. It's not a bad head game but just a bit of fun. Besides, it's none of her business to know. But there's also no reason for her *not* to know. She's just fun to mess with!" He grinned at her, his eyes full of amusement.

"Well, let's see how long we can go then!" She framed his face with her hands, pulled him down so she could quickly kiss him again. "Okay, I need to get going here. Duty calls, you know?"

He nodded. "For me too. Thanks for your help with Cappy. This would be so much harder without you around."

She smiled as she walked out of the stall. "I'd say nearly impossible." At his humble acknowledgement of the simple truth, she added, "But I'd do anything for a friend!"

When they left the barn, Ty headed up to the office as Ripley headed down to her RV. Both smiled all the way to their destinations.

Chapter 20

Thursday, September 3

Ringing the doorbell, Ripley waited while her heart raced in anticipation. When Ty opened his door, he hauled her in, kicking the door shut with his foot. He wrapped his arms around her and kissed her senseless.

Laughing, she hitched herself up, wrapping her long legs around his hips as he leaned her against the door. She placed soft, quick kisses all over his face before she returned to his mouth again.

When they finally pulled apart, Ripley tried to get her breath back, happily noticing he was in the same condition.

"Hi there, Sugar!" He grinned at her. "I see you found my house okay." He hugged her tightly, just holding her close.

She squeezed him back, resting her head on his shoulder. Had she ever done this with any guy she'd dated before? she wondered. None came to mind.

Leaning back in his arms and cupping his cheek, she said with a straight face, "Well. If I'd known *that* was waiting for me, I'd have run *all* the red lights to get here!"

He laughed as she slid back down to the floor to stand on her own two feet. "C'mon, I'll show you around."

The first place he took her to was a nice, all-around home gym that was built onto the back of his house and attached to his garage. Her eyes took in all the machines and equipment he had and the three walls of mirrors. *This* would explain his fit body!

The fairly large area of blue gym mats stumped her so she asked, "What do you do on those mats? Wrestle?"

"No. Kickboxing, martial arts, and lots of other self-defense skills."

"Who do you work out with?"

"I can do the kickboxing by myself with the stand-alone there. I just roll it onto the mats if I want to use it. Otherwise, I work out with Morgan."

Ripley was genuinely surprised. "You and Morgan kickbox each other?"

He nodded. "That and other self-defense skills. We finally got tired of hitting the hard floor, so that's why I got the mats after I hired Josh to build this place. I earned lots of reward points on my credit card. These mats and mirrors weren't cheap."

"Why her? Does Josh come?"

"Normally it's just me and Morgan. We've been working out since nearly the beginning of her hiring me. Morgan was alone out in the middle of nowhere before she got The Darrells. But they may not be around, so she needed to be ready. And she still comes around because it's something you need to keep up with.

"I felt she needed to know more than just how to shoot a gun. Same idea as the dogs... She may not have a gun on her if she got attacked.

"I've taught my female relatives too. Women really need to know how to take care of themselves. Besides, working out together is great for keeping in shape, and it relieves stress. Josh will pop over now and then. He prefers the stand-alone because it doesn't kick back!"

He grinned at her laugh. "Morgan and my cousin Channion are a great match to watch. She doesn't hold back! A few years before she married Josh, so this wasn't built yet, Chan came out for a visit. We invited her over, and somehow the visit turned into a sparring match.

"I warned him she was very good. He either didn't believe me or was worried about hitting a woman. Well, she knocked his socks off!" He laughed heartily at the memory. "After that, he applied himself a little more. Chan took it very well, and the three of us still laugh about it."

Amused at the story, Ripley smiled. "Morgan shoots too?"

"She's a great shot. Excellent eye."

"Is there anything she *can't* do?" she asked in earnest.

He cupped her face for a moment. "Don't be jealous, Sugar. Seriously. And I can teach you too. Shooting, well, either you're good at it or not. That being said, it's also just practice. We normally go to a shooting range.

"Again, she's out in the middle of nowhere. There's a boatload of reasons why her having a gun, and knowing how to use it effectively, is needed. Whether it's for her own protection, having to kill a snake, or God forbid, put a horse down in an emergency."

Ripley had to agree.

Ty took her hand as he led her back into the house.

Besides the real-life, stunning Western pencil drawings by an extremely talented artist who signs his work 'Shoofly,' he had a small, tasteful display of photos of who she assumed were family.

Her eyes paused on a photo of him on a gorgeous palomino. The deep golden coat, and the three white socks and stripe down the horse's nose, gleamed in the sun. The creamy white mane and tail were long and flowing. Looking closely, she could see the wind was blowing them just enough to add realism to the picture.

"Holy moly! This is a beautiful horse. Is he Morgan's?"

"No, he's mine. He stays in Quail Run near Morgan's horse, Bombay. His name is Monte. I'm sure you've seen him... No? You need to get out of your RV more, Sugar. We should go riding sometime."

"We should... when Morgan's gone." They both grinned. "How in the world could I have missed seeing this horse? He reminds me of when I was a kid, I went to this horse show. The Shriners were there, and they all rode palominos. Another team at another show rode all blacks. They were drill teams.

"In regards to Monte here, I really only go up to the office, see Cappy and the rescues, or walk the trails. I guess that's why I haven't seen him. I simply haven't gone inside Quail Run except for my first day there. But you're right. My work seriously needs to take a back burner for a while!"

Her gaze continued over the photos. She smiled and pointed. "Who's this? You two look like you're having a great time!"

Leaning over her shoulder, wrapping an arm around her waist, he smiled. "This is my cousin Channion at his house when we were obviously kids. We've been best friends, more like brothers, since childhood. He's my partner in crime and closest confidant besides Morgan.

"He's a detective back in Illinois. He got married a few years ago to an absolutely terrific woman. Raina's a musician with a voice that'll blow you away. She has a website with her music on it. I could give it to you in case you want to listen to her. You'd like her, I think.

"She's funny, direct, and feisty. Raina has a strong personality with a generous heart. She's extremely selfless and has the courage of a hundred men. She's similar to Morgan in certain ways."

"I'm not sure if that's a good thing or bad thing right now!" she joked.

"It's all good, Sugar." He grinned. "But you can be glad Raina's not here right now because I doubt either one of us could get by her for very long. And for sure not both her *and* Morgan! Nothing seems to get by her. Both Channion and I say she'd be an incredible detective or interrogator. She can read between the lines of what's *not* being said as well as any trained investigator."

"She's never met Morgan?"

"No, but I've invited Channion and her out here since they got married. They know they're welcome anytime. With Chan being a detective, it's hard for him to get time off. Especially long enough to make a trip across the country. He and our Uncle Ron are partners, and they're always working on some case or another. I imagine Ron is bound to retire sometime fairly soon.

"Raina gives music lessons, sings in a bar, and travels all over for concerts. She's not like mega famous, but she's traveled quite a bit so her name *is* getting known. Her schedule can be hectic too.

"It'd be nice if they could make it out here. They will, sooner or later. Probably later with the way things are looking. But Chan's been out here over the years before he got married, so Morgan and Chan know each other pretty well."

He answered her questions about his large family. As Ripley listened to him, she caught the softer tone in his voice.

As she walked by his recliner, she noticed a book on the table beside it. Puzzled, she reached over and picked it up, flipping through the pages. Surprise showed on her face when she realized why it looked so different. "You read books in Spanish?"

"Sometimes. It keeps me sharp, and I like reading in Spanish. It's a beautiful language."

Ripley nodded. "It really is. Are you fluent in it? I guess you would be if you can read an entire book in it."

Ty answered, "Pretty fluent, but I still need to resort to a dictionary sometimes. Watching movies and shows in it helps."

Ripley stared at him for a moment before making sure she understood him correctly. "You watch TV and movies in Spanish? Not in English?"

"I do both. Since no one else at the Center speaks Spanish now, and we really don't get many Spanish speakers there, I figured to keep it active in my mind. If you don't use it, you lose it."

Impressed, she put the book back where he'd left it. "How'd you learn it in the first place?"

Ty motioned for her to sit on the couch and joined her before replying, "We had an employee named Carlos—"

"Naturally his name would be Carlos!" she interjected with a smile.

"Naturally!" He grinned back. "But Carlos *was* Mexican, and he spoke fluent English. He was about forty or so when he worked for us. Great worker! Reliable, mature, had a talent with the horses, friendliest guy on earth with a terrific sense of humor! Skinny as a beanpole.

"He had this quirk that drove us nuts though. It could be triple digit heat, and he'd be wearing three long-sleeved shirts. And one was usually a thermal. You know, an insulated one like long johns? *Man!* It made me sweat to death just looking at him!" Ty laughed in remembrance. "Alexis only worked a little while with him before he left, but I'm sure she'd remember him.

"Anyway, I asked him if he wouldn't mind teaching me his native language. I knew some from over the years, but I wasn't fluent in it. And I forgot quite a bit since I wasn't using it.

"It was his suggestion to only listen to the radio, TV, and movies in Spanish. Or other times, to have it in English with Spanish subtitles, or vice versa. Once I got going, that's when I began trying to read and write it more. It was a process, still is. I started with children's books. The pictures helped a lot!

"He was a very patient teacher, only speaking to me in Spanish. This meant it took a lot longer for work to get done because I had to figure out what he was saying. And, of course, I had to speak only in Spanish to him. I'm sure there were days when Morgan wanted to clobber both of us for work taking way longer than it should've!

"I *do* remember one day she warned us that although she paid by the hour, she stopped paying us at all at a certain time. So we'd better be finished on time unless we were okay working for free!" He laughed as he recalled those long-ago days. "If we were in a hurry, one of us would resort to English before she got mad. We're probably the reason she switched from hourly to a daily salary!"

Ripley laughed, imagining it. "I can't see her *ever* being mad at you... or anyone really!"

"It doesn't happen too often. She's got an impressive tough side. Don't let her smile and easy-going nature fool you. Being a female owner who works with the general public has made her even tougher.

"The quickest way that I've seen to set her off is to have a male customer ask to talk to her manager. They look to me because I'm a man and just assume I'm over her. I just point to her to back her up. She resents it, but she also appreciates me just tossing it back to her without saying a word to help her out. If I did, it'd just undermine her authority.

"I do remember this one time, this chauvinist kept asking to speak to her manager. Since I *am* that, I said this situation needed to be handled by the owner. This jerk agrees. So I pick up the office phone and call Morgan—who's standing right beside me. She pulls out her phone and answers."

Ty shook his head, remembering the look on that guy's face. "Doing that sent this guy into a *tailspin*. He swore, and he fumed. But he finally left just in the nick of time as I was ready to bodily escort him out. We put him on our blacklist.

"I admit working for Morgan has really opened my eyes to misogyny. I knew it existed, of course, but seeing it play out in real time is... I don't really know if there's one word for it. Disgusting? Archaic? Offensive? Like our talk in Phoenix, remember?"

She nodded as he went on, "And I recall Carlos telling me about some of the racist things he went through too. I wasn't raised that way, so it's always been a bit baffling to me how people can be so painfully ignorant. Even now as a grown man, it's puzzling. But some people definitely are. It's always been that way, I guess."

"It sounds like your parents raised you right. They should be proud of that."

Ty smiled. "I'll let them know you said that."

Ripley smiled back before she asked, "Morgan doesn't speak Spanish?"

"Some. She was picking it up a little, but she really didn't have the same time or interest as I did. She mainly memorized key phrases. She uses her phone translator if I'm not around. But oddly enough, we really don't get many Spanish speakers out there. Or, most likely, they just speak English."

"That's something I really wish I'd done when I was younger. They say if you learn a language as a kid, your brain just soaks it up. But as an adult, it's a lot harder. But some people have a knack for languages. I've met people who speak five, even eight, of them. It blows my mind how they don't get them mixed up!" She shook her head in bewilderment just thinking about it.

She continued, "To me, the world's too small to know only one language. In my opinion, Americans need to teach other languages starting in elementary school. We all need to be fluent in more than just English. And some Americans can't even speak proper English! Poor grammar drives me nuts."

She sighed. "It's one of my regrets—not learning Spanish more than just from school. I did try a few times over the years though. I love hearing it." She wiggled her eyebrows. "And it's kinda hot to know you speak it!"

Ty chuckled before saying with a straight face, "I'll be sure to remember that." He nodded before saying, "We agree on something else too. Americans *are* lazy when it comes to other languages. Or maybe it's not so much laziness because it's simply not available, as you said.

"Young minds *could* pick it up so much easier in elementary school. Languages are really a lost art, and the arts have lost a lot of funding over the years in our educational system. *That's* something the politicians should be focusing on—making our educational system much more practical and complete.

"We're falling behind, I'm afraid. It's a shame, maybe a disgrace, that we don't push learning languages far more. You're one hundred percent correct in saying this world is too small to not know more than one. It doesn't matter that English is universal.

"It *is* laziness to expect others to know English while we don't care to learn theirs! Knowing another language opens up a world of job opportunities too."

She nodded. "I know some sign language. But like you said, you don't use it, you lose it. I had some friends teach me some years and years ago. It's the third most popular language in the States. Did you know that?"

Ty thought about it for a moment. "It's actually a bit odd to think of it as an actual language. But it *is* one, isn't it? It's used to fully communicate to a large and diverse population. Interesting."

Ripley said, "Knowing so many international people myself, knowing their language, even attempting to speak it, shows them respect. Respect toward them, their country, heritage. I think they really appreciate it."

With a straight face, Ty said, "Well, how about I teach you some Spanish while I wait to be put on your speed dial?"

Ripley laughed. "And maybe I can teach you some sign."

"Why not? I've always been good with my hands."

THEY HUNG OUT AT his place for a while before deciding to go into town to eat. They could maybe catch a movie, or just drive around to see some tourist spots. Everyone was meeting up later for dinner at The Neon Moon, so they had time alone first. Ripley had taken the entire day off to spend with him, and they planned to make the most of it.

As they walked through town hand in hand, they took their time browsing. Block after block they walked, taking in the local flavor by stopping in the little shops.

They'd just walked out of an art gallery when Ripley's heart stopped. She was looking across the wide street after some cars went by when she spotted a silver truck that read *Harmony Hills Equestrian Center* on the door. It immediately hit her that someone they knew could be watching them.

Ripley shrieked, "Ty! The truck..."

"Yeah, I just saw it myself. Act natural, Sugar!" he said, his eyes scanning the windows of the stores. When he felt her begin to remove her hand from his, he gripped it tighter. "No, Ripley. If we're caught, we're caught. There's nothing to be embarrassed or ashamed about."

"I know, but..."

Ty said, "They're in the sub shop across the street—Josh and Morgan. I don't think they saw us yet!"

As he was talking, he quickly swung her around. Both now laughing like kids, they quickly headed back the way they came. They were hoping to get around the corner where they'd be out of sight.

Ripley had the gall to tease him. "If we're not ashamed or embarrassed, why are we running in the opposite direction, Sugar?"

"I was just trying to respect your wishes!" he joked back.

His phone buzzed on his hip. He released her hand so he could answer it. He groaned, but then he grinned. Ripley noticed and was about to ask him about it when her phone rang. Not answering it, she saw him shake his head in mock defeat, showing her the screaming text message from Josh's phone: *U 2 R BUSTED! GET IN HERE!!*

Her phone began ringing again. She pulled it from her purse and saw the Caller ID. "Crap! It's Morgan!"

His eyes sparkled with humor. "Might as well answer it, Sugar. We got caught!"

Giving in, Ripley answered. Morgan must've called right back, otherwise it would've gone to her voicemail. Acting natural, Ripley said, "Hello?"

She immediately heard Morgan's voice, amusement clearly coming through. "Hey there, Ripley. Why don't you turn right back around and join my husband and I for lunch? And be sure to bring your cute friend with you."

"I'm sorry, but you're calling outside of my office hours," Ripley began, smiling when Ty laughed.

Morgan's laughter came through loud and clear. "Get over here, and don't dawdle!" Morgan hung up.

Ripley slipped her phone back into her purse. Glancing up at Ty through her sunglasses, she scrunched up her face, stomped her foot, and cringed. "Man! It's like being caught by your *dad!*"

Ty laughed, completely agreeing. "Why is it worse to meet my friends—people we *both* know—for lunch than me meeting your friends, and more of them who I'd never met before, for dinner?"

She adjusted the strap of her tank top as she thought about it. "I have no idea!" She stomped her foot again, saying, "Dang it! We're going to get grilled to death in there, aren't we?"

Reaching for her hand, Ty kissed the back of it before he nodded. "Yes, ma'am. But we'll survive. Remember, they're friends. They won't hurt us." He grinned again at the look on her face. Prepared to face the music, he turned them around to walk back toward the sub shop.

"They have really good cookies there at least," Ty announced as they waited to cross the street.

For some reason, his offhanded comment made her laugh. Was she getting hysterical in her nervousness?

Ty noticed his friends watching their progress as they crossed the busy street. "We're toast, Rip!" he teased her. "Please just don't leave me alone with them, okay?"

She groaned good-naturedly and gamely walked by his side. "Should we just grab our lunch here? Kill two birds with one stone?"

"Might as well."

"I once heard they have really good cookies," she deadpanned.

Ty laughed as he opened the door.

When they entered, they saw Josh and Morgan sitting there, side by side, eyeing them both intently. They nodded to them and got in line to order food.

She said, "Before we order and get grilled ourselves, I'm heading to the bathroom." When she turned to go to the little hallway that led to them, he followed. She jokingly asked, "Afraid I'm making a run for it?"

He grinned. "You'd set off the emergency alarm if you tried that door, and the windows are too small to crawl out of. I think it's safe to say you won't make it. I'll wait for you in line."

After getting their food and drinks, they walked over to the booth where Josh and Morgan were patiently waiting. Ripley thought it was so romantic and cute how they sat next to, and not across from, each other. That little gesture squeezed her heart. They were the most adorable couple she could think of!

Sitting by the window, Morgan pointed to the booth seat across from herself and Josh. Trying to keep a straight face, she said, "Fancy meeting you two here. Sit down, won't you?"

At Ty's nudge and smile, Ripley slid in first so she was across from Morgan.

As Ty slid in beside her, Morgan said, "This is *such* an interesting development, isn't it, sweetheart?" She turned her bright, humor-filled green eyes to her husband.

"It certainly is, sweetheart. And here you were only a short time ago wondering about this very thing happening." Josh's broad grin spread across his handsome face.

Ty raised an eyebrow. "You wondered about us meeting for subs?" His friends laughed. Ty looked at Ripley, saying with a straight face, "We may as well eat. These two will go on and on for a while. They'll let us talk once they wind down. It might be a while since I know Josh is pretty excited because he texted me in all caps. He knows better."

Smiling, Josh got up to refill his and Morgan's drinks while Ty and Ripley began eating.

Morgan said, "Hurry, honey! I have to wait until you're back, y'know."

They all laughed.

When Josh sat back down, Morgan immediately said, "So. You two hooked up." She playfully wiggled her fingers at them. "How long *have* you two been seeing each other?"

Calmly drinking some tea first, Ty replied, "A while."

Josh asked, "Why keep it a secret?"

Ty answered, "It's not, and we weren't. It was just easier to keep it between ourselves. If we went our separate ways, then no one would be bothered or upset for either of us. Plus, there'd be less barn gossip and endless speculation."

Ripley interrupted, "That's not wholly true. It's because we didn't want to be grilled like high schoolers caught outside of curfew."

Ty grinned at her, his eyes filled with humor. "I thought it was because you didn't want to be seen as one of my many loyal and faithful groupies?" He teased her about one of their Phoenix conversations.

Ripley chuckled. "That too!"

Morgan and Josh laughed.

Josh drawled out, "Aww... Now, Ripley, we wouldn't grill either one of you guys. We like you both too much!"

Her raised eyebrow plainly said she didn't believe him.

Josh smiled broadly. "Okay, *maybe* a little. It's just a surprise. Morgan thought she sensed something but wasn't sure. Honestly, we both *like* the idea of you two as a couple. Morgan knows you better than I do, Ripley, but I really like what I know of you so far!"

A chip in her hand, Ripley asked, "You were talking about us behind our backs? How rude." She tried to sound appalled, but her new friends knew she was teasing.

Morgan smiled. "Only in a good way. I seriously like you and have from the start. You've been *such* a help with the horses. You have a natural sense with them, and they trust you. Look at Cappy!

"You get along with people, you pay your rent on time, you take care of yourself and your things, you keep the area around your RV clean as a whistle. You work, and you're responsible. You have a great sense of humor, and it seems like a good head on your shoulders. Josh says you're a keeper because you take out the trash, and you're pretty."

Josh laughed as he put his arm around his wife's shoulders. Ripley and Ty laughed, knowing this was all in good fun.

Ripley mused, "You two have been pretty chatty."

Ty grinned as he looked at Josh. "Is that your only stipulation on who I date? That she takes out the trash and be attractive?" He took another bite of his sub.

"Doesn't hurt," Josh replied cheerfully. "Besides, it worked for me!"

They laughed.

Morgan persisted on learning their details, at least some of them. "So, how'd you get together? And when, exactly?"

Ty shook his head, pointed his finger at his longtime friend. "Now *that's* a secret!"

Chapter 21

Since she'd caught them, she wasn't letting them off the hook so easily.

Morgan prodded again. "Okay, you've been dating for a while. Is this just a for-fun thing, or is it more like a could-be-serious-thing? Are you an item or a fling?"

Neither Ty nor Ripley answered her.

Josh spoke up, "Well, in their defense, Morg, that's an impossible question for either to answer in front of the other. You're putting them both on the spot, aren't you? I'd have to say neither of them really know yet, anyway, as their relationship is too fresh. Ask something else."

"True enough." She tried again. "Ripley, you said you weren't planning on staying for long. You never said how long you were planning on staying. In my eyes, you can stay as long as you'd like. You're business to me as well as being a nice person I'd like to call a friend. Now that you're dating my best friend, I just have to ask you... What are your intentions?"

Ripley choked on her sub. Reaching over, Ty whacked and then rubbed her back with a small grin on his face. Stalling, Ripley took her time chewing and finally swallowed. She took a drink, considering how to answer.

Glancing at Josh, who smiled at her with his brown eyes lit with humor, Ripley asked, "Shouldn't she be asking the guy that question? Who asks the *woman* that question?"

Ty teased, "That sounds kinda sexist, Ripley. Aren't we against that type of thing?"

Ripley rolled her eyes, but she also had to admit he had a point. It can't be double standards.

Josh shrugged. "Well, in this case, the *guy* is her longtime friend. She probably already knows his intentions, more or less. *You* are the new person here. My wife is just an equal opportunity kind of person."

The three friends waited expectantly for her answer.

Ripley looked at Ty and said, "These cookies better be worth this!"

He laughed as he reached down and patted her leg. "They are."

Finally, Ripley said carefully, "It's too early for either one of us to know for sure. That's what dating someone is all about, isn't it? To see where they go from there, assuming they're working out? Not everyone does. There's only one way to know, and that's to spend time together. We just met, as we all know.

"When I have to go, Ty and I will cross that bridge at that time, but that'd be between him and me. As Josh pointed out, our relationship is new so we're moving along at our own pace." She tilted her head slightly as she looked from Josh to Morgan, adding, "I imagine just like the two of you did."

Ty caught on to her saying *when* she goes and not *if*. That bothered him, but it wasn't like she hadn't been upfront about it. He actually knew this before he even went to Phoenix, so he couldn't place any blame on her for it. His plan of action was to simply help her change her mind.

Morgan and Josh caught what she'd said too. They each threw an automatic, quick glance at Ty.

Morgan pressed her further. "When we met that day at the restaurant, I think you mentioned you could work from anywhere you wanted to. If you and my best friend became seriously involved over time and he asked you to stay here, would you?"

Although Ty felt that question was better asked by himself, he still waited for her answer. He saw Josh look at him, reading the quick flare of hope for him in his eyes.

Ripley considered before answering honestly, "If we did, then yes, I'd consider it. I don't really have a home, Morgan. I don't have anywhere specifically to go back to. There's no landing zone that's calling me back to stay there. I've been in some wonderful places, but I've never been anywhere that felt like home to me. Whether it was the place or the people, nothing has fully captured my heart to make me want to *live* there. There's a place I do go back to fairly often that'd be the closest thing to a home I have, but I have yet to feel the need *to* stay.

"At this point, I'd have to say if Ty and I decided to further our relationship, and this is where he wants to be, then I'd be hard put to argue or try to change his mind. He's happy here... I can clearly see that." She rested her hand on his knee, gave it a little squeeze. "And I mentioned to you just last week how much I liked it out here, so there's that for a possible beginning.

"But mostly, I'd never want to take anyone from what made them happy. Life's too short to not be doing what you love, where you love doing it. There's always the option of a compromise. But at this point, I'd say I'd be fine here. That could change in the future, of course. But for now, it's the truth."

Morgan nodded, breathed out a sigh of relief. "I have to say it'd break my heart if Ty ever left me and the Center, Ripley. But as a realistic adult, I have to accept the fact that maybe someday he might, for any reason. I don't own him after all. He knows how much I value him, so if he ever left, I know it'd be a very difficult decision for him. But I'd have to support him. It's his life, and I can't be selfish and want to keep him to myself. We can still be friends wherever we may live. I'm sure Josh would agree?"

Josh nodded, knowing if Ty ever did leave Morgan, it *would* break her heart. She'd mend, of course... At least to an extent. And obviously she loved him, and he wasn't going anywhere. But she and Ty's history was complicated and confidential, and no one but him knew all about it. Would Ty ever confide in Ripley about his past? If he and Ripley stayed together, would he be compelled to confide in her? At least *some* of it? Ty had to keep quite a bit to himself. *Could* he trust Ripley?

Could *they?*

Ty said, "I *do* love it here and would never want to leave. However, it's not all about me when another person and their desires or needs are involved. Compromises are a part of relationships just like Ripley said. We all know this. That's another bridge to cross if we get that far along.

"Right now, Ripley and I are still learning about the other. There's no pressure, no expectations between us at this point. And we don't want any *put* on us... from anybody. We both know we could simply drift apart and go our separate ways at any time. That's true of any relationship.

"We just plan to remain friends of some sort and not trash the other should we decide we just won't work. We may not, but we won't know if we don't try. So for now, we're just enjoying each other, and what we both can bring to the other." Looking at Ripley, he said, "And that's where communication is essential, right?"

Ripley agreed. "Absolutely. I already told Ty I'm really rusty at relationships. I'm probably going to try his patience and drive him nuts. And he may do the same to me... Probably will. Relationships are a two-way street after all. But I'm giving it my best shot to just be me, the person I am. And hopefully he's doing the same.

"And if—when—we irritate or disappoint the other, we'll have to deal with it if we feel the other is worth it. Right now, I feel he is... Which is why I'm willing to be interrogated by his best friends in a sub shop on our day off and outside my normal business hours."

She smiled at their grins before explaining, "I can accept this because I already know that you all care deeply for each other. Frankly, I'm quite envious of the relationship you all have. My friends and I are very close in some ways, but you all have something... I don't know... It's intangible, so it's hard to put into words.

"But just so we're all on the same page here, I'm just going to say it. As long as you don't get *too* involved and nosy, it's good with me. This relationship is between me and him, not me and all of you. I value my privacy very much and protect it much like Morgan said the day we met about her own. We all have our boundaries, and we all need to respect them. But you questioning me about us right now? I'm good with that."

Ty reached over, held her hand in his. "My friends are loyal, Ripley. I wouldn't expect them to act any other way. You'll learn this about them, if you haven't already. When it comes right down to the nitty gritty, they'll always be there. *We* will always be there for each other. In time, this can apply to you too. But I'm also confident enough to venture to say in some respects, it already does."

Josh nodded. "He's right. You've already shown some of your character, your compassion, and your dedication to what matters to you. You have admirable traits. As far as I can tell, you've had no reason to *try* and impress us. Maybe you're fooling all of us, but I don't think so. You came as just a short-term renter, and now here we are. Why else would you have done what you've done if that wasn't who you already really are?"

Both Morgan and Ty silently agreed as Josh went on, "We stick together. My best friend and his wife, meaning Damien and Laura, are the same. We always have room for one more loyal person. But it's a process, a position that's basically earned. We all have to work at it because all relationships take effort. We aren't a special, elite social club by any means. We're just friends in the best definition of the word. We all know what it's like to be on our own, and we prefer to know we have true friends who have our backs.

"We've all had disagreements over the years. We don't agree on everything political, things like that. But we always remember we're each entitled to our own feelings and opinions. We just accept each other for who, and what, we are.

"Fighting and arguing over something isn't going to make the other person just instantly agree anyway. You can never sway a person over in a negative war of words. They'll just dig in their heels whether they really want to or not. Egos can be a terrible thing. Sometimes the details can be the real issue, but not the big picture. We look for our common ground.

"And while we like to challenge each other intellectually, we don't want discord. We all want to grow old together, knowing we all have someone who has our back even then. Rocking away on a porch, sharing tales and stories, is our end goal.

"In the case of Damien and Laura, if something ever happened to them, Morgan and I would take in Sasha. It's already legal. It's been cleared with their families because we've talked it all out. We make a point to spend time with Sasha so she knows us, and we know her. As her parents, we'd be the same age as her own, and we can keep them alive with her because we're such close friends. We know how they'd like her raised, what goals they want her to reach someday.

"We're family. It takes work, forgiveness, patience, and humor. The best relationships are worth all it takes to maintain them."

Ripley nodded. What would it be like to have friends like this, knowing there was someone there always backing you? Even if you're dead? Just because they loved you and cared about you? She wanted to be a part of this so badly, it made her heart ache.

But Josh was right. Relationships like that are built upon trust and history. It all took time. There really wasn't any other way. Time is the biggest resource of all and often the most wasted.

Morgan saw Ripley's facial expression, and it made her own heart ache. She had an instinctive notion that Ripley was lonely, and possibly even a little bit lost. Looking for a home for herself and still not finding it, no matter what she did, who she helped, or where she went. A person could be strong, independent, and smart and still be lost and lonely. Because she herself had been in a very similar situation, Morgan knew she could only be there for her.

Trying to get their lunch back on a lighthearted note, Morgan said, "Well, I'm satisfied! I wish the best for you two. If it doesn't work out, then it just doesn't work out. Like Ripley said, that's what dating is all about. And I really hope we can all remain friends no matter what happens. And that we can work through any awkwardness if there is any. If it *does* work out, I'll be so happy for you!" She took a sip of her drink before saying to Josh, "Now then, perhaps we should let them eat in peace?"

Ty said dryly, "That's *it?* That was pretty short and sweet, wasn't it?" He took a bite of a chocolate chip cookie as he waited for her to reply.

Ripley nudged him. "Maybe on *your* side it was. She didn't ask *you* anything!"

They all smiled at her comment.

Morgan shrugged her shoulders as she took another sip of her lemonade. Turning to her husband, she said, “I’m so glad we just happened to run into these two today! I think it’s time for us to get back to work now though. Do you think your truck is done at the shop by now?”

“If not, it should be pretty soon. Give me a lift, and we’ll see if it’s ready. We can stop at the store on the way.” Turning back to Ty and Ripley, he asked, “We’ll still see you both at The Neon Moon tonight, right?”

Ripley smiled. “Sure. We’re not skipping town!” As Josh and Morgan prepared to leave, Ripley added wryly, “And have fun talking about us after you leave.”

Josh grinned. “Oh, we will.”

After they left, Ripley released a long breath. With a grin at Ty, she confided, “Okay. A little rough there in the beginning. But overall, I think that went better than I expected!”

Ty nodded. “I told you we’d survive.” He leaned over and kissed her temple. He then flashed a grin before adding, “Even so, I think now is a perfect time to move. Do you have room in your RV for me?”

Chapter 22

THE NIGHT WAS FULL of surprises.

When Ty and Ripley arrived at The Neon Moon hours later, Damien and Laura were waiting in the lobby. Josh had already let Damien and Laura know of the new dating couple so they had to go through a second mini-interrogation. And Ripley finally got to meet Damien. It made her inexplicably happy to meet another male friend when she didn't have hay in her hair like when she'd met Josh and Ty. She still couldn't believe that'd happened.

Josh and Morgan finally arrived with Toby and Maya walking in right behind them. Since The Neon Moon was a hangout for all of the Harmony Hills crew, Toby and Maya had just decided to stop by on their own. When Josh saw them pull up, he invited them to join them.

Deciding to just eat in the bar area, they found a table large enough to accommodate them all. Ripley looked around, now understanding what Morgan had meant the day they'd met. Thursday was karaoke night, and the place was already buzzing. She'd forgotten Morgan had told her that, and since she hated singing in public, she hoped to bypass that part of the entertainment for the night. She would've chosen somewhere else if she'd remembered the karaoke part! Well, that didn't mean *she* had to sing though.

Waitresses tend to love regulars, so Margo was all smiles when she came over to their friendly table. Ty introduced Ripley to Margo, who was a lot shorter than Jo. Ripley was intrigued that Margo's hair was almost as long as she was tall. When Margo left them, she tried not to stare.

Laura noticed, saying, "I know what you're thinking as I had the same look on my face, Ripley!" She laughed as her eyes followed Margo for a moment. "Margo looks so defenseless too. But let me tell you, there's a lot of shazam packed into that little body of hers. And she does not put up with any crap from anyone!"

Ty grinned. "Not true. She puts up with ours all the time."

Laura relented. "To an extent, yes, but we're all good-natured people. She doesn't mind the friendly crap. Plus, we always tip her really good."

Ripley said, "Meaning you pay her off."

Laura laughed. "Shamelessly!"

When Margo served their drinks and took their food orders, Maya eyed Laura. After Margo left again, Maya continued to watch Laura, wondering why she looked different. And noticed she and Damien kept tossing a look back and forth to each other. And wondered why she wasn't... Suddenly, Maya blurted out, "Oh my gosh! You're not drinking alcohol tonight... Are you..." she let her voice trail off.

Damien and Laura both smiled broadly as Damien put his arm around his wife's shoulders. Laura nodded, happiness shining from her eyes. "Yep. Sasha is going to be a big sister in about seven more months! Next March is our expected month to begin diaper duty all over again. We found out for sure just yesterday and were planning on telling you all tonight. You beat us to it, Maya!"

As Maya looked so apologetic, Laura quickly reassured her, "It's okay. Don't feel like you let the cat out of the bag. It's fine!" Even though her eyes were filled with excitement, Laura also looked hesitant. She added quietly, "Well, we *wanted* to tell you, but it's still early yet. You know the first trimester is iffy... And with our past difficulties, it's scary to say anything, you know, in case..."

Damien pulled her closer to his side in comfort. "But we're among supportive friends. If we can't rely on these guys for support, who *can* we lean on?" He kissed her temple. "We'll all be fine, honey."

Only Josh, Morgan, and Ty really knew how many years they'd been trying to have a family. They all figured Sasha was their one miracle baby, and the pregnancy had been really hard on Laura. Hearing she was pregnant again was both a happy surprise and a big worry to their friends.

Morgan grabbed her hand, squeezed it in understanding, saying softly, "You're not alone, Laura. You know that, right? We'll be here for you."

Laura mouthed a silent "Thank you" to her friend.

With congratulations coming from everyone, the happy, expectant couple settled into answering questions about the baby, and Sasha's reaction to it.

Laura shook her head. With some hesitation, she explained, "We're not telling Sasha anything at all. If I lose the baby, how do I explain that to a little girl in a way she could understand? If she thinks she's going to be a big sister, and is actually excited about that, then if I..." She shook her head again, took a deep breath.

Damien squeezed his wife's hand in support before saying, "Laura and I decided to just not say anything at all. So if you all happen to be around Sasha, please, please don't say anything at all to her, okay? *When*," he squeezed Laura's hand again as he looked into her eyes, "the baby comes, then it'll just be a surprise for her.

"As Laura gets bigger and bigger," he said, teasing his wife to lighten the mood, "we'll just say Mom's gaining some weight, but just not why. If Sasha was older, much older, then we'd tell her. But she's so young, why burden her little innocent mind with possible worries?"

Josh rested his hand on his childhood friend's shoulder and looked at them. "We understand. We've got your backs like always. You both know we're all here for you, anytime, for anything. Let's just enjoy the news, the moment, and think only of positives here, okay?"

Damien and Laura both nodded. She said, "It's scary. Since we weren't planning on this, we're just hoping it happened for a reason. We're not telling anybody at all. No co-workers, and no family. We just want to keep this under wraps, you know?"

With confidence, Morgan said, "Laura, you know it's more than possible to have this baby. You already accomplished it because you have your little girl. Concentrate on that, and know it can be done. Not everything is in our control, but it doesn't always have to be. Everything happens for a reason, even if we don't know the *why*. And I know that's no consolation, but sometimes it's the only way to see things. Don't put any pressure on yourself.

"You've got Damien to take care of you, plus all of us. You guys just ask if you need *anything*." She looked at everyone there. "And we'll all respect your wishes and keep this to ourselves. Tell no one at The Center or anywhere else."

Everyone nodded. With Ripley being new to this group, she didn't know about the heartaches this couple had gone through, but she was catching on quickly. And although she herself had never wanted kids of her own, she could empathize with those who did. It had to be brutal, to wonder on a daily basis if you could bring a new life into the world, or lose it... Not having the ability to save it. She couldn't imagine the trauma and heartache.

Changing the subject, Damien asked Toby, "So when are you and Maya here going to tie the knot and make it all official? You've been together for years and engaged for a couple of months now. What're you waiting for?"

Toby replied, "Nothing in particular. I guess we can tell them now, right, Maya?" She winked at him so he continued, announcing, "We're already married."

There was silence at the table. Morgan finally choked out, "*What?* You got married and didn't even tell us? We weren't invited? How *could* you? I don't believe you."

Josh studied the couple before saying, "No way you two did something like that. If you did, you either just got fired or at least got a huge pay cut!"

Laura and Damien echoed Morgan's questions, but not Ty and Ripley.

Ripley was too new to the group to be that upset. She also wondered if it were true as she remembered their reactions when they announced their actual engagement that morning in the kitchen. The joy and support they got from their coworkers and friends made it hard for her to believe they'd leave them all out of their actual wedding. She just couldn't see them eloping.

Ty didn't believe it simply because he was sure one of them would've let it slip. If they'd told Alexis—which he was positive they would've done right away—*she* would've let it slip within five minutes of getting out of her car. He also figured they were too excited to *get* married to not want to tell everyone they *were*.

With a shrug and a pointed look at her fiancé, Maya said sternly, "I *told* you they'd react this way. Are you going to listen to me next time?"

Toby smiled and kissed her hand. Keeping it in his own, Toby admitted, "Okay, okay... We *didn't* get married yet. If it was up to me, we would've been to Vegas and back by now. Maya thought that was too unromantic though. She insisted we find a time for you guys to 'share in our happiness' with us." Toby raised his fingers and crooked them like quotation marks when he said the last. He laughed when Maya playfully smacked his arm.

Seriously but with a twinkle in her eyes, Ripley said, "You were wise to wait, Young Ones. Otherwise, you were looking at an untimely demise, I think. I'm *so* glad I can just enjoy the evening now."

They laughed, appreciating her humor.

Maya said, "Well, we're keeping it pretty small. Maybe just around twenty people or so... if that. We picked the date." She paused, then blurted out, "It's two weeks from now. So, um, Morgan, we both need to request at least a few days off, if not more, if you can spare us." She smiled at their boss.

Morgan raised her eyebrows. Grinning, she said, "You'd better hope there's nothing major on the books already!"

Maya explained, "It's open. We just checked the book again. It's the only day no rides have been booked yet. And everyone is in town, including you. You're normally off judging shows or something around this time, but you're not so..." Her voice trailed off. "Do you think you can do this for us? It's a Sunday. We'd really like everyone there. I mean, *you're* the reason we met."

Morgan nodded. "I'll do my best to make it happen." She smiled and said, "My wedding gift to you is each other!"

Ty said, "Hey! *I* was the one who gave them permission *to* date!"

Toby smiled. "You just gave us permission to not have to sneak around... Dad."

They all laughed at his remark.

Humor in his eyes, Ty asked, "*Two weeks?* Not months or years? That's not much notice. What if *we* aren't available in two weeks?"

Maya gave everyone there a hard look. "You *make* yourselves available. Got it?"

Ty laughed. "Got it."

Laura teased, "You're not gonna be a bridezilla, are you? You kinda sound like one already."

Ripley added, "If you need something, you *ask* for it. Keep in mind if you turn into a bridezilla, we'll all find something else to do that day!"

Maya smiled. "It's crazy to think we were coworkers that turned into friends, then boyfriend/girlfriend. Then we turned into fiancée/fiancé... Now it's bride and groom..." Maya gasped, "I'm having an identity crisis!"

They all laughed at her as Toby hugged her to his side.

Maya smiled, looking from Ty to Ripley. "You're coming, right, Ripley? You'll still be here in two weeks? We were going to invite you anyway, so don't think we see you as just a plus-one now. It's actually another reason why we picked such a quick date. Will you still be here?"

Ripley sighed. "Yes... As far as I know. I *do* have to leave for Texas soon, but I can put it off until after you're married. Just don't delay it any, okay?" She gave Ty's hand a reassuring squeeze.

Toby nodded. "You bet. We need to get this thing over and done with!" He instantly howled when Maya grabbed his knee and squeezed it hard. "*Maya!*"

She smiled sweetly. "What he *meant* to say was he can't wait to marry me and build a great future and life together."

Everyone laughed.

Straight-faced, Damien told Toby, "Okay. You're gonna need a few pointers from us married men. We obviously need to get together really soon."

Margo came then and, with a couple of trips, delivered their dinner plates. She took another drink order and made sure they were all satisfied before heading away to her other tables.

Throughout the informal dinner, Ripley could feel again the bond these friends had made over the years. They had history between them... Which was convenient for her as they all insisted on regaling her with stories about Ty. He took it all in stride.

Soon after they finished eating and Margo had topped off their drinks again, singers began signing up for karaoke once the DJ announced he was set up and ready to go. Morgan nudged Ripley, asking, "How about you? You game?"

"Uh, not really. I hate to sing in public. Remember I told you that when we met? I can speak in public... But singing? No. Hard no."

Laura joined in, insisting, "We all have to! We're pals here. It's how we bond. Besides, it's so much fun. You just gotta go up!"

Ripley smiled and shook her head. "No. But I will fully support each one of you."

"For Ty?" Laura pleaded.

"Definitely not. He'd run the other way!" she joked.

"I'd never do that, Sugar."

"You say that now," she retorted. She took hold of his hand that was resting over her shoulder, lacing their fingers together.

Laura grinned, determined to win. She batted her pretty eyes, saying, "For me? An expectant mother? As a congratulations gift? A good luck charm?"

Ripley actually shuddered as she looked at the pleading blonde. Ty felt it and laughed. Kissing her hair, he whispered in her ear, "You're gonna have to do it at some point. You might as well get it over with!"

Cornered and coerced, Ripley finally agreed. Laura's face shone like a beacon.

Damien smiled and said proudly, "That's my wife! She has a way with people, doesn't she?"

"So did the Nazis," Ripley said under her breath.

But Ty heard her and laughed again. When she looked up into his amused eyes, he smiled and shook his head at her. She rolled her eyes in resignation.

The women went up first to the DJ's book, flipping through the pages of available songs. Morgan, Maya, and Laura picked theirs fairly quickly, filled out the paper slips and tossed them into the little box for the DJ to pull from. Ripley took her time, her nerves on edge, as the three women patiently waited with her and suggested songs. She kept shaking her head, dread making her stomach feel tight.

Feeling her phone vibrate in her purse she still had slung across her body, she automatically checked it. Julia. She always answered for the spunky Julia. "Hey! Save me, Jules!"

"What are you into *this* time, Ripley?"

"I'm with some friends, and they're making me sing. In public! In a bar!"

Morgan, Maya, and Laura laughed good-naturedly at her.

Julia did too. "No sympathy on this end, Rip. You've got a great voice! I don't know why you're always hiding it." Pause. "Hey, is this a girls night out thing, or are there men around?"

"It's co-ed," Ripley replied, speaking loudly over the music.

"Is Ty around?" Julia asked casually.

"Yeah."

"Really? Let me talk to your handsome fella. Give the phone to him."

"Jules..."

"Come on, girl. Let me talk to him. Now!" Julia prodded her.

"Okay... Hang on. He's at the table, and I'm not... Give me a minute here." Turning to her new friends, she said, "I'll be back in a second." Seeing their skeptical looks of not believing her, she added, "Promise."

Ripley squeezed through the crowd to get back to their table. Her phone to her ear, she tried to find out why Julia wanted to talk to Ty. When she stopped beside him, the men's conversation stopped. They all looked up at her expectantly. Resting her hand on Ty's shoulder, she said, "Julia is insisting she talk to you. She won't talk to me. Would you mind?"

Josh asked curiously, "Who's Julia?"

"My best friend as well as a business associate."

Puzzled, Damien asked, "How does she know Ty?"

Ripley grinned at Damien. "What can I say? The man gets around."

Ty grinned as he took the phone from her hand. He teased his friends, "*I'm* still a man of mystery." He spoke into the phone, covering his other ear to hear better in the loud bar. "Julia? Ty here. Do you miss me?"

Julia's laugh and excitement came through the line. "Ty, I'm so glad you two are still together! Can you talk, or can she hear?"

"We're in a bar on karaoke night, Julia. No one can hear!"

Laughing, she said, "Go someplace quiet. Don't let your girl follow."

He got up, saying to his friends, "I can't hear her. I'll be right back. Ripley, go pick out your song while I chat with her for a minute." He playfully shoved her back toward the other women who were still waiting for her. She looked more than a little reluctant to leave his side. "Go on now!"

Although wondering what Julia wanted with Ty, Ripley dutifully walked back to Morgan, Laura, and Maya to find an unwanted song.

"What's on your mind, Julia?" Ty asked from a quieter cove.

"I just wanted to say I'm glad you two are dating. Ripley's a wonderful person, but she doesn't always let people in to know how wonderful she is. Do you know how great she is?"

"I'm learning more and more every day."

Julia paused, choosing her words with care. "I can't break our confidences, but I just want to say you're very good for her. She needs a man like I think you are, so be patient with her... All right? Don't give up on her. She's... complicated in some ways. But she'll open up to you more and more as she learns to trust you. She listens to her gut more than anything else, more than *anyone* else, so it may take her some time to really be open with you."

"I'm a patient man."

"Good! I hope to see you guys again sometime soon. Since I was sitting here thinking about her, I wanted to see how she was doing. And if she was still in Arizona." Julia paused again before saying straight out, "Rip's supposed to head to Texas in the very near future. Did she tell you this yet?"

"She's mentioned it." Ty's hand tensed a little on the phone. Always talk of her leaving.

"Ty, do you know why I know you're special?" Julia asked sincerely.

"No, but I'm all ears," he replied.

Julia explained, "The biggest reason is because she's still there. Ripley's never been known to stay at a stop this long. She's been there months now. She's staying there this long for you."

Ty wanted to believe Ripley's best friend. But since she wasn't here, how could Julia be so certain? "I'd like to believe that's the case, but do you know about the rescued horses? How the one is incredibly bonded to Ripley? I have a feeling she's staying as much for the horse as me. This horse and her have a remarkable bond."

"Yes, that's true. Cappy, right?"

"Yes."

Julia mused out loud, "She probably could've made other arrangements in regards to Cappy. But yes... You're right. She's stayed there for him too. It would've broken her heart to leave him unless she knew he was on the road to a better life.

"But I know my friend. You've... intrigued... her, and that's hard to do. I'd bet everything I have that the *equal* reason she's stayed there this long is you. You're inadvertently opening up other life choices for her, and she's obviously open to considering them. This is heady news!"

"You think so?"

"I'm sure of it! Another thing that points to you is that she took today off... as well as all future Thursdays. I honestly can't think of another time when Ripley took an extended, regular full day off for any reason. I've told her to over the years to balance out her life more, but she's always wanted to be available for everyone.

"Anyway, she told me this only a couple of days ago in a personal email. She also did an email blast to everyone saying she was taking off on Thursdays until further notice. And to find out she's with you makes me very happy!"

Ty couldn't help but smile. Hearing this news from Ripley's best friend really meant something to him. He felt he and Ripley had a whole lot going for them. This information seemed to confirm his feelings. Their relationship was still so new though. He was an adult who knew things could change in an instant.

Julia said seriously, "I trust you to not mess with my girl, Ty. It'd be out of her character to be with a man who would, but people can get duped so easily. You don't seem the type of man to do that, but one never knows.

"But our business is a people business, and we tend to learn to read people. You just didn't strike me as anything but decently good, interesting, and fun. You didn't come across as a player or a liar to me. You better not hurt my friend by using her. Don't make a liar or a cynic out of me, Ty."

"I'd never deliberately hurt her, Julia. Either our relationship will work out, or it won't. But it won't be from lack of our doing what we can to make it work. And doing it by being ourselves. With her traveling all over the place, we're just trying to build a foundation while she's here. I don't want her to leave. Since I knew she traveled when we first met, I have to accept that she will. We'll cross that bridge at some point soon, it looks like."

Apparently satisfied, Julia sighed before saying, "You're a good man, Ty. Just give it time, all right?" Julia decided to move on to another subject. "She mentioned she's to sing in public. She *hates* to do this more than anything else I know about. If she's stalling over a song title, pick one for her. She has this voice that's just beautiful, but she rarely sings in public. It's crazy. Her confidence isn't strong in this area so you need to encourage her.

"She's a great networker, a savvy business gal, but she doesn't like to sing in public. I don't know why, but just don't let her back out of it."

"I'm not. Another friend coerced her, so she's stuck now!"

He could hear the smile in Julia's voice when she said, "That's the best way. It's also about the *only* way! Let me give you some songs for her to do." She listed songs she'd heard Ripley unwillingly do before, but that she did well.

Ty chuckled at her exuberance. "I'll do that. I wish you were here. Thank you for the tips. You obviously know your friend well. She's so confident in everything else, it does seem odd she isn't in this area. But we'll work her out of it!" He smiled when he heard Julia chuckling. "Well, it was great talking with you again. We should talk more soon." He looked through the doorway at his friends. "Do you want me to go get her now?"

Julia laughed loudly. "You bet I do, but not for me. You go get her for yourself! Sweep that girl off her feet, but don't you *dare* drop her on her ass! My girl deserves respect. You be sure you give it to her. You hear me?"

Ty laughed before clarifying, "Yes, ma'am... But I *meant* did *you* want to talk to her now?"

"Of course not. It's her day off, so I wouldn't want to bug her!"

"Then why'd you call?" he asked with a grin.

"You're smarter than that. You know it was to make sure she was with you. That's all I need to know. Now, hang up this phone, and go have some fun with her!" Julia promptly hung up.

Ty figured that was her way of saying goodbye and smiled. With a light heart, Ty stood there thinking. Before he changed his mind, he scrolled through Ripley's *Contacts* to add Julia's information to his own phone.

Just in case he ever needed to call someone who knew her.

Chapter 23

THEY'D DESERTED HER, AND she couldn't be happier. Ripley was hoping to stall long enough they'd change their minds about making her sing. Or so she could come up with an alternative plan... like slipping out the door. The only reason she hadn't yet was because she wasn't a coward. And because Ty drove them and had the keys.

When Ty re-joined his friends, Ripley wasn't there. Morgan smiled and pointed to her across the room. He made his way through the crowd to her. "Having trouble, Sugar?"

She nodded. "I *hate* to sing in public. Seriously." After turning the pages over and over, she tried another tactic. "How about we go somewhere, just the two of us, and make out like teenagers instead?"

Ty rubbed her back. "We'll definitely do that later. Relax, Sugar. Singing is just talking in a rhythm. You talk in front of people, right?" When she nodded, he asked, "Then what's the big deal?"

"It just *is*, that's all. People don't usually judge, or even remember, you for a speaking voice unless you sound like Minnie Mouse or Goofy. But they always remember someone's singing voice!"

He thought about it, coming to the conclusion she wasn't wrong. "Well, we're all friends. If you stink, we'll still like you. If you don't, we'll like that much more about you. You're a winner in either case. I hardly think you'll get run out of the bar. Have you heard some of the others tonight?"

She turned on him, a glimmer of triumph in her eyes. "A-ha! *See* what I mean? You just proved my point!"

He laughed and shrugged his shoulders. "And yet they survived. You will too."

She went back to going through the book. After a minute, she glanced at him again. In an exasperated tone of voice, she asked, "Can't I just pay all of you off instead? Like you pay off Margo for putting up with you? I can pay cash!"

Ty flashed a wide grin at her. "No. We can't be bought because we have ethics."

"So you're saying Margo doesn't?" she shot back. "Maybe I should tell her that in case she doesn't know."

He laughed. "Sugar, you're thinking about this way too much. Just pick a song you know, sing it, and it'll be all over. Isn't there a song you sing in the shower? Or driving down the road? Pick something you know that makes you happy, or that you're comfortable with. This isn't a singing competition you have to win."

He kissed her temple, leaving his lips there for a couple of extra seconds before he handed back her phone. Those sweet, tender touches always made her heart skip a beat.

Snapping out of her stupor when the DJ announced a new singer to come up, she asked, "Didn't Julia want to talk to me?"

"No." With that, he winked at her and walked back to their table.

ONE BY ONE, THEIR names were randomly called to sing. Each time her name wasn't called, Ripley breathed a sigh of relief. The place was pretty busy so she was hoping her name simply wouldn't be picked. With some luck, the DJ would pack up and leave or the bar would close. She was impressed at how well her new friends all sang... which just added more pressure on her. They could at least carry a tune. She was enjoying herself because they were up there, and she wasn't. Some of the other singers she didn't know made her cringe inside.

Ty kept ordering more alcohol for her to keep her loose. Morgan noticed what he was doing and shook her head.

When Ty went to use the bathroom, Josh followed him. Ty glanced at him when he followed him through the door. "What? Are we girls now?"

Josh smiled, his eyes alight with humor. "Hey, I just wanted to say if you keep pouring the booze down your girl, she won't be able to stand up straight let alone walk onto the stage and sing coherently!"

Ty grinned broadly. "You're not paying enough attention. She's nursing them and barely that. I think she's on to me!"

Josh shook his head in mock dismay. "I just never pictured you to be a guy that'd liquor up his girl for a good time."

"I'm not, and you know it." Ty shook his head. He walked over to the sinks and washed his hands. "She just needs a little courage in a shot!"

"More like a pitcher," Josh replied as he washed his hands.

As they walked back, Ty stopped at the little table with the song books on it. He motioned for Josh to wait with him while another person filled out a card, slipped it in the box and walked away. Flipping through the songs, he found what he was looking for. Filling out a few of the slips of paper, he tossed them into the box.

Josh's mouth gaped open. "Ty! You can't do that to her!"

"Sure I can. It's taking too long. This just gives her more of a chance to get up there sooner rather than later. It'll ease her anxiety if she just gets it over with. Besides, as much money as I'm spending on her drinks tonight, I'll be poor soon."

Seeing the humor in Ty's eyes, Josh still warned him. "You're taking a gamble, you know."

"That's all life is, Josh. One big gamble, and I'm ready to throw the dice."

Ripley was talking to Laura about anything but her pregnancy when she heard the DJ call her name. She froze in mid-sentence.

Laura smiled at her. "Go on, Ripley! You can't be any worse than anyone else!"

"You're a real support, Laura."

With their smiles propelling her forward, Ripley reluctantly went to the stage, taking the mic from the DJ.

"You ready?" he asked her.

Shaking her head, she replied, "I'd rather be executed."

He laughed good-naturedly and reminded her of the song title.

"That's not the song I picked out."

He handed her the paper. "Is this you? Maybe I called the wrong person. Are there two of you?"

Ripley read the slip of paper. Twice. "That's my name all right. There's no way there are two of that name in here. It's just not my handwriting."

The DJ smiled. He'd seen this happen before many times. "Are you still game?"

Ripley shot a look over at Ty, who was just watching her with a casual look on his handsome face. She saw Josh lean over to say something to him. Ty nodded, smiling as he replied. Josh shook his head at him before leaning back and talking to Morgan. Morgan shot a look of reprimand at Ty. He just smiled back.

Game? Yeah, two could play this game, Ripley thought. The challenge got her blood pumping through her veins. Turning to the DJ, she said, "You bet. Crank this puppy up!"

With a wide grin at her sudden spunkiness, the DJ cued the song. Announcing her, he said, "Okay, for the first time ever on stage tonight we have Ripley singing 'Fire'! Let's all give her a big hand and a warm Neon Moon welcome!"

The audience did as requested as Ripley walked over so she could see the screen. She smiled a bit nervously and wiped her sweaty palms on her shorts. Her look changed to a slight glare when her gaze rested on Ty. He just smiled back at her and raised his thumbs in the air for support.

The music began and Ripley just focused on it, shutting out everything else.

When she began singing, her friends were surprised. They assumed she'd sound awful based on her reticence to sing in public and were only prepared for that... Not for her voice to be what it was. As she continued, they broke out in a raucous roar. She was really getting into by then, using her shoulders and swaying to the beat. She even threw sultry looks at Ty now and then. Not needing to see the words, Ripley walked across the stage, playing to the crowd. When it ended, the whole crowd was on its feet, cheering and whistling. She smiled before she walked back to the DJ.

The DJ took the mic as she held it out to him with a shaky hand. "Wow... That was awesome! Why would you rather have been executed?"

"Because it would've saved me from having to kill the man who signed me up because murder is still illegal."

The DJ laughed before he called out the next name. When she reached their table, Ty grabbed her, kissing her soundly. She wrapped her arms around his neck and kissed him back, much to the delight of their friends.

When she pulled away, she reprimanded him. "Don't you *ever* do that again, mister!"

Unrepentant, he grinned as he still held her. "Sorry, Sugar, but I plan on kissing you like that a whole lot more!"

Their friends heard, of course, and laughed.

Ripley pulled out of his arms, saying, "You know what I'm talking about."

But she smiled and accepted the congratulations from her friends. Their enthusiastic and genuine responses made her think maybe she wasn't all that bad. But she still didn't want to go back up there and do it again anytime soon. As in ever. She told Laura she'd better have twins because she wasn't doing any more singing favors for her. Laura laughed and hugged her, thanking her for the good luck.

By the end of the night, Ripley decided she was never, *ever*, going to let Julia and Ty talk again. Not unless she was there to monitor their conversation from start to finish. Being called back up on stage two more times to sing, one of those times to sing the song she herself had chosen, Ripley was over her fear of singing in public. At least for tonight.

Ripley was slightly perturbed Ty hadn't respected her wishes about singing. But neither had her best friend. Or her new friends. She wasn't sure who to talk to first about it. She figured she was overthinking it, and it wasn't even a battle to fight. It was harmless. And it wasn't like she hadn't done it before. What'd be the point in blowing it out of proportion?

It was Morgan who began calling them Riptide. Like a celebrity couple, she combined their names. It caught on immediately among their group, and they had a feeling it'd stick.

As the night went on, Ripley realized she was having a fantastic time. She genuinely felt welcomed and comfortable in their group. She felt accepted.

She was also pleasantly surprised that by some sort of silent agreement, they'd all stopped drinking alcohol completely. Everyone switched from their mixed drinks, beer, and shots to soft drinks and tea. Obviously, Laura had been drinking tea or water the entire night. This puzzled Ripley until she recalled Morgan telling her months ago that none of them would drive if they'd been drinking. It simply wasn't worth the risks.

The way Ripley saw it, that made Laura their Designated Driver if someone couldn't drive home safely. But being responsible, they'd *all* stopped drinking alcohol well in advance and switched to non-alcoholic drinks. She'd never seen people do this, at least not an entire group.

Ripley pondered this new development. She was against drinking and driving wholeheartedly. She *had* wondered earlier about them driving home since everyone except Laura was drinking. And once she came to the conclusion they'd all stopped drinking alcohol on purpose, she wondered if they were just as safety conscious as she was? Or was it because they were almost all business owners in this community and therefore pretty well-known? Were they consciously protecting their reputations and their businesses?

In the end, she didn't care. But she had to admit to herself, it impressed the socks off her. The business friends she'd have dinners with were specifically chosen because they were also responsible. One of the biggest reasons she didn't go out in groups was because of the drinking—and the inevitable after-drinking results. She didn't want to deal with drunks, plain and simple. And dealing with all the ridiculous drama that came with group outings, especially when people had been drinking, made her balk at going out with them in the first place. But this new group of friends wanted the night to end on a safe note too. This in turn made her *want* to spend more time with them.

As Ty drove back to his place, where her car was still parked from that morning, Ripley would look at him from time to time. The longer she was around him, the more she liked. He honestly didn't do anything that truly drove her nuts or got on her nerves. At least, not yet. He wasn't perfect, but he didn't do anything that really annoyed her. And except for her not wanting to sing in public issue, he'd shown true respect to her in every other area.

And everyone there had *also* pushed her to sing, she reminded herself again. It truly wasn't a major deal in the scheme of things after all. He still respected her in everything else. No other man she'd known had done that. None.

She wondered how they'd be affected when she left for Texas. It was going to be soon now. And what about Cappy? Was he truly in a better position to trust men now? Would it even make a difference in the long run? She fervently hoped so. She dreaded leaving both man and horse. The deep heartache surprised her.

It'd occurred to her before that both she and the abused horse had been repeatedly and deeply hurt by men, effectively erasing their trust in them. Wasn't it odd that both Cappy and she herself were now struggling to put their trust and hope in the same man?

With an inward sigh, she knew she had a lot to think about when it came to Ty Stanton from Arizona. She finally closed her eyes, resting her head on the truck seat.

Sensing her inner struggle, Ty reached over, lacing their fingers together. He just held her hand in silent comfort and support as he drove down the road.

Chapter 24

EVERYONE KNEW THE NEXT two weeks would fly by. With so much to do and to plan for, everyone was kept busy from dawn to dusk.

For Ripley, it was particularly bittersweet knowing she'd be leaving soon. She was so thankful she'd met Morgan that day as her life had truly been changed. And while she felt it was for the better, she still resisted the changes happening too quickly.

The other woman whose life was changing was Maya. Unlike Ripley, Maya was ready to further her relationship with her guy. Of course, she and Toby had been dating for a number of years now.

They originally thought to just continue living together, worrying that getting married would somehow ruin what they had. They'd seen it happen to so many others, they didn't want to take the chance. But they finally decided to get married for themselves. After all, they also knew many happily married couples like Morgan and Josh and Damien and Laura.

The day after their wedding announcement, Ripley took a break from her work and headed up to Sunset Ridge. Sitting on a picnic table with Maya, Ripley learned she and Toby didn't really have the extra money to take a honeymoon. Neither was upset about it, not really, but Ripley knew all newlyweds wanted one. Who'd prefer to go back to work rather than going on a honeymoon?

Considering an idea, Ripley asked for places they'd like to go to someday if they could. As Ripley soon found out, Maya had lots of places in mind.

Waiting for Maya to take out her next ride, and knowing Toby was still out on another, Ripley met with Morgan when they were alone. Morgan was more than willing to work with her on a little project for the newlyweds. They called Laura for her assistance, knowing they didn't have much time to pull this together. Pulling their personnel records, Morgan gave Laura all the information she needed. The three agreed it was best to keep it as a surprise for the engaged couple.

Ty and Ripley went on dates as often as they could though still careful to have their own personal time. Sometimes, if her work day wasn't too busy, she'd just walk up to the office and hang out with him and Morgan. Ripley was learning how the trail-riding business was run as she sat there, watching and listening when customers came in and rides were sent out and returned.

She also learned quite a bit about Ty just by watching him interact with the general public, and how he cared for the horses. It said quite a bit about his character and personality in the way he handled people and animals.

Ripley took the horses to the water troughs, and she scooped up manure to help out. She even got to groom some horses early one morning while Bo and Drew saddled them. Another night, she and Ty fed the horses themselves so the wranglers could have an early night. She was completely enjoying being hands-on with horses again. And Cappy followed her around like a puppy when he was out and she was around.

Silently, Morgan noted her presence around the barn. She appreciated the effort her best friend's girlfriend was making. Ripley was also the only one who ever had.

One night, Ty stopped at Ripley's RV. After she opened the door at his knocking, he asked, "You all done working for the night?"

"As a matter of fact, I am. Why?"

Instead of answering her, he said, "Put your shoes on. Come with me."

The Center was surprisingly empty and deserted for the rest of the night. Riding in his truck back up to Quail Run, he told her that Josh and Morgan were out on a date so the place belonged just to them. The last boarders had already left, and being so close to Morgan's closing hours meant no one else would be coming out.

Ripley wondered what was going on as she followed him into the barn. Sliding his hand up the wall by the barn door, he turned on the lights and led her down the long aisle. "The alarm is already off," he mentioned as they walked in. "Head on down to Monte. I'll meet you there."

She ran her hands down Monte's golden neck as she waited. She looked curiously at Ty coming back from the tack room carrying only a bridle in his hands. Monte sniffed her hair, blowing gently on her cheek. Smiling at the horse, she kissed his velvety soft nose.

Opening the stall door wider, Ty slipped on Monte's bridle and led him out into the aisle. Knowing Monte was fine to ride double and wouldn't buck them off, he motioned for her to swing up.

She happily grabbed some mane, and with Ty's help, she swung up, careful to not kick the horse as she swung her leg over his rump. With hardly any effort, Ty easily swung up behind her, got settled, and nudged his horse into a walk. As they walked out the large barn door, he leaned over and turned off the lights.

In the light from the moon and stars, they rode around the property and onto the short trail. Seeing them, The Darrells joyfully joined in the spontaneous night ride. Monte wanted to run so Ty allowed him to break into his slow, easy canter. Ty heard her laughing in pure enjoyment as they moved with the rhythm of Monte's strides. When he brought Monte back down to a walk, she sighed deeply.

With his strong arms around her waist, she leaned back against his chest. Now and then, Ty would simply lean around a bit and place a soft kiss on Ripley's cheek or neck. She always sighed when he did that, he noticed. He loved wrapping his arms around her as much as she loved it when he did.

As they rode Monte in the moonlight, it felt as magical to him as that night up in the mountains in Phoenix. When he told her that, she agreed wholeheartedly.

As Ty slid off Monte's back when they returned to the barn, Ripley knew she was falling hard for this man. She just didn't know what to do about it. She had to re-evaluate her future, and she refused to rush into anything. She sat on Monte while Ty turned on a light.

She finally slid off herself, resting her arms over Monte's warm back for a moment. A smile on her face, she turned to Ty. Her heart nearly stopped at the longing she saw in his eyes. And when he moved in slow and captured her mouth with his, she couldn't stop herself from kissing him back, letting her feelings pour into the kiss.

He ran his fingers over her hair, trailing them down her back. Ripley leaned closer to him, reveling in the surging emotions he could make her feel. When he pulled back, it was all she could do to *not* do anything she might regret later. She leaned up to kiss him again before she wrapped her arms around him and just hugged him. She felt him reciprocate.

After a minute, Ty kissed the top of her head. Still holding her, he said gently, "I love you, Ripley." He felt her tense up, but he didn't let her go. More firmly, he repeated himself, "I love you."

She pulled back but kept her arms around his waist. He saw the tears in her eyes and watched as she blinked them away.

As he suspected she would, she first tried to deny it. Softly, she said, "You and I haven't known each other long enough to know for sure. You can't love me, Ty."

"I do," he said softly.

Her eyes were locked onto his. Her heart beat so quickly, she could barely breathe. She shook her head at him.

"I love you, Ripley Capilano."

She immediately disagreed again. "No, you don't. You just *think* you do. It'll pass. Trust me." But she still didn't break eye contact with him. She simply couldn't.

Ty read the mixed messages in her eyes and in her voice. Her words were shoving him away, trying to keep some distance between them. But her eyes were drawing him right back in with their hope. Hope she probably didn't know she was conveying to him. He'd hold onto that.

"I'm a grown man. I think I know what I'm feeling and the differences from mere infatuation." He ran his hands over her hair a few times, wondering how he could convince her. "It's all right to just give it time to sink in. My feelings aren't shallow, so they aren't going to simply fade away.

"And I'm not asking you to tell me you love me right now either. I don't want you to say it unless you mean it... And you may never. I accept that, Ripley."

Her breath hitched again, and she took a mental step back. "I won't hold you to what you just said. Don't worry about it, okay?"

She swallowed as her eyes searched his face for any sign of relief at her statement. She didn't see any. He would've felt relief if he said he loved her by accident, even by design, but then wanted to take it back, wouldn't he? And that relief would've shown on his face, wouldn't it?

"I'll give you all the time you need, Ripley. I know we haven't known each other all that long, but when you know, you know. And I think you feel there's enough there already to know it's more than possible.

"But there's still no hurry with us at all, all right? Neither of us are in our twenties anymore. We've moved through our lives alone, but now maybe fate has put us together. I'm in no rush with you because you're worth the wait. I just thought you should know."

She cupped his cheek with an unsteady hand while looking into those penetrating eyes of his. "You're right when you say we haven't known each other that long. It's only been a couple of months or so. You might be infatuated with me, but you're not in *love* with me. You can't be."

"Josh and Morgan knew in practically one meeting."

"We're not—"

He interrupted her, "No, we're not. And we've also had more than one meeting, so don't discount that fact either. We've had way more time together already than they had before they knew. Time isn't the issue, Sugar. What we feel is." He kissed her lightly on the lips. "The lack of time doesn't make it less true though."

Thoughtfully, he said, "But maybe you're right. Maybe it's not really love. Tell you what... I'll think about it some more, and let you know."

Reverse psychology worked wonders with some people, he knew.

He was inwardly pleased when he saw the expression on her face. She couldn't hide her disappointment or hurt at his last comments. He leaned down, kissed her again, feeling her respond. Leaning his forehead against hers, he said, "Okay. I'm done thinking about it. I'm certain I love you. I guess you're stuck with me, Sugar."

Running her fingers through his hair, their heads still leaning against the other's, she laughed. She believed him—at least she truly wanted to. But she also knew she couldn't say the words to him yet. She had to be sure herself, and she was far from it.

She stepped away, stopping when she felt Monte's big body at her back. Ripley looked at the man standing there, watching her. Softly, she said, "I don't want to hurt you, Ty. It's the last thing I'd ever want to do. But I just can't say it back to you, not unless I'm certain myself. Once I tell you, then you'll know you're stuck with me too."

Nodding, he cupped her face gently with his hands. "That's all I want, Ripley. I'm not going to rush you. You need to be sure yourself. I don't want to hear it unless you're positive in your gut. Fair warning though. Once you tell me, I'm for sure not letting you go."

With a smile, she nodded. Ripley lifted her hands, cupping his handsome face. Running her thumbs over his cheekbones, she pulled him back to her and kissed him with a passion that came from deep inside her. She felt his instant response, and if Monte hadn't moved and bumped into them, jostling them, she wasn't sure when they would've stopped.

No matter how much they kissed or touched each other, he still never pressured her to go any further. It just wasn't what either wanted yet.

The fact he'd respected her feelings from the very beginning was almost overwhelming to her as she rarely heard about any man doing that. The fact she'd found a man who respected her, who she also respected, was almost enough to make her throw caution to the wind.

But yet she didn't. Couldn't.

She'd once heard that it takes closer to a year and a half before someone *really* knew another. And there was so much she was cautious about, she simply had to stay the course. She had to take her time and keep herself grounded.

She'd always wondered when people said knowing who to love and marry would be the hardest decision they'd ever make. Looking at the man standing there with her, Ripley still went with her gut response.

To her, if it was truly real, it should actually be the easiest.

Chapter 25

Since Ripley just carried her phone everywhere she went, Ty was also learning how her business worked firsthand. Unless she needed her laptop, she was free to roam. If they were alone, she'd often put her phone on speaker so he could hear both sides of the conversation. Her friends at their first dinner had explained it all in-depth to him, but hearing and seeing it in action was more interesting.

From the health and financial stories he heard from people he'd never met, he was impressed with what her company did for people from all walks of life. She definitely had more security than he did in many ways. Thank goodness he had retirement accounts set up, but would they be enough? How could one be sure they'd be taken care of when they could no longer work? Could he live off his retirement when his paychecks stopped coming in?

Damien had told him Ripley had sponsored him and Laura into her business. Since Laura had more free time and knew more people, Ripley spent more time helping her get them started. Laura was also taking the nutritional shakes as her prenatal at Ripley's suggestion. Damien said Laura was already feeling much better with this pregnancy than she had with Sasha's.

It was interesting to Ty to watch how his lady worked with people. She wasn't pushy, nor did she chase after them. She simply approached them, set up a time to meet with them and went from there.

She knew many people made fun of, even derided, network marketing businesses. They had talked about this over dinner one night at his place. Sure, some *were* scams. But the people who condescendingly said *all* of these businesses were scams normally were the people who failed—or never even tried one. Most just didn't follow the plan or give it enough effort or time. It *wasn't* a get-rich-quick business. In fact, it was usually the opposite.

The company she'd been with for a long time was fully legit. The hundreds of thousands of people who'd been doing it for decades around the world just in her company alone *proved* it wasn't a scam. And yet, Ripley said, she had numerous people still scoff at her. She never argued with them or even tried to change their minds. She just left. Her time was too valuable to waste. She had far more security than any one of those who spoke from ignorance.

Ripley ignored the naysayers who said it was "a pyramid scheme," knowing they missed the blatant irony when they went to work the next morning for someone else. *That* was a true pyramid scheme. They worked to make someone else rich.

No employee at their job would ever have the chance to earn more than the owner... or even their boss. How many could start their own businesses from their current one as an employee? They could be fired or laid off with absolutely no warning whatsoever. And rarely did a boss or owner actually care about what happened to their now-former employees. And if they stopped working, or simply missed work, that meant no money coming in at all. No work, no income, no money. Just bills. As she often said, "You can't pay bills with excuses."

Working for others meant you had residual bills but not residual income. Ripley had no real bills, but she *did* have plenty of residual income. She just didn't tell Ty how much.

At least in her business, *everyone* had a chance to make as much as anyone else including the person who sponsored them. Ripley didn't lie or exaggerate anything about the business. Instead, she went in-depth on how hard it could be because, yes, it took work. It could be a real struggle. It took consistent work, motivation, dedication, and even some luck.

But then there were the rewards. Ripley lived a free life now. She was financially secure for life. She didn't even need to work. She *chose* to work as much as she did, but she also took off whenever she wanted. She was very well-traveled, and she had a network of positive people to connect with. She could work wherever she wanted to, whenever she wanted to. She *chose* to continue to help others because someone had once chosen to help her.

No one was perfect in network marketing. No one was perfect *anywhere*. Although anyone could do network marketing, it also wasn't for everyone. What job was?

As she told Ty, everyone could work at McDonald's, but that didn't mean McDonald's was for everyone. Same for a bank, a store, and any other business. A person just had to find what worked for them.

Some people she sponsored didn't even do it as a business. They just wanted or needed health benefits. Others had small businesses, bringing in just a little extra per month. She also had some who took it as seriously as she did and had large businesses. She had her goals, and they had theirs. She just tried to help them get theirs accomplished.

Ripley felt she and Ty were learning about each other with no worries or thoughts about how much the other made. And she wanted to keep it this way as long as she could. She wanted to be sure they had a firm foundation to stand on first. She didn't let Ty know how much she earned or about her financial status at all. He didn't ask. She didn't offer. She didn't know what he earned either. She didn't ask. He didn't offer.

To Ripley, relationships weren't about how much either made. That was superficial. She was far more concerned and interested in what really mattered.

RIPLEY CUT BACK ON her workload for more free time. She split that time hanging out at Sunset Ridge with Ty and with the rescues. Ty and Ripley continued to work with Cappy together, hoping to get him as solid as they could before she left.

Ripley found Ty one afternoon leaning against the fence. He was watching Cappy and the other rescues enjoying the sunshine, a breeze gently moving their manes and tails. Stopping beside him, she said, "Hey, handsome. What's on your mind?"

Cappy had stopped and turned at the sight of Ripley. Looking very much like he was debating on whether or not to walk over to her, Ty couldn't help but smile. "That horse has radar when it comes to you, you know that? I didn't even have to turn around to know you were behind me. He told me."

She smiled as the horse began walking toward her. His ears were up, and his gait was a happy walk. "I'm not surprised. He loves me! And what's not to love?" she joked.

Cappy stopped directly in front of her, greeting her with his soft muzzle blowing on her cheek. She ran her hands down his sleek neck a few times. Cappy just soaked in the attention she gave him. Ripley kissed his soft muzzle as he nuzzled her hair.

"I can't say how much I'm going to miss this guy when I go! It seriously breaks my heart just wondering where he might end up. All of them, really. They are just furry individuals who deserve a loving home. I wish they could all just stay here. But I *really* wish I could just steal this guy when I leave!"

Ty nodded. "We're all in the same boat. Morgan and I have tried everything, but it's just not in our power. We also have Matt and Dell trying to help us. But to the courts, they're just part of another case number."

Ripley looked up at Ty as she ran her hands around Cappy's head, noticing he was still head shy when she got near his mouth. Ty noticed it too.

He sighed. "That right there is what I was thinking about when you came over."

"His being head shy?"

"Yeah. He's not so bad when it's a halter though. We can mess with his ears, but his mouth is another story. Do you think they used chains on him?"

Ripley considered it. "Well, it'd make sense, wouldn't it? He's mean, aggressive, prone to attacking. Loop a chain over his gums through his halter to teach him a lesson and to gain some temporary control? Maybe. I don't know how they could get that close, but I'm sure they did.

"Women don't normally resort to those measures, but men do. Sorry for the stereotype. I know women can, and some probably do, so don't think I'm being sexist there. If so, that could be a part of why he hated men."

Ty replied honestly, "It's probably true in many cases, and I won't take it personally. It'd be truer especially if he was stuck with cowboys or insensitive men. You know, the ones who think they have to be mean, alpha males. The ones who see a horse as just a tool. Most cowboys don't think like true horsemen who want to work *with* the horse and respect it.

"Most horses just want to please a person. It's their nature to want to please. Thankfully, there's been progress in this area over the decades thanks to men like Monty Roberts, John Lyons, Ray Hunt, Buck Brannaman, and so many others."

"You know your horse whisperers," she said happily.

He smiled. "Morgan has gone to some of their clinics over the years, and then trained me from what she learned. She's also sent me to some so I could see it done in person. It was probably more for a tax deduction, but it was still a paid mini-vacation for me." He grinned when Ripley laughed. "It's really interesting. I've also watched their videos and read their books—in English."

She chuckled as she gently held the horse's head, studying it until he pulled it away. Apparently satisfied with the attention he got, Cappy walked away, his tail swishing at flies as he joined his other equine friends. They silently watched as the horse walked away.

Softly, she mused, "I didn't see any scars on his mouth. Unless his mouth wounds healed?" She turned to look up at Ty, who was leaning against the fence again, staring out at the horses.

Ty thought about it some more. "If he were a bronc, they usually wear halters and not bridles with a bit. Using a chain on his gums, or even over his tongue, since the chain can be looped through the D-rings is probable. *Why* does man have to be so cruel to innocent animals? It hurts my mouth, and my heart, just *thinking* about it."

"Mine too," Ripley agreed. After a few moments, she had another thought. "You know, we may be looking at this from the wrong angle."

"How's that?"

"I'm just throwing this out there, okay?" At his nod, she said, "Have you watched him eat? I mean, *really* watched him eat and chew? Besides the treats we've given him?"

Realizing they hadn't, not really, made him furrow his brows. Instantly catching on, Ty asked, "You think it's his teeth?"

"Yeah, but it's just another angle. It'd explain why he doesn't like his mouth to be touched. The day we tried the bridle, he about shoved it back into *our* mouths, remember?"

Ty said thoughtfully, "And it could explain his aggressive behavior. Tooth pain can be extremely painful in humans and is known to be just as painful for a horse. Make it even worse by shoving a piece of hard metal in his mouth, then add the tugging or jerking of the reins? *Of course* he'd react violently. How could he *not?*

"He can't verbally explain his pain. If no one bothered to look, he fights against the pain so they beat him up, making it all just get worse. The cycle simply continues until he just associates men with intense pain and mistreatment." Ty shook his head sadly. "It makes me sick just picturing it."

Ripley nodded, saying softly, "Same here. Having those images in my head can literally haunt me." Her heart squeezed tightly just picturing it. She knew she had to get it out of her mind before it was all her brain would dwell on. She offered, "It could be an abscess, or maybe just sharp edges that need filed down. Maybe food is getting stuck between his teeth. Malnutrition maybe making his teeth or gums hurt?"

Ty grimaced. "I can just see Doc jumping at the chance to float that horse's teeth!"

Ripley laughed.

Just then, Morgan walked toward them from the barn, the cordless phone clipped to her belt. "Hey, you two. Mind if I join you?"

Ty motioned her over. "Not at all. Grab yourself a board to lean on. We were discussing Cappy, and what's with his head shyness. What if it all boils down to his teeth?"

Morgan leaned against the fence beside Ripley, thinking it over. She'd picked up on Ripley's go-to phrase and said, "Well, hell. *That* would explain an awful lot, wouldn't it? Toothache, abscess, biting the inside of his mouth..." She shook her head. "How stupid of us to not think about that sooner. We should've!"

Ty sighed. "Ripley's the one who thought about it, so that makes her the smartest one of us—*if* that's what it's all about. She could be wrong, but I don't think so. If it was an abscess at the time, it could be gone by now. But that *could've* been how his aggressive behavior started. On the other hand, it could be recurring. Either way, it's still worth a shot to take a look."

Ripley nodded. "It's just a theory of mine, Morgan. What are the odds of Doc coming out soon to float his teeth, or do a mouth exam?"

"For Cappy? Slim to none," Morgan deadpanned.

BUT MORGAN DID HAVE Dr. Shamis out almost immediately to determine Cappy's dental issues. Since *he* had returned her coffee mug, she joked, she chose him to come out.

When Dr. Shamis arrived, he joked that he thought about permanently closing his clinic right after Morgan had called him to come out. They all appreciated his reticence and laughed as they walked into Grand View.

Dr. Shamis was pleasantly surprised to see that Ripley was still there. He was far more surprised when Ty led a docile Cappy from his stall. The experienced vet couldn't believe the drastic change in Cappy's behavior. He swore it was a different horse, and they were all just messing with him. It took a good fifteen minutes for them to convince him it was the same dangerous horse from before. He even looked for the suture scars from the wreck.

Finally, Ripley held Cappy's head so the vet could check his teeth. He whistled when he saw the problems. "You did right by calling me out here! He's got some hooks and ramps that need taken care of. Has he been quidding?"

Ty nodded. "After Ripley questioned it being his teeth, we watched him actually eat. Sure enough, he had partially eaten food, even some balls of it, left in his tub. It probably took him hours to eat anything!

"You know, so often we just toss in the feed and move on. His weight looked good, and his feed was always gone, so we didn't think much about it. Now we all feel lower than a snake."

Dr. Shamis nodded in understanding. "There's no blame, Ty. At least he's getting the help he sorely needs now." He looked again at Cappy, calmly standing there. He even had his ears up as he listened to the people talk. "I still just can't believe what you've been able to do with him! His transformation seriously needs to be a documentary."

Morgan smiled. "The credit most definitely goes to Ripley. She's got a rare bond with Cappy here, and it's made a brand-new beginning for him. She made it possible for Ty and Josh to work with him. The only way I could be any happier is if I got to keep them all. I'm scared to death to hear what's going to happen to them. We all are."

Dr. Shamis asked, "You still don't know anything yet?"

Everyone shook their heads.

Dr. Shamis frowned before saying, "Well, let's get him sedated and get to work on giving him a better life. Then we'll check on the others while I'm here."

With assistance from them, the vet spent the next several hours checking and floating all the teeth of the rescues that needed it. As it turned out, only two didn't need a float. Dr. Shamis also checked them over from their previous injuries, very pleased with what he was seeing. He was relieved at how well the gray mare was doing. Her eye didn't seem to bother her at all. Her other injuries had healed nicely too. The gelding with the bad leg was moving as he should as well.

Before he wrote out his bill, he gazed at the people there. He said sincerely, "You know, I've been doing this for a lot of years, and I've seen a lot of horses in a lot of places. Some places I've had to report they were so bad. Other places are all right. And then there's here.

"I think these horses had a guardian angel looking out for them when that truck got hit. When I got the emergency call about that wreck, they didn't know where to take them. Who could get them, assuming they didn't all need put down? I told them right off to call you, Morgan. Thank God they did.

"I remember what these horses looked like, and the worry we all had for them. *Now* look at them! You all have done just an amazing, spectacular job with them. You've loved them, gave them health care, fed them, worked with them. You've let them all just be a horse in the safest environment they could ever have asked for.

"I just want to say thank you, from the bottom of my heart, to all of you for what you do here. And for what you've been able to do for these horses.

"We don't know what the future holds for them. But with what you've done, especially for Cappy, you've given them all another chance. You've transformed their lives. If there's any justice out there, they'll let you keep them, Morgan. Or at least allow you to buy them.

"But no matter what, just know I hold Harmony Hills in the highest esteem of any place I've gone to. Any time I've come out here, it's never been less than impressive. But what you've done this time with these horses is just really extraordinarily special."

Morgan was so touched by the vet's words, she got tears in her eyes. "Thank you, Doc. It means more than you know for me to hear that. It's better than a five-star review! Maybe you can do one of those too." She smiled through her tears when the vet laughed. "But seriously, thank you."

"You're welcome, Morgan." He opened up his clipboard and took out his receipt pad. "Now then. I'll just write up your bill here, and then I'll be on my way."

Ty moved the plastic chair closer to him. Dr. Shamis gratefully sat down, happy to be off his feet. Quietly, they watched him write down what he did.

As the vet wrote his bill, which wasn't any of her business, Ripley went down to give some attention to Cappy. She was dreading the time she knew was coming. The time when she had to leave him was fast approaching. And Ty.

But she hurt far more leaving Cappy because she didn't know what was to become of him, where he would go. She couldn't just call him to check in. What could she do to save him? Anything? She opened his stall door. Although still slightly groggy from the sedative, he poked his head out. She pet him as he rested his head in front of her chest, trusting her to always be there for him.

Dr. Shamis looked up for a minute. He glanced down the aisle, seeing Cappy and Ripley together. He figured he was looking at Cappy's own guardian angel right there.

He wrote some more before he tore off the copy for Morgan. He put the rest of his things away before handing it to her. She looked at her bill, then back at him.

"What do I owe you, Doc?" Morgan asked, confused.

"It says it right there, Morgan. You've got thirty days to pay in full."

"It says twenty dollars... I don't understand..." She looked up at Dr. Shamis again.

He sighed. "I can't find it in my heart to charge you for this trip. For everything you've done, this is my 'thank you' to *you*.

"Their names and descriptions are written down for their medical records, and I'll get the individual sheets out to you in a day or so. I'm just not charging you for them. You called me out for only Cappy anyway. I *volunteered* to check the others, if you remember. The twenty bucks is just so my accountant doesn't yell at me too much."

Morgan smiled, tears in her eyes again. "Can I hug you?"

Dr. Shamis smiled. "Only if Josh doesn't mind."

"He won't. If he does, he'll get over it."

She smiled through her tears as she hugged the man who let her know she'd accomplished one of her Life Goals: Building Harmony Hills to be the best.

Chapter 26

Patience was a virtue, whether working with abused and rescued animals or cautious humans.

Mel, Kat, and Morgan worked with the other rescue horses when they could, leaving Cappy to Ty, Ripley, and Josh. To test the sorrel's willingness to accept a different man around, they'd have Toby, Drew, Rory, or Bo come over more often than before. Morgan had Rick, her patient blacksmith, come out and trim the rescues' hooves.

Gaining Cappy's trust, he no longer shivered, attacked, or broke out into a nervous sweat at the mere sight or sound, or even a touch, from any man. He was beginning to cooperate and work with them, building a relationship with all humans for the first time in a long time—if not ever.

Like Cappy and Ty's relationship, Ripley and Ty's was simply a work in progress. There was give and take on both sides. It took patience and compromise, but they knew the rewards were too promising to pass up on.

After they dealt with Cappy's dental issues, the real change began in the horse. The constant irritation and pain gone now, he was able to focus more on the positive aspects of letting humans work with his head and mouth. While he'd still sometimes pull his head away, they all figured it was merely a conditioned response by this time and hoped he'd work out of it.

Ty and Josh had Cappy line-driving like a dream. Hooking the long lunge lines to his halter or bridle, they safely walked behind Cappy, steering him all over the property. Soft hands and soft tugs allowed Cappy to keep a soft mouth. And he'd accepted the bridle and saddle with less issues than anybody expected. Morgan had been tempted to have an ambulance on hand in case Ty got bucked off the first few times he rode him, but Cappy showed no real signs of wanting to buck. Ty felt his back hunch up a bit the first few times, but he patiently worked it out of the horse.

Surrounded by loving people, the abused horse had almost no other choice *but* to trust them in the end. They simply gave him no reason to *not* trust them. They instead gave him the space, time, and love he so desperately needed.

With Josh being a first-rate rider, he also rode Cappy. As with Ty, Josh felt Cappy hunch his back a little, but he never put forth the effort to buck, bolt, or rear. Also like Ty, Josh was pleasantly surprised at how responsive and smooth Cappy was to ride.

Maybe their assumption that he'd been a rodeo bronc was wrong. And if it wasn't his teeth and the resulting pain causing his behavioral issues, they just weren't sure what else would've made the horse so hateful of men.

They'd probably never learn the truth of the horse's background. They just hoped if he didn't end up back on his way to Mexico, he'd have a real chance at a better life now that he'd learned to trust people in general, men in particular. They all prayed he didn't end up with someone who ruined all of their efforts and made his life hell again.

When Ripley walked into the barn to meet Ty, she saw Cappy on the cross-ties, decked out with a Western saddle and breast collar, with a bridle over his halter. "Hi sweetie!" She kissed Cappy's nose.

Ty turned the corner, greeting her with a smile. "Hey, Sugar! You wanna go for a walk with me? You have time?"

"Off for the night." Looking down at her shoes, she asked, "Will these do?"

"Yeah. You ready?"

"Sure." Looking at Cappy who was stretching his neck toward her so she'd scratch his forehead, she smiled. "Ah, are we walking, or is he?"

"All of us. I wanted to see how he'd do out in the real world. You game?" He unhooked the cross-ties from Cappy's halter, letting the ropes swing down to the walls.

She nodded, falling in beside him as he walked the horse down the aisle. Cappy looked excited to be out of his stall and walked jauntily beside Ty.

"I have a distinct feeling you're just using me," she said, humor in her voice. "I'm here to save your butt if he decides he doesn't like the real world, aren't I?"

Ty flashed a grin at her. "Something like that!" He explained, "We've been on his back here in the round pen and in the large outdoor arena. But we need to see what he does in the desert, a different environment. We'll take him out, and see what he does. I think he'll be fine."

"Me too."

They slipped on their sunglasses as they went out into the bright sunlight. For extra head protection, he wore his cowboy hat like usual, and she wore the new ball cap he'd given her. She'd smiled when she saw the Harmony Hills logo on it. He'd said it was a keepsake just for her.

As they turned toward the trail, Ripley asked, "Is there water in the saddle bags?"

"Yeah. You know Morgan would kill us if we died of dehydration."

Once on the trail, Cappy wanted to see everything at once. He was like a kid in a toy store. His intelligent brown eyes seemed to be looking everywhere, but he rarely spooked or startled. He walked alongside the two people like a dog. They were all just out for a nice stroll. Ty updated her on the rescues' status and told her what he and Morgan had been told earlier about the case being in court now. She nodded, thinking it over.

Soon after that discussion, Ripley broached the subject that was forever between them. "I have to leave for Texas right after the wedding, Ty. Surprisingly, I really don't want to, but I promised those people I'd be there. I never break a promise if I can at all help it. And then I have other stops after that in the South and East, so my time here is coming to an end."

She was surprised at the hurt she felt knowing she was leaving the Center and her new friends. Saying it out loud now to her boyfriend made it even more real. She felt a stab so sharp in her chest, she actually tried to rub it away.

"Well, I knew it was coming." Ty also felt a stab of pain in his heart thinking of being here now without her. He instinctively knew it wouldn't be the same. She'd changed things, and it couldn't go back to the way it had been.

She glanced at him but couldn't read his facial expressions due to the sunglasses and hat shadowing his face. Gently, she said, "I did tell you this is what I do. And everyone knew I was only planning on being here for a little while. I've stayed far longer than I meant to, but I'm good with that. It was a mix of staying for Cappy and for you, Ty. At this point, though, the Texans are wondering if I forgot about them."

He nodded. They continued to walk in silence, listening to the crunch of their own shoes mixing with Cappy's bare hooves on the sandy, sometimes rocky, ground. They couldn't always walk beside each other due to the cacti and bushes in their way, but once they side-stepped it, they were side by side again.

Finally, Ty stopped, asking Cappy to stop with him. The horse did immediately, and Ty automatically praised him before motioning for Ripley to get up in the saddle.

"What? You want me up there? No way. I signed Morgan's papers. I'm not supposed to..."

He smiled. "Get up there."

He checked the cinch, then helped her into the saddle, adjusting the stirrups for her legs. "Just don't be nervous so he doesn't pick up on it."

"I'm not. I just don't want to get into trouble with Morgan."

"You won't."

Cappy looked back, his nose sniffing her shoes. Satisfied she was who he thought was up there, he swung his head back around, waiting for a command. She smiled at Ty, who smiled back.

"Walk." Ty clucked to the horse, who eagerly began walking alongside him.

As they walked, Ty said, "Back to us. You know I want you to stay. I know you have to work. But you can work from here, so why won't you? You *have* been."

Ripley thought out her words carefully. "Yes, I can. But I can't see people in person from here for meetings and trainings when they live somewhere else. In-person trainings are more effective. And, yes, I have been working from here.

"But I gave my word to see these people to help them get their businesses going strong, as much as I can help them anyway. Most of it is simply up to them. But having someone new come in and do trainings is a real motivator. I love motivating and training people."

He nodded, having heard her do it many times just over the phone. She was really good at what she did. As he and the horse walked along the trail, he asked, "Does anyone else in your business do this?"

"Not that I know about. But everyone else probably has a family or a home."

"You have me. You have all of us." Ty paused, looking up at her for a moment. "Am I just not enough for you, Ripley?"

Her heart instantly cracked. "Oh, no! Ty, that *isn't* it at all. You're more man than I've ever thought to find. It's just... I've been doing this traveling training thing for so long now, it's become expected of me. Yes, I can stop doing it. But I told a whole lot of people I'd come visit them. It's *why* I live in an RV. I've been to a whole lot of places, but my list is still fairly long. It takes a long time to travel, train, get people started, move on again.

"This trip has been in the making for over a year, Ty. Long before I even met Morgan. I fully expect to be on the road for another eight or nine months, at least. Honestly, it'll probably be longer than that."

"Will you come back here?"

"I'd love to, but I can't say when. I can *always* visit, Ty."

Ty felt his heart ache at her words, but at least she was being honest. She wasn't being coy with him, and he had to respect that about her.

They walked along in silence. Ripley watched Cappy's ears flicker as his broad head swung from side to side to look at his surroundings with interest. Ty shoved Cappy's head out of his way a few times just so he could see where he was going. Ripley smiled every time Cappy blocked Ty's view.

He stopped the horse and turned to look up at Ripley. "Okay. I'm just going to leave the lead on him, but you're going to do all the steering and controlling of him from up there now. You got the reins?"

"Yeah." With a smirk, she asked, "By controlling him, you mean keep his head from knocking you over or blocking your view?"

He grinned. "That's it exactly."

They began walking again. Ripley shortened the reins a bit more to keep Cappy's head from his excessive swinging. She knew his eyesight was fine so she figured he was simply curious in his surroundings.

"He has a nice, smooth stride, doesn't he?" she asked after a few minutes.

"Yeah, Josh and I talked about that. His canter? So smooth you could fall asleep up there." He paused before asking, "Will you go to Toby and Maya's wedding with me?"

"Of course. I never thought I wouldn't. Why would I go with anyone else, or go alone?"

"Just making sure. It'd be rude of me to not ask and just assume." He motioned for her to stop and dismount.

"I appreciate that. Thank you for asking," she replied before she swung down.

Looking at her, he asked her straight out, "Why can't you stay, Rip? After this Texas trip, why can't you just come back, and stay here with me? Why won't you?"

She ran her hand down Cappy's smooth coat while she thought it out. Softly, she admitted, "I want to. I just don't know if I can."

"What does that mean? Why *can't* you stay with the man who loves you?"

She looked at him, tears brimming in her eyes and sliding over. She wiped them away with her finger before they trailed below her sunglasses. It was the second time he told her he loved her, and it pierced her heart just like the first time.

Ty saw the motion, knew he'd made her cry. It made him feel awful, but he was already feeling awful himself. He reached up, removed the sunglasses and saw the tears spilling over some more.

She finally answered, "Because I just don't know for sure. And it's a lot for me to take a chance on. I just want to *know.*"

"Know what?" He removed his own sunglasses and hung them on his shirt like he always did. He wanted direct eye contact with her, for her to see his eyes as he saw hers.

"That you really *do* love me. That you actually *want* me. That you *need* me. That they're not just words to make me stay here longer. Ty, we haven't really known each other that long. It seems like it, but we really haven't."

He studied her, wiping away her tears with his thumbs. He asked softly, "Why don't you believe me when I tell you I love you? Just because of the short time we've known each other?"

Her answer was immediate. "Because I've been told that before. And it's never once held true. Not a single time."

He sighed, remembering their past conversations. "Did you ever love them?"

"No."

"And what about me?" he asked softly. "Do you love me, Ripley?"

She hesitated, saw the look flicker across his face when she did so. *Because* she did so. "I think I do, Ty. But it's not enough for me to *think* I do. I need to *know* I do. You are by far, hands down, the best man I've ever known. And I love so much *about* you."

Ty leaned down, kissed her softly. He reached up and moved her cap out of the way and kissed her again. Cappy shook his head, yanking them apart. But Ripley held on to Ty and pulled him back to her. When they stepped back, she cupped his face with her hand, rubbing her thumb across his cheek.

Ripley tried again. "Let me try to explain my thought process to you, okay?"

He nodded, leading them to a small boulder off the trail to sit on. Automatically, he checked all around it for snakes. Finding it clear, he sat down on it, motioning for Ripley to join him. Cappy seemed content to stand there, looking around, enjoying the sunshine, and the warm breeze blowing through his mane. Ripley adjusted her cap.

She told him about one of her previous boyfriends, how he was even similar to Ty in some respects. And how it all ended, leaving her feeling used. "To say he burned me bad is an understatement. He burned me to a crisp. There's a bit more to the story later on, but it ended the same way yet again. And he's *not* the only man to treat me this way. I'm sick of it, *all* of it, and them. Done. I've been alone since, and I've been so much happier."

Ty couldn't believe someone would say and do those things to a woman like Ripley... or to any woman. This other guy was one of *those* guys who did damage to a woman that made them not believe it when someone like him told her the same thing. He knew men like that himself. Players. He sighed, realizing again her trust issues were legit. What was he supposed to do to convince her to stay? That he loved her?

Ripley watched a zebra-collared lizard sunning itself on a nearby stone for a moment. When it scurried off, she continued, "But I still slept with him. I didn't mean to, didn't even really want to. I could blame it on a single, potent drink, or me just wanting to live life. But those are really just excuses. I was weak. I knew what I was doing.

"I just thought that maybe it was worth the chance. To live life, sometimes you just have to take a chance now and then. To not worry about what's running through your head or gut all the time. To this day, I can't pinpoint it. I was just weak, and I didn't stand up for myself. I regret very much sleeping with him. I just wish I could go back and change everything that happened! Even now, I'm so ashamed, mad, and resentful. It's still so hard to face it, to try and move on from it."

It was hard for her to admit her feelings, but she had to. She looked at Ty, tapped her chest. "Inside, I died. For a personal confession here, I can live without sex. I don't need it to function on a daily basis. Maybe it's because I just haven't had that deep, emotional connection I *need*, the way it *should* feel. So, I live just fine without it. Sex is a lot of work, it's messy, it's easy to use someone for it, and that someone was me. I never really saw the rewards of it.

"Now, that being said, I do leave this open for change. It's possible I'd love it with the right man. Maybe that's you, Ty. But not until I'm ready. Not until it feels like it should. When I feel I can trust enough." She took a breath, released it. She hated feeling so vulnerable! "And I'm sure men probably hate to hear that from a woman, but there it is."

After a moment, he asked, "Have you seen him since?"

"No. I hate that the friendship we had for ten years was now gone just because of this. He was always one of those people I enjoyed being around the most. Like us, we could talk about any subject, and we joked. And then? Nothing. Nothing but lies."

"I'm not him." Ty knew it was an obvious statement, but it was the only thing he could say.

"I know that. I really do. But with you, I feel in some ways the way I did with him. The whole love-being-with-you feeling, being-so-compatible-with-you feeling is so very similar. But it's *stronger* with you, more..." She searched for the words she wanted. "Relaxed? Authentic? Deeper? You're already so much better than he ever was!

"But now I've gone so long without dating anyone, inside I just feel... dead. It's been calmer, safer being on my own. Yet when I'm with you, everything inside of me just seems to start working again. I feel like I'm coming alive inside again. But I also feel I still need to be cautious and not be in any hurry.

"I *love* what we have right now. I don't want it to end, and I'm scared it will. If it does, I'll be scarred for life." She cupped his face with her hands, her thumbs running over his cheekbones as she looked into his warm eyes. "I don't want to lose you or what we have going."

He took hold of her hand, turned it, and placed a kiss in her palm.

She let out her breath in a swish of air. Softly, she said, "That. When you do that..."

He smiled at her tenderly.

Ripley kept his hand in hers, lacing their fingers. "To give you hope, and to bare my soul even more, I'll admit you do things to me that I haven't felt in years. And all of them are amazing. I can stay up late at night just remembering what we've done together, conversations we've had. I so often recall your hugs, your kisses, and it just makes my heartbeat race! I've caught myself working on something, and then all of a sudden you're in my head and I'm smiling."

He smiled at her, nodding, letting her know he'd been experiencing the same.

"I make one of my shakes, and it sits on the counter for an hour because you got into my head—"

"Just an hour?" he teased. "I must be doing something wrong if it's only an hour."

With a grin, she chuckled. "Yeah. More or less. Remember I'm a very focused individual, so an hour is long enough!" She looked at his hand that was joined with hers. "And I don't want to let those feelings go. I don't want to let *you* go. I would love to have you love me! But I need to know you *want* me too. And that you *need* me. Love, want, need. They aren't the same. I only want to be with someone who can honestly say and feel all three of those things and not just one or two.

"I need to know if I'm going to put my heart on the chopping block, make huge changes in my life, I have a solid reason to do so. It's not that I'm afraid of being hurt... It's more that I want to know it was *worth* being hurt. So if it all doesn't work out in the end, I can at least say it was worth it. That we had a marvelous time, and we gave it our all. It just wasn't meant to be. No blame. No fault.

"I don't want to have regrets and be filled with guilt, self-loathing, and, worst of all, resentment. I don't *ever* want to resent you or myself over us. I do with others, and I can't get rid of it. I've tried, but I can't. I'm just doing what I can to prevent it with us."

Ty knew he had to bare his soul too. It had to be a two-way street. Like her, he found it hard to say.

He said softly, "You could hurt me, Ripley. You alone have the ability to rip my heart right out of my chest. It's really hard for me to admit that to you. It's not just because I'm a man, but because I don't ever recall another woman who could do to me what you could do. And do it so easily."

Touched deeply by his honesty and vulnerability, she squeezed his hand. "I never, ever want to hurt you, Ty. But I'm terrified I will, and you'll never forgive me. I hate that feeling!"

Tears came to her eyes again. He could see the torment in them.

She shook her head. "I'm sorry I'm so screwed up for relationships! This is why I need to go slow, don't you see?"

Ty gathered her close, tears misting his own eyes. He wanted her so much, knowing she had to come to him on her own free will. To him, Ripley was the one thing that could, and was, filling up that void in his life. He never thought he really had one, but he did. This woman unknowingly not only made him fully aware of it, but also how deeply the void went.

Although Ripley was savvy, compassionate, beautiful, intelligent, independent, fun, and strong, she was also a bit of a lost, wounded soul. She was very similar to Cappy, he thought suddenly. No wonder they'd bonded. Neither felt they could trust a man. And who could blame them?

On the other hand, wasn't he the same? Didn't his past teach him to never fully trust anyone, otherwise it could cost him a life—possibly his own? Only a select handful of his friends and family even knew of his past. He'd always used a cover story to mask where he was, what he did. The less people who knew of his past, the safer he was. And the safer those he knew about were too.

Guarding his secrets, his past for so many years, not allowing himself to really let any woman get close, hadn't he himself evolved into a lost, wounded soul too? With the exception of Morgan, who was an altogether different situation, he could never let a woman get too close.

He and Ripley, and the eleven rescued horses, were all just lost souls looking to have their hope and trust resurrected. And not be let down in the end. They were all rescues, he figured.

Although able to live life just fine, he was still searching for that *one* thing that completed him. Whatever it was that could fill that void he now knew was there, somewhere deep inside. Someone or something he could fully trust and lean on that was there just for him. Wasn't that exactly how Morgan had felt when she'd met Josh years ago? He wanted that inner healing *she* had now. He'd never seen her so settled, so genuinely happy until she and Josh got together. Could it ever happen to him? With Ripley?

As they sat there on the boulder, her leaning against him, his arms around her, one thought continued to run through Ty's mind: Could he trust Ripley with his past? He just didn't know. He felt it was just too soon.

When he realized that, it smacked him in the face that he needed the same confirmation about her that she needed about him.

It was humbling to realize they were in the same predicament. And it was equally humbling to realize that although neither one of them were young, starry-eyed kids having these issues, they still were. Perhaps that's *why* they were. They were mature adults, knowing love doesn't always conquer all.

As he thought everything through, Ty just gave her the time she needed to gather herself together, simply holding her in the sunlight until she settled again. And it gave him time to settle again too. She wasn't the crying type, and he knew she kept a tight rein on her emotions. She snorted out a laugh when she felt Cappy's soft muzzle blow on her cheek like he was comforting her.

Ty smiled as he got the same impression himself. Cappy felt connected to the woman, so Ty figured the horse *was* offering her comfort. She reached up, stroked the soft side of his mouth as the warm horse breath blew gently across her face. He noticed Cappy no longer jerked his head away when she touched it. He smiled to himself. Another hurdle crossed, he thought.

When she reluctantly moved away from Ty, Cappy lifted his own head out of the way. It was like he knew she was all right again. Running her hands over her face, she said, "Two of the best guys ever right here in my lap, and I can't hold onto either one of you!"

"You can me, and we're still working on Cappy here." Ty stroked her arm, studying her.

She rested her hand where his neck and shoulder met, her thumb rubbing his neck. "I know I've said this before, and I'm sure you're tired of hearing it, but I just need time. I just want to be solid myself because I feel if I *am*, then I hope this'll prevent me from hurting you. Does that make sense? Can you just be patient with me?

"I'm really trying here. And by *trying* I mean I'm making attempts, not that I'm testing your patience. Although, I'm sure I'm doing both."

"You are." He smiled when she playfully slapped his arm. "But I'll be here because I love you. And I *do* want you in my life. I'd never love someone I *didn't* want in my life. And I do need you to make my life more complete, more whole. I feel complete when we're together, Ripley. And, I guess, even when we're apart because I know you're here in my life. It's like I know we're already together because our hearts are.

"And echoing your feelings, I'd hope you'd love, want, and need me too. You're correct saying they aren't the same things. I guess it's something I knew, but I never put into words before. I want to be those for you too.

"I'm still not going to rush you, Ripley. But I also won't chase after someone who doesn't want me back. I believe you do, though, and that makes all the difference to me. I need you to come to me on your own terms, when *you* are ready.

"I know I started all of this between us even though I knew you were a short-term resident here. But something about you just hooked me. And I'm still glad I took the chance of going to Phoenix. We have something special going here.

"I can only say I hope my love is strong enough to be able to withstand you being gone, not knowing if you'll just move on without me. Out of sight, out of mind, you know? I believe my love is strong enough, but I won't pine my life away for someone who doesn't know if they even want me at all. How long am I to wait before I decide it's just not going to work? It's hard on me, Ripley. I can't gloss over that."

She nodded, appreciating his openness with her. "That's what I'm working out, Ty. And I *do* want you in my life. Don't doubt that. I've been on my own for so long, it's foreign to me to think about needing someone. But it doesn't mean I don't want to."

They sat there on the boulder, each in their own thoughts.

Ripley felt she needed to give him more of herself, more than just words. Something each could look forward to like an end goal. After thinking it through, she said, "As I've explained, I feel obligated to finish up this list of mine. I promised these people, and they're depending on me. But it doesn't mean I have to do it all in a row, meaning going from one place to the next, to the next, with no real breaks. Even though that *is* why I bought my RV," she added ruefully.

"I'm going to go out on a limb here, for my faith in *us*." She squeezed his hand in hers, feeling his answering one. "I won't add any more visits to my list. Assuming we're still together then, and we're committed to what we have and building it even more, how about this? About two trips before my current list is done, how about we sit down and talk it out? If you and I, well, if we decide we want to stay together and plan on making it permanent, then we'll go from there."

Hope leapt from his heart to fill his entire body with the intangible wave of it. She was thinking far out, looking and speaking toward the long-term. Of permanency.

He asked, "So for these upcoming work visits that you have planned already... Are you thinking of coming back here, to me, in-between them? Or are you thinking of just being on the road non-stop until you get them done? And I just wait here until you are?"

She considered. Cappy stood beside Ty now, apparently realizing they weren't leaving this boulder anytime soon. Cocking his hind leg, he got comfortable and looked ready to take a snooze in the sunshine. Ty ran the lead rope through his hands as he waited for her to answer him.

Finally, Ripley replied, "These Texas ones would be better to just do in a row. Then I'm supposed to head East, so it just doesn't make sense for me to drive back and forth. I specifically planned my visits on a route to make it most efficient."

She looked at the mountains as she thought it out. "Maybe I can leave my RV for a while, fly back here, then fly back to my RV, and then move on to the next. I can drive my car to an airport, park it there, fly here, then do the reverse going back. I want you to know I'm willing to make this work between us, Ty. I'm willing to do my part."

Ty appreciated what she was willing to do for them. He loved her for making the effort to work out something. That meant she was taking their relationship as seriously as he prayed she was... As seriously as *he* was.

He asked, "What if I helped in this compromise? What if I flew out to meet you when Morgan can spare me? I do have vacation time with her. She likes you, so even if I didn't, getting extra time off from her isn't a problem unless we have a lot going on all at once. I won't abuse our friendship, but she's flexible.

"Even if it's just for a couple of days at a time, Ripley, we could still see each other. It's not fair for you to be the one having to come back to me just because I'm the one with a home and job that doesn't move."

She smiled, saying, "That'd be good too. You can stay with me in my RV, or we can get a hotel room if that's more comfortable. We can take turns, with it being understood overall it's easier for me than you to make the trips. I know how busy you guys are here, and you're a huge part of it running the way it does. Morgan depends on you. That hasn't escaped my notice."

"I don't know if I'd say *huge*, but my being here certainly helps." Ty looked at her for a moment before asking, "We're good then? When you leave soon after the wedding for Texas, you'll not just leave me sitting here in your dust? Humiliated, having people take pity on me? We'll still talk, text?"

"You bet. As often as we can."

"And you'll come back to me, Ripley?"

She knew he didn't just mean their current geographic location. Looking at him, she said without hesitation, "Yes. I just can't say right now when precisely that'll be, but I will. Can you handle that?"

With a sigh, he replied, "I guess I'll have to. As long as we honestly and regularly communicate with each other, we can do this."

She nodded in agreement. "Yes, we can."

Ty could only be there for her. Knowing all he knew about her, starting from the first day when he discovered her sleeping in sand to comfort abused horses, he knew she was worth it. From their talks and the time spent together, like now, he knew she was worth the effort of making their relationship work.

She was a successful businesswoman, but she kept her promises to everyday people. That was most certainly one of the reasons *why* she was so successful. She paid *attention* to people. She truly listened to them. She loved to laugh.

And she also went out of her way to try not to hurt him, knowing all the while she already was. But also knowing it tore her up. She wasn't immune to what she was doing. She was just trying to do the right thing for both of them. He had to respect that about her.

He pulled her close, hugged her. When they pulled away, he said, "We'd better be heading back."

Nodding, she stood up, brushed her hands over her butt automatically to clean off any dirt. Both of them slid their sunglasses back on.

"Hang on," Ripley said as she removed the bottles of water from the saddlebag, handing one to Ty.

She twisted off the cap and drank most of it while Ty drank all of his. Cappy leaned his long neck over to them, his lips trying to get to the bottles, making them smile. She poured the rest of hers into his mouth, with most of it just running out of his mouth and down his chin, but he seemed satisfied he got some. When they were done, she put the empty bottles back in the saddlebag.

As they began walking again, Ty reached over for her hand.

"You bring a certain amount of peace to me," Ripley said as they walked along. She squeezed his hand in hers. "Thank you for being able to do that."

"You're welcome. That's something you also give to me. I just wish I could give you more."

"You do, Ty. Just let me figure out how to manage it all."

Chapter 27

Sunday, September 20

The day of the wedding started off overcast. Nobody could believe it.

When Maya walked into her kitchen, her mom Georgette was there waiting for her daughter. A cup of warm coffee in her hand, Georgette smiled. "Don't worry, dear. I already checked the weather channel. It's supposed to clear up by afternoon."

Hugging her mom tightly before pouring herself some coffee and adding creamer to it, Maya smiled. "Leave it to me to have the one overcast morning. Since everything is inside, it really doesn't make a difference. But, well, the sun just makes it seem... cheerier. I want my day to be perfect, Mom!"

"You're marrying a man who's perfect for you, honey. A wedding is just an event. A marriage, a happy one, is the most important thing to focus on. You know I love your Toby. I have high hopes for you both."

Maya's lips trembled in a bid to not cry at her mom's words. "I do, too, Mom."

As predicted, the sun was out by that afternoon. When Maya saw the bright rays shining down from heaven, she rejoiced. Her mom laughed in happiness and joy with her daughter. Having the sun back out just seemed to lift her spirits even higher than they were. She was getting *married* today!

"You look gorgeous!" Alexis gushed as Maya walked through the door in her wedding gown. "Toby will be wishing he'd asked you sooner. *And* glad he didn't whisk you off to Vegas because he would've missed seeing you in *this!*"

Alexis walked around Maya to see the entire dress again, her smile wide and bright. "It's even more beautiful than in the store at the last fitting. You're going to knock him out, Maya, with a one-two punch!"

Maya smiled at her friend. "You've always been so supportive of us. I appreciate that, Alexis. I really do."

Alexis gave her a carefully thought-out hug, worried she'd mess up something or get caught and tear something else off.

Georgette walked in and her hands flew to her face in happiness. She exclaimed, "Oh, my darling Maya! Look at you... Oh, your daddy would be so happy for you." She cupped her daughter's face. "And so proud." She kissed her daughter's cheek.

Maya nodded, tears threatening to spill over. "I know, Mom. I wish he was here. I miss him so much, and today especially. But I've got *you* here with me, and that means the world to me."

Her dad had died of a heart attack the year before, but Maya took solace in knowing he'd approved of Toby. She knew her dad had truly enjoyed Toby's company during the couple of times they'd met.

At his funeral, Toby had been a rock. She'd never forget that about him. He was there for not only her, but for her mom, when they needed someone the most. He'd simply stepped up to the plate without being asked and took care of everything for them both.

Even after they'd returned to Arizona, he'd made sure he checked in with her mom on a regular basis. They still spoke on the phone at least weekly even now. If Maya hadn't already loved him, she would've fallen for him then, completely.

Alexis scolded them, "Hey. *Hey!* None of this sentimental stuff until *after* the ceremony. I was a nervous wreck doing her makeup the first time, and I can't take a chance on having to do it again!"

With a gleam in her eyes, Maya said, "I agree. And since I'm already in this gown, you're not gonna get the chance to stain it by accident. And it ain't coming off until tonight!"

"MAYA! YOU LOOK *STUNNING!*" Morgan had slipped back to see Maya before the ceremony began.

Her smile beaming, Maya opened her arms to hug her longtime boss and friend. "I'm so glad you hired Toby all those years ago, Morgan. Who knew he'd end up being all I ever needed or wanted?"

Morgan smiled and teased, "Well, as I said before, consider him my wedding present then. I'll just go ahead and take back what I got you!"

Turning to Georgette, Morgan held her hands in support for a moment. "Georgette, you look radiant yourself. You must be so excited."

Georgette smiled. "Thank you. I am. But it's always hard for a mother to let her daughter go. But it's just another step, another chapter, in our lives."

"Yes, it is." Turning to her longest employee, Morgan shook her head, smiling. "Alexis, you look fabulous! You wear that at work, and I'm positive your tips would increase enough to pay for grad school!"

Alexis laughed. "If I run out of grants and can't get a loan, I might give it a shot!"

Maya asked, "Have you seen my groom?" She smiled in joy. "I have a *groom!* Who would've ever thought it?"

"And soon he'll be a *husband!*" Morgan happily replied. "And *yours.*"

"I'm a *bride.* And I'm going to be a *wife!*" Her hands flew to her face. Maya still hadn't quite realized those terms belonged to her now. It was all apparently sinking in though. "Those are so different than just *girlfriend.*"

Alexis smiled. "And right now, you're also still a *fiancée!*"

"Oh... I'm having another identity crisis!" Maya exclaimed, sending them all into fits of laughter. She put her hands to her cheeks again. "I thought I got through it at the bar that night, but apparently not!"

Grinning, Morgan shook her head. In reply to Maya's original question, she said, "No, I haven't seen your *groom* yet. But I wouldn't worry. The bachelor party was under control from what I heard from Josh when he rolled in at a reasonable hour."

"I'm not really, but one never knows!" Maya said.

Morgan shook her head again, saying cheerfully, "Besides, Ripley gave him an early wedding present. Ty made sure he got it."

Curious, Maya asked, "What was it?"

Morgan smiled as she walked to the door. "Thick socks."

She winked at Maya and slipped out the door. She heard their laughter as she walked down the aisle to *her* husband, scooting by him and taking her place between him and Ty.

When the music began, everyone turned around in expectation. Georgette walked down first, escorted by Bo. Then came Toby's parents and sister, who sat next to Georgette so she wouldn't be sitting there all alone. Next came Alexis, escorted by Drew, the Best Man.

After Alexis and Drew took their places at the front of the church by the little altar, she smiled at Toby and nodded. He smiled broadly and nodded back.

When the music began for the bride's processional, everyone stood up in anticipation and in honor of the bride. With the sunlight beaming through the stained-glass windows, Maya looked gorgeous as she walked through the rainbows toward her soon-to-be husband. The shower of colors across the aisle landed against the white dress and veil as she slowly walked up the aisle.

She'd joked at their rehearsal it was a short walk to a long song so she was going to walk slowly.

Ripley looped her arm around Ty's waist and leaned against his solid body as Maya walked slowly up the aisle, her face radiating her happiness. He loved the fact Ripley felt so comfortable with him as he reached down to hold her hand at his waist. He smiled as Maya looked over and grinned happily at them.

As the ceremony went along, Ripley tried to picture herself being married. Before, it was hard for her to even imagine it. But now that she'd met Ty, that picture was beginning to become a little more clear and real to her. There was even an image of it being her and Ty. What would they be like as a married couple? Would they stay as happy as Josh and Morgan? Damien and Laura? Her own parents? What would their wedding be like?

She finally put the thoughts out of her mind, focusing on the two who *were* getting married.

She got tears in her eyes at the sweetness of it. Ty squeezed her hand when he heard her sniffle. She'd come prepared and used a tissue to dab at her eyes. Morgan held out her hand and wiggled her fingers over Ty's lap. Grinning, Ripley put a couple of tissues into her hand. Kim, sitting behind them, needed one too. Ripley passed a couple back to her. When Kat and Mel, also sitting behind them, looked at her, she just gave them the rest of the tissues she had. Ty chuckled softly.

When it was time for the rings, Toby turned to Drew for Maya's. Drew checked his left pocket first, pulling out the flask that Ty and Josh had given to them earlier. He handed it to Toby, asking him to "Hold it just for a moment," even offering him a sip while he waited for the ring to be found.

Soft laughter came again, with some worrying the minister would be offended at the lack of anyone being all that solemn at a wedding ceremony. But he didn't appear to be bothered at all. In fact, he looked to be enjoying himself.

When Drew checked his other pocket, he pulled out the pair of thick white socks Ripley had sent to Toby as a joke. She grinned when Toby turned to look at her with a mock frown and shook his head. Drew took the time to unravel the item so everyone knew what they were. Ripley could hear people laughing, whispering, "Socks in case he got cold feet!"

After Drew handed the socks to the minister saying, "Here, you can keep these," which made everyone laugh, he began looking for the ring again.

Maya was laughing, but she had this somewhat nervous look on her face too. She wasn't sure what else Drew might pull from his pockets. After all, the guy did have four of them.

With a flourish, Drew withdrew the ring from his inside pocket. He handed it carefully and reverently to the grinning Toby, who handed back the flask, saying, "Don't need it. Not today!"

Maya had to wipe the tears from her eyes while Toby's vows went off with no problem. Toby repeated the "With this ring, I thee wed" with a serious tone and slipped the ring onto Maya's finger.

When it was time for Maya to say her vows to Toby, the tears of sweetness became tears of laughter when Maya had to ask the minister to repeat what he'd just said because, she admitted, she was daydreaming. Even the minister laughed and dutifully repeated the words.

Her face pink with embarrassment, she listened this time and repeated them back. She'd heard her mom's delighted laughter from the front row, and it helped calm her nerves.

Toby grinned at her and held eye contact the whole time—which seemed to fluster Maya more.

When Alexis handed Maya his ring, Maya's hands were shaking so much, Alexis worried she might drop it. With their luck, it'd get lost, and they'd be crawling around on their hands and knees looking for it. She was just relieved *her* part of keeping the ring was over with. It was all on Maya now.

But Maya held onto the little piece of jewelry, sliding it down Toby's ring finger. When it stopped at the end, she squeezed it, whispering, "This ring had better *never* leave this finger."

Both the minister and Toby smiled broadly at her words.

Toby whispered back, "Yes, ma'am. Yours either."

They both laughed when the minister whispered to them, "Those are the best vows I've ever heard!"

When the minister finally announced them husband and wife, they both turned to walk back down the aisle. The minister cleared his throat, stopping them by asking, "Don't you want to kiss your bride?"

Toby, apparently flustered himself now and just following Maya's cue of facing the audience, quickly answered, "Yeah! I sure do!"

He grabbed her and kissed her passionately to the laughter and cheers from their family and friends. When they finally walked down the aisle, everyone continued clapping and cheering.

During the receiving line, Ripley noticed the couple was beyond happy. She hugged them both, whispering her congratulations in Maya's ear.

Maya said, "I'm *so* glad you stayed for us, Ripley. We both really are thankful you stayed a little longer just to be here with us."

"I'm honored you wanted me to be here. Thank you for inviting me."

AFTERWARDS, SHE RODE WHILE Ty drove her car—she claimed it was cleaner for their good clothes than his truck probably was—to the reception. He suddenly pulled into a small, empty lot, parked the car but kept it going for the air conditioning. He smiled as he had to remember how to put a Prius into *park*.

Ripley asked, "What're we doing here?"

He looked at her for a long moment. He finally said, "I want the very first thought and answer that comes to your mind when I ask my question. Deal? Promise me."

Her heart in her throat suddenly, she could only nod. Her heart beat faster, and she tried to focus on what he was going to ask her.

Softly, he asked, "What were you thinking as the ceremony took place?"

With a slight hesitation, she replied softly and honestly, "That maybe one day that could be you and me up there."

He smiled, his eyes locking onto hers. "That was mine too. It's good we both were thinking along the same lines, don't you think?"

Ripley shook her head. "I'm sure most people think that."

He immediately disagreed. "No, they don't. I've taken others to weddings, and I've been *in* weddings, and I never once thought that about any one particular woman. Until you.

"Answer me honestly again. Have you ever pictured yourself getting married to any other man, or a date you were with while at a wedding?"

She had to think back. She hadn't been to a wedding in years, so it took some time. Looking back, she considered.

Ty gave her time, letting her sift through her past. After a couple of minutes, though, he asked, "Has it been *that* long for you to attend a wedding? Or are you afraid to tell me?"

"Actually, it *has* been a while. And I only had a date for one or two. And no, I never pictured myself up there with him. I've never pictured myself getting married to *anyone*."

He commented, a touch of satisfaction in his voice, "Until today with me."

Ripley quickly glanced his way, startled. "Yes."

He smiled again, unbuckled his seatbelt so he could lean over. He framed her face with his strong hands. "You know what's happening, Sugar? You're letting your brain override your feelings, your subconscious, your heart. Inside, you're thinking long-term with me. And that's enough for me. For now." He pulled her as close as her seatbelt allowed, and smiling, met her lips with his.

Ripley, trapped in her seatbelt but feeling a power build inside of her, ran her hand over the side of his face, back into his thick hair, as she returned his kiss. When she finally pulled back, she smiled at him, passion lighting up her eyes. She tried to get back the breath he stole from her. "You get to me in so many ways. How do you manage to do that?"

"It's because you love me. If you didn't, I couldn't," he reasoned, saying it tenderly. He took hold of her hand, kissed her palm before just holding on to it.

Simple truths were always so poignant.

He let go of her hand after a moment, and Ripley sat back in her seat, adjusting her mauve-colored skirt around her legs. Her heart pounding, she looked out the window for a minute before looking back at him. He just nodded. The tenderness and love shining from his eyes nearly broke her resolve to remain level-headed.

The truth hit her right between the eyes.

He was right. She *was* in love with him. But was it enough?

Chapter 28

Thursday, September 24

He knew she had to go. She'd told him time and time again.

Although he'd still hoped she wouldn't, Ripley had left yesterday. The place seemed incredibly desolate and empty without her RV parked there, but not nearly as desolate as his heart felt at that moment.

Morgan reached over to untie Bombay. Glancing at Ty, she waited until he landed lightly in his saddle on Monte before handing him Roman's lead. They were going to lead Josh's buckskin horse on their ride to give him some exercise. She'd put Roman's bridle on over his halter in case one of them decided to ride him.

"It's your choice of trails this time." She led Bombay away from the hitching rail and checked the cinch before mounting up.

Ty shrugged. "Nothing else to do this afternoon. Long trail?"

"Sure." She knew the long trail was often used when they needed to talk about something.

Taking advantage of an early afternoon off, they decided to go for a ride. It was this, going to the shooting range, or working out. They both opted for the peace and quiet. They'd asked if Josh wanted to come, but he was still swamped with work.

The newlyweds were off on their all-expenses-paid honeymoon to Hawaii, courtesy of Ripley and Morgan with Laura's expert assistance through her travel agency. Work was a little busier, but nothing they couldn't handle. There was plenty of staff, so everything was running smoothly. Leaving Bo and Drew in charge since it was a slow day, Morgan and Ty decided to take advantage of it.

Together, they trotted away from Sunset Ridge heading toward the trail head, veering off in unison on the longer trail. The Darrells romped alongside the three horses, their tails wagging happily. With the dogs being older now, they both took care to not wear them out.

Ten minutes later, they were able to ride beside each other. Morgan inquired, "You okay?"

"Yeah."

"Miss her?"

"Yeah."

Morgan considered what to say next. "It's not the same with her gone, is it? I'd gotten really used to seeing her place down there and seeing her around the Center. She was so good with the horses too. They'll be another incentive for her to get back here. Ripley doesn't strike me as a person who gets attached to something like this, just to leave it all behind and forget all about it." Morgan said more firmly, "She'll be back, Ty. I have faith in what you two have going."

He ran the reins through his fingers a moment. "We all know the rescues aren't a permanent fixture though. And we'll still talk on the phone and email. It's just an adjustment."

Morgan whistled for the dogs to stay within her range of vision. They both trotted back at her call. She reached over, laid her hand on his arm. "Hey, it'll be all right, Ty. I feel it in my bones."

"That's old age creeping up on you." He sent a grin her way, knowing she was being the friend she was and trying to cheer him up.

She chuckled. "That may be part of it." She was silent for a while before asking curiously, "Okay. I have to ask. Did you run background on Ripley like you did Josh?"

Ty nodded. "Yeah. I had to. I myself needed at least the basics to make sure she was real, clean, and didn't have a criminal record. I needed to know she was legit and not a mole or an agent. If she is, her record was set up pretty well and looks airtight. They agreed she needed checked out just in case we do go further for both my protection and for those I protect.

"But I told them to tell me only the basics. In essence, the info I got was just a typical background check a landlord would run, with a deep focus on her being real. The only thing they added a little more info on was her financials. It wasn't a red flag, more like a yellow one that went green. They didn't give me specifics but said she was set up very well, and that it all looked legal. They checked all of her tax records and said it all looked completely legit. Her company is too. Her spending habits are thrifty. Like Josh, no gambling problems, debts, or anything like that.

"The Agency knows more, but they didn't pass along anything else except what I asked for. Any type of red flag would've been passed along to me immediately. And this also pertains to you because you were her landlady. I just did the background check for you... without you knowing."

Dryly, Morgan commented, "Appreciate it. Especially now that she's gone."

He smiled before he said, "I wanted to learn about her as we went along. I didn't want there to be anything between us that could come out later. So with any luck, she won't know about the background check I ran on her. I want it to be honest and fair between us. And it's hard to not look deeper when I can, but that's not fair to her. It's wrong to pry into her life and background when she has no way to do that to me without me knowing."

"I agree, Ty. Don't do it. If she found out, it'd be a serious breach of trust. I don't feel she'd ever be able to work through that." She looked at her friend, saying, "You might have more knowledge of this than I do, but I have the distinct feeling she's been hurt or betrayed. Something that keeps her from just jumping in with both feet, all the consequences be damned. She's almost as cautious as I was."

He sighed. "Yes, she's had some experiences in her past. We've talked about them. I told her I'd never do any of what she went through. She trusts me not to. I intend to keep my promise even though I'm not perfect, and I'll probably hurt her too. But I've never done what happened to her, so that part isn't that hard to uphold.

"She's open and willing for there being an *us*, and that's all I want. She's worth it to me, Morgan. She really is."

Morgan nodded, her gaze wandering over the mountain views before she checked on The Darrells. They were walking behind them, taking their time sniffing things. This was the peace she loved out here.

She finally said, "I've watched you over the years, you know. I want you to be happy like I am now since I found Josh. Or rather, he found me." They both smiled. "He's filled this void inside of me. A void I think I knew I had, but it deadened me inside so much I felt... The best word is *hollow*.

"I could be wrong, but I think you have a similar void in you. And I only say that because Shane had it. He told me I filled his void of loneliness, of having someone just for him to come home to. Someone who he didn't need to keep secrets from, at least what he did anyway. He had someone he could trust, be open with.

"He once told me I allowed him to breathe. I've never forgotten how that statement hit me like a ton of bricks. It was the best compliment he could've ever given me, you know? Since you were both agents, I can only assume you'd have a void too."

Ty knew his best friend was perceptive. This confirmed it once again. "You're right. On all of it. That's something I realized not too long ago—that I had a void, and just how deep it went. I knew there were times I'd feel lonely, wishing my life were different... probably like most people.

"But I didn't really get how *deep* it was until Ripley. More so after I began to realize there was enough between us that could take me further into a relationship than anyone else before her. I had to really analyze that."

She nodded in understanding.

They rode for a minute before he told her, "You fill some of my void, Morgan. You do, and you have for many years. It really helps that I don't have to hide my past from you anymore, that I can trust you with all of that. It's been a relief, and a huge weight off my shoulders. I guess you could say you've allowed *me* to breathe too.

"I know you credit me for being there for you, but you were always there for me too. You still are, and it doesn't go unnoticed.

"And you know, Josh also fills some of my void. He's the first male friend I've had out here, not counting our staff. He actually brought that to my attention. Since he also knows about me, the two of you are even more special. But there's still an open space there. Something tells me Ripley could completely fill it."

Several minutes passed before Morgan turned to ask him a question, but she stopped short of voicing it.

Ty noticed her hesitation, and then answered her unspoken question softly, "Yes, I do."

She looked at him, a bit startled. "Yes, you do what?"

"Yes, I love her. Isn't that what you were going to ask?"

"Yeah." Her eyes got misty with tears as she looked at him. "You love her? Like the marrying kind of love?"

"I'd like to think so. And I think she loves me, but she's not sure what to do about it yet. Mainly because we *haven't* known each other that long. She's correct about that. But like you and Josh, when you know, you know. And because of that time issue... well, that's a part of it... she refuses to say it to me. And she won't until she's ready, but when—*if*—she does, I'll know I have her.

"But I do love her, and that's what I kept reminding her this past week. It's probably for the best she *did* leave though. While I'm sure I do love her, maybe I shouldn't have told her yet because it may not be enough."

"How so?"

"What do you think would be holding *me* back? Name the big one."

"Trust. Can you trust her with your past?"

"Bingo." He gave Roman a bit more lead so he could walk around the brush they were approaching. "I just don't know. And until I do, I can't... and won't... say a thing about it. Since I rarely have anything to do with it now, there's really no need to bring it up."

"Except for the trust issue, Ty. It won't be like it was with us because I already had experience with it." Morgan sighed, thinking. "If you *don't* tell her and somehow in the future—assuming you got married or just continued in a relationship—she found out, she'd wonder why you never told her. It'd boil down to a lack of trust between you. And without trust, you won't have a leg to stand on.

"And if you take that giant leap of faith and *do* tell her, then you'll be looking over your shoulder. You'll always be preparing yourself for that what-if of you breaking up. And can you trust her to keep it to herself forever? Or would it slip out by accident or in the heat of an argument?"

"Yep, that's exactly what it boils down to. Every guy I know in this line of work has this same huge issue. It's not easy to know what to do. Some guys have been burned, and others got lucky. Shane was lucky because he had you to rely on."

After they stopped to let The Darrells rest if they needed to, she said, "I think Ripley could be your Josh. It's still early, but she has a lot going for her. It took Josh and I almost two years to get to the point where I was ready to marry him. He had the patience of Job! But he never pushed me in anything.

"It might be that you'll go through the same thing with Ripley. I couldn't help it, and she probably can't either. You just need to be prepared to wait until she's ready like Josh did for me."

He nodded. "Right now, with her leaving and not knowing if she'll return to me, I can't see the reasoning of telling her. I just can't, Morgan." He paused with an uncharacteristic hesitation before he asked, "How did you know you could truly trust Josh with your past? What made you take that plunge? You did it far sooner than I ever thought you would too."

Morgan thought back. Finally, she replied, "You."

"Me?" He sounded genuinely surprised.

She nodded. "I trusted you and your instincts. *And* my own. Of course, my hand was forced because of the trial. But I trusted you in your faith, judgment, and belief in Josh. I knew in my heart that if he didn't pass your personal criteria checks, gut feelings, and get your full approval, you'd never have let him near me. But you did. You never even once tried to warn me off or away from Josh. If anything, you did the complete opposite. I got *so* lucky finding Josh."

Seriously, he said, "If he didn't pass my scrutiny, I would've found a way to make sure he stayed away from you."

Softly, she said, "I know. And I'm thankful you never had to, so very thankful. It's hard to imagine my life now without Josh in it. I do love him, Ty. And I know he loves me. Besides Shane and yourself, he's the best man I've ever known. He *is* the best. And I do whatever I can to never take him, and what we have, for granted. I got a second chance, and I don't want to blow it. I don't live on a pile of eggshells, but I'm just aware of the alternatives."

He nodded. "Yes, I know. And I'm equally as thankful you have Josh. I used to really worry sometimes if something happened to me, who would you have? Suddenly, Josh came along, and then Damien, Laura... then Josh's family. You have a new solid set of friends outside of work... and me." He paused before confiding, "I just wonder if that love you and Josh have is a card that's somewhere in my own deck."

Morgan reached over, grabbed hold of his hand in support. "It has to be, Ty. It just has to be. You are the absolute best friend ever. And not only that, one of the most upstanding humans I've ever known. Don't give up. It may or may not be with Ripley. She has my vote though. I really do like her, and I approve of her. I just wish she'd settle down here for you. It really needs to be her choice, you know?"

"Better than you really. I can't pressure her, and I can't make her. I also told her I won't run after someone who doesn't want me."

"No, you can't do that. You could do a really fast power walk though!" She caught his grin and squeezed his hand before letting it go. "If she doesn't come to you on her own free will, your relationship wouldn't be as strong as it'd be if she did. A relationship is work enough without having to wonder about why you're together."

"We all agree on that."

"But she *does* want you. I'm a woman, so I can give you the female's perspective on this. I've seen you together. I've studied you two like bugs under a microscope."

Looking at her, Ty smiled. "Somehow that doesn't surprise me."

Morgan chuckled. "It was only fair since I know you did it to me and Josh. I was really just watching your back. I think she's the real deal. She's a hard worker, clean, responsible, has a talent with horses and people. She also seems honest, and she's got a great sense of humor. She has an adventurous spirit—you need someone like that. From what I can tell, she handles money well which is very important. She prefers Pepsi over Coke, and even chews with her mouth closed. She's got class."

She added the last comments to make sure he was listening to her. When he grinned, she knew he was, so she happily continued, "She made the effort to spend time with you, even scooping up manure. What woman who doesn't want to be around a man does that?

"And I've seen the way she watched you, heard the happiness in her voice when she talked about you. It wasn't faked or forced. She'd have no reason to do that anyway. If she didn't *want* to be with you, all she had to do was tell you. Or even simply unhook her RV and drive off in the middle of the night."

He nodded slightly. "That's about what I've been telling myself."

Morgan decided to add some more support for her friend. "And this long-distance relationship thing? She said she'll come back to visit now and then, right? And you *know* I'll let you go visit her when I can. And distance doesn't always matter, not when there's a firm foundation already built. You guys are just going to build on that foundation you've already started, but do it by being apart. There are actually some positives to that."

Ty nodded. "That's what we were trying to do before she left. Build that solid foundation so we had one but still have the personal space we both needed. Working with Cappy made for great opportunities for that."

After a few minutes, she said, "Let's stop here. Let me get on Roman so he gets some more loving. Plus, The Darrells can rest again for a minute."

After she called her dogs over, she dismounted from Bombay. She reached into her saddlebags for the reusable bottles of water and the squishable dog bowl she carried. She poured some of the water in the bowl for them and gave the other bottle to Ty. She finished off the bottle she shared with her dogs, then checked their feet.

Ty asked, "They okay?"

"Yeah." She dumped the water from the bowl over a barrel cactus once she was sure the dogs were done drinking. She shoved it and the empty bottles back into her saddlebag before she handed Ty Bombay's lead.

"Let's see how he reacts when I'm on Roman," she joked, stroking her horse's neck. "Or do you want to ride Roman instead?"

"Nah. I've got your temperamental kid."

Ty helped her swing up on Roman. With a laugh, she eventually got settled on Roman's bare back. She took the lead from his halter that he also wore and draped it over his neck. She gathered his reins and patted him. "I used to be a lot more athletic than that!"

Ty laughed as he now held onto Bombay's lead and adjusted his reins for Monte. "Well, I'll allow that you *were* kinda pinned between them when Roman moved over and squished you."

She laughed as they began walking. She soon scolded her own horse from Ty's other side. "Bombay! *Quit* that!"

Bombay had a jealous streak in him when he saw his mistress on, or even with, another horse. He began tossing his head and balking instead of walking along like usual. He gave Morgan what could only be considered a snotty look.

Ty gave his lead a firm pull and got Bombay up beside him. "Bombay, behave yourself!" With a chuckle, Ty tugged on his lead again. "Such attitude!" he teased.

"It won't kill him to see me riding Roman. It's not like I left him alone. He's still with me!" She looked over at her Thoroughbred, who was decidedly giving her a look of disgust. "Gotta love his personality though!" She laughed heartily at her horse's jealousy.

Bombay's look got darker when he saw Morgan patting Roman's neck and talking to him. Ty noticed it and laughed. "He's not going to let you pet him for a week once we get back!"

What he said was probably correct. Bombay had a human personality in many regards. If he saw Morgan with other horses, he'd ignore her for days at a time, deliberately walking away when she came to see him. Once he got over his pouting, though, he'd follow her like a puppy. He'd even come running to her when she called his name.

As they rode along in silence for a few minutes, Ty tugging on Bombay's lead now and then, she said, "Fate may say it's not Ripley. I hope it is though. But if not, if you don't find your gal... Well, you've always got me. I know it's not the same, but you take what you can get sometimes!" She gave him a grin to keep it light.

He genuinely smiled back. "I'll take you any day."

They rode on together, two friends with a shared past looking toward a promising future.

Chapter 29

Monday, September 28

They looked like the Brothers Grimm. Deputy Matt Harvey and Humane Society Representative Dell Shannon walked up to Morgan early the next week.

She was helping riders dismount from the three-hour long trail ride. Making sure their legs were steady enough to support them before letting them walk away on their own accord, she took her time. She watched as the people walked stiff-legged toward the picnic tables. Almost everyone walked just like that when they dismounted from this long ride, she told them with a cheery smile. Then she recommended they walk it off and not sit.

When Morgan saw the two men coming toward her, her insides clenched together in a knot. They waited discreetly for her to become available. Morgan called out to Maya, back from the surprise honeymoon, to come finish up with the horses.

Maya came over immediately, saying nervously, "I'm praying this is good news. They aren't smiling though. My heart is pounding out of my chest!"

"Mine too." Morgan handed the lead ropes to Maya before walking over to the two men. "I guess you have news?"

They nodded to her, motioned for her to walk with them.

"They finally got a verdict?" she asked, cutting to the heart of the matter.

Matt nodded. "Yeah. The part that concerns you are the eleven horses, of course." He smiled. "Good news first. The judge has awarded you compensation in full for the receipts and charges you filed in court. The original shipping company is required to pay you immediately for all services rendered. You should be hearing from their lawyer or bank within the next couple of days. The judge ordered for you to be paid immediately for everything up to now."

She smiled a little. "Well, that's good, of course. I'd rather hear about the horses themselves. They aren't going to confiscate them and send them back on their way to the slaughterhouse... Or are they?"

Dell shook his head, but he also didn't look optimistic. "Not exactly. Because of all of the broken laws and regulations that were found, the judge was pretty upset. He's not returning them to the shipping company *or* to the guys who bought them at auctions up north." His pause did not bode well to Morgan. She was right.

"But he also isn't going to let you just keep them since you're being reimbursed to the penny for what you've personally paid. And he won't swap the horses for your fees and charges. We had a lawyer ask him already, and he said no. The lawyer is a very good one, but the judge still wouldn't budge."

Morgan's heart ached when she asked softly, "So what *did* he say?"

With disappointment in his voice, Matt replied, "He ordered them to be sold at another auction. All proceeds are to be split between the victims in the crash on top of the insurance they're getting. Whatever it is, it gets split. The lawyers will get the receipt of the sales, and then divvy it up per court order."

"*What?*" she cried out. "Why should *they* get the money from the horses? That doesn't make any sense, Matt! None! Doesn't the judge realize these are innocent horses that are being stressed out here? What could happen to them doesn't matter to him? Isn't he supposed to be for justice?"

Morgan also understood what else he was saying. Or rather, *not* saying. Her heart hurt as it all sank in. "Sell again at auction, where the most consistent bidders are the meat market buyers. They weren't awarded back to the original company, but they'll most likely just end up with another one."

Both men nodded.

Thinking, Morgan asked, "What if I just bought them? Not a swap, but a buy? Can I do that?"

Matt shook his head. "No. The judge's orders were clear and explicit. They must be sold at public auction next month." He paused, wondering how to say this next part. "There's one more thing."

Morgan knew it wasn't going to be good news. Trying to be professional, she firmly asked, "What is it, Matt? Just tell me."

He looked around, hating to say it. "Per the orders from the judge, you and any direct, paid employee, or a person in immediate relation, as in an immediate family member, of any employee of Harmony Hills are not allowed to bid on the horses at auction. Neither can we. Basically, anyone directly involved with the horses are banned."

Stunned into speechlessness, Morgan just gaped at him.

Matt and Dell both shook their heads in true disappointment.

Finally, Morgan asked softly, "But why? Why would he do that?"

Matt answered, "Because he figured you were being compensated in full for your expenses. Also, I think he was attempting to keep this all separate. Maybe to not allow you to be compensated in full for your expenses, which were quite substantial, then allow you to turn around with that same money just to buy them back for yourself. Which means you'd use them here at the Center to then make a future profit off them.

"However, it *doesn't* say in the court order someone *else* couldn't buy them. And what *they* do, well, that's their business at that point. It's just mainly you, your employees, and any immediate family members that can't buy them. In essence, as tough and unfeeling as he came across, there's a part of me that thinks he did it more for appearances. But he left a slice of opportunity in there, thin as it may be.

"I almost got the impression he did this on purpose, knowing something we don't. I could be wrong. Do you have a boarder, or someone who's close to these horses, that could afford to buy them all? Or even a few? Or maybe a bunch of your boarders could do it together?"

Morgan shook her head. "I don't know anyone who'd have the funds to buy them. Or whether or not they'd try to sell them back to me. Obviously, I'm not privy to the private financial details of my boarders, so I have no clue if someone has money to burn. As long as they pay board on time, we never have any issues.

"I mean, since Josh and Ty are excluded, there's no one else I know about who could even try to get a loan to buy them. How would they know how much to get a loan for since at auction you never know what they'll bring anyway?"

Dell added, "And to make matters worse, he ordered a large reserve on each horse. If the reserve isn't met, the horses are to be shipped to another auction until the reserve *is* met. This is to continue until all eleven are sold. Who knows how many auctions these horses could be sent to! Their conditions could worsen as they went, making it harder and harder for them to bring in the reserve."

Morgan shook her head. "This is ridiculous! We've taken great pains to rehab these horses! They know us. They know the Center. They feel at home here. *Here* they're loved and safe!"

Both men nodded.

Looking away, Morgan worked to hold back her tears. Her heart was shattered. All the work they'd put in was most likely done in vain. There had to be *some* way to save them. These horses deserved better!

Matt sighed. "Anyway, I have the papers from the judge. They're solid and clear, Morgan. Before we came here, we sat down again with the lawyer and his associates. We went through it line by line, looking for that loop hole. The best I got was that judge knows something we don't, or he just doesn't care.

"The auction is to be held next month. It's actually only two weeks away from now. At the time the horses leave your property, namely your care, your expenses end. You'll be compensated in full until the horses are delivered at the first auction lot. If I were you, I'd charge as much as you think you reasonably can for transportation. And don't forget about the return mileage, meals, and labor."

Morgan nodded. "Oh, you can count on that!" She blew out a shaky breath to get control of herself. "I think I'll charge for pain and suffering too. Do you think I could get away with that?" She had a sudden thought. "But what if they *all* don't sell at this first auction? Who gets them until the next one?"

Matt replied, "That's an excellent question, and I'm glad you asked. I forgot to mention that. I'm sorry. Any that don't sell, you have the sole authority to return them here. You're required to then take them to the next available auction, and so on until all are sold. Any more accrued expenses you'll be compensated for so keep a record like you did before."

Dell looked at her. "You've got two weeks to think of something, Morgan. The Humane Society can't do anything. With donations being lower than they've been in years, we simply can't afford to do it. Not to buy eleven horses, transport them, feed them, board them, do vet and hoof care until we hopefully find them an approved home. We can hardly find homes for the ones we already have."

He added with a frown, "We've also already contacted local rescue centers, but they're in the same fix as we are. Money is just too tight. No one can afford to over-extend themselves any more than they already are. And there are people who are still just letting their horses loose all over the state not realizing, or caring, most of them will die!"

Matt and Morgan nodded, knowing this was truth. Many domesticated animals didn't know how to survive in the wild. Some made it, but it was more cruel to do that to them.

Matt handed her a large, thick envelope. "This has a copy of the court's orders. The documents you'll need when you take them to auction, the form *they* need to fill out and send to the court, along with the document giving you the sole authority to bring back any that don't sell are also in there. I'm sorry, Morgan. I know you love these horses more than anything, and you're scared for them. It's just out of our hands."

"Thank you. I'll read these over later when I'm alone and not distracted."

Nodding, they left her standing there in the shade as they walked back to Matt's cruiser.

"He said *what?*" Ripley couldn't believe what Ty was telling her. She was sitting on her couch in her RV near Abilene, Texas after working all day and doing a training earlier that evening.

"We can't keep them. The judge ordered them all sold at auction." Ty went on to give her all the details and stipulations. "In my opinion, I think the reason the judge put such a high reserve on them is to discourage the meat buyers from wanting to buy them. They want the cheapest horse flesh they can get. They'll possibly avoid bidding on these eleven because it'd make it harder for them to recoup their expenses and still make a profit."

Thinking about it, Ripley had to agree. "But it also makes it harder for anyone else to buy them. However, I think you're right. He was hoping someone with money would buy them, thereby giving them a better chance of a real life. The problem is most horse people with money aren't buying unregistered stock from auctions but from horse breeders instead."

He agreed. "Now that Morgan has had time to sit and think it all through, she may agree with me too. She had me come up to the house once we closed today. We went through it all. I just got home a few minutes ago. Josh will probably see it that way, too, whenever she tells him. He was working late again."

Ripley asked, "Do you know exactly where they're to be sold? And when? What the reserves are?"

"Of course."

"Give me the exact details. Or you can email the information to me."

"I have it right here. Want it over the phone?"

"Sure. Hang on a second." Reaching over, she grabbed her notebook and turned to a fresh page. With pen in hand, she headed to her little table. "Okay. I'm putting you on speaker so I can write easier. Give me everything you got."

Chapter 30

Saturday, October 17

It rained the morning of the auction. Morgan asked Josh how was she supposed to keep from crying over the rescues when even the angels in heaven already were? He just hugged her, knowing her heart was as broken as his own over them.

The staff of Harmony Hills felt the rain was appropriate. No one was smiling or joking this morning as their moods were as depressing as the weather. Although rain was welcome in the desert, it just wasn't welcome today.

Since it was so early and still fairly dark outside, Morgan and Toby backed up the two trailers into Grand View for more light for safety. It also helped to keep everyone dry. They began loading the horses after they ate their final breakfast there. Morgan insisted they be fed well.

With Ty manning the Center, Morgan drove the first trailer with Alexis coming along to help out. Morgan couldn't help but remember that night when they got the call it was Ripley with her. Toby and Maya were again following behind with their own GPS set to the auction lot in case they got separated.

Hours later, they pulled into the auction yard. Following the signs, they drove to the stockyard buildings and holding pens. After using the restrooms inside the main building, Morgan led the four of them into the office. She presented the court documents, the health papers from Dr. Shamis, and the auction's required paperwork she'd downloaded at home to pre-fill out with Ty and Josh.

The middle-aged lady behind the tall desk looked through everything, checking details and records. She licked her fingers to turn the pages easier. "Okay. It all looks in order. Thank you so much for being so thorough and prepared, Mrs. Wright. It helps everything run so much more smoothly when people do it correctly.

"Sign these papers, here and here"—she pointed to the lines—"to release you from the horses once they get unloaded. If any don't sell, come back in here, and I'll fill out this form, okay? We'll send this copy here to the judge for you to show your compliance. You probably want a copy for your records?"

"Yes, I would. Thank you." Morgan took a deep breath. She gripped her hands together to keep them from shaking.

"Smart lady. I would too." The lady took the paperwork to a copier in the corner. She handed the fresh, warm copies to Morgan. She then slid the originals into a manila file folder. She turned to a young man sitting in the corner watching a small television. "Randy, can you go with Mrs. Wright here? Unload eleven horses. Here are the tags for them."

"Sure." A young man with short brown hair who looked to be in his mid-twenties, wearing a Stetson hat and Wrangler jeans, got up. He nodded to them as he got the tags and papers. After Morgan got the receipts, Randy led everyone back outside. He showed them where to go with the trailers.

Alexis started crying as soon as she climbed in beside Morgan in the truck. Morgan knew Alexis had been holding it in on the drive up. Once they arrived, she saw the tears glimmering in the young woman's eyes. Morgan was on the verge of falling apart herself, but she didn't have that luxury. This was all too real now.

"I know, Alexis. This is breaking my heart too." Morgan reached over, rubbed her back. "But you have to be strong about this. We're adults, and we can't be creating a scene for everyone to watch, okay?

"Just think of something else to distract yourself if you feel yourself falling apart. Think of something that can make you happy. Think about graduating, and what you want to do once you do. Or what you may want to stay in school for. You can cry all you want to on the way home, okay? Just do your best to hold yourself together here."

It was like Morgan hadn't said a word as Alexis blurted out, "I just can't believe we have to do this. It's so *wrong!* Morgan, you can do anything. Can't you stop this? You can do it... I *know* you can!" She grabbed some napkins from the glove compartment to blow her nose.

Humbled by the faith from the young woman, Morgan had to shake her head. "No, I'm sorry to say. Rules and the law apply to me too. There's nothing I can do except what I'm forced to do now. I know how you're feeling. Believe me, I know. But they have a chance, Alexis, for a better life. You have to remind yourself of that now."

Morgan started the truck, preparing to follow the young man to the pens. "Now pull yourself together, Alexis," Morgan said firmly. "You're representing Harmony Hills."

While Alexis tried to pull herself together, Morgan followed Randy. When he signaled to stop, she put the truck into *park* and turned off the engine. They followed him to the back of the trailers to begin unloading the horses. After they received their ID tags, they were led into the holding stalls for the buyers to look over.

Randy commented, "It's a nice change to have horses that unload this good. Some of the ones we get are more than a little dangerous. In this job, I never know what's gonna be coming at me from any trailer! I'm always hopin' the driver will warn me, but many don't."

Maya said sadly, "That's because we spent months working with every single one of these horses. We rehabbed them and especially worked on trailering. They were rescued from a semi crash, and it wasn't easy gaining some of these horses' trust again."

Randy looked over at her. "Oh, man! I heard about that. It was on the news a few months back, right? These are the same horses?"

Toby nodded, adding a quiet, "All the ones that lived."

Randy nodded, understanding in his eyes. "I bet it's really hard to let 'em go, ain't it?"

"Very much so," Morgan said. Hard? It's killing me, she thought to herself.

Randy was sympathetic as he said, "I'm sorry. It's so easy to become attached to 'em. They ain't just animals to you, are they? They're like furry people, right? I can tell by the way y'all look."

They all nodded.

"I understand. There are times I hate workin' here because I can't stand the not knowin' of what will happen to 'em once they're sold. We try and vet our buyers, if that's any help to you. We try to only let legit buyers bid. We even run their names by the sheriff's office and the Humane Society... Anyone who might know more than what's put on paper."

Morgan nodded. "I know you guys do. And for those of us who love these furry people, we appreciate it. But it's still excruciating to let them go..." Her voice trailed off before it cracked. She turned and prepared herself for the hardest one yet.

When Morgan led out Cappy, Alexis couldn't take any more. Before bursting into tears again, Alexis headed straight for the truck, hopped in, and slammed the door. Morgan was hard put to not follow her.

Maya and Toby had faces of sorrow as Morgan led Cappy to his small pen. He was looking around with his intelligent eyes. It seemed to Morgan he knew exactly where he was and what went on here. It was apparent to Morgan this wasn't his first visit to the auction yard as Cappy broke out into a sweat almost instantly. He was an auction lot veteran. And it'd never gone in his favor. Morgan prayed he didn't revert to his old ways here.

The three kept an eye on Cappy, noticing his rolling, white eyes and his worried eyebrows. His intelligent and ever-expressive eyes kept resting on Morgan like he was seriously asking her: *Why are you doing this to me again? Haven't I been good? I tried to be good. I really did! Don't you want me? Why don't you want me anymore? What did I do wrong this time?*

Besides feeling like she was completely betraying Cappy's trust in her—which she *was* being forced to do—Morgan never handled goodbyes without crying.

Feeling deep guilt eating away at her heart and her composure, Morgan choked back a sob as she stroked the horse's neck. She blinked back the tears and bit her lip to keep from crying. She was a grown woman, dang it. She did *not* cry in public *or* in front of her employees. She blew out a few deep breaths as she stroked Cappy's neck and silently apologized to him, over and over.

Toby noticed his boss was fighting a good cry. He transferred his gaze back to the horse. Trying to think of something to distract her and his new wife, he said, "I wish Ripley was here."

Unfortunately, it was the one thing that made it worse.

Maya nodded, tears now spilling over her eyes. "Me too. This would just crush her heart, wouldn't it? After all the work she and Ty put into Cappy, here he is again! All of them *trusted* us to take care of them, and look what we're doing to them now. Damn that heartless judge!"

Maya wiped her eyes as more tears ran down her cheeks. She felt like running to join Alexis but refused to leave Morgan alone as the sole female. She had to stay and offer solidarity to her and to the horses, she told herself. Or die trying. "I'm so sorry, Morgan. I told myself I could get through this and not fall apart."

Morgan could only nod. A few tears falling freely now, Morgan just kept apologizing to Cappy. Maya cried softly beside her. Toby had to leave so he didn't cry too.

People came by, assessing the horses to see if they wanted to bid on them. Morgan and Maya got many looks from people, but neither cared. Cappy stayed right beside them, never once leaving their sides. He knew what was going on, and in his fear, he stayed with the only two people he knew he could trust. Knowing this just made it practically unbearable for Morgan to take. Maya went and gave some loving attention to the other ten horses there, leaving Morgan alone with Cappy.

Morgan had several heroic scenarios rolling through her mind... Of her whisking Cappy away, if not all of them. Or of one of her boarders from the Center who could legally buy them come swooping in at the last minute. She'd talked to some of her boarders, but no one seemed able to help. Her heart was shattering at the thought of any of these horses ending up in the wrong hands again, but most especially Cappy. She even wished she'd forced the vets to swear they'd *all* died from their injuries. Then she could keep them and love them the way they should be loved.

Cappy's gaze stayed on Morgan as he stood beside her. They were betraying that trust by not keeping him. That's all Morgan could think... Because it was true.

They finally had to leave him. Morgan kissed his nose one last time, telling Cappy it was also from Ripley and Ty. She went to the other horses, kissing each one, petting them. Walking away, she quickly and resolutely wiped the tears from her cheeks, straightened her shoulders. She was the one in charge here so she needed to be strong. Maya had Toby to lean on while here. She wished Josh were here with her, but he was working on the business complex. He'd really wanted to come, but she'd told him he had his own business to run. This complex was a huge opportunity for him, so she'd insisted he stay behind this time.

Toby had moved the trailers from the un-loading area. He met them as they were heading back to the parking area, looking for him. Alexis was with him, her eyes red and swollen from crying. Feeling ashamed for acting like a child, Alexis apologized to her boss as soon as she saw her.

Morgan hugged her, saying, "We're all hurting here, guys. We just have to pray these horses fall into the right hands. Not all buyers are bad ones. Remember some of ours *I* bought from an auction. We just need to focus on that. I'm not the only nice person out there looking for a good horse. Think positive thoughts."

They all tried to. Debating on whether to stay there and wait to eat, or go somewhere nearby and come back, they felt obligated to stay and see what transpired.

"I'm not done yet!" Morgan stated angrily as they walked back toward the building where the auctioneer would do his best to get the highest prices. "We are *not* just going to drop them off and abandon them. I want to know *who* is going to buy these guys. I want to meet them and make it clear of their backgrounds. I'm going to give these horses a fighting chance!"

THE TWO MEN DISCREETLY watched them from a short distance away but were close enough to see their tears and hear Morgan's resolve.

Jerrod looked at his companion, studied him for a moment. "This is tearing her apart. Are you sure you want to take this chance?"

The other man nodded even as his own heart was torn in two for more than one reason. "It's too late now either way. And we have the back-up plan in place in case it doesn't go the way we're hoping it does." He watched as the four people walked into the large building again. He let out a short huff of air to stay focused on his task.

Jerrod asked quietly, "How can you even do this to her, Storm?"

Silently, Storm stared at the doorway she'd walked through just a moment before. Finally, he replied softly, "Because this test isn't for her. It's for another."

AFTER USING THE RESTROOMS again and washing away their tears, Morgan bought them some concession food and drinks to tide them over. She got a program as Toby led them to nearly the top of the metal bleachers to watch the proceedings. They nibbled on the food that tasted like sawdust in their mouths.

Some of the horses going through were going for dirt cheap prices. They all figured those were the meat buyers... but not necessarily.

"Remember they try hard here to prevent the meat buyers from getting them," Morgan repeated this optimistic thought over and over to her crew. And to herself.

When their horses began coming out, their hearts broke all over again. Morgan saw one bidder sitting all alone near the front flipping through pages and skimming the program as the first horse, the gray mare, was brought out. Morgan was too far away to see what kind of papers he had. She'd noticed he hadn't bid on any other horse yet and assumed he was just waiting on a certain one he had an eye on. She was surprised when she saw him raise his hand to bid on the mare.

He and another couple of bidders kept raising the amount. The auctioneer saw a bidding war in the making, and his energy spurred them on. Finally, the other two bidders waved off. The man below them clinched the winning bid. Morgan made a note in her program of the bidder's number so she could track him down afterwards.

But how could they track down eleven different people before they all left if they all sold? she wondered, almost in a panic.

Alexis sat there in a daze as so much of her trust and innocence of the world was lost during that one auction. Working since she was so young until now for someone like Morgan, who put the horses first no matter what, to seeing her first auction was a shock to her system. The conditions some of these horses were in, and how cheaply some people thought their lives were worth, opened her eyes and broke her heart.

In her mid-twenties now, Alexis just never really realized what parts of the world and life were all about. She lived at home, went to school, and worked at Harmony Hills. It'd been her routine for years. She'd never really gone out to do anything life-changing like this before in her life.

Alexis wanted to go back to the Center and hug every horse they had. With her eyes now opened, she had a profound, new respect for the rules Morgan had regarding her horses and how they were to be treated. She wanted to thank and hug Morgan, too, for being who she was. And Josh and Ty because she knew they felt the same way about all animals.

"SOLD!" the auctioneer called out, breaking into her thoughts.

The man with all of the papers nodded at the auctioneer and made a note on the papers in his lap. He set those papers aside just to pull some more out of a folder sitting beside him. A woman soon walked up to him. As he spoke to her, she nodded and smiled. She walked away, making a note on her clipboard. He had just bought a horse that wasn't one of theirs, Morgan noted.

As the sale progressed over the next few hours, it occurred to Morgan that that one man was bidding on every single one of their horses that'd come out so far. There were other bids, of course, but he consistently raised them. Morgan knew what the reserves were on every horse of theirs and just kept watching, helpless, as the reserves were met, and the bids were raised.

The auctioneer just went on to the next horse. And the next and the next.

Maya had also caught on to the man below them and turned to Morgan. "Hasn't that man in the gray shirt down there bought all our horses so far? He just bought the Haflinger. If not, it sure seems like it."

"I was thinking the same thing, honey," Toby said. "Have you noticed, Morgan?"

Morgan nodded. "I've been watching him too. He's also bought one that wasn't ours. Afterwards, let's see if we can meet him, all right? No hysterics if we hear something we don't want to hear either."

They all nodded. Hours later, the auctioneer closed the sale.

Morgan had pulled out her smartphone earlier, opened up the notes app and made a note of every horse the man in the gray shirt had bought. She wanted a backup to her program notes. She checked it again now.

Fifteen total, with *their* eleven being included. He'd bought every one of their horses. Did he know they all came from the same place? Morgan wondered as she watched the man organize his papers and slip them all in a binder. The woman with the clipboard had come back out, chatting with him as he gathered his things. Once he was ready, she led him away.

As everyone began leaving, Morgan and her staff rushed down the bleachers to catch him but lost him in the crowd. Knowing the process, Morgan led the way to the Cashier area. They waited impatiently until Maya caught sight of him. They saw him as he was signing his name on all of the papers. He'd shown his identification to the smiling clerk, who'd made notes on more paperwork. He then apparently paid for the horses, as the clerk then stamped the paperwork, smiled, and shook his hand before giving him the papers in an envelope proving he was the new owner. She then handed some papers to the same woman they'd spoken to themselves when they'd checked in. Morgan assumed it was to send to the judge's office showing her compliance.

Waiting outside the office for the man to exit, they practically pounced on him the second he walked out the old wooden door that had once been a bright white but was now a dingy, dusty beige.

Morgan greeted him, "Excuse me, sir? I'd like to ask you about the horses you just purchased."

The man stopped, smiled warmly. "Yes?"

"We were wondering what you were planning on doing with them? Where they were going?"

He began to walk away to a quieter area, out of the way of the pressing crowd, motioning them to follow him. When he stopped, he turned to answer Morgan's questions. "I have no idea. I didn't buy them for myself, but for a friend who was unable to be here on such short notice. It's up to them. I was asked to be here, buy these horses, and transport them to another person's place for them."

Morgan needed more information. "Do you mind if we have your friends' names and contact information? You see, we've been working with most of those horses you bought for months now. We've put a lot of love, time, training, and patience into every one of them. One in particular. Some had been abused, and some injured badly in a wreck on the interstate. We just really want to be sure they're loved and cared for. If I could just talk to whoever bought them and explain..."

The man shook his head in regret. "I'm sorry, ma'am. I'm not at liberty to do that. However, if you give me *your* information, I'll pass it along to them both. My friends are animal lovers. Please don't worry about any of these horses being sent to slaughter, left in a muddy lot, or a cramped stall with moldy hay for the rest of their lives. They'll be treated even better than Black Beauty when Joe Green found him again. None will be abused. You can trust me on that. They'll take great care with them." He looked Morgan in the eyes when he spoke to her.

"Do you know that for *sure?*" Morgan pressed him. "It's breaking our hearts to let them go. If I could just talk to the owner, it could relieve my mind. All of our minds."

"I'm sorry, ma'am. If you give me your contact information, they can contact you. I can't say *when* exactly, but I will stress to them your concerns."

It was the best they could do, so Morgan went through her purse, took out two business cards. Handing them over, she stressed, "We really and truly want to hear that our horses are doing well and are happy. That's our utmost concern."

Curious, he asked her, "If you're so concerned for them, why did you sell them?"

"They aren't actually mine. We were contacted by the local authorities about a wreck on the interstate months ago. My equestrian center is the biggest one around that could handle that many horses at one time, especially at the last minute. They've been at my place since we got them out of the wrecked semi-trailer that night.

"We've rehabbed them over the past few months, hoping to give them a chance at a better life. We think they were on the way to a slaughterhouse, but they're too good of horses for that! They all have such potential and wonderful personalities.

"Per court order, I wasn't allowed to purchase any of the horses, nor were any of my employees or relations to any of my employees. We were forced to bring them up here this morning. We just want to know they'll be treated well. It's truly breaking our hearts to let them go! I'm seriously willing to buy them back if your friends are open to that, okay?"

The man nodded in understanding. He saw the tears from the young woman's eyes standing behind this lady he was talking with. And the sheen of tears in the other woman's eyes too. He tucked the cards in his shirt pocket, patted it. "I promise to pass along your concerns and your information to my friends. Please, don't worry over them. They'll be treated with love and care."

Morgan said, "Please, I can give them information on each horse. We have photos and videos of their training. They tie, lead, load, trailer, and ride. We even gave them baths. And wormed them too. We just trimmed their hooves about a week ago, and they did fine. And I had my vet out, and he floated their teeth.

"One horse in particular, the tall sorrel gelding, has been abused by men. It took us a long time to help him trust men again. He's fine with a woman, okay? If he doesn't take to a man, *please* just bring a woman over. He had a dental issue, and he just got abused horribly because no one took the time to figure out what was wrong. He doesn't deserve to be beaten ever again! Here's his tag number." Morgan showed the program in her hands to him, pointing to Cappy's number. Then she again practically begged him to have his friends call her.

His eyes, full of sorrow, locked on Morgan's again. "We'll take great care of them, ma'am. Nothing could rip them away from us. As God is my witness."

They all thanked him, not wanting to see the horses loaded up and driven away. Their hearts just couldn't take that.

With heavy hearts, but with hope flaring inside that the horses would be in a good home, they finally headed back to theirs.

As Morgan and her staff left the building, Jerrod and Storm watched them. Even after they were out of sight, the two men still stood there.

Jerrod finally broke the silence. "It seems like she passed your test. This makes you feel better, right?"

Storm nodded. "Of course." With a slight smile softening his features, he added, "Whatever you said to the judge to make him add this requirement seems to have worked."

Jerrod grinned. "I've been told I can be quite persuasive at times. And it was all legal and clean. It was merely a strong suggestion I gave him." After a moment, he asked, "Do you want anyone to pass along the news?"

Storm shook his head. "No. This was just a way for me to have his back. Besides, it's not completely finished. There's still more to come."

Jerrod nodded as he observed the hustle and bustle of the auction house as people mixed with animals. He finally ventured a question to his friend, asking softly, "Don't you think he'd want to know?"

Motioning for them to leave, Storm's walk was slightly jerky with his limp. After a few moments, he replied, "He'll never know."

Chapter 31

Thursday, November 19

Weeks later, Morgan still hadn't heard from whoever bought the rescues. It made her fuming mad one minute for believing that man and absolutely devastated the next.

The papers she got from the auction office didn't list the buyers. They just confirmed she'd done what she was forced to do. She wondered if she could get his name from the woman she'd given the papers to. Normally they weren't allowed to give out personal information, but maybe she could give Morgan *something?*

But life went on, and she had a business to run. Kat and Mel were gearing up for the upcoming shows Morgan had planned as they gave lessons. They'd both been gone for a few days, taking some of the students from Harmony Hills to a two-day show at another facility about five hours away. They had all placed well, and Morgan was cheered by their success.

Toby and Maya were still living in wedded bliss. Their happiness was a shot of the much-needed emotion injected into daily life at the Center.

Alexis, so affected by her time at the auction, began volunteering at the Humane Society with Dell Shannon when she had the time. And she was also thinking about switching her major to be a veterinarian or something like that now. After all, she'd already taken nearly every required class. Discussing it over with her parents, she then discussed it with her other set of parents—Morgan, Josh, and Ty. Encouraging her, they were proud of her wanting to have a life with purpose. One that would benefit animals from her own compassion was even better. Ty suggested she ride along with Dr. Shamis to see if that was really what she wanted to do. Josh and Morgan agreed.

They all also agreed it was good for Alexis since she came from a fairly sheltered background. They knew she was growing up and maturing more now as she saw the world for what it could be. Alexis was quite intelligent and getting hands-on experience would help her be more balanced. The fact she wanted to be spoke volumes for her character.

And then there was Ty, who obviously missed Ripley. To his credit, he wasn't moping around. He was too mature for that, but he also tended to just go home and not out with them as often as he did before.

Ripley, now in San Antonio, kept herself going by throwing herself into her work. The times she worked with Laura over the phone were the hardest because Laura simply reminded her of Ty and the rescues. Laura told her of all the ways Morgan and Josh were supporting her with her pregnancy. From watching Sasha, cleaning the house, cooking meals, and just being there for her and Damien, their unfailing support was inspiring.

Ripley missed Ty even more than she'd expected. If she let herself have down time, she was miserable. Nights were both her saving grace as well as the bane of her existence. It was normally at night when she and Ty talked to each other. And other times, it was when she and Julia talked. If she didn't talk to Ty, then she could hardly sleep for missing him. In the mornings, she was worn out and looked worse than when she went to bed the night before. She told herself she was pathetic.

It'd been almost eight weeks since she'd left Arizona. She was surprised at how much she wanted to go back. She was stretched out on her couch, her feet propped over the arm as she watched TV, but she soon dozed off. When her phone rang, she rolled over so quickly to grab it off the floor she almost fell off the couch. Her heart was racing in anticipation of it being Ty.

When she saw the Caller ID, her excitement dimmed a little, but she was still happy to take the call. "Hey there, Steve! How're my kids doing?"

"The kids are doing great. They're outside playing right now. I think they miss you. It's almost time for dinner, but I thought I'd call you first. When are you coming home?"

"I'm not sure. It's been a while since I've been there, hasn't it?"

"Yeah, it has been. Mom and Dad said to tell you hello, by the way. They were asking about you again. Thanksgiving is coming up next week. Do you think you can make it here, or do you have other plans?

"Your parents are coming. It's been a while since you've seen them, hasn't it? And the Ricardos, some other Capilanos and Ceravolos are planning on being here too. It'll be a crowded house complete with an eclectic mix of Italian, Spanish, and slang American dialects. It's sure to make us laugh cider out our noses!"

Ripley laughed heartily. "That was a long time ago, buster! And it hurt too." She sighed. "I just don't know yet. It'd be terrific to see everyone again, but sometimes it's just nice to not travel, you know?" She smiled while she thought about Joe and Lilly, Steve's parents. "Tell your parents I said hello, too, okay? Are they doing all right?"

Steve said, "Yeah, Mom just left for Maine to visit her friends for a few days. She wanted to see them before winter set in and didn't want to wait for spring. She's been worried about Della. Dad dropped her off at the airport this morning. She asked about you before she left. I told her I'd call and ask you. So? I'm asking."

Ripley paused, thinking. "I want to head back to Arizona soon, so maybe I can make a layover there with you. I'll check my schedule to see how it plays out. I talked to Mom earlier today, and she mentioned she and Dad were planning on being there with you guys. I told her the same thing I just told you. It's just a 'maybe' right now."

Steve considered her words for a moment before inquiring, "Back to Arizona? Aren't you in Texas right now? What's back in Arizona? More work? I didn't think you ever went backwards that far for work."

At her silence, he laughed. Excitement in his voice, he said, "No. Way. *No* way! You found a guy, didn't you? Did you find yourself a *man*, Rip? Did my girl find herself a man? A real live one?"

With humor and love in her voice, she replied, "As a matter of fact, I did. A real live one! What of it?"

"Nothing. Nothing at all. I just won't sleep at all tonight thinking about this turn of events!" He paused, wonder in his voice when he spoke again, "So he must be pretty dang special if he caught *your* attention."

With a bit of nostalgia in her voice, she confided, "Yes, he's special. He sent me flowers for my birthday, Steve. Can you imagine that? He had a big, beautiful bouquet of them delivered right to my RV door here in Texas. He took the time to figure out where I was, and then found someone local to get them to me. If that doesn't make him even more special, I don't know what would."

Steve smiled to himself. Could his cousin actually be *in love?* She'd never really cared about flowers from a guy before, at least that he could remember. "He sounds like a guy I can't wait to meet! You know we have to meet him to run him through the Italian character test, don't you? Do you think he's brave enough to pass it?"

She laughed at his teasing. "Yes, he is. I have no doubt he'd do it with flying colors too. Besides, he's made it past all of my own tests so far. If you could, Steve, *please* don't mention him to any of the family, all right? I didn't tell Mom either. I'm scared it'll jinx us, you know?"

"You got it, cous. I won't say a word to anyone. You know you can trust me. Friends like us gotta stick together!"

"That we do. Thank you." She paused and smiled. With a bit of seriousness in her tone, she added, "And I think you'd really like him. The two of you could hang out and be buddies in no time flat. I'd really like that if you two could hit it off. He's such an amazing person, and I'm a bit overwhelmed still at him picking me out of all the women he could have."

Steve was serious when he replied to her, "Ripley, you're an awesome person on your own. You do so much for people with most of them not even knowing it's you doing it. You have love, compassion, humor, determination, and loyalty. *That's* what he sees in you. And even though only those close to you know all that about you, he obviously picked up on it.

"And for me liking him? Probably. I can't imagine you going out with just anyone. He'd have to toe the line for you to give him the time of day. You're one of those women if you got a diamond engagement ring, you'd go have it appraised first."

"I would not."

He heard her snort and smiled. "So, when do I get to meet him? Will you bring him here for the holidays, or will that be a jinx thing? Does he know about your kids, by any chance? Would he like to meet them all?"

She laughed. "As a matter of fact, he does. Well, in a way... He just doesn't know they're mine. Or that I have more of them."

"How is *that* possible?" Steve asked. At her silence, he said, "Oh, no. You're up to something, aren't you?"

"You know how complicated my life is, right? Nothing is ever simple with me." She heard him laughing. "As it turns out, we first met *because* of these recent kids, but prior to them becoming mine.

"I want to wait to make sure all the court orders are clear before I let any of them know what happened. I don't want anyone put on the spot in case the lawyers figure out I'd been living there. The judge was pretty explicit about who could buy them, so I don't want to have any leads going back to them yet. Everything is clear as far as we know, right?"

"Yep. We have all their papers, your money obviously was good at the auction, and the lawyers are most likely sending out the checks to those involved. It's been, what? Just about a month now?" He checked the calendar, verifying. "Yeah, it's been five weeks since the auction. I'd say you're clear. You might want to hold off a little longer, maybe a few months, if you really want to be sure. Courts sometimes move slowly."

"I'd prefer to do that, but it's been hard on me to not say anything to them. Especially since Morgan repeatedly asked for who bought them to contact her. She's probably worried sick to her stomach or irate as a protective mama grizzly. Possibly both. But I just couldn't take the chance of saying anything yet. I might just have to play it by ear.

"I know when your dad went to the auction for me that they were really torn up about his buying them. If I was there, I'd have bawled like a baby! Knowing these people like I do, I can only imagine how much it broke them in pieces to be forced to sell them at an auction."

"About as much as it was breaking you... So, when are you coming home? Are you bringing your guy?"

"Man, you're *such* a nag!" Ripley joked. "I'll let you know when I know—" She heard her Call Waiting beep and took a quick look at the screen. Her heart sped up at seeing who it was. "Steve, I've got a call coming in I need to take. Do you want me to call you back?"

Steve, being not only a cousin but a great friend, knew Ripley Capilano *despised* Call Waiting and *never* took that incoming call. She *always* let it go to voicemail. She felt quickly hanging up on one person just to talk to someone else was flat-out rude, no matter who it was. When it happened to her, she seethed. So for her to tell him she had an incoming call that she *wanted* to take? He knew it had to be the man she was seeing.

Didn't love just conquer all? he thought with a wide grin. And that made him feel a little ornery so he simply kept talking to her on purpose.

"Actually, Ripley, I wanted to check with you on these horses' worming schedule. Do you want me to worm them anytime soon? Or are they okay for a while?" He had to fight back his laugh as he knew the last thing she wanted to talk about with her boyfriend calling was worms.

"What?" Ripley couldn't believe Steve had to discuss parasitic worms. *Now?* She heard the beep again in her ear of an incoming call. Dang it! She felt obligated to keep talking with Steve because he *was* taking care of all of her horses, so she forced herself to answer him. "Read the vet papers, Steven! I'm pretty sure they were wormed at the Center. I can't imagine Morgan letting something like that slide."

She only used his full name when she was peeved at him. Fighting back his laughter, he said casually, "Oh, yeah... I guess I could've checked that. Sorry. But if they need it, do you want me to go ahead and do it?"

"Only if they need it. But I'm sure they're fine." She thought about it. Actually, it had been a few months, at least. No, she thought again, they should be fine. She'd bet Morgan wormed them just before they left her place to protect them. That's how she was. "Anything else?"

Steve wasn't finished needling her. "Well, yes. Are any of these mares confirmed in foal?"

Silence.

Ripley knew she'd missed Ty's call and would need to call him back as soon as she got done with Steve. Wait. *What* did he just ask? "What makes you think they're in foal?"

"Well, either they're fat or pregnant. And you know how those feed lots and holding pens can be like. They sometimes just throw all the horses in one big pen together which allows for lots of horsing around!"

Laughing at his pun, she finally replied, "No, none are in foal that I know about. Geez, Steve. *You'd* be the one to know more about that than me anyway! What do I pay you for? They didn't look fat to me when they were at Morgan's. Maybe you're just feeding them too much. Cut back on feed costs, Steve-o! Do they *look* pregnant in any other way?" She hoped not!

"Oh, well, you know I hadn't had time to really check them myself. It was just a thought I had." He figured her boyfriend was waiting for her, so he decided to let her off the hook. He loved to tease his cousin. He also knew if he took it too far, her own revenge could be lethal. She had a sense of humor she didn't mind using to her advantage. "Well, Ripster, my dear. I guess I'll let you call your boyfriend back now."

Ripley was silent for a moment. How did he...? She gritted her teeth when she figured it out. "You did that on purpose, didn't you? Asking me about parasitic worms and pregnancies?"

His laughter was contagious, and she couldn't stop herself from joining in. "Steven Michael Ceravolo! You'd better hope I *don't* come up there anytime soon!"

He was still laughing when he bid her good night and hung up.

With a grin still on her face, she called back her boyfriend.

Chapter 32

Wednesday, December 30

Drinking hot chocolate with extra marshmallows, Morgan looked at the clock again. Holding back a smile, she commented innocently, "Man. Time is sure flying by today, isn't it? It seems like we just walked in the door, and now it's... just after ten-thirty."

Shooting her an exasperated look from his new desk where he was prepping year-end paperwork, Ty held back his grin. She'd been needling him all morning. He'd told her last night as they were leaving that Ripley was flying in later this afternoon. It felt like time was crawling along like a three-legged turtle on ice. Leave it to Morgan to tease him about it.

Watching him with a sparkle in her eyes, she said, "I don't know why you're even here working. If it were me, I'd have asked off."

Ty gave her a look that conveyed he was going to throttle her. "You could've *offered* me the day off, being my best friend and all."

"You *volunteered* to work the first half of the day, if not all day."

"You said you'd *pay* me. *And* you could've said no need to."

"Could've," Morgan agreed as she leaned back in her chair with her mug. She blew on the hot liquid before taking a careful sip. "But then all you'd be doing is sitting there at home, watching the clock. Minutes ticking by slowly... tick, tock, tick, tock." She demonstrated by moving her index finger back and forth as she spoke. "At least by being here, you can make some money and use up the time much more constructively."

He shook his head, but she saw his grin when he looked down at the papers.

Still all innocence, she went on, "If Ripley needs a place to stay, let her know she's welcome to one of my spare rooms. Maybe even yours. Josh and I won't mind having her over. If she doesn't want to stay in the house, there are a couple of empty stalls down at..."

Quick as a flash, Ty grabbed a rubber band and shot it at her with total accuracy. She squealed in laughter as she ducked in case he had more, quickly putting her mug on her desk. Just as she was ready to shoot one back, the office door opened, and some customers walked in for the eleven o'clock ride. She dropped the rubber band as Ty stood up, welcoming the five people to the Center and handing them the waivers to sign.

Once they were set up, Ty mentioned they could hang out at the picnic tables by the portable heaters. As soon as the door closed behind the last person, he turned and leaned over her desk. Morgan leaned forward so they were almost nose to nose.

Trying to sound firm, he asked, "Did I ever tease you about Josh?"

"I don't remember."

"I didn't." His eyes were full of humor, so she wasn't intimidated at all. "And you know she doesn't need a place to stay while she's here, Morgan. She's staying with me."

Grinning, she said, "I just thought I'd offer."

Josh walked in then, seeing them squaring off over her desk. With a wide smile, he asked, "What's she done this time?"

Shaking his head, Ty asked, "Haven't you had enough time to get your girl here trained to be more respectful toward others?"

"Oh. So now she's just *my* girl, not *our* girl? What's up with that? Besides, she was *your* best friend long before I came into her life. Haven't *you* had enough time?"

Morgan smiled as she swiveled her chair back and forth. She toyed with the rubber band as she replied to her husband, "Sweetheart, I was only offering Ripley one of our rooms while she was here. And Ty, well, he just got all bent out of shape about my offer of hospitality!"

Ty added dryly, "She also offered two of the stalls."

Knowing his wife was teasing their friend mercilessly, Josh walked over to her. After he kissed the top of her head, he placed his strong hands on her shoulders. With a glint in his eye, he said, "I'm holding her down now, Ty. What form of punishment would you prefer this time?"

A customer walked through the door at that moment. Ty gave a look to a smiling Morgan. "Lucky you. You just got a reprieve."

THE SUN WAS BARELY still shining in the cold winter air as Ty drove his truck down the highway toward the airport. He had to engage the cruise control so he wouldn't speed and get a ticket.

As a grown man, he was a little surprised at how excited he felt knowing he was going to see his girlfriend soon. Seeing Ripley again just felt different from seeing a friend or family member after time apart. A different part of his heart beat just for her. The past three months felt like forever. Love is love, he figured.

Parking at the small, private local airport, he went inside to wait for her. When he saw the small, white airplane slowly descend in the now-dark sky and land smoothly on the runway, he caught himself smiling. He waited impatiently for the plane to taxi to the building and let Ripley loose from its confines.

Finally, the plane's side door was opened after the metal ramp was in place and locked down. He caught himself smiling again before he even saw her. He watched the passengers walk down the metal steps and head to the building where an employee held open the door. Once inside, Ripley saw him at once. With a huge grin, she ran and jumped right into his arms, her legs wrapping around his waist.

They hugged each other tightly before their lips met. Both were grinning like idiots when he finally let her slide down and get her feet back on the ground. Stepping back, she said, "Excuse me, sir. I thought you were someone else. I'm here to meet my outrageously handsome boyfriend. I wonder if maybe you've seen him?"

"Forget about him. Take me instead!" He laughed. "I sure have missed you!" he said before hugging her again.

"Me too," she admitted as she held him close.

Not letting go of her waist, he reached down to grab her carry-on bag that she'd dropped when she'd run to him. They waited with the others for the baggage to be unloaded, walking over to get hers when she saw it.

As they walked toward his truck, they held on to each other's hand. She carried her bag while he rolled her suitcase behind them. Deciding to test the waters, she said, "Ty, I have so much I have to tell you while I'm here."

"Yeah? Will I like it?"

"I hope so." She was nervous at just the thought of telling him all of it. But Julia was right. She might as well do it now, and then they could go from there.

"Do you want to tell me now or later?" he asked. He'd caught the slight anxious note in her voice. Glancing down, he studied her.

Grinning, she said, "Later. I don't feel like talking right now."

Stopping at his truck, he let go of her suitcase and wrapped his arms around her again. Laughing in happiness, she pulled his head down and kissed him. When they pulled apart, she said, "I can't believe how good it is to see you! I thought today would never get here."

Appreciating her honesty, he put the suitcase and her bag in the backseat and opened the door for her. "I feel the same way. Knowing Morgan would show me no mercy, I didn't even tell her you were coming until last night. She razzed me all morning long. Josh had to come in and save me."

She waited for him to slide behind the wheel before asking, "So are we avoiding her then?" she joked.

He laughed. "The thought crossed my mind. But I know if we did, she'd just show up at my house looking for us. We'll get together later on though." Driving back toward his house, he asked her, "Are you hungry? Did you want to get something to eat?"

"Besides feeling worn out, I'm famished! How about a burger or something? Or we can just grab whatever you have at your place, if you have anything. Then maybe later we can go out to that Mexican restaurant we wanted to go to before. If not tonight, another night's okay. Unless you have something else planned. I'm open to suggestions."

"Sounds fine to me. I didn't really make any plans as I figured we do so well at just bumbling along. Why mess with a good thing?" With a smile on his face, he reached over and took hold of her hand, squeezing it in his.

There was just something about holding each other's hand as they drove down the road.

Opting to eat at his place now and maybe go out later, he stopped at a drive-thru for burgers and fries. After they ate at his house, they sat together on the couch talking and catching up. It wasn't long before Ripley began to fall asleep beside him. Ty saw her eyes closing and her fighting it, so he helped her by telling her it was completely fine to take a nap. He simply grabbed one of his pillows at the end of the couch, and wrapping his arms around her, he lowered them both down. She was asleep in less than a minute, snuggled up against his warm chest.

Placing a kiss on her head, Ty felt wonderfully at peace. Holding her in his arms, Ty soon dozed off himself.

Later that evening, both voting to just stay in, they ordered from a local pasta restaurant. Ty drove in to pick it up while Ripley returned a couple voicemails she got while they were napping.

When she was done with her calls and he still hadn't returned yet, Ripley decided to take a quick shower. Plane rides always made her feel grimy for some reason, especially when she rode on more than one of them. And even worse when you had to get up at three in the morning to make the first one on time. A shower would also make her feel more confident when she talked with Ty later. She grabbed clean clothes from her suitcase and headed off down the hallway to the bathroom.

Feeling refreshed after her shower, Ripley opened the bathroom door, letting the residual steam roll out. She knew Ty was back from the smell of food wafting down the hallway. Dropping off her dirty clothes in a bag by her suitcase in the bedroom, she made her way to his kitchen, following the scent of food like a cartoon character.

Ty was leaning against the counter with a glass of wine beside him, simply waiting for her. He smiled when she walked in as a wave of pure happiness washed over him.

She couldn't help but smile back as she walked right up to him, wrapping her arms around him. She rested her head against his chest as he rested his chin on top of her head while his arms folded around her.

He smiled after a moment. "You just can't keep your hands to yourself, can you?"

Ripley grinned. "Maybe I'm just handsy!"

He laughed, remembering the comment her friend made during their first dinner.

They just held each other, both soaking in the feeling of finally being together again.

Later, Ripley was again cuddled up against him on the couch. Both were feeling relaxed as they talked, listening to Neil Diamond on low from the stereo system.

She figured now was as good a time as any. Closing her eyes, she just soaked in the feeling she felt at that moment, memorizing it. Just in case things changed after she began talking. Taking a deep breath and slowly releasing it, she said, "You know how I said I had some things to tell you?"

"Yeah. Are you ready to tell me?"

"Yeah." She sat up, adjusted her position so she could face him. She grabbed a pillow, hugging it to herself so she had something to do with her hands. "It's hard for me to bring up this subject because it always has a way of changing peoples' view of me. They always tend to act differently around me after they know, so I don't normally bring it up with people outside of my business. But I've discussed it at length with Julia...who sends a very cheery hello by the way"—Ty smiled broadly at her—"and she said for me to bring it up with you to see how you handle it."

Ty, his interest piqued now, studied her. He could tell it was important to her, and that she was quite reluctant to bring it up. He thought using some humor might help her. "Are you already married to a couple of guys you forgot to tell me about before you left?"

"I'm sure I woulda remembered at least one of them if I was," she replied with a grin.

He acted like he was thinking. "Got kids with different last names?"

"Dozens," she deadpanned.

"Well, I guess those are some of the big ones for me to know about—"

She blurted out, "But I'm rich, like fairly wealthy. So." She abruptly stopped talking.

The only sound in the room for a moment was the music playing in the background. Ty just looked at her, thinking. The Agency had given him hints, but he'd refused to ask for specifics from them. "Rich, huh? How rich are you talking?"

She took a breath before saying, "Like I probably don't need to work anymore if I don't really want to. At least for a really long time, I imagine. I've built my business up for years, and it's residual income. I could just live on my monthly paycheck, assuming nothing goes insanely wrong. But I've also invested and saved a lot over the years, just in case. Since I like what I do, I still tend to work a lot. I'm sure one day I'll slow down and enjoy it more, probably retire early at some point." She scrunched up her face, waiting anxiously for his reaction.

When he still didn't say anything, she asked quietly, "Does it bother you if a woman earns more than you do? If *your* woman earns more than you do?"

Ty shrugged a shoulder. "Well, I assumed long ago we weren't exactly on a level playing field. I guess the manly side of me would prefer to be the one who earned more because, well, the man always just wants to be able to support his family. And generally that meant he earned more than his wife, if she worked at all. But on the other hand, I'm not about the money. And times have changed. We aren't living in the fifties and sixties, after all.

"Sugar, I assumed you were well off. You have a very nice RV and stay in expensive hotels. I've never heard you once talk about money, or needing to wait to pay rent to

Morgan. Your friends alluded to how much money you earned the very first night I met them, remember? It didn't matter to me then, and it still doesn't. You caught my interest well *before* I ever met them, remember? Before I even saw the inside of your RV.

"If you're happy, then you're happy. I'm happy with what I have."

"Seriously? You really don't care?" Ripley closely watched his body language.

Ty shrugged his shoulder again. Trying to be honest with himself, and her, he took another moment to evaluate it. "Sweetheart, as long as I, or we, can make ends meet, with some left over, I'm fine. Have some put away for emergencies and hope it's enough.

"Morgan is a woman, who happens to be technically also my boss. She makes way more than I do. I know how much she earns, and it's never bothered me. Not even before we became best friends. Of course, I *want* her to earn a lot more because that's job security for all of us.

"Knowing a woman earns more than me doesn't make me insecure. Now, I know men who *would* have a big issue with it, but I don't. If it's a legitimate career choice and not illegal or immoral, then a woman has every right to earn what she wants. As long as it's not thrown in my face or used to make me feel less of a man, than it is what it is."

She pressed on. "But how do you feel about *me* earning more? It's more personal, isn't it?"

He leaned against the couch, thinking still. "In terms of you, my woman, making more than me?" He sighed. "Well, honestly, it bothers me in only a slight way. But that's really just in the traditional sense, I mean. Again, as long as you don't throw it in my face, try to emasculate me, I really don't mind. If you do that, then yes, it would *become* an issue.

"Remember I told you the bulk of my family is in law enforcement? We're hardly independently wealthy doing that, so it's not something I've ever dwelt on. There are a lot of other jobs that pay far more than law enforcement does. I've simply grown up knowing that fact. And I was raised to live within my means.

"Many of the wives in my family earn more than their husbands. I know for a fact a few wives are in the medical field and certainly earn more than their husbands. My Aunt Janet worked and made more than my Uncle Ron. She saved and invested almost everything she earned while they lived on his salary. They were frugal even with their daughters. They now have a nice nest egg. She's now retired, and he still works. When he retires, they'll be set up mainly from her earnings and not just his own retirement. It works for them.

"I love what I'm doing, and where I do it. I have a respectable income from Morgan. She pays me more than she probably should, plus she gives me vacation days, personal days, and benefits. She splits my insurance costs. She set up a retirement account for me a long time ago and has a matching program. Morgan does this for all of her full-time people. It's just one reason she has an incredible retention rate with her workers. She cares for them long term. She even has some benefits for her part-time staff.

"What do I have to show for it? Well, I have my own house, my own truck. I have a healthy retirement account, and I have some savings put away. I don't live paycheck to paycheck, have a great credit score, and I'm happy with where I'm at in life. My truck is almost paid off, and hopefully my house will be all mine within the next ten or so years since I pay extra every month.

"Other than those two things, I'm debt-free. I even give to a few charities on a regular basis. I go see my family and friends at least once or twice a year, and it doesn't mess up my finances at all.

"Sugar, if you earn significantly more than I do, then I'd say you're earning it. I know the hours you put in. And you travel thousands of miles to help others succeed. I hope you're being paid well for what you do. And if you've worked hard and long for it, and that's what your reward is, I'm proud of you for having the work ethic to do so.

"As my dad told me, 'Some people are so poor, all they have is money.' It took me a while at the time to understand what Dad meant, but I finally figured it out. Money isn't everything."

Stunned, Ripley sat there. She looked closely at his face, wondering if he was just being nice about it. Maybe inside he was secretly doing mental victory dances because he'd met a rich woman but knew to not let it show. Or maybe Julia was right about him. She didn't think he'd care all that much. To her, Ty just didn't seem the type of man who'd get bent out of shape about it. But how could Ripley know for sure?

After a moment, she asked, "So if I made, say about a million dollars per year from my work and investments, you'd be okay with that?"

His heart sped up in his chest thinking about it. "Well, you'd definitely be earning more than me!"

"But would it bother you?" she pressed.

"Is that how much you make?"

"Would it bother you?" she pressed again.

"No."

"Why not?" Her facial expression showed her confusion.

"Because, Sugar, I fell in love with you. *You.*" He reached over, pried her hands away from the pillow he noticed she was gripping like it was a lifeline. Holding her hands firmly in his own, he said, "The woman who'd sleep in sand for an abused horse who needed her. The woman who'd give up sleep for two days to answer requests to help with a lonely, scared horse. You're still grounded enough to scoop up horse manure. You have such humility and selflessness. That's who *you* are, Ripley, on the inside.

"I love your humor, laugh, smile, heart, and compassion. You have a zest for life, a terrific attitude. You have a strong work ethic, and you're honest. I admire your independence and personal strength. And you not only motivate people, you *inspire* them. You inspire *me.*

"I also know that no matter how much money you may make, you still feel obligated to help others attain success too. You didn't forget about, or brush aside, those damn Texans when I asked you to stay with me, if you'll recall. And as Josh said, you're pretty and take out the trash!"

She laughed and squeezed his hands which still held hers. He smiled back before he got serious again. "I know you're selfless and love to give to others. Morgan told me after you'd left that you paid for Toby and Maya's honeymoon, and that it was all your idea."

She broke in, "But she pitched in..."

He smiled. "She pitched in some spending money so they could enjoy it. You paid for everything else from the plane tickets, island tours, the hotel, everything. I know Laura had to work magic to make that happen on such short notice too.

"They told me all about it when they got back. I think they're still in awe, to be truthful. To be given a complete honeymoon as just a gift really blew their minds. You made a lasting memory for two people who you barely know. That's who *you* are, Sugar."

She smiled warmly. "They're a fun, sweet, hard-working couple. Thank you for letting me know that they loved it. It worried me a little they'd see it as charity or something, but Morgan assured me they'd accept it as a wedding gift and not a pity gift. She was to present it as coming from a bunch of us, so it'd seem easier for them to accept. I'm still assuming that's how she did it.

"I constantly checked the weather reports after I left here, hoping they weren't having a hurricane blow through!" She simply glowed in the knowledge she'd made someone happy.

Ty could see her sincerity in her glowing eyes and smiled back, kissing her hand. "What else? You have an earthiness I find extremely appealing. And your affinity to a suffering animal speaks volumes. You also caught on about Toby and Maya and their announcement. You have a way with people. I've heard you on the phone with them.

"In a nutshell, if you make a million a year then I love the fact you want to be loved and accepted for who and what you are on the inside and not for your bank account. You've had to work hard and long to earn that, I'm sure. That's determination and tenacity. That makes me *more* proud of you!"

He paused for a moment. "Now, if you make considerably *less* than a million a year, I'm sorry to tell you I may just hold out for someone else who makes more than that. After all, I *do* have high personal standards to maintain."

Believing him, she leaned forward and placed a tender kiss to his lips. He deepened it, pulling her closer to his body. She willingly came to him.

He whispered against her mouth, "And I love how you respond to me, Ripley. And I love how you're open with me, trusting me." He placed a soft kiss to her cheek before just holding her. He felt her breathe out a huge sigh and simply melt against him. She tucked her head under his, her fingers playing with his hair at the back of his head.

She pushed gently against his chest a moment later, saying, "Thank you, Ty. Rich people always have to be on the lookout for those who want to take advantage of them. Julia was positive you weren't one of them. I didn't think you were, either, but it's hard to know for sure. I don't want you to look at me differently because of it, okay? Can you do that?"

"I understand." Taking a chance, he went on, "If we keep moving along here in our relationship like I hope we do, I'll gladly sign papers that says we keep what we've earned on our own. That way, you don't have to worry about it. You'll know I love you for you, not your money.

"We'd sit down and compromise on bills and such so it wouldn't be all me or all you. We'd be a team, yet still have individual independence." He intertwined their fingers, watching her body language react at what he was implying.

Ripley realized he was alluding to a prenuptial agreement. Her heart sped up at the thought of being married to him. The thought had crossed her mind countless times, but she just pulled herself back to the present, not ready to take that step just yet. Unable to speak, she just nodded.

He said, "And just remember I told you I loved you long before this moment. That proves I love you as a person and not for your money."

They sat there quietly for a minute before he asked, “Was that all you wanted to tell me? That you were dating a poor, humble, working man and are over the moon about it?”

Ripley laughed before saying, “There’s just a *little* more I need to tell you.”

“Okay. I think I’m ready. Should I grab some more wine first?”

“You might need more than that once you hear the rest.” Sitting there, she tried to figure out the best way to broach this next topic. She finally hit on it. “Well, do you remember how a little while ago you asked if I had any kids?”

His eyes squinted a little, his mind racing. “Yeah. *And*...?”

With a small smile, she said, “You *might* want to know I just adopted fifteen more of them.”

Chapter 33

New Year's Eve

She didn't deserve such a handsome man. That was too bad because she was keeping him anyway.

Her heart skipped a few beats when Ty came out of the bedroom in black dress slacks and a deep purple dress shirt. He wore nice black dress shoes instead of the boots she was used to seeing him in. She'd had the same reaction when she'd seen him dressed up for Toby and Maya's wedding.

Work jeans and dusty boots, pressed dress slacks and dress shoes, dingy camping clothes and beat up tennis shoes, facial hair or clean-shaven... The man just had the body and look for anything, she thought to herself as he walked toward her, buttoning his cuff. He'd decided to keep it slightly more casual and didn't wear a tie.

When he saw her in her classy, form-fitting dress with a flowing skirt and high heels, he smiled in appreciation. Her long, dark hair was twisted and held together with a decorative hair comb. The length of it trailed over her shoulders. His heart kicked in his chest as he took in the vision before him.

"Look at *you!* You look like a million bucks!"

She raised her eyebrows and just gave him a look, her hands now on her hips.

When he realized what he'd said, he laughed. His eyes twinkled in delight when he said, "That was just a figure of speech, Sugar! I swear... Please don't make me think before I speak, Ripley. It takes away all the fun!"

Believing him, she smiled and twirled. Her skirt billowed around her. "Will this do?"

He whistled and said, "You are simply gorgeous. The local police will use you to stop traffic later!"

She laughed. "Thank you, babe. That's the best compliment I've ever had!" Looking him over again, she smiled. "They might do the same to you! You are one fine looking man, Ty Stanton."

Smiling, he picked up her trench coat from the chair and helped her into it. He leaned down and placed a kiss on her neck. In a whisper, he said, "And you're one stunning woman, Ripley Capilano."

When he slipped into his leather bomber jacket he removed from his hall closet, her heart kicked like an angry mule in her chest. She *loved* men in leather bomber jackets.

"Sweetheart..." she murmured as she ran her hands over his broad shoulders and chest, sighing deeply. "You've just found my weakness." She leaned up and kissed him, both lingering over it. With a wink, she said, "We'd better go now."

With a broad grin, he handed her the small bag she wanted to take before he set his alarm, locked and closed his door and followed her down his sidewalk.

THE COOL EVENING BREEZE blew Ripley's dress and long trench coat around her legs as she walked by Ty's side down the block toward the restaurant. With their arms looped around the other's waist, they talked as they took their time walking down the street, enjoying the cooler temperature. As they neared the Mexican restaurant, they saw Josh and Morgan crossing the parking lot beside it.

Ripley said, "Why didn't you park closer to the restaurant? There's plenty of space over here still."

He pulled her closer to his side. "What use is it to have you wear those sexy heels if I can't enjoy them?"

She laughed at his reply and was still smiling when their friends spotted them. They welcomed her with open arms. Seeing them all dressed up again like at the wedding and not in jeans and dusty boots was still a shock to Ripley's system. Josh and Morgan also had the look for anything.

They ate authentic Mexican cuisine under the little white lights stretched across the patio with the Spanish music adding to the exciting New Year's Eve atmosphere. The four of them shared stories, caught up with each other and joked.

Ty swept her away to dance to the Spanish music, Josh following with Morgan. Their table and the dance floor were in the outside portion of the packed restaurant under heaters, so they were comfortably warm even with the occasional cool breeze that blew.

Ripley leaned close to the warmth of Ty's hard body, his grip firm on her as they danced under the stars. As she followed his cues, she asked, "Did you know every date with you is better than the one before? I'm never going to be able to top anything you've done yet. You know that, right?"

Smiling, he said, "Well, you picked the restaurant tonight so this is a shared date idea. And I have to say I've not had any as enjoyable as the ones I've spent with you. It must just be us, don't you think?"

Ripley smiled warmly. "That must be it."

He said, "And I bet one day you *will* think of something to try and top my best date. Although I still think our first one was one of the best, you're right when you say they've all been great in their own way. No one here knows when it was, by the way. That's still just for us, okay?"

Ripley grinned and nodded.

"In regards to you trying to match, even top, any of mine? Well, it's going to need to be something extravagant, you know. It'll need to just blow my mind. Needless to say, I'll be looking forward to it!" he teased her.

"Thanks for not adding any pressure!" she joked back as she ran her hands up and down his back.

"We're not in competition with each other, Sugar. Anything we end up doing together, I'm sure will be just fine and sincerely accepted."

Having an appreciation for the Hispanic culture, Ripley loved the music being played and wondered who it was. It gave Ty the answer he was looking for on what to get her for a gift while she was there. He knew they sold the CDs in the gift shop, so he'd have to get in there before it got any busier or closed. It'd be a perfect reminder for her of their New Year's date after she left in a few days.

When the four of them decided to return to their table, Ripley decided to break the news to Josh and Morgan about the rescues. Ty had said last night that everyone still worried about them, so she didn't want to delay the news too much longer. As long as they kept it to themselves, all should be fine. The fun part was deciding *how* to tell them.

After they sat down, Ripley reached into her small bag she purposely brought tonight for this announcement. She pulled out her tablet and turned it on.

Keeping a straight face as Ty watched her, humor in his eyes, Ripley announced, "Hey, you two. I have some news that Ty assured me you'd want to know." She tapped an icon on the tablet, and then waited as a website loaded. Thank goodness for free Wi-Fi, she thought happily. "Give me just a second here..."

Morgan took a sip of her wine, glancing at Josh. He didn't seem to know what Ripley was doing but from the satisfied look on Ty's face, he at least knew. Morgan asked, "What is it? Something good?"

Once the site was up, Ripley just asked, "Have you ever heard of a place in New Mexico called 'Just One More'?"

Both Josh and Morgan shook their heads. Josh said, "No, I've never heard of it. What is it?"

"Well, when Ty told me on the phone how the judge ordered the rescued horses to be sold at auction, I—"

Morgan interrupted in her excitement, "*Ripley!* Did you *find* them? Are they okay? Where are they?"

Josh leaned forward, too, his eyes intent on Ripley's face. "You found them, didn't you?"

Ripley smiled broadly. "Yes. They're doing very well. Even Cappy is behaving himself so all that effort with him was not wasted. This is where all eleven are for now..."

She turned the tablet around so Josh and Morgan could see the website she pulled up for Just One More. Josh gently took it from her hands so they could see it better, laying it on the table between himself and his wife after she moved their glasses, plates, and the candle out of the way.

Happy and relieved tears in her eyes, Morgan said enthusiastically, "Oh, I can't believe you *found* them! But *how?* I couldn't track them down myself. That man I gave my cards to swore he'd have the new owner contact me, but they never did.

"He lied to me, or the new owners refused to... Which is just damn rude and heartless! How did you find them, and when?"

"Well, it's a bit of a long story..." she began. She stopped when Ty laughed. With another smile, she started again, "Let me explain what Just One More is and does. It's an equine facility that specializes in rehabbing horses, giving them another chance at a good, productive life.

"It's not necessarily a sanctuary, but more like a training facility. Or a distribution center if you want to look at it another way.

"Horses brought in could be from auctions, ex-racehorses of any breed, ex-show horses, shut down summer camps, or sometimes when someone has to move and simply can't take their horse with them. And there is the occasional case of the owner dying and the executor or the kids don't know what to do with the horses, so they come to Just One More.

"Once the horse has been worked with, vet checked for health and evaluated by the staff, then they're ready to find a new home. The staff is very selective, and a contract is signed by every new owner. It says if they ever can't keep or no longer want the horse, it's to be returned to Just One More or to a place approved by them. The horse's welfare is always the top priority.

"New homes have been therapeutic centers for the physically or mentally handicapped, stables to be used as lesson ponies, a few have become trail ponies, some have gone back into the show world, some to horse camps, a few have been placed with wounded soldiers, and a few have recently gone to help at a facility that works with autistic people. A couple of minis went to a place that uses them for nursing home visits.

"And I know the staff there are talking with a local jail or prison for non-violent offenders to create a program for them to work with the horses. Or they just go to people who want a good horse. Oh, and a few even went on to become involved in the Border Patrol. And I think there was one or two that became police officer mounts way over in Tennessee. But each and every place is fully researched and checked out first."

Morgan and Josh glanced back down at the website. He asked, "It sounds like a super place. What does the Just One More mean exactly? I'm sure it's on here somewhere, but do you know? You seem to have done your homework on this place!"

Trying to keep a straight face, Ripley answered, "Yeah, I do. Just One More means a few things, but mainly that's how many they'll take when someone's in a crunch and comes to them for help."

They all smiled as she continued, "It's for just one more home to find. Just one more move to make, or just one more chance they need."

Ripley and Ty watched as their friends scrolled around the website, listening to her comments.

Finally, Morgan asked, "So how in the world did you find them, Ripley?"

Ty grinned as he waited for Ripley to drop the bombshell.

She smiled at him, knowing he was ready to burst. "The man you spoke with, Morgan, was Joseph Ceravolo. He helped to transport them to a friend's place until Just One More could make arrangements to pick them up and get them to their place in New Mexico."

Ty leaned back in his chair, getting comfortable and waiting for Ripley to stop dragging it out. He grinned again and shook his head at her.

His brown eyes fully directed at her, Josh asked, "How did you find the name of who she spoke with? He didn't even give my wife his name."

Ripley shrugged. "Well, Uncle Joe was just doing what I told him to do and say. He knows better than to oppose my wishes."

Dead silence.

Ty laughed at their expressions. He was fairly sure his looked similar to theirs last night when Ripley told him. But he didn't have the lead-in they were getting from her.

They both sputtered, but Morgan won out in asking her, "Wait. *What?* Your uncle just *happened* to be there and bought them? All of them, plus a few more?"

Ripley smiled. "Nah. That'd be too much of a coincidence, don't you think? He was buying them, if you remember, for a friend who couldn't make it on such short notice."

Josh seemed to be working it out in his mind. He leaned back in his chair, slowly putting it all together. His suddenly shocked glance went to Ty, who nodded, grinning. Josh's glance then went to Ripley, who was now leaning into Ty's side while his arm wrapped around her shoulders. She looked at Josh but stayed quiet.

Josh was still trying to comprehend it all, wondering if he was understanding it correctly. But from the looks from Ty and Ripley, he apparently was.

He looked at his wife, who hadn't caught on yet. That was odd as Morgan was normally quite astute. He figured it was the little shock of hearing about the horses and finding out Ripley had 'found' them. That judge caused a lot of caring people a lot of sleepless, tear-filled nights.

Looking at the website on the tablet, Morgan said out loud, "Okay. I think the wine is slowing me down here. Y'all might want to cut me off for a while so I'm not wasted before midnight even gets here."

The other three laughed at her and waited for her to figure it out.

Morgan asked, "Your uncle bought the horses for a friend?"

Ripley nodded. "Well, yeah, I'd like to think so," she teased, making Ty laugh and Josh smile.

Morgan continued, "And *that* friend owns, or at least runs, Just One More... which is in New Mexico. And this is where all eleven are right now. Right?"

"You're hot on the trail, Morgan," Ripley encouraged her line of thought. "Stay on it!"

"Ripley!" Ty laughed. "Quit it!"

Josh smiled when Ripley just shrugged her shoulders.

Morgan looked up, wondering what was so funny. “Does your uncle also live in New Mexico?”

Ripley nodded. “Yes.”

Josh grinned, knowing he was guessing correctly. He looked at his wife before he took away her glass of wine. “Sweetheart, I’m cutting you off until eleven fifty-five! Your brain has completely shut down. It’s embarrassing!”

Ty and Ripley laughed good-naturedly while Josh shook his head at his wife, who just flashed a smile at him. Distracted again as she scrolled through the website, Morgan simply said, “Okay.”

The others just smiled again.

Morgan looked up, saying wistfully, “I’d really like to talk to the people who own this place. Who owns Just One More?”

Ty smiled broadly as Ripley said simply, “I do.”

Chapter 34

Morgan was speechless. She sat there staring at Ripley like she was Samantha on *Bewitched* and just suddenly popped up right in front of them. Ty simply ran his warm hand up and down Ripley's bare arm as they waited for the other two to regain their ability to think and talk coherently. Although Josh had figured it out, he still looked a bit shell-shocked since she confirmed it so cheerfully.

Morgan looked over at Ty. He didn't seem surprised at all. "You knew? This *whole* time?" she asked in disbelief. He *knew* how worried she'd been about them!

He shook his head vehemently as he denied her implication of his keeping this a secret from her. "Not until last night when she told *me*. I was just as shocked as you two are. Trust me on that. I never saw it coming!" He chuckled as he remembered.

She believed him. Now looking at Ripley she said, "I'm waiting for my brain to process all of this! *You* own a horse facility too? That's how you know about horses? I always wondered but just never asked. And you bought these eleven... Where did you come up with that much money, Ripley? I was there, so I know how much they cost!"

Ripley nodded, took a long drink of her wine before answering. "Yeah, well, if it wasn't for that judge's high reserve requirement, I could've bought them for far less. But they're worth it to me."

Morgan suddenly remembered what she'd said earlier. "I'm sorry I called apparently your uncle a liar, and apparently you as rude and heartless."

"I believe it was '*damn* rude and heartless,' wasn't it?" Ripley teased her. "I get it. Think nothing of it."

She paused as she thought out how to answer the rest of the questions Morgan had posed. "Well, see, this is where it gets really tricky for me. I don't like for people to know certain things about me. I'm a private person about some things. I'll just say I had the money to purchase the eleven. Uncle Joe was told under no circumstances was he to leave there without all eleven... *especially* Cappy. If he happened to see any more really needing to be saved, that we could rehab, he could get more. He did. He added four more to our eleven. I'm sure he would've bought them all if it wouldn't have gotten him fired. But it's *so* hard to say no and not buy them all. The guilt is horrendous.

"Because of the judge's ruling regarding the horses, I had to be sure none of you knew *I* was the buyer. It was a strong possibility he'd look into who bought them, and if he ever sent someone out to speak with you, you had to have complete deniability. If he checked the paperwork, which I'm sure some lawyer did, Uncle Joe was the buyer. He used funds I gave him through Just One More.

"I wanted to be sure all was clear through the courts before I told you. Trust me, it's been hard! The judge's orders were pretty clear. Since I *had* been living there and was dating your manager who's obviously an employee... I just didn't want there to be a loop hole one of us missed and have the judge refuse the sale.

"Honestly, I suggest we keep this between ourselves for another month or two, just in case. You could maybe tell your staff where they are. Or even say the owner finally contacted you because that's the truth... I even came in person! But just don't mention *I* bought them... Just for a while longer."

The other three nodded, understanding her position. Their concern was mainly for the horses after all. There was no way they wanted to jeopardize their current safe status.

Pulling one of the chip baskets closer to him, and then the famous cheesy salsa dip the restaurant made, Josh said, "I guess Ty called you, let you know the court's decision, then you sent your uncle to Arizona to buy them. Then what?"

Ripley leaned forward to grab a couple of chips for herself and dunked them in the tasty dip. She immediately slid the second chip and salsa bowls closer to Ty before she answered, "Well, after about... Let me think here..." She ate the chips, thinking of the timeline.

Ty leaned forward, and seeing him grab some chips, Ripley smiled at him. Knowing he couldn't stand hearing other people crunch chips or nuts, he was getting some for himself to block it out. She sometimes had to do that too.

Morgan smiled, now realizing why Ripley moved the chips closer to Ty. Ripley was truly learning about him, Morgan happily thought. It's the little things that really matter.

Ripley said, "I guess they were at a mutual friend's place, where he originally took them, for about four or five weeks before we could move them to New Mexico. It may have been a little longer. Let's see, the auction was in October..." She thought about it and shrugged. "Whatever. They're in New Mexico now!" She smiled. "I don't do math when I've been drinking wine. Man, this stuff *is* potent!" They all laughed at her as she grabbed another chip and washed it down with the last of her wine. "Crap. Now I'm out. Honey, wanna share yours?"

"No." Ty laughed as moved his glass away from her.

Smiling in appreciation, Morgan said, "See? It's *not* just me!"

They smiled at her as they waited for Ripley to begin speaking again.

Ripley finally continued, "We had to make room for another fifteen at once and had some others that were leaving, so it took a little time to work it all out. I keep a very small staff on hand to keep costs down, so we had to be patient. Once we were ready, some of my staff drove to get them to take them back to Just One More. They've been there about seven weeks now and have adjusted very well. They arrived about a week or so before Thanksgiving... So, yeah, that sounds about right on the timeline.

"Joe, Lilly, and Steve really run the place for me. They're my uncle, aunt, and cousin. I'm really just a silent partner anymore. It was my idea to found the place, got it going, hired Joe, Lilly, and Steve, then later a couple others, to staff it. They keep me in the loop overall, and when I can, I go visit.

"I went there for Thanksgiving to see the horses—and a whole lot of my family. They insisted I come back. So yes, I have seen them all and can personally verify they're doing well. Cappy seems to be in heaven. That's probably a true statement based on what we think his life was like previously. It was wonderful to see the rescues again especially the ornery one! Steve and I even rode him and another gelding while I was there. No problems at all.

"I'd told them all about Cappy so they had a heads up, but they assured me he's not been negative in any way toward men since they got him. And Morgan, Uncle Joe said you'd mentioned it to him as well. That was great of you to do! He *really* respected you for that. Your concern was genuine and impressed him."

Josh smiled at Ripley. "You know, we were all really looking forward to seeing you again, but *this* just makes your visit even better!"

Ripley smiled warmly at him. "Thank you. I can honestly say I've missed this place. In a lot of ways, it was, *is*, the closest thing to feeling homey to me that I can really remember. I mean, the place in New Mexico is mine and technically I use it as my address, but it doesn't really feel like *home* to me. I love visiting, seeing my relatives, the horses, but it's always fine with me to leave. Maybe it's because I've just worked so long and hard and wasn't really there for so long? But being *here*, it feels different to me. Trust me when I say I think about all of you a lot."

Morgan could see the conflict in her eyes since she was right across from her. Knowing not to pressure her into staying for Ty, Morgan knew she had to change the subject. She asked instead, "I suppose you normally try to sell the horses you get then? You don't just try to keep them all, or do you?"

Ripley grabbed the lifeline Morgan tossed her with gratefulness. She answered immediately, "The point of selling the horses is to make the place more self-sustaining rather than being a financial drain. We have fundraisers, but much of the income needed comes from regular donations and definitely through sales.

"We added a gift shop—you can see it online there—and that brings in a little bit. That was actually more for fun for Steve and I than a serious income avenue. Although, Aunt Lilly has shown in the reports it *has* been building over time. I think if we tweak it more, it could really start turning in some money. She's been promoting us online quite a bit the last year or so. She has a real knack for online stuff. I just let her do whatever she wants to do."

There was wonder in Morgan's voice when she said, "I still can't believe this. You own a horse place like mine. It's hard for me to get that. You never let on..."

"No. Nothing like yours, Morgan. Mine is more like a halfway house. Your place is like a Super Walmart!" They all laughed at her analogies. "The majority of my horses don't stay forever. If they're old, injured, something like that, then yeah, probably. If I kept all of them, we'd always be struggling to make ends meet because we'd be more of a sanctuary. But I have contacts who can take in senior horses if we can't swing it. We don't turn away any needy horse."

Josh asked, "So how'd it start?"

"In the very beginning, I bought a sweet mare from an acquaintance who was moving and couldn't take her. I kept her at another friend's place so her horse had company. Then there was another one. And so on. Once I got the idea to make this a business, I found an old, rundown property and fixed it up.

"Soon after, I hired Joe, Lilly, and Steve to run it for me because they seriously needed the work and a place to live at the time. Confidentially here, Uncle Joe had lost his job due to the economy, Aunt Lilly was tired of where she was, and Steve is my buddy who I knew would love being there and gaining experience.

"My uncle losing his job was very difficult for him. He couldn't find work anywhere else. Aunt Lilly was still working, but it wasn't enough to pull them through for too long. Steve helped, but he was planning on going to college full-time to finish off his degree. He'd been going part-time for quite a while even before his dad lost his job.

"They all love animals, but mainly I hired them because I know I can trust them unconditionally. I'm closer to those three than my own parents, so it just made sense to hire them for my foundling project. I mean, my parents and I get along just fine, but they just aren't into animals much at all. I never even had a dog or cat of my own.

"Again, just between us, giving them a place to live while building a business for animals, well, I think it helped them keep their pride, you know? A small chunk of what they make I just apply toward letting them live there. I only really do that so they feel like they're pulling their weight. No charity. So it's really *their* home, not mine. They can do pretty much whatever they want to with it.

"It's a mental and emotional thing when someone's older and loses their job suddenly. The stress alone can cause depression because they feel they aren't valued anymore. I think they both know that may be why I also asked them, but we've never discussed it. We don't need to."

Her friends nodded in understanding.

Morgan said softly, "That was very kindhearted and sweet of you. You're probably correct that asking them to handle this for you picked them up, gave them a purpose again, doing something they apparently loved to do. You saw it from their perspective as much as your own."

Ripley replied, "I tried to. It's been working out great for all of us. And to top it off, Steve is now a talented veterinarian, so he takes care of the horses that come and go. He opened his own clinic near there so he has an independent income, so it's not just my horses. He wouldn't have enough to do if that was the case. He has a couple of assistants now that help out.

"He has his own little house about twenty minutes from Just One More, so he isn't a grown man living with his parents still. He *had* been living there to save money, and for the convenience between working there and going to school. Well, until this one day I told him he'd never find himself a girl if he lived with his parents." She grinned. "He was gone in less than a month!"

They all laughed heartily.

"Did he find someone?" Ty asked, amused.

Ripley shook her head, smiling. "Nope. Not yet. A fact he brings up almost every time we talk! There aren't a lot of choices over there, I guess."

Her friends laughed again.

She didn't add she was the one who paid for Steve's education, and he pays her back a little per month. She insisted he didn't need to, but he insisted he did. She decided it was important to him to do, for his pride, and to feel he earned it himself. They finally agreed on and set up a monthly payment program. He'd taught her a thing or two about male pride, and she was thankful for the lessons.

Ripley ate a couple of chips and took a drink of water before she went on, "The only drawback I worry about sometimes is Joe and Lilly *are* getting elderly. You'd never know it if you met them because they're mobile and still mentally sharp. However, I'm also realistic in knowing at some point in the future, I'll need to find someone younger, and just as honest and loyal, that I can rely on.

"Steve, who's just a little younger than I am, hasn't mentioned wanting to leave. If he ever does, that's something else I'll need to figure out. But for now, they're there. And they're not just running it but enjoying it."

Josh said, "It sounds like an excellent operation on a few different fronts. You're a planner and a doer like Morgan. You guys could maybe bounce ideas off each other on some things."

They discussed in general Morgan buying them back, but they figured to save the details for another day.

Josh was the one who asked the question she was hoping they wouldn't. "So are you rich or something? I mean, for you to have bought the horses, and then ship them to New Mexico to a facility that you own indicates you must have money. Plus, you travel all over in an RV, and now you're taking off from work to fly back here to spend time with Ty. I'd have to say you're pretty well off. It doesn't matter to us, and I don't mean to pry, but are you?"

The three saw how the question made her a little uncomfortable.

But then a thought hit her. She wanted to belong to this group, right? What difference did it make to her if they knew how much she made? Ty was fine knowing, so it stood to reason they'd be fine too. Laura and Damien were probably figuring it out through the business end anyway. Logic said Josh and Morgan would find out at some point. So why not now?

Ripley looked at Ty, who nodded in encouragement. She answered, "The answer to your question is *yes*. I'm wealthy through my work, so it's not old family money. It's taken me years to get where I'm at."

Josh thought about it before commenting in approval, "Wealthy, huh? I never would've guessed it by what I know of you."

Morgan smiled at her, nodding in appreciation and understanding. "That's exactly what she wants. She wants to be known by her character, her actions, not her bank account. She doesn't want people to know she has money. It always changes things, doesn't it?"

Ripley smiled genuinely at Morgan. "I see the wine has worn off!"

Josh grinned before teasing her, "To respect your wishes, then, we'll be sure to treat you poorly."

She laughed at his wit. "Please do. I'd appreciate it. And I'll do the same to you guys!"

Her three friends laughed.

Their busy waitress stopped by to check on them, so they ordered more wine and desserts. The woman somehow turned away with a flourish even though the space on the patio was limited due to the crush of people partying.

Ripley smiled. "This has been quite a year for me, at least the past six months or so! When you think about how all of this came about, it's crazy, isn't it?

"Morgan, you and I randomly meet. Then you offer me a space at your place. What are the odds you'd even have a spot for an RV? Most horse places I know don't, but you do. Later, when I joined you for a fun evening, we instead end up rescuing eleven horses! The very next morning, Ty and I meet. Soon after, he and Josh agree I'm pretty enough for him to date. Oh, and because I take out the trash. Details matter.

"You have a horse place, and I have a horse place. And somehow the two are now connected. This world of ours is pretty small, isn't it? It's always intriguing to me how *one* simple decision can just snowball into something entirely different. Something never expected or even considered!"

They all agreed.

After a minute, Ripley remembered something. "Morgan, I almost forgot to bring this up! Uncle Joe tried to give you clues to help ease your mind, if not practically telling you who bought them. He knew you couldn't really know yet, but he said your worry for them broke him down. I was curious if you caught them at all?"

"He did? What were they?"

"Guess not!" Ripley joked, causing them to laugh. "He said he mentioned something like they'd be taken care of like Black Beauty when Joe Green found him again. Although his name is Joe, *I'm* Joe Green, I guess. Surely you read that book? What little kid who loves horses hasn't? It was in reference to the original groom of Beauty's, who later finds him again, and then keeps him forever. I actually thought that one was brilliant myself. He figured, as horse people, you all would know that story."

Ty deadpanned, "Well, I never read it. Thanks for spoiling the ending for me."

They all laughed.

"I'm sorry, honey! I think you're kidding, but if you're not, I'll buy you a copy before I leave... Maybe in Spanish!" Grinning still, Ripley continued, "And Uncle Joe said something like nothing could rip them away from him? Rip... Ripley."

Morgan tried to remember back to that day. "I actually do recall the Black Beauty reference, but I missed the rip one. Those were great clues. Tell him I wish we'd picked up on them to save ourselves the heartbreak!"

Josh deadpanned, "She's no good at charades or Pictionary either."

Morgan lightly shoved her husband, laughing. "I'm *usually* sharp! We were very distraught at the time. It was devastating to let them go. I think I get a little bit of slack here, don't I?"

Josh sighed dramatically. "I suppose."

Smiling, Ripley took her tablet back from Morgan, shut it down, and put it back into her little bag. Not trusting the larger, boisterous crowd to leave it while they went back to the dance floor, she asked a passing waitress if she could put it somewhere safe.

"We have lockers for a quarter in the back where we take breaks. You want to use one? It should be okay."

"That would be great!" Ripley said. She and Morgan got up to follow the waitress, stopping at the bathrooms after they were shown where to go. Morgan tossed her purse in with the bag so they didn't have to worry about it when dancing.

When midnight rolled around, the four of them celebrated with joy and happiness bringing in the New Year together. Going with the restaurant's requirement of counting down in Spanish was amusing amid all the drinkers there, but they managed to pull it off.

When Ty wrapped Ripley up in his arms and their mouths met at the stroke of midnight, Ripley knew this was the best New Year's Eve she'd ever had.

She'd once read that whatever you're feeling at that stroke of midnight was the springboard for what was to come in the upcoming year. With the love she felt for Ty in her heart, she wondered how much better could it get?

Josh pulled her away from Ty while Morgan was playfully swung into Ty's arms.

Toasting each other with their flutes of champagne, they all looked forward to the coming year.

Chapter 35

Late February

Calculating the time zone difference in his head, Ty picked up his phone, hitting a number he had on speed dial. He waited for her to pick up, and when no one answered, he was prepared to leave a message.

He almost missed he was suddenly talking to a live person when she finally answered with a breathless and happy, "Hello, handsome!"

"Hey there, gorgeous! Have you missed me?"

She laughed good-naturedly before answering. "Of course! As does Channion. We were just talking about you the other day. Were your ears burning?"

Ty smiled. "Not any more than usual. A lot of girls talk about me when I'm not around. You know how it is."

"Yeah, yeah. Keep talkin' like that, and you'll be alone forever."

"Who says I'm alone anymore?"

She jumped right on it, just like he knew she would. "Oh, don't tell me... Ty! Did you find someone? Who is she?"

He smiled at the excitement in her voice. "You just said to *not* tell you. Do you, or don't you?" He paused, adding, "I also didn't realize you'd be so... surprised... for me, Raina. I'm not sure how to handle this. I feel a little bit offended by your attitude."

"Stop stalling. Tell me." Raina sat down on the couch, got comfortable. "Does Channion know about her?"

He laughed. "Maybe it's best I stay single if this is what happens—"

She interrupted him. "Maybe? *Maybe?*" As usual, Raina picked up on the smallest things. "Are you seriously thinking of marrying her?"

"It's crossed my mind." So many times, he'd lost count.

Raina was silent for a while before venturing, "So, have you asked her yet? Discussed it at all?"

"In very general, broad terms only, and no in regards to the asking. We're still just dating, learning as we go, but I feel the potential is there."

"Oh, Ty! I'm so happy for you! You know we have to meet her to make sure we approve, right? I sure hope we do, but if she passes your criteria, we probably will. So." Raina paused for dramatic effect. "When should we all meet? What's your schedule like?"

His cousin's wife could always make him laugh. He asked, "Is that what it'll take to get you and Channion out here? Why do I have to keep coming to you?"

"As a matter of fact, that's *just* what we were talking about the other day. Channion has vacation days piling up since he and Ron have been working non-stop over here for what seems like forever. And I was thinking I should take some time off myself. I think the two of us need to get away on a little retreat.

"Following that lovely train of thought, we were discussing the possibility of making a little trip out West. It won't be for a while yet still, but we're planning on it. What do you think?"

"I'd love to see you guys out here! Family is always welcome. You know that. Just give me a little heads up to be sure I'm around."

"Wonderful! I'll let him know." She waited a beat before asking, "Was there another reason you called? Or did you just want to talk about your ears burning? Were you looking for Channion? If so, he's out on a homicide case, according to his recent text. Or was it to run your girl by me, and see what I thought?"

"I have a mom for that, Raina, but thanks!" Ty heard her chuckle before he said, "But I did call you for a particular reason. I'm not sure you'll want to do it, but I've thought about it and decided it wouldn't hurt to ask. If you don't want to do it, you just say so, and there's no problem, okay?"

"No. I still love my husband like crazy, so I won't run away with you. Sorry!" she said cheerfully.

Ty chuckled. "I know you do. And I'd never ask that, mainly because I know you'd say no. I'd hate to be shot down like that. It's hell on my ego. Not to mention my stellar reputation with the ladies." He heard her laughing on the other end.

"Not to mention what your lady friend would think about it!" Raina laughed again. "Okay, Ty, seriously. What can I do for you?"

"Would you be interested in doing a performance out here as part of a fundraiser?" he asked. "You just said you wanted to come here for a vacation, but maybe now you could do both?"

"Really? A fundraiser concert? Hmm. I don't see why not. It'd depend on when, and what the fundraiser's for. I won't do a show for something I don't like or support. If it's political in any way, not a chance."

"Don't blame you there. Stay clear of the politicians!" Ty paused, knowing this might be the part she'd not want to get involved with. Knowing her past still haunted her a little bit, he had to tread lightly and just feel her out.

"It's a fundraiser to help support horses and finding them new homes." He waited, and when she didn't answer him right away, he added, "Raina, if this is too close to you yet, you just say *no,* and there are no hard feelings whatsoever. You understand me?"

She was still quiet, but he patiently waited. Finally, she said softly, "Tell me about it."

He did. In-depth so there'd be no surprises, he told her everything from the wreck that first brought the horses to Harmony Hills, to the court-ordered auction, to about Just One More, and their quarterly fundraisers. He even told her his girlfriend was the one who'd founded Just One More, but he'd had no idea about that until recently. Any question she asked, he answered truthfully.

He was hopeful she'd do it mainly because she hadn't said no... Yet. "If you want to think about it, that's fine, Raina. It's just a thought I had. If you want more information, you can go to Just One More's website to see for yourself. If you decide not to, then you just say so. If it's still too close to home for you, Raina, you just tell me."

"Okay. You know I will." She paused before asking, "What's the website?" Raina headed over to her laptop to pull it up. As she browsed the website, she asked a few more questions. Over an hour later, she said, although a bit nervously, "Okay. I'll do it. When are you thinking?"

Now Ty paused before answering. "Are you *sure* you don't want to think about it some more? I haven't even mentioned it to my girl, so you can take all the time you need, Raina. I came to you first."

"If I think about it, Ty, I'd probably change my mind. Once I say I'm going to do something, I do it. My gut says to do it, and you know how I feel about listening to my gut."

"Yes, I do." He wondered if he should've checked with Channion first. But knowing his best friend and cousin, he'd just say it was his wife's decision. "I'm not pressuring you, darlin', but let's grab our calendars and see what dates are open for you. That'll give us something to work from."

"Got one right here." Raina flipped open her day planner. "When is the earliest you want to look at, and we'll go from there?"

Chapter 36

Sunday, June 5

The plane landed with a slight shudder, bounced lightly before it continued down the runway. Its speed gradually decreased as the pilot applied the brakes and lowered the flaps even more. Taxiing to their gate, the plane took him one step closer to seeing Ripley.

When the seatbelt lights turned off, and the cabin lights popped on, Ty was ready to spring from his seat and mow down everyone in his path to get out the door first. He held himself back and minded his manners instead.

Before he pulled down his own bag, he even assisted an elderly lady in getting her bag down from the overhead compartment, knowing the bags had undoubtedly shifted in the turbulence. Seeing the elderly lady was still shaken, Ty also carried her bag and helped her to the tarmac to be sure she was all right. She thanked him with a sweet smile and patted his hand.

Once he was sure she was fine, he headed to the restrooms. He impatiently walked among the other people who were weary from the plane ride. Turbulence was especially rough during this trip until the pilot was able to fly around the edge of the massive thunderstorm. Ty hadn't minded it himself, but he judged from the looks on many of the faces from his flight he was definitely in the minority.

Reaching the bathroom, he felt refreshed after he splashed cool water on his face after washing his hands, raking his wet fingers through his hair. Drying off his hands with the rough brown paper towels, he grabbed his carry-on bag and hurriedly headed out the door.

His flight to Ripley had been delayed five hours due to the sporadic and sometimes violent June storms rolling across the Midwest. Normally he didn't mind delays, but this time he did because it'd been just over two months since he'd last seen her when she'd visited him again in Arizona. At that time, she'd *had* to come to him there so she could see Damien and Laura's month-old newborn boy, Jacob Alexander, so he insisted the next trip was on his dime. At this rate, they'd never get together. But between their many phone calls and texts they were closer than ever.

This trip was especially important to him as he was planning on telling Ripley about his past. After talking at length with his best friends and confidants Channion and Morgan, he decided to take that leap of faith.

But it was during a ride that he and Josh took that really tipped the scales. Josh told him it was now or never. They couldn't go forward unless she knew all of it. Josh knew that personally because he and Morgan had gone through the same thing when they got together. Except it was Morgan's past that had to be dealt with, which also involved Ty to a great degree. And still did today.

It was a huge and even dangerous risk telling Ripley, but Ty felt it was something that needed to be discussed. He had faith and trust in Ripley Capilano. He could only hope to the high heavens his instincts weren't steering him wrong.

Ty knew he loved Ripley, and he knew he wanted to marry her someday. She had three more visits left on her list. True to her word made last September, she hadn't added any more to it. It seemed like a lifetime ago when she'd made that promise to him. But one thing he'd learned about his lady early on was she didn't break her promises.

They'd talked more about getting married in very general terms. It was always more along the lines of saying they wanted to stay together, make a life together, wanting their relationship to grow and be permanent. But the *M* word was just never uttered by either.

And he had yet to hear the words from her he needed to hear the most. She still hadn't actually said "I love you" to him.

Oh, Ty knew she did, but she just wouldn't say it. Not until her last personal reservation was gone, because, as she told him, "Once I say it, that's it. No turning back. Once I say it, I'm yours. Yours forever, Ty. I'm simply making sure, for both of our sakes." Then she kissed him until he couldn't think straight anymore.

Yes, indeed. He loved that woman to the moon and back.

As he came down the carpeted slope that led to the luggage carousels, he saw her making her way against the crowd toward him. With a big smile, he met her halfway, catching her when she practically leapt into his arms. He kissed her and felt her immediately respond. His heart felt like it was going to burst with happiness at having her in his arms again.

When she took a step back, she said, humor lurking in her eyes, "I'd like to point out that as the stereotype goes, it's usually the woman who runs late. What's your excuse, you handsome devil?"

He kissed her again before saying matter-of-factly, "I was outnumbered, Sugar. Not only is Mother Nature a female, but so was my pilot. And both were very good at their jobs—with my pilot winning in the end. God bless her!"

She laughed heartily. Arms around each other's waists, they headed for the parking lot.

Ripley happily chatted with him as they walked through the rain-soaked parking lot there in Tennessee. She'd taken off the next few days so she could focus only on her man.

She'd told Julia that morning while they talked on the phone that she was already dreading the day he had to leave for home, and he hadn't even arrived yet. Julia agreed she had it bad for the man, and that she couldn't be any happier for her friend.

When Ripley pulled up to her RV in a nice park set up specifically for them, Ty smiled.

She noticed it as she turned off her car and unfastened her seatbelt. "What?"

"Your RV. As crazy as it seems, your RV feels familiar to me... Like an old friend. Even like home. I see the appeal of having one. No matter where you may be, you're still... home. It's a comfort, isn't it?"

"Well, I've always said 'home is where your stuff is.' And we've spent enough time in it together for it to be at least homey for you. And for me, it *is* my home. Your house feels the same to me. We have two homes. The only thing is, you never know for sure where your other one is!" she joked as they got out of the car.

She unlocked, then held open the door for him as he walked up the steps with his bag, setting it down by the little dining room table so it'd be out of the way. Following him in, she then automatically locked the door and turned around.

They didn't last more than five humming seconds after that before they ended up in each other's arms again. With a laughing squeal coming from her, Ty had her flat on her back on her couch.

With an almost frenzied rush, she yanked off his t-shirt, tossing it across the room, almost knocking over her lamp. It rocked back and forth a couple of times before somehow staying upright. With a chuckle, Ty whispered, "Easy there, Sugar!"

"Shut up!" She laughed as she brought him back down to her. She ran her hands over his broad back, loving how he felt to her. She missed him so much when he was away. It took all her will power to hold back the happy tears now that they were together again. She heard his laugh when they rolled off the couch and landed with a thud on the soft rug on the floor.

"Better." She smiled. "There's more room down here." She swung her long hair out of the way as she leaned back down to kiss him.

It was a long while later when he leaned up on his elbows, looking down at her beneath him. He tucked her hair behind her ears before he leaned down and kissed her again. Looking into her eyes, he saw her passion. Trying to keep a straight face, he commented, "Apparently you're happy to see me."

She smiled before saying in a serious tone, "Beyond words."

She trailed her fingers around his muscled shoulders, then up behind his ears and into his soft, thick hair. She missed running her hands through his hair. She often found herself wishing he was around just so she could. Softly, she admitted, "I miss touching you when you're not with me."

Lying now on his side, his head propped on one of his hands, he looked down at her for a long moment. His other arm rested across her belly. Had he ever felt this content? Ty wondered.

"So how come I'm still not on your speed dial?" he asked thoughtfully, now combing his fingers slowly through her hair. He watched the strands fall smoothly to her shoulder.

"For basically the same reason as the other," she said softly, referring to why she wouldn't say she loved him out loud. She knew he understood her. "For the record, you're making it extremely difficult for me. Don't give up hope, babe. You're wearing me down!"

She smiled as she looked into his eyes, cupped his cheek with her hand. "Just *don't* start speaking in Spanish to me because you *know* what that does to me!"

"Dame un beso, mi amor," he said immediately, grinning. *Give me a kiss, my love.*

She grinned back, knowing this phrase as he'd been teaching her some Spanish over the phone. "Okay." She pulled him back down, both laughing.

She knew she loved this man, if for no other reason than he still had not pressured her to have sex with him. Sure, they'd go pretty far like they did just now but still no sex. Heavy petting is what a friend of hers would call it, she figured. Just thinking about it made her heart begin racing again. She fought to keep herself grounded even as she knew she was on the verge of flying. They both knew it was just a matter of time.

They'd been dating for ten months now. True, they'd been separated much of that time. But in a time when most people ended up in a sexual relationship on their first or second date, she and Ty could sleep together and could have some incredible make-out sessions, but they still hadn't had sex. And the fact he wasn't pressuring her in any way really blew her away. And he never once threatened to leave her because of it either.

She constantly heard and read stories from so many women about how their dates expected them to have sex immediately. Either as just an expectation, or even as payment for simply taking them out. Sex for dinner. Sex for a movie. Sex for *anything.* What was wrong with men nowadays?

One friend had told her it wasn't even a date at all. It was a so-called male friend who gave her a ride now and then who got furious when she wouldn't "pay" him even though she'd give him a little gas money. He didn't want her money; he just wanted her body. He'd presumed the whole time he was racking up points for sexual favors!

Her friend had immediately set him straight. He'd then left voicemails and sent texts cussing her out for allegedly leading him on. She still kept them all on her phone and also printed them out. She'd even had to block his number as he'd constantly text or call her. Scared, she'd let her friends know what was going on, and then went to the police... Just in case.

Ripley shuddered at how men disrespected, used, and abused women so horribly.

But not *her* man.

With the fact being that they *had* been separated for long periods of time, they learned about each other with no pressure of becoming more physically involved. Their relationship wasn't built on sex like so many others were. Sex simply got in the way, and then it became expected. Once that boundary was crossed, it was nearly impossible to back up and resume the relationship without giving in again. Sex simply changed everything. And to them, casual sex was not the same thing as love. Neither confused the two.

She refused to have a superficial relationship like that ever again.

What they'd learned about the other through countless emails, texts, and phone calls over the months they were apart just solidified what they learned about each other in person. It was adding layer upon layer, all built upon a firm foundation. They had a great thing going, and she didn't want to mess it up before she was ready to go any further. And he respected her for it. And better yet, he agreed with her.

Ripley cleared her mind of thoughts as she ran her fingers over his back. She loved the feel of his rippling muscles. He wasn't built like an extreme bodybuilder, which she found unnatural and a turn-off every time she saw a guy who was way *too* ripped. She didn't want a man who looked and felt like a beetle. Ty was just in excellent shape and had strong, defined, toned muscles from doing physical labor, working out in his gym, and playing games like basketball.

As his skillful mouth moved to her neck, she whispered, "Yep. You're making this really hard on me, you know. But just not yet..."

Hearing her soft words, Ty lifted his head. With tenderness, he brushed her hair back from her face, just gazing at her. "It's a good thing I love you for your money then, huh?"

Seeing the amusement in his eyes and the grin he was fighting to hold back, she knew he was teasing her, and she responded in kind. "Well, I'm glad I'm good for something!"

"Good for nothing," he teased again.

She laughed. "Well, at least I don't cost you anything then."

He kissed her lightly on her mouth. "And yet, I'd give you everything." His look turned serious again. "You know I love you, right, Ripley?"

Tears sprung to her eyes. His sweet words always pierced her heart. "Yes, I do, Ty. Just don't stop."

"Don't see it happening anytime soon." He tenderly kissed her again, and then pulled away from her. He walked across the room and picked up his shirt from the floor. Tossing a knowing look her way, he adjusted the lamp's position before slipping his shirt back on.

She grinned as she stood up, running her fingers through her hair to straighten it out. "Let's get you set up, shall we? Then we can decide on what we want to do while you're here. I wrote down some options, but we can do anything you want to."

He bent down to grab his bag and followed her toward the bedroom. "*Anything?*" he teased.

Ripley laughed. "We'll see."

Chapter 37

Wednesday, June 8

It was the night before he left that Ty told Ripley about his past. He didn't want to tell her too soon in case it ruined his trip. But he also didn't want to tell her just before he left because that wouldn't have been fair to her.

Ready for bed and relaxing in her little living room with the CD music from their New Year's Eve dinner playing in the background, Ty decided it was now or never. Had he ever been so nervous about anything? Even his first op wasn't as nerve-wracking as what he was about to do. At least, not that he could remember.

It was probably true because he was so much younger and fearless back then. He used to run on adrenaline and challenges, the thrill of the game. The older one got, the less fearless they became, he mused. Experience could do that to a person sometimes too.

She was sitting cross-legged on the floor between his legs while he sat behind her on the couch, rubbing her neck and shoulders in one of the best massages she thought she'd ever had. She'd found he gave wonderful massages the last time they were together. The man had magic hands.

"How's that feel?" he asked, hearing her moan yet again as her muscles loosened up.

"Like heaven," she said with feeling. "I could let you do this to me forever."

"Just say the words," he responded softly. She reached over and rubbed his bare leg with her hand but said nothing in return. After a few more minutes of massaging her shoulders, he said, "Your muscles may be sore for a little while from working out those knots, but then you'll feel better than ever."

Placing a kiss on top of her head, he said, "Ripley, I have something really important I need to talk about with you. It's something I had to say in person. I guess now is as good a time as any."

"You do?" Her heart was instantly thundering in her chest.

For a split second, she was absolutely terrified he was going to say he was moving on without her. That he was tired of waiting for her to make up her mind. She tried to hide her panic from her face in case he could see it. She had to close her eyes, fighting back the dizzying head rush she felt.

That singular moment was a life-changing one for her.

It told her just how much she loved Ty Stanton, fearing to her very bones that he was going to leave her. But she couldn't tell him *now* because this was *his* moment, not hers. She opened her eyes, looked straight ahead at her wall to compose herself and held her fear at bay. If he said he was leaving her, and she told him right now that she *did* love him, would he believe her? Or would he think it was just her saying what he wanted to hear in order for him to stay?

Ripley didn't know what to do, and her heart was racing in her indecision.

Wordlessly, she just nodded. She tried to get her thundering heart to slow down. She took another breath before asking, "What is it you wanted to tell me?"

Wondering what went through her mind there in that odd moment of silence between them, he hesitated.

"Come sit up here with me." He waited until she did so. He looked at her, really looked at her. His gaze didn't miss the slight fear in her eyes. "Are you okay, Sugar?"

She just nodded, scared to speak and scared to hear what he was going to say.

After a moment, realizing she wasn't going to say anything further, he decided to move along. He asked seriously, "I can trust you, right, Ripley? Are you able to hold in confidence something crucial? Promising to never tell another soul. Ever?"

"Of course." Okay, she told herself, *that* didn't sound like the intro to a break-up conversation. Looking deeply into his eyes, she said firmly, "You *can* trust me, Ty."

He waited a beat before saying, "For what I feel we have going between us, I don't want what I need to tell you to be a secret from you. I always want there to be honesty between us, Ripley.

"For us to move forward together, I'm prepared to share a part of myself with you. A part that you *must* keep to yourself. I feel if I don't tell you, and it comes up in the future, it could cause you to think I don't trust you. So I can only take a huge leap of faith here and hope I'm not making a terrible mistake in sharing this part of me with you."

He paused again. "We've known each other for almost a year now. I think I've ascertained correctly that you're trustworthy especially on things that are very important to others."

She nodded.

He paused again before saying, "I know this may sound far-fetched, but it's the honest truth. It's not a joke or a story I'm making up. I need you to understand that."

She nodded again. "You can tell me whatever you need to, Ty. I *promise* to keep it to myself."

Ty had to trust his gut. His heart thudded in his chest as he debated telling her one final time. This could—and most likely would—change everything.

His mind made up, he said, "There's no easy way to say it, but I'll try. Before I began working at Harmony Hills, I had a completely different career. For most of my adult life, I've been an undercover agent for an international agency. I'm pretty much retired now, but technically I'm still active. My assignments are still confidential and for good reasons.

"To this day, I protect dozens of people with my absolute silence by people not knowing of my past at all. It *must* be kept this way. If it got out, it puts not only me in real danger, but all of them too. I trust you to keep this completely to yourself—forever."

Shocked, Ripley was speechless. Was this a joke? Something to intrigue her with that was all made up? Could he prove it to her? But studying him, she had to admit he appeared to be very serious. His dark gaze was level and direct while his voice had taken on a slight edge.

Finally, she was able to ask softly, "Which agency?"

He shook his head. "I can't tell you that. I worked for them about fifteen years before I finally left. I was deeply involved in a crime world that most people don't know even exists. Everyday people you see could have links to the underground, but you just don't know it. That's the whole point, of course. Mafia, human traffickers, weapons dealers... Anyone could be anything.

"Anyway, not too long after I left, they asked me to work on a part-time basis, you could say. And I agreed."

She waited for him to speak again, but he stayed quiet. "Why did you leave?" Ripley asked in a soft tone. She laid her hand on his knee, just letting it rest there in silent support.

Knowing he couldn't tell her the real reasons, he thought for a moment before still truthfully replying, "Looking back, it was most likely burnout and disillusionment. And I wanted a normal life where I didn't have to live with the lowest or most corrupt of the human race.

"I'd become so accustomed to seeing the world as just a place with a possible ambush coming from every corner, knowing I couldn't trust *anyone*, that I'd forgotten who I used to be.

"I rarely saw my own family or my few trusted friends outside of my work. I was worried I'd be followed one day and lead them right to my family's front door. It was safer to stay away from them, using a different name to hopefully prevent leaks that'd lead back to them.

"My own family has *no* idea what I did, Ripley. Only a select few do, and they're sworn to secrecy for life. It doesn't matter that most of us are in law enforcement in one form or another. They simply cannot know. So they don't. It's safer for everyone this way.

"And I knew, too, that no matter how long I worked, no matter what all I, or all of us, did, it'd just never end. It'd never really be finished. While there's some job security in that, it got old. It got to the point where it didn't make sense for me to do it anymore. It was major burnout that I simply couldn't shake off like I'd been able to do before.

"Ripley, I'm now entrusting you with my secret. Never can this information be revealed. It's not only my *own* life that I'm protecting, but the lives of a whole lot of other people. They trust me to never reveal their secrets, their lives, their whereabouts. And I never will.

"If it got out that I was an undercover agent, Ripley, I'd be running for the rest of my life. I'd always be looking over my shoulder, wondering if I was walking into a trap. I'd never be, or feel, safe. Neither would you. They could use you to get to me. That's fact. It stands to reason, if they don't know about me, then they don't know about you. Staying alone over the years has always been safer for me, but then you came along. You changed things for me, Ripley.

"As it stands now, I've been out long enough I don't have quite the same feelings as I did before. The ones I had of being watched or followed. There are still a whole lot of people who'd love to get their hands on me, and I'd rather die to avoid the torture for the information they'd want. I know too much about too many. Do you understand?" His voice was dead serious, and his eyes never left hers as he spoke.

Still stunned, she could only nod her head.

He let out a deep breath and simply waited for it all to sink in. The music played in the background as she processed what he'd told her.

Her throat and mouth dry, she finally asked, "So you're still with them, still... active, but you really just work for Morgan?"

"Yes. I've been working at Harmony Hills for Morgan for a long time now. It's safe for me there. It's safe now for me to visit my family and friends. I can now tell those who are close to me where I work, and what I do. Before, when I was fully undercover, none of that was true or even possible.

"I love it at the Center, and I don't plan to leave it... or Morgan. Besides being technically my boss, she's one of the absolute best friends I've ever had. One of the few people I can truly trust. We've gone through a lot together. It'd be very hard to leave her there, on both a personal and business level.

"There's still *nothing* for you to be jealous about, though, Ripley. Morgan and I have only ever been friends, but we're tight. We've never once been together romantically. We've never slept together even though some people think we have.

"It helped immensely when she married Josh, but people still made assumptions from before then. She won't put up with gossip, so those people aren't around anymore. I made sure I told you this at the very beginning of our relationship, but I just want to emphasize it again now."

Ripley nodded, recalling him clearly telling her this, others mentioning it, and she'd seen it herself. He and Morgan *were* tight. She'd even asked Josh about it once when they were alone after working Cappy. He'd assured her there was nothing for either of them to be jealous about.

Ty paused. "Are you scared? I'd not let anyone hurt you if I could ever prevent it. You *are* safe with me. It *is* safe to be with me." He prayed he was right.

Ripley didn't know what to say or do. She felt so amazingly petty now for thinking her secret of being rich was so heady. Ty was in a life-or-death situation. She'd never felt so humbled in her entire life.

What was it like to live with that over your head at all times? That someone could discover you, and honest to God want to *kill* you? And for you to be ready, and willing, to die simply to protect others?

She told him her thoughts, forcing herself to be honest and truthful, softly but with strength. He answered her questions and concerns for a good hour or so. She realized this was a burden *she'd* have to carry now. Was she strong enough? She thought she was. She hoped she was.

Ty watched her carefully. He'd been reading her body language since he'd begun speaking. When she'd spoken, she'd sounded calm, accepting, thoughtful. She wasn't in a panic mode, nor was she so scared she was asking him to leave... which had been one of his worst fears.

"Do you have any other questions?" he asked.

"Do Morgan or Josh know?"

Shaking his head, he replied, "I'd never say. If I said yes, you'd be tempted to discuss it with her or them. One day when you *thought* you were alone, you'd bring it up. And it'd take only one person to overhear by accident. This is *not* a topic for discussion by anyone, at any time. Do you clearly understand that? It must stay with *only* you.

"I'd also never say because anyone who knows, *they* could then be in potential danger as well. No one knows who *else* knows with a few exceptions for necessity. It's a safeguard for me and everyone else. Maybe someday I can impart with some more information, but not right now, Ripley. I can't."

He looked at their fingers laced together for a moment before he said softly, "I know it's a heavy burden to carry. It was a difficult decision to make to tell you for more than one reason. I needed to be sure we had enough between us *to* tell you. And to be able to tell if you were strong enough to carry my secret. I believe you are.

"Once we end this discussion, it can't be brought back up unless we're absolutely certain we're alone and secure. We'll come up with a code just between us that signals we need to bring it up when we're positive we're alone.

"You may *think* we're alone, but all there needs to be is a single person to overhear and to spread it. It might surprise you just how quickly a secret like this can spread. It's an uncontrollable wildfire in high winds. I've known of others who weren't so fortunate and were found—and *killed*.

"It's not a joke. It's very real. Ripley, I need you to fully understand that it takes only one person to kill me. Do you understand how important this is?

"If, for some unknown reason, we *ever* go our separate ways, I *need* to know, Ripley, that you will keep this secret to yourself until you die. If you end up hating me for some reason, or you get mad at me, I beg you to please not use this against me in any way.

"It's not just about me, but so many others. No one, I mean, no one, can ever know. You can't tell anyone. Not your pastor, your mom, Joe, Steve, Julia, whoever." He held her hands tightly. "I'm trusting you with my life, Ripley."

The trust he must have in her left her breathless. She was stunned. And humbled. And proud. She couldn't let him down.

Leaning forward to kiss him, she whispered, “Forever silent, Ty. You have my promise. You can trust me. *Thank you* for trusting me.”

Chapter 38

Thursday, June 9

They slept in the next morning, knowing it'd be another two months before they saw each other again. That's when the fundraiser would be that featured Just One More and the rescued horses at Harmony Hills.

August wasn't the best time in Arizona due to the heat factor, but it was the best date they could come up with that worked with Raina Scott, Morgan, and Ripley's work schedules.

Ty had hours yet before his plane left to return him to Arizona. To make his stay longer, he'd chosen the latest departing flight, knowing he could sleep through the night on the plane trip back to Arizona if he needed to. Besides that, the time zone changes would work in his favor. He also had part of the next day off to get home from the airport, unpack and unwind before heading to work. Morgan would tell him to just stay home if it wasn't busy though. She said she'd let him know.

Now, still here in Tennessee with the rain coming down in sheets, neither felt like getting out of bed. Except to go to the bathroom or get something to drink, they refused to leave it. Warm and cozy with each other, they just shared pillow talk, wrapped together, listening to the rain, and later, dozing off.

At a crack of thunder and a brilliant flash of lightning, Ripley awoke suddenly. Getting her bearings, she felt Ty's arm around her waist, keeping her warm and close to him even in sleep. She lay there quietly, just relishing the feeling of having him beside her, knowing this time tomorrow he'd be gone again. She wiped a couple of tears from her eyes at the thought. She slowly turned over to face him, not wanting to wake him up.

While he slept, she studied him. She loved to watch him sleep. Knowing what she did now of his being an undercover agent, she saw him in a completely different light. Thoughts filtered through her mind as she gazed at him. She respected him before, but now? What words could she use to describe her feelings about this man? She swore to herself she'd never tell a soul, no matter what.

She wondered when she should tell him she loved him. Just telling him seemed so... well, plain. She thought of all the times together they'd shared, all the original dates he'd thought of—especially their first secret date in Phoenix. She smiled just remembering it. The guts and courage it took for him to do something that brave still left her in awe. It took nerve to do that.

That's when it came to her that *this* was her opportunity to do something special to show him she had the same courage. The chance he took last year was still bigger than her doing something now because *now* they were already together and in love. Unless it was something extravagant that'd blow his mind. She smiled, remembering their New Year's Eve conversation.

Still, it was the thought that really counted. While she knew he'd be overjoyed and beyond happy to just hear the words, she wanted to do it justice. She also wanted to be absolutely sure, especially with his recent bombshell news. She wanted to be settled with that more, in case a thought or feeling popped up later that she wasn't feeling now. But she actually felt solid about it.

Adjusting her head and hair on her pillow, she looked at him, thinking. With her finger, she lightly traced his face. He still reminded her of somebody she couldn't place, and it drove her crazy sometimes. She idly wondered what he'd look like when he was older. She'd seen pictures of his parents. His dad looked somewhat like an older version of Ty, so she bet he'd still be just as handsome himself. She hoped to be around to see it firsthand. She smiled at the thought.

At another crack of thunder, Ty opened his eyes just to see her looking into his. Adjusting his head on his pillow, he just looked at her, wondering what had her smiling. He could see the love in her soft expression. He wished she'd say the words because then he'd *know* he had her for life.

The thought filled him with so much hope, he smiled back. He could picture them together years from now, doing this same thing. If only she could. He still felt it was right telling her of his past, so they could hopefully have a future. A future that included this.

They heard the rolling thunder as they lay there, actually felt it reverberate through the RV. There was another brilliant flash of lightning that shone like a flickering spotlight outside the windows. Ripley automatically glanced at the nearest window, but of course neither could see out as all of the blinds were pulled down.

Ripley loved storms. Generally, the worse they were, the more she liked them, barring a tornado since she lived in an RV. It wasn't exactly safe being in a home on wheels. She'd turned on the weather alert radio before they went to bed, just in case.

She knew Ty loved storms, too, especially being from Arizona where big storms weren't exactly the norm. He'd told her how much he loved the monsoon season and the occasional winter storms. And how he'd sit and watch the storms roll over the mountain ranges. She'd soon learned a lot of people down there shared the same sentiment.

Now, they both automatically looked up as the rain just fell in torrents. Ripley said over the noise of the falling rain, "Wow. That skylight better not start to leak, or we'll drown in here! If this keeps up, babe, your flight could be cancelled or at least delayed. What do you think about that?" She had to talk louder to be heard over the rain pounding their sanctuary.

"Fine with me! I could stay here all day and night with you." He smiled at her, saying, "Unless you're sick of me and can't wait for me to leave?"

"Are you kidding? How could I ever be sick of you? I..." She caught herself. She couldn't believe what she just about said.

Neither could Ty.

"You... *what?*" he asked tenderly.

She bit her lip, inwardly cursing herself. And not knowing why she was.

Ty rolled over on top of her. His hands gently brushed her hair away from her face as his body weight pinned her to the bed. He saw the misty tears in her eyes and wished with all his heart she'd just admit it.

"You know you love me, baby. Why don't you just say it? Stop torturing yourself." And me, he thought. He placed tender kisses on her forehead, her nose, and her cheeks. "You know I love you."

Ripley had to give up something: Her irrational self-control or her heart. Since he already had one of them, she made her choice rather easily.

Under the dual assault of the exciting thunderstorm pounding down on them, and Ty's pure, overwhelming love, she really had no way to hold back any longer. Cupping his face tenderly in her hands, she said gently, "How about I show you instead?"

Chapter 39

Tuesday, August 16

The sun was shining brightly as the large silver plane's wheels touched down with a bump and a skid on the dry Tucson runway. The heat sent shimmering waves upward from the pavement, distorting everyone's ground-level view.

A full flight, it seemed to take another hour before everyone was able to get their carry-on luggage and disembark. Hand in hand, they walked through the tarmac, stopping at the restrooms first.

As they made their way toward the luggage carousels again, she couldn't stop smiling. "Oh... It's so *good* to be here!" Her big smile turned toward him, she practically squealed in excitement. She reached over and took hold of his hand again.

"It took us long enough, didn't it?" he agreed, grinning. He squeezed her hand as they walked with the crowd.

She smiled as she looked around. "More than. Man, I'm *so* excited! I hope nothing goes wrong."

"Like what?"

She shrugged. "I don't know, just nothing. There's a lot going on... I just want it all to be perfect!"

"Don't jinx it, sweetheart," he joked.

As they turned the corner where the density of people began thinning out, they saw the tall, dark-haired man by the wall. A huge smile spread across his face when he caught sight of them, and he quickly made his way through the few people in his way so he could get to them faster.

She let go of her man and headed straight into the arms of another.

"Hello, darlin'! It's so *good* to see you in my neck of the woods finally!" Ty swooped up a happily squealing Raina in his arms and hugged her tightly. Her arms returned his embrace. He grinned at Channion, who stood there shaking his head at him, acting exasperated with his wife. But his own wide grin betrayed his true feelings.

Ty held out a hand to shake Channion's even as he still held Raina in a close hug. His cousin just laughed and shoved it aside. "Let go of my wife, you scoundrel!"

Ty laughingly obliged and tightly hugged his cousin, who was much more like a brother. Their lifelong bond was tight and unbreakable.

Backing up a step, Ty took a good look at him. He nodded in silent confirmation of what Raina had told him on the phone the day before. Channion and their uncle Ron, Channion's partner, had been working long, stressful hours the past year. This trip was something he seriously needed.

Raina worried he was going to burn out, or worse, be too tired to think straight if he couldn't take a break somewhere far from home. With him being a cop, she was truly concerned his judgment could get impaired from his grueling schedule. She was terrified to think of what could happen if he wasn't in top form.

She'd confidentially told Ty the day before of her fears when she'd called to confirm their flights. "Ty, I never want to see my husband on the news for an accidental shooting, or something worse. Ever since he got promoted two years ago, dead people see him more than I do. He's coming to Arizona with me even if I have to kidnap him, or go in person and tell the chief he's taking some time off. He looks worse now than at the family reunion, and he was there only one day, remember?

"Unless I miss my guess, Janet is about ready to do it for Ron too. Since they both got promotions, it's been non-stop work!"

Now personally seeing the exhaustion etched in Channion's face, Ty said with concern, "You surely look like you need a vacation, Chan. You look like you've been turned inside out!"

Ty cupped his cousin's head, studied him closely. His cousin was a tough man who didn't break easily, so to see this look on him didn't sit well with Ty at all. Channion looked even worse than when he'd worked Raina's case when she was being hunted by criminals after saving a deputy's life. Ty would be sure to make him rest while he was out here.

"Does Uncle Ron look like you too?" Ty asked when his cousin didn't immediately reply to his comments.

Channion smiled and shrugged his wide shoulders, saying, "Not at all. Raina assures me I'm *much* better looking." His wife and cousin laughed, but Channion knew what Ty was asking. "Probably. It's those so-called budget cuts that've taken away my officers like they've done.

"My darling wife here is ready to go on the warpath again with the chain of command. We all know she's more than capable of doing it. Of course, since the higher-ups also know this from past personal experience, my guess is they want to avoid having to deal with her at all costs. So *that's* why my detectives and officers are supposedly being returned to me. If not soon, I'll sic her on them myself!"

Raina nodded and rubbed her husband's back as Ty smiled at the thought of her taking on the corrupt and greedy politicians of Illinois. For her husband, he didn't doubt she'd do it. As a matter of fact, she *had* already done it before they were even dating. Going on the warpath as his wife would be even more impressive.

Raina stated, "I've already been planning my attack strategies. I have various scenarios rolling around in my mind. I might share them with you while we're here to get your input, if that's all right?"

Ty grinned. "Whatever it takes if it's for Channion."

With a deep sigh and a look at his wife, Channion continued, "Thank you for this getaway for us, Ty. I know Raina is working here for a few days, but it's still a vacation. We're both sorry we couldn't make it out here sooner. We really wanted to."

Ty shook his head. "Hey, it's okay. You're here now, right? No need for apologies. I completely understand. We're adults now, and we all have responsibilities. It's just great that you're finally here!

"Morgan is almost as excited as I am, and she can't wait for you to meet her husband. And per meeting Raina, Morgan's chomping on the bit. She wants to see who took you away to matrimonial bliss!" Ty teased.

Channion grinned. "Same applies. I want to see what guy passed not only your tests, but hers!"

Turning back to Channion's wife, Ty studied her. Raina, in contrast with her husband, looked positively radiant. This time, he took a moment and read her shirt. `Hi, Uncle Ty!` He noticed the words were in a cartoon bubble coming from...

"*Oh! Darlin'!* Are you...? *Seriously...?*" Without thinking, he placed his hands on the sides of her belly, looking at her with joy on his face.

She laughed at his expression once he figured out she was pregnant. Channion laughed too. They knew Ty would be ecstatic for them. She patted his hands now on her waist, saying firmly but with humor shining in her eyes, "My belly is *not* community property, but I'll make an exception this time for the kiddo's uncle!"

"I'm so sorry. It was just a reflex..." He wrapped her up in his arms again, now feeling he should be careful of hurting her. Ty kissed her cheek before he hugged his cousin again. "I'm so happy for you both! Geez, Raina, I'd not have asked you to come flying across the country if I'd known you were pregnant."

"That's why we didn't tell you. I really wanted to see you while I was still just me and not carrying ten pounds of diaper bag and thirty pounds of kid. My fearless husband may not be carrying on this trip of ours, but I sure am!

"And I have about six months to go. Besides that, we set this all up before my husband was home just long enough to pay me some attention!" She laughed when Channion lightly tapped her head to tell her to shut up.

Ty laughed, looked at her again while he held her hands. "I can't believe I'm gonna be an uncle to your kid, Chan. You're gonna be a *dad*. Wow. After all this time..." His voice was full of wonder.

Channion grinned. "Yeah, I know. You can only imagine how Janet reacted when we told her and Ron!" Channion laughed good-naturedly. His wife looped her arm through his as they all began walking. "We were so afraid Aunt Janet would be popping over in the middle of the night, just walking in with ideas, gifts, and whatever, we almost changed the code on our security system."

As they walked over to get their luggage, Ty glanced at them, wondering if he was being serious. It seemed he was.

Raina nodded, her eyebrows raised, and her eyes big. "Oh yeah, Ty... Janet has gone over the edge. I opted for moving, but Channion vetoed that. He said he didn't have the time to pack and didn't want to leave everything behind. I even asked about Witness Protection, but he said we didn't qualify now."

She smiled as both men laughed. "I'm sure Janet respects us enough to not come barging in our house. Man, I *hope* she does anyway!"

With a long sigh and an affectionate pat to her barely-round belly, she mourned, "If Stephanie or Sabrina would have a kid right now, I'd *really* appreciate it! Her own daughters having a kid would totally take away some of the pressure.

"Although I'm out here working, trust me, I'm really on vacation too. Actually, I feel more like we've run away from home!"

Ty laughed heartily. "You two are welcome to stay as long as you like! Give me your return tickets, and I'll shred them for you as soon as we get home."

Raina suddenly stopped walking and turned to him. Grabbing his arm, she interrupted his thoughts asking, "Hey! Where's your lady love? I'm dying to meet the woman who was able to snag *you* off the market!"

Ty took a breath, knowing what was going to happen next. "She's not here."

By his tone, she asked, "What does that mean? Do you mean she's not here at the airport? Or not here altogether?"

Preparing himself, Ty said, "Not here altogether." At their dual looks of disbelief, he hastily added, "Yet."

Grabbing his arm again, Raina pulled him out of the way so others could get by. Channion followed, perplexed himself. Her face showing her surprise, she asked, "Are you telling me I agreed to do a concert for a fundraiser for *her* horse facility, and she's *your* girlfriend who you love to pieces, and she's not even here? Do you *expect* her to be?"

Ty's first thought was there was a hormonal pregnancy rage coming on, but then realized it didn't have anything to do with hormones. He was asking himself the same questions, and he for sure wasn't pregnant!

Ty thought long about his answer before he opened his mouth. His trust in Ripley was absolute, but *man!* She was putting it to the test right now. Since they'd made love that day in Tennessee two months ago, they'd only talked a couple of times. And the last time was the same week he'd arrived back in Arizona. That's when she said she needed to break all contact with him but to wait for her, to be patient, to trust her. They weren't breaking up at all, she assured him. She just needed the space.

His heart hurting, he didn't really have a choice. He told her he loved her again and would be here for her before they hung up.

Since then, he hadn't heard a word from her. Nor had Morgan. Not a single word.

Now, the fundraiser was going on at Harmony Hills as they'd planned out. Her Aunt Lilly in New Mexico was a devil with details and had it all worked out with Morgan in no time at all. Morgan was having a blast hosting the fundraiser. Lilly and Morgan looked at this fundraiser from every possible angle, and both agreed immediately on holding it at Morgan's.

But they'd also decided months ago to leave the horses at Just One More until closer to the fundraiser, so they'd have more impact coming in. Morgan indirectly sent money to help pay for their care so they wouldn't be a burden to Just One More's budget. She could even use it as a tax deduction since she sent it in as a donation. How they spent it wasn't any of her business. It was theirs.

Besides, not only was this where it all began, and where it was ending for the horses, Harmony Hills was established and well-known all over the southwestern states. It'd be sure to have a gathering just from Morgan's name alone. And her clout would add even more validity to Just One More's facility.

The other day when the horse trailers pulled in with the eleven horses, the place went up in cheers. Having bought the horses back from Ripley, except for Cappy, they were finally back where they belonged. Ripley said Cappy wasn't for sale as he'd chosen her to be his human. She'd decide where to keep him later on, she'd said. Morgan had nodded in understanding.

Now, with the fundraiser only three days away, his own family's arrival stirred up those feelings again.

Returning his attention back to Raina, who was still staring expectantly at him, Ty said, "Okay. All I can say right now is I wish you were still single, Channion. No offense, Raina, darlin'."

They both laughed, but neither let him off the hook either.

Raina asked, "When was the last time you spoke with her?"

Ty sighed. "Two months ago."

Channion broke in. "Whoa. Did you two have a fight?"

"No."

"Are you *sure?* Because I've learned from my lovely wife here, we don't *always* think alike. And while *I* may not think we had a fight or a disagreement, that doesn't mean *she* doesn't think it."

Ty smiled when Raina leaned up and kissed her husband soundly. Channion smiled when his wife pulled away and patted his cheek.

"See *why* I love him? He's one of the smartest men I've ever met!" Raina wrapped her arm around her husband's waist.

Ty replied, "No fight. I'm positive. Ripley wouldn't walk away from a fight anyway."

"She knows you love her?" she asked.

"Yes, at least she should by now. It was also the last thing I told her."

Ty was feeling slightly uncomfortable under the interrogation of Raina. She was too whip smart to not figure out more. Channion would figure it out on his own, too, but his gut said Raina would do it first. Not just because she had incredible instincts, but because she was nosier.

Channion asked, "Well, what did she say?"

"Do we really have to talk about this? Here? Ever?"

"Yeah, we do," Channion stated firmly.

Giving his cousin a look of betrayal, Ty finally said, "Fine. In summary then, we discussed this fundraiser. She was excited and happy Raina had decided to do it. And she said she needed some time to herself. But she also said to not give up on her, just to have faith and trust in her... which I do."

They both just looked at him in suspended silence.

Finally, Channion said with compassion, "Oh, man. The 'needed some time to herself' phrase... Ty, you know that's the kiss of death right there! I'm sorry, man." He looked all sympathetic for his cousin. He even patted his shoulder in consolation.

Raina scolded him, "Honey, it is not!" At his *Seriously? Are you kidding me?* look, she amended her statement, "Not *always*."

"Thanks, Raina," Ty said dryly.

"Normally, I may agree with that statement. But she added the other on there, so that could just mean she needs some space to..." Raina looked hard at Ty, understanding coming in a flash. With a flat voice, she said, "You two had sex, didn't you?"

"*Raina!*" Channion hissed at his wife. He clamped his hand over her mouth, looked over at his cousin in apology.

"Seriously, Channion. I *really* wish you were single right now!"

Channion laughed even as he felt like duct taping Raina's mouth shut. Undeterred, she pried her husband's hand from her mouth before she said, lowering her voice, "Ty, you didn't! You said you weren't going to... *Why* did you?"

Channion grinned at her. "*Really*, sweetheart?" She smiled, shooed him away. He laughed at her attempt to shush him, but then stopped laughing abruptly, saying in wonder, "Whoa. Hold on *just* a minute... You two were talking about... Why didn't you call *me?*" he asked his cousin.

Fighting back her grin, Raina answered instead, "You were *working*, sweetheart. I do understand that you had no other choice, so it's all right." Her husband shook his head. Her attention back on Ty, she said, "Well?"

"You're worse than my mom, you know that? Geez, Raina!"

Holding back a grin, she stated, "I'm practicing to *be* one. Right now. So?"

Channion laughed heartily as Ty rolled his eyes and looked away, but both men knew she wouldn't let it go. Ty explained to his cousin, "First off, your wife and I *didn't* talk about this subject in detail. It was inferred, and then answered in general terms in response to a few dozen questions she'd asked."

Channion smiled and nodded, knowing his astute wife was like a hound dog when she caught whiff of something... *anything*. And once she did, she never let it go. She didn't know the meaning of the word *quit*, which he loved her dearly for most times. And for which he was positive his cousin hated about her right about now.

He wrapped his arms around his wife from behind, pulling her closer so she could lean back against him. He kissed the top of her head as he waited for his cousin to continue.

Since the subject had been broached, Ty explained to Raina, "It was mutual. There's more to it than that, but that's not any of your business. So that's all I'm going to say about it."

"*And...*" she prodded, holding back her smile. Attempting to respect their privacy, she also sensed there was more to the story.

"And later that day, I boarded the plane that brought me back home."

Raina's mouth dropped open. She sprung away from her husband, exclaiming, "Ty Stanton! I thought so much more of you! How *could* you? You slept with her and then *left* her all in the same day?"

He glared at her. "Knock it off, Stewart. It was between two consenting adults, who'd been dating each other for a year at that point. I'd say I showed her far more respect than most any other guy I know, present company excluded, of course."

"Thanks, cous," Channion said.

He honestly did feel bad for Ty, and he certainly wasn't sure what to make of his girlfriend at this point. It was most likely just a private matter between them, he decided. To help Ty out, he looked at his wife to tell her to drop it, but she beat him to it.

Raina apologized profusely, "I'm sorry, Ty. Really. Dang these hormones! I didn't mean that to sound so bad... But..." She shut her mouth at the dark look on Ty's face and instead wrapped him up in a hug. She wiped the tears from her eyes and blew out a breath. "These hormones are hell. Okay. Moving on. What happened next?"

Ty took a deep breath, relieved no one was around them to overhear this conversation. He felt like a lovesick teenager talking with his parents. If he didn't have so much respect for Raina, and didn't love her like another sister, he'd have told her to mind her own business. But the truth was, he needed someone to talk to. Someone who *didn't* know Ripley personally. Maybe a fresh viewpoint was needed. Love *was* blind after all.

"Ty? What else happened?" she asked again.

He knew he was in for it now. Looking straight at her, he said, "I asked her to marry me."

Chapter 40

THEY STARED AT TY.

Almost afraid of the answer, Channion asked, "Well? What'd she say?"

Ty sighed. "Nothing. She just cried, hugged and kissed me goodbye, and my plane left fairly soon afterwards. I honestly didn't even mean to ask her then. It just kind of came out."

Raina asked gently, "And that was the last time you talked to her?"

"No, we talked twice more that week. The second call was when she said to trust her, be patient, and give her time. We've had no contact at all since then, per her request. I'm just respecting her wishes, knowing she has good reason for it."

Raina refused to let her husband be right. This was Ty, and he *loved* Ripley! Something told her it'd actually be all right. She had great instincts, according to these two men, so she thought she'd use that to her advantage.

"Hey," she said to Ty, placing her hand on his cheek. "It's all fine. Trust me. You two and Ron have always remarked on my amazing psychic abilities, so don't—"

Channion interrupted, "Whatever, sweetheart. We never said they, or you, were psychic!"

Nonplussed, she said with a twinkle in her eyes, "You will soon! And I promise I'll only use my powers for good."

Ty smiled broadly at her comments so that made her feel better. "Seriously, Ty. Ripley will show up. And even if she doesn't happen to show up for the fundraiser, I'm positive she'll come back for you. After all, I've never known you to hang out with an idiot before."

The cousins laughed heartily. Grinning, Ty said, "I see your wife still has a way with words, Chan. No, my girl is far from being an idiot, God love her!" He laughed again. "Thanks, Raina."

"It's my pleasure, darlin'." She looked around, suddenly noticing practically everyone else had left the area, and it was just them. Their luggage was still waiting for them on the carousel which had even stopped turning by then. Wow. How long had they been there?

She took a deep breath, and let it out. "Now then, it seems we've all been updated with current and major events that pertain to us. And since we're reassured all's well, at least for the time being, I say we get moving. Let's grab a couple of carts to haul all my junk, and then find somewhere to eat. Ty's little bundle of joy here is making me hungry. Either his tiny little tummy is growling, or mine is.

"I'm craving some Chinese like crazy. Is that all right with you guys? Do you have a good Chinese place around here, Ty?"

Ty burst out in laughter at the look on Channion's face.

Channion shook his head. "Great. That's just great. Her hormones are buzzing around so badly, they're messing up her memory." Looking at his wife as he placed his hands firmly on her shoulders, he asked, "Sweetheart, if you can't keep straight who the father of your kid is, how in the world do you expect to remember the words to all of your songs?"

Raina's laughter rang out as she walked with them to get their luggage. She took hold of her husband's hand as they walked. Remembering a funny story, she turned to Ty. "Hey, if you two ever *do* have a fight, or at least a stupid argument—and you will—let me talk to her. I'll tell her how to sort it out."

Channion glanced over at his wife and retorted, "Oh no, you won't!"

Ty grinned, knowing it had to be good if it was between these two. "What happened?"

Raina chuckled. "It's bound to happen with you and Ripley. It happens to *all* couples, but I *still* can't believe it happened to us. But it sure enough did." She sighed dramatically. "It was all over a pack of gum. Can you believe that?"

Channion looked at Ty, shrugged, and nodded. "It was just one of those things."

Pausing from loading a suitcase on a cart, Ty raised an eyebrow. "You two lovebirds fought over a pack of *gum?* Are you messing with me right now?"

Raina giggled. "I know. Crazy. Stupid." She smiled at Ty before she began to explain. "What happened was this... I was going into town, and being a loving wife,"—she gently elbowed her husband when he laughed—"I asked Channion if he wanted me to pick him up anything. It was like his first day off in weeks, and I simply thought to save him from going into town himself, see? He was chilling at home, and he seriously needed to.

"Anyway, he said to get him a big three-pack of a certain kind of gum. The *blue* pack."

Channion interjected, "I was pretty specific about *which* blue one."

She continued like Channion hadn't said a word, "So I get home and happily hand him the three-pack of gum. He gets upset and says it was the wrong one. It was a *green* pack of gum. I apologized, wondering myself how I could've messed it up as I knew what kind he normally bought. I told him it was just gum, chew it anyway. Hardly a big deal, you know?

"Anyway, he doesn't let it go and keeps asking me *how* could I have not bought the one he wanted?"

Ty smiled as Channion shrugged his shoulders again as Raina went on, "So then *I* get upset, go to our bedroom, shutting the door to cool off, right? A few minutes later, here he comes. I think he's going to apologize, offer me comfort, you know? But *no!* He jumps right in again about me buying the wrong gum. He made me cry!"

Surprised, Ty admonished him, "Channion Scott! *You?* You made your wife *cry?* Shame on you."

Channion tried to keep a straight face when he replied, "Yes, I did. But in my defense, I still blame that crying part on PMS."

Raina said sternly, "Oh, it was. You're absolutely right on that, darlin'... Except it wasn't female that time around. Men have it, too, as you so obviously proved that day."

Ty laughed when his cousin grinned but didn't reply to his wife's dig. As they loaded the last suitcase onto the cart, he asked, "Did he apologize to you? Because if not..."

She smiled as she tightened her ponytail. "Yes, but it took a few days. Now we can laugh about it, but at the time, it wasn't funny at all. It's just dumb, little things that happen that seem to be the *worst* arguments. But no one can win *because* they're so dumb!

"Then, when you look back at it, you shake your head wondering what the big deal was in the first place? That's marriage, I guess. We never once did that until we got married. Stuff like that just needs to be worked through now."

Confused, Ty asked, "So how does this apply to me and Ripley exactly?"

"It's more for Ripley, I think." Channion laughed, his eyes sparkling in amusement. "When I didn't apologize fast enough for her, she took matters into her own hands."

He laughed heartily again. "I'm working my tail off at work, right? I'm dealing with druggies and murderers. A couple of days later, I'm engrossed in stacks of paperwork on a homicide case to prep for court, and Diggs plops down this *huge* bouquet of flowers on my desk. I look up, and ask him what it was for?

"Diggs replies he wasn't sure. It was just delivered downstairs and had my name on it. Since he was down there, he decided to save me the trip to get it. The delivery girl just said to tell the recipient he'd better *not* come home without it!"

Ty laughed until he had tears in his eyes. He looked at Raina's grinning face. "So you bought your own flowers, having them delivered to him at work just so he could bring them home to you?"

Raina nodded. "I thought it was a nice gesture for him to do, don't you? It was terribly sweet of him to bring me such gorgeous flowers. I'll just say that we had a very romantic, lovely evening and night after that."

Giving her a stern look at her last comment which just made her grin, Channion then added, "You did it to humiliate me and teach me a lesson!"

Since he was now smiling, Ty figured he wasn't that upset about it. At least, *now* he wasn't anyway.

Channion added, "And I still haven't lived that down yet. Every now and then one of the guys, or even Ron, will make some crack about buying some flowers on the way home. Even Chief Coutts had something to say about it. Another time, someone left a small plastic vase of flowers on my desk. I still don't know who did that. Or someone will leave a card or note with flowers on it on my desk. Too bad those cards never have money in them!"

The three of them smiled as they wheeled the two carts out of the airport terminal toward the parking lot. With a big grin, Ty said, "I think it best if I keep Ripley away from your wife while she's here, Chan. I don't want her unduly influenced."

Channion smiled and said lightly, "Since she's not here yet, I don't think you need to worry about that."

Ty replied, "For some reason, I feel that's going to change. Unless I miss my guess, she'll show up at some point."

He only hoped he wasn't losing his instincts.

Chapter 41

Harmony Hills Equestrian Center was humming with activity. Morgan was happily running her business as usual while Ripley's amazing Aunt Lilly set up the fundraiser. It was basically ready, so now they just needed to wait for the day to arrive.

Morgan promoted this fundraiser for Just One More like it was for her own facility. She did so by insisting Lilly and Joe be the ones on TV as it was more for their facility than Harmony Hills. She figured they could also permanently link the story to their own website for future use. When they all tried to talk her into being on TV, she'd refused firmly but always with a smile. Morgan also ran radio ads.

She went out of her way to promote Raina Stewart-Scott as well. She even managed to get her on the phone during a live radio spot. The Harmony Hills website's Home page announced this huge event too. Morgan created a special, temporary page that gave a link to Just One More's website, and then did another page just for Raina. She'd had Raina email her link as well as photos and song information so she could make it nice for her too. Morgan Wright never let an opportunity like this go by without taking full advantage of it. She wanted recognition for everyone.

And Lilly Ceravolo was her biggest fan.

Because Josh's parents had been horse rescuers themselves, they flew out early from Kentucky to support it in person. It was a grand excuse for Patrick and Annabelle to see not only their son and his wife, but also Damien and Laura. Since they were like Damien's other set of parents, they were also excited to see Sasha again, and now baby Jacob.

It was just like having a family reunion.

The one fly in the ointment was the biggest fly of all: Ripley Capilano. She had yet to return any of Morgan's calls, emails, and texts. It was so unlike her, Morgan was actually getting worried.

When she gently discussed this with Ty the other day, he didn't seem all that upset or worried about it. Not overly happy, but still not that upset. That was also when Ty revealed *he* hadn't heard from her in two months either. At her shocked look, he kissed her cheek, told her not to worry about him, and walked out the door to help the returning riders dismount.

Ripley's relatives said all was fine, and that Ripley was probably just swamped with work. Her cousin Steve just smiled and said they didn't really need Ripley anyway. All she did was get in their way and give them more work to do. But he'd said it with a twinkle in his eyes, so Morgan knew he was teasing her.

Morgan had offered her other spare room and sofa bed to Ripley's family, but they'd politely thanked her and explained Ripley had already paid for some really nice rooms for them locally.

But they did accept her invitations for dinner every night. They even came up for breakfast a few times. They insisted on coming early every morning to feed and clean up after the rescues until after the fundraiser was over. During the day, they'd go visit local sites to have a little vacation themselves, sometimes with Annabelle and Patrick going along too.

And they also insisted on either buying some of the food, or at least pitching in some money for it. Feeding that many visiting adults a few times a day was bound to get expensive, they said. Josh and Morgan graciously accepted their contributions, knowing it'd allow their guests to feel more comfortable if they could help out. They'd learned that from hosting his parents, who did the same thing. Morgan stressed they could all do their laundry there any time they wanted to.

The two elderly couples got along great because they could relate to each other. Josh remarked to Morgan one night before bed that he felt like they were starting a Senior Living Center. Grinning, Morgan admonished him.

Having Ripley's family over so much gave Josh, Morgan, and Ty a chance to learn more about Ripley even in her absence. Her three relatives were naturally personable, truly outgoing, and had unique senses of humor.

They were a family of contradictions to Ty. He knew these three relatives ran Just One More and that Steve was also a caring, talented veterinarian. Knowing she'd want professional, serious, and responsible people running her business, it seemed odd that the three of them were rarely ever serious at all. They seemed to thrive on telling jokes and teasing one another. They rarely were seen without a friendly smile on their faces or a welcoming glint in their eyes. Ty could tell it wasn't forced or just a show they were putting on.

But yet, for all their play and fun, Ty couldn't find any fault with the results of their work. Grand View was perfectly clean at all times, and the horses glowed from their grooming. While they worked, they were quite organized, efficient, and jovial. The horses seemed to enjoy their company as much as the Harmony Hills gang did.

Ty could see where Ripley got her sense of humor from. Liking Steve almost instantly, Ty and Josh took him out on a ride in the mountains one evening so he could see the area. The three men talked, joked, and shared stories on about every topic that came up between them, whether it was horses, work, sports, or Ripley.

It was a given that Steve and Ty were mentally sizing the other up. Steve was intensely curious about this man his cousin fell hard for while Ty was curious to learn more about Ripley, her background, and her family.

Ripley had told him she considered Steve as one of her best friends, all the way since childhood. It was interesting to Ty that while Ripley had questioned him about *his* best friend being a woman, she *herself* had a best friend who was a male—cousin though he was. He wondered if she ever realized that contradiction.

Although her family was a breath of fresh air, Ripley's continued disappearance puzzled her new friends.

Even laidback Josh found himself now wondering what she was doing. He'd seen firsthand what Ty and Ripley had going and couldn't imagine anyone better for Ty. He wanted Ty to be happy like he and Morgan were, and Ty seemed to be showing that happiness himself the longer he dated Ripley.

Josh recalled the day he and Ripley were alone. She'd asked him about Morgan and Ty's friendship. He'd reassured her they were only friends, nothing more. He'd also told her that *she'd* caught Ty's attention immediately—which was a first in Josh's knowledge.

When Ripley had asked why he thought that, Josh had grinned. "Why? He brought you up to our house the very first morning he met you for *breakfast!* He's never brought *any* woman to our house for *any* meal—even on game night. Never."

Ripley had insisted Josh was reading more into it than he should. He'd just raised his eyebrow at her, letting her know he didn't think so. When he'd joked maybe she had a sort of animal magnetism that caught the immediate attention of both Cappy and Ty, she'd said, "Well, as long as the correct one got gelded, I'm okay with that!" They'd laughed until they had tears in their eyes.

But now her sudden status of not being in communication with any of them was so odd and so unlike her, Josh understood why Morgan was concerned. But he also knew Ty very well, so he just figured there was more going on than Ty wanted anyone to know.

Out of them all, Ty was the most private although Morgan wasn't too far behind. And both had their reasons. But Josh figured Ty was a grown man and let him be. Just in case, though, when the two of them had taken Roman and Monte on a long ride a couple of weeks ago, he did let Ty know he was there if he wanted to talk or just needed a sounding board. Ty had thanked him, knowing his offer was sincere and anything said would be held in confidence.

Obviously having the most to lose, Ty had also been concerned about Ripley. Wondering if she was truly all right, he'd texted Julia one evening. He said he was respecting Ripley's wishes, but he just needed to know she was safe.

Julia had immediately texted back that she was, that she was just coming to terms with her life and making serious decisions.

She'd insisted that Ty "Just hang in there, and all would be completely fine." She'd also said she appreciated his respecting Ripley's wishes.

Ty had thanked Julia for letting him know. He felt much better knowing Ripley's best friend was in contact with her for sure, and she wasn't in a hospital or something somewhere.

But now with this major fundraiser coming up in three days, one of the guests of honor was still missing and hadn't been heard from in two months. The three longtime friends just put their faith in the woman who'd recently entered their lives, feeling in their hearts it'd all work out.

Chapter 42

Wednesday, August 17

Raina just couldn't keep her mouth shut. "*Wow!* This place is... incredible! This is where you *work?* It's... huge!"

Raina looked out the truck window as Ty pulled through the main gate to Harmony Hills. He smiled in pleasure at her reaction as he drove to Sunset Ridge, rolled down the windows a bit, and shut off the engine.

They were to have that day off as well until band rehearsal that evening, but Raina decided she wanted to see how she reacted to being around horses again. Using the local band from The Neon Moon, they had only a couple of days to work through songs. They'd spoken on the phone, so she felt they could probably pull this off. She'd also sent them a link to her website so they could listen to her and get an idea of what she normally did.

The place was buzzing with people and horses. Raina watched two big German Shepherds trotting over to some people sitting at a picnic table.

Channion smiled as he opened her door and helped her from the truck. "I tried to tell you it was, sweetheart. It's hard to describe, and the website doesn't quite do it justice, does it?"

She shook her head, trying to see everything at once. There was even a food truck here. She assumed it was a permanent one since it had a large lidded garbage can and tables strategically placed around it.

"Ty! Is that you?"

Hearing his name, Ty turned and smiled warmly at the elderly woman who didn't act her age coming toward him. "Hey, Annabelle! How're you doing today?" He hugged the older woman to him, and then introduced her to his guests. "Channion, Raina, this is

Josh's mom, Annabelle Wright. She and her husband Patrick live in Kentucky and are horse people too. They came out to help make sure things go smoothly."

With her genuine, engaging smile, Annabelle exclaimed, "Oh, you're Raina Scott. I've been hearing quite a bit about you." She saw how Raina rested her hand over her belly in an unconscious gesture and said happily, "Oh! You're going to have a baby, too, aren't you?" At the expectant couple's surprised looks, she smiled. "I knew it just by looking at you. How *wonderful!* Congratulations to you both! Is this your first?"

Raina smiled. "Thank you, and yes."

Annabelle said to Raina, "I still remember with my first I had the most *insane* cravings for Yoplait yogurt. I couldn't get enough of it! Patrick joked he was going to buy stock in the company." She next looked at Ty, her eyes sparkling. "My, my... Between her and Laura, what are you going to do? Just think if we got Josh and Morgan..." She wiggled her eyebrows, making them all laugh.

Ty grinned, holding up his hands in a defensive gesture. "Hey, don't be looking at me for advice there, Annabelle! The three of us do have our boundaries, and I for one respect them."

Annabelle smiled. "Well, I have to respect that, don't I? But it sure would be nice if you talked them into it somehow, Ty. If anyone could, it'd be you!"

Confused, he asked, "Really? How exactly would I do that?"

Her eyes full of humor, Annabelle shrugged. "I don't know, but I bet you do! Think on it, and see what you can come up with. Make it snappy while you're at it."

They laughed at the older woman as she grinned at them.

Raina asked, "Who's Laura?"

Ty replied, "Josh's best friend's wife. She'd be you if Channion was Damien, and I was Josh."

Annabelle shook her head. "I'll let you decide if he's right or not. Morgan just sent out another ride. She was on the phone when I was walking out the door if you're looking for her. It's been pretty busy here today."

Ty replied, "I want to give Raina and Channion a quick tour first, and then show them the rescues."

"Of course! This is a very impressive place and deserves a tour. It was wonderful to meet you, Channion and Raina. I can't wait to hear you sing live!" With that, Annabelle headed toward the house.

Ty bypassed Sunset Ridge and the busy trail rides for the moment and led Channion and Raina toward Grand View. He looked at Raina, hating to ask but doing so anyway, "This isn't going to be too hard for you, will it, Raina? Seeing horses in person?"

She shrugged her shoulders before licking her lips as she looked around. "Right now, I'm fine. I'd rather get it done now than later. The wondering is making it worse in my head. That's why I wanted to come out early, remember? I didn't realize it'd be this busy though. But we're here now, so..."

Ty said, "Well, Grand View will be quieter. Only the rescues are in there. We'll be putting them out later so they can play and get exercise." Glancing at his cousin first, Ty then asked her, "You remember my own horse is a palomino, right? Just in case we see him later?"

She stopped. "No. I'd forgotten about that... Um... Let's just wait on seeing him for right now, but show me the others. I'll be all right." She hoped.

Channion held her hand as they walked toward the largest barn where the rescued horses were being stalled. Ty led them inside Grand View, his heart feeling at peace, knowing the rescued horses were back home to stay.

He'd been here, of course, to help unload them. Knowing they were so connected with Ripley nearly killed him because she wasn't there, especially when Cappy was unloaded and led into his old stall. It just wasn't the same without her here if they were.

The first person they saw when they walked in was Steve. He was filling up the water buckets, happily whistling along with the radio. He turned and saw the people heading toward him. "Oh, hey there, Ty! How goes it? Looks like we got us some tourists here, huh?"

Ty smiled. "Not quite, but sort of." He made the introductions, "This is Dr. Steve Ceravolo, veterinarian extraordinaire per his own words, and this is my cousin from Illinois, Detective Channion Scott and his wife—"

"Raina. My goodness. I've been listening to your music on your website. Your voice is amazing! Can I call you Raina?" At her smile and nod, he went on, "Call me Steve. Yes, you have a wonderful voice, and I can actually understand the lyrics!

"Oh, I took it upon myself to test out the sound equipment on the stage just this morning once they got it all set up. I even sang a few pieces to a small audience to make sure everything was working up to snuff."

Knowing already he was a jokester, Ty asked, "What happened?"

Steve shrugged his shoulders, rolled his eyes. "Oh, nothing a couple of bushels of rotten tomatoes couldn't have said nicer."

They all smiled at him and followed him to the next stall.

Raina steeled herself before she looked inside. A bay gelding with a white stripe down his face was munching on his hay, looking over at her with his ears up. Channion, still holding her hand, squeezed it to remind her she wasn't alone.

She went up the stalls, one by one, reading their names and seeing the pictures of what they'd looked like when they'd first arrived after the wreck. It took most of her willpower to focus on these horses, knowing they were not hers. Hers were gone, for about four years now.

For all her recovery from what she went through years ago, being around horses was the one thing she was having the most trouble with. In all honesty, it was the *only* thing she was having trouble with. No therapy had worked its wonders with her yet.

Had she forever lost the ability to be around horses? Why couldn't her mind just relax enough to let her remember the pure joy they'd brought her instead of this torment?

When she got to a stall with a sorrel, she stared. Flashbacks zipped through her mind as she stood there. She felt a small rush whip through her mind.

"Raina?" Channion squeezed her hand again. "Raina."

She faintly heard her name being called. Pulling her gaze from the horse that faintly resembled one of her own, she looked at her husband. "What?"

"Steve asked if you'd ever been out West before?" Channion saw the signs of her unease.

"I'm sorry, Steve. My mind just... wandered off a bit there." She blew out a breath before pulling herself together to answer. "Only as far west as Oklahoma, but I've been to South Dakota. I'm not sure if you count that as west or north? But this is my first time in Arizona. I can't wait to tour it while we're here!"

Steve could tell something was happening, but he wasn't sure what. The other two men were watching Raina like they were ready to protect her or something. He caught onto her slight nervousness and saw the light sweat breaking out on her forehead. He didn't think it was from the heat.

Trying to keep it light, he said, "Well, I guess it's still north even though you went to only the south one. Even though we're south of north, it's still considered the West! The *Southwest*, to be more accurate.

"My parents and I have gone around a bit ourselves... usually in circles since Dad refuses to use the GPS." The three smiled, appreciating his lightening it up. Steve happily went on, "I totally see how those Bible people wandered around and around for forty years in the desert. Dad had us so far out, I think we found some of their sandals."

The three laughed.

"Where'd you find this guy again?" Raina asked Ty, who was grinning.

"He's Ripley's cousin from Just One More in New Mexico. He and his parents drove the horses over. Apparently Steve led them here and not Joe because they actually made it on time!"

Steve laughed, appreciating Ty's humor. "That sounds so plain, Ty, my man." He turned to Raina and Channion, comically bowed before saying, "We really blew in here on the gentle force of an Easterly Wind."

"Sounds like fun." At the mention of Ripley, Raina asked, "So Steve, do you know if Ripley's coming? I'd love to meet her!"

He smiled, his gaze flickering over them to rest on Ty last. "It's hard to say with the ole Ripster. Growing up, she did whatever her gut told her to do. We just got to saying 'Let-'er-Rip!' because it opened the door for all sorts of possibilities. That girl entertained the hell out of us kids growing up!"

He turned off the hose nozzle, wiped his hands on his shorts, and stood there with a quirky grin on his face. "Ya gotta understand something. The ole Ripster is a grand pal of mine. Since we were kids, I could talk to her about anything... Even *girls!*" They all chuckled at the wide-eyed expression on his face.

"And after we'd talk about them from sun up to sun down, to me it really boiled down to this—I just really wanted to find a gal who knows which songs *not* to talk over when I'm listenin' to 'em! The danged thing is, I haven't found her yet! I bet *you* would know not to do that, wouldn't you?" he said to Raina.

The three of them couldn't help but smile and laugh even though all three caught that he didn't answer the original question.

Ty studied the man, wondering about his evasion. Was it because even *he* didn't know if Ripley was coming? Or did she tell them all to keep quiet for some reason? They obviously listened to her, if Joe's behavior at the auction was any indicator. He was told not to say a word, and he didn't. Not one. Did she do it again this time?

A short man walked in with a smile just like Steve's plastered on his face. "Oh, hey! You're back!" He was looking at Ty when he made the statement.

With a quick grin, Ty said, "Thanks, Joe. I was wondering where I was."

Joe laughed and slapped his leg. "I sure like you, Ty. Who're these people?"

Ty introduced him to Channion and Raina. After a few minutes of friendly conversation, Raina thought she'd try with the elder Ceravolo. Giving him a smile, Raina asked, "So, do *you* know if the ole Ripster is going to blow in here like a wild tornado anytime soon?"

Ripley's uncle stared at Raina a moment before he started laughing until he had tears in his eyes. Steve laughed too.

"If she does, that's just the way she'd do it!" Joe looked at Raina again, gently took her hand and twirled her in a circle like they were dancing. Even with the faint scars on her face and arms, she was a pretty little thing. And she had a beautiful smile and a light in her eyes. He liked her on sight.

Joe said, "She's a sharp one, this Raina is. She sings like a songbird, she's pretty as a mountain sunrise, and she's got a wagon load of humor." He glanced at Channion almost suspiciously but with a twinkle in his eyes. "You her husband?"

Channion smiled widely, nodded his head. "Yes, Sir. That I am, and proud to be too."

"Well, that's just too bad. Too bad all around." He gave a dramatic sigh and looked at his son. "Steve, you best keep lookin' then. It wouldn't be right at all to steal her away from a loving husband like him." He changed subjects without taking a breath. "Your mom's waiting by the truck. We're ready to go when you are." With that, he tipped his hat to them and ambled right out the door.

All three grinned and looked at each other when they once again realized they didn't get an answer.

Steve jerked his thumb in his dad's direction. "I gotta go along with them in case he starts driving in circles again, okay? It drives Mom nuts... No pun intended!" Steve walked out behind his dad, dragging the long hose behind him to roll up.

Channion said softly, "Smooth family there. Neither answered you, sweetheart. I'm surprised you didn't push it a bit more."

Raina just shrugged. "First impressions, I guess. I preferred to be professional."

Her husband looked at her in disbelief. "It's still unlike you, but okay."

She laughed and rubbed his back.

Channion turned to Ty. "If your Ripley is anything like these relatives of hers, I just don't know what I'd think if I were you!" He grinned as he slapped his cousin on his back.

They were just reaching the end of the row when Alexis came into the barn. "Ty! I thought I'd find you here. Boss lady saw your truck and wants to see you. Pronto!"

Ty replied, "I'm off right now."

Alexis shook her head. "If you're on property, you're eligible for work. She knows you're here, so there's nowhere to hide." She grinned at him.

Channion and Raina laughed at her comment while Ty shook his head. Looking over, he admonished them, "Don't encourage her!" Turning back to Alexis, he said, "Tell her I'm coming then."

"Nope. *I'm* off right now, and I'm not heading that way. Here." She tossed him her radio. He caught it in one hand as she said, "Hey, Channion! It's so great to have you back out here! It's been like *forever*. You must be Raina? Welcome to Harmony Hills. Gotta run because I can't be late. Later!" With that, she took off, her hair trailing behind her in the breeze.

As she left, Ty wondered, "What is going on around here? I feel like I'm in the Twilight Zone, or I fell down a rabbit hole. That was Alexis, by the way, Raina. She's one of Morgan's original employees and has been here for years. And as she just proved, excels with communication skills." Channion and Raina laughed as he clicked on the radio. "Morgan, where are you?"

Raina shook her head. "Wow. Imagine a place so big, the workers actually use radios!"

Channion shrugged as he said with a straight face, "Well, they don't do any good unless they answer."

"Sorry, darlin'!" Morgan's voice came from behind them. "The radio just seemed too impersonal to use when I was so close to y'all. Alexis pointed the way as she was leaving."

Channion turned at the sound of the familiar voice. With a big grin, he caught Morgan in a bear hug. "Hey, darlin'! It's wonderful to see you again! How've you been?" He stepped back as he looked at her, holding her hands still. "Looking as great as ever, I see. You just don't age, do you?"

Morgan grinned. "Of course I do. Just not as fast as you've been losing your near vision!"

She turned to the woman watching her with curious eyes and shook her hand. "You must be Raina. Oh, I'm so thrilled to meet you in the flesh! Thank you so much for coming out for this event. Seriously, I'm so happy you agreed to come. And you're as beautiful as Ty said. Leave it to him to find all the pretty ladies!"

Raina laughed. "Yes, it's one of his many gifts all right!" Raina couldn't take her eyes off the woman standing beside Ty now. Channion had told her long ago that Morgan was the total package, and she saw now firsthand what he meant.

The woman was flat-out gorgeous with a tight figure to boot. And those amazing green eyes! She had a fun laugh and a beautiful smile. And she owned this place. Raina transferred her gaze to Ty and fleetingly wondered the same thing everyone else had: How had Morgan and Ty *not* ended up as a couple? They looked great together.

Raina said, "Well, first off, thank you for inviting me."

"I didn't. Ty did."

"Oh. Well... He always did have good taste!"

Morgan laughed and looped her arm around Ty's waist. He rested his arm around her shoulders and grinned. Morgan nodded. "Yes, he does."

"So you don't want me to thank you for me being here?" Raina ventured.

"Holy cowbells, Ty. You're right. She *is* a sharp one." With a smile aimed right at Raina, she said, "Nope, but thank you for the courtesy. I came down here to thank *you* for coming here. I've heard so much about you, I've actually thought about heading to Illinois to meet you. And to catch up with your cute husband here. You've been a stranger for far too long, Chan! I'm glad you let your wife come out with you anyway."

"I feel a little nervous now that I'm here," Raina admitted. "This is a little different than what I've done before. I'm sure it'll be fine once I get situated, and we go over everything."

Morgan shook her head. "Don't be nervous. We're a laidback bunch out here. And when we have parties, we tend to attract the same. Don't add *any* pressure to yourself knowing we want this fundraiser to just knock it out of the park for these horses!"

Morgan winked at her, and with her smile still in place, looked from her to Channion. "I talked to Annabelle just a minute ago on the phone. She told me you two were taking the plunge into parenthood. Congratulations!"

Channion smiled, wrapped his arm around Raina's waist. "Thank you, Morgan. And we came here as soon as we could. We just wanted to surprise you, that's all."

"You being married was surprise enough. No need to wait to get pregnant, too, to come out." Grinning, Morgan added, "And Channion, you two could've made a baby out here just as easily as back there. The surprise would still be nine months away. Don't wait so long in-between visits next time!"

Smiling, Raina said, "By the way... Speaking of making babies out here... When *we* were speaking with Annabelle, she asked us to ask you to *please* make her a grandbaby. She really, *really* wants one from you and Josh. You need to make her happy. It's the least you can do, isn't it? So, you know... Get to it. Chop, chop!"

They laughed at her order.

Morgan groaned in mock dismay. "Oh, isn't that just great? She's already got you on her side! She *does* have two biological daughters who have kids of their own already. Kindly remind her of *that* next time she brings it up!"

Smiling and tugging on her hair, Ty said, "But, Morg, she wants one from *you two!* Josh is the apple of her eye after all. You should gift her with at least one, don't you think? Keep the family name going since he's the only son?"

"Not you too!" Morgan groaned again, but her eyes were alight with humor. "We'll see. Don't hold your breath though. On the other hand, if my man and I don't show up for this shindig, it could be we changed our minds by giving in to all this peer pressure!"

They laughed at her comment. Morgan looked up at Ty, her eyes still bright. "And by the way, don't forget *you're* the only son in your family too."

"But Annabelle doesn't want a kid from *me*," Ty retorted. "We're talking about *you* right now."

"Chicken." Morgan accused him with a grin. Excitedly, Morgan asked, "So, have they seen Cappy yet?"

"No. Steve and Joe were here and just left. We got to talking about… I'm not really sure what," Ty replied, grinning.

Morgan nodded. "I know what you mean. Lilly is a trip too. She's like a New Mexican Dirt Devil. She just goes and goes and goes."

Ty nodded. "They're definitely related!"

Morgan grabbed Raina's hand, pulling her along. "C'mon! I want you to see Cappy. He's a gorgeous specimen of the horse world, and the sole reason Ty and Ripley met when they did!"

Morgan mentally kicked herself for mentioning Ripley but figured it was too late. Besides, facts were facts. Raina glanced up at Ty, but he didn't seem to mind. He dropped back and walked beside Channion.

Morgan stopped at the last stall. "Look, Raina! Isn't he a beaut?"

Chapter 43

Obediently, Raina looked into the stall. Both time and her heart just stopped. The tall horse looked right at her and seemed to pierce her very soul.

In slow motion, like she was in a dream, she watched as the horse walked right up to her.

Unable to tear her eyes away from his mesmerizing brown ones, Raina just leaned her head against the bars. Cappy raised his soft nose, blew gently on her face. She automatically blew back. Cappy returned the favor again.

It was then that Raina smelled a familiar scent. One she hadn't smelled in four years. Old, repressed memories came rushing back so quickly, she felt dizzy and grabbed the stall bars. Before she could stop herself, she began crying.

"Oh no! Raina, what is it? Are you okay?" Morgan asked, genuine concern in her voice. She put her arm around her shoulders.

Channion and Ty both knew what was happening. Channion quickly hugged her to him and just let her cry it out. When he first caught sight of the horse himself, he *knew*. It smacked him as hard as it did her.

The resemblance was stunning. This Cappy looked exactly like her own sorrel, Royal Rodeo (pronounced row-day-oh). But it was really those eyes. Channion saw them immediately and *knew*. This horse's eyes had the same soft, yet piercing, incredibly knowing, and deep understanding look in them that her Rodeo had had. There was just something about those eyes.

Ty, having never seen her horses in person, just knew she'd had a sorrel and a palomino which is why he'd asked about her seeing Monte. There were far more sorrels than palominos, so he didn't think seeing a sorrel would trigger her memories as much as seeing a golden palomino would.

It took a few minutes for Raina to get it out of her system. She finally pulled away from Channion, wiped her cheeks with her hands, and turned toward the horse. She again leaned against the bars. Cappy seemed to know she needed comfort and quietly stood there, softly blowing on her cheek.

Seeing Cappy do this to Raina reminded Ty of the day he and Ripley took him on the trail for that walk. He'd done the same thing to her while they sat on that boulder. Horses were such sensitive animals. Some, like Cappy, seemed to know they needed to comfort a human now and then.

Cappy had a tender, kind soul inside that large body of his. He ended up being a gentle giant. Who would've thought it possible from the horse they'd first met?

Morgan ran her hand up and down Raina's back in comfort. "You okay now?" she asked softly.

Raina nodded, whispering, "Yeah... Thank you. I'm sorry for... that, Morgan. It was just a rush of memories I wasn't prepared for."

Morgan understood completely. Still rubbing her back, she whispered, "There's no need to ever apologize for a broken heart, Raina. You take all the time you need. And if you ever want to talk, you just come and get me. I mean that." Morgan studied her closely. "You sure you're okay?"

Raina nodded just as Morgan was requested at Sunset Ridge via the radio. She answered the call immediately. "Coming. Give me just a minute."

She wanted to get them all back on even footing so Raina wouldn't be embarrassed. Morgan turned to the guys and said cheerily, "Duty calls, so I gotta run. Bring 'em up to the house for dinner after rehearsal, Ty. Well, unless y'all have other plans? If you do, cancel them."

"We'll come," Ty replied as she backed away. "Do you need anything?"

"No, thanks. Mom and Pops are at the store now. We'll have enough to feed an army when they get back! I'll see you guys later... And you'll get to meet Josh!" With that, she turned around and headed out the doors.

Ty went to get something for Raina to blow her nose with.

Channion studied Raina as he comforted her. "You good, sweetheart?"

"Yeah... I can't *believe* I did that! I'm *so* embarrassed... But can you see it, Chan? Can you see what I do? Rodeo had the exact same..." Her voice trailed off as she wiped her face with her hands.

"Yes. As soon as I saw him, I knew." Channion kissed her hair.

"He's a spitting image of Rodeo, isn't he? And can you *smell* him? There's this certain scent... The same look, eyes, and scent... It's like they're identical twins, or my sweet Rodeo was reincarnated into Cappy here."

He wrapped his arms around her and simply held her.

Returning with some paper towels, a couple of them wet with water from the hose, Ty saw them talking. Watching from a little distance away, he knew love when he saw it. And he missed it for himself.

Where, he thought yet again, the hell was Ripley?

Chapter 44

MORGAN COULD HEAR THE band rehearsing as she swept out the tack room that evening. When she heard the familiar ringtone, she quickly propped the large broom against the wall to answer her cellphone.

"Hello?" When she heard the voice on the other end, she cast a quick glance toward the office. "No, it's okay. I can talk." She walked out of the barn and headed toward the outdoor arena for privacy. "So, if you're finally calling me back there must be a reason. What's going *on* with you? If you were here right now, I'd kick your ass!"

Ripley wasn't surprised at the hint of anger as well as disappointment in Morgan's voice. But her first concern was not for herself. If his best friend wanted to eat her alive, she sort of deserved it. She could handle it. But first, she had to ask, "How's Ty doing?"

"I'll tell you if I feel you should know. You first." Morgan's voice was firm and unbending.

Ripley let out a breath. "Look, Morgan, let's cut to the chase. I don't know what you do or don't know here. Either way, it's between Ty and me... Not him, me, you, and everyone else. It's *our* relationship. And neither one of us need to be supervised, no matter how well-intentioned anyone may be... Or think they are. We're both adults.

"But if it helps you to know, it all works out in his favor. I never meant to hurt him or even myself. But I also had to know a few things first, and I couldn't think straight when I was so close to all of you. Especially Ty.

"I needed complete space and freedom to just be me like I was before you and I met. I needed that to know if I was still who I was before. If not, then to come to terms with how I've changed. *And* if I was all right with how my future will change if I make certain decisions, if I was ready for it. For me to do all of that, I *had* to break contact with you all. Sorry for not returning any of your many, many messages, but that was the space I needed to take. I didn't mean to make you mad or concerned.

"But really all I did was go back on the road for my last visits. The ones I was upfront about with Ty from the very start. He knows when my list would end, and where I'd be when it did. You cannot hold that against me, Morgan. It wouldn't be fair to be pissed at me for doing my job. This job helps pay the bills." She knew Morgan would understand where she was going with that statement.

Morgan did but still said, "Yeah? Well, I can still be pissed at you for other reasons." She paused. "Where are you now? You'd better be on your way here, I can tell you that!"

"Well, here at the tail end of my little personal vision quest, I ended up at the big ditch."

"The big ditch?" Morgan asked, confused. "What and where is that?"

Ripley laughed at her confusion. "The Grand Canyon... It's in the northern part of this western state called Arizona. I thought you of all people would've heard of it before. It's been here a little while, you know."

Morgan laughed. "Oh. I've never heard it called that before. I'll have to tell that one to Josh. He'll get a kick out of it!" She leaned against the fence. "So what's going on?"

Ripley said, "Please, Morgan, tell me... Is Ty hating me right about now? Does he wish he'd never met me?"

Morgan heard the sincerity in her voice. "He's hurting, Rip. He comes to work, and he hangs out with us but not as often. He goes home alone. He still smiles, jokes, talks, and works, but he's hurting. I've known him far too long to miss how he's feeling. He recently gave me a partial rundown after your last talk, and that was about it.

"He may have spoken to Josh. It's a guy thing, and as close as we are, he'd possibly want a male shoulder to lean on. He also may have spoken with his cousin Channion since they're really tight.

"But he's *my* best friend, Ripley! I can't *believe* you did this to such a terrific, all-around guy as him. What were you *thinking?*" Her voice got harsh again as she saw her best friend in her mind. Taking a breath to calm herself, Morgan sighed. "And he doesn't hate you, Rip. He's not cursing the day he met you or any day after. Well, at least, not that I know about. There've been times *I* have though.

"But I'd have to say he misses you a great deal. He's just trying to be patient and hopeful that you're coming back to him. And coming back to him on your own accord with no pressure from him or anyone else."

Morgan watched as a ride crested the ridge on its way back to the barn. Toby was guiding it, and Maya was in the office, so she could keep talking.

"As his best friend, I need to ask you... Are you going to hurt him more? Are you going to tell him you're through and moving on? Because if so, you need to do it *now.* And do it cleanly so he can begin to move on himself. I don't want him humiliated anymore by you. I can't stand to see such a good person go through this much longer. And I won't. I'll tell him I talked to you, and I'll tell him myself to move on if I think you're even *thinking* of messing with him anymore."

Even though it was faint, Morgan thought she heard a sniffle on the other end. Was the stoic Ripley crying? After a moment, Ripley finally answered. Her voice was slightly strained as she replied, "No, I'm not going to tell him we're done. We never were, Morgan. And I refuse to let him go. I never will.

"I've never known a man who was so hard to just get out of my mind. He's had a place in my heart for so long, it's hard to remember what it felt like when he didn't. We're both hurting by being apart, Morgan. But I needed to know *how much* it hurt before I could truly grasp my feelings. And to be as sure as I could about them."

Because she felt Morgan needed to understand, and because she knew she really wanted her friendship, she opened up to her while she had the courage to. "You know how sometimes you think you know someone, and you think your feelings for them are real because they're so strong? But when you go your separate ways, the hurt only lasts a little while?

"Sure, maybe sometime in the future you think of them and wonder where they are, or what they're doing. But you don't *really* miss them? You just know inside somewhere that it was for the best? That you can even be *relieved* you're not with that person anymore?

"It's different with Ty. It *always* felt so different with him. I needed to know for myself that it *was.* When we got together, I don't know if I really let myself think it all through. Or maybe, I thought about it too much. That's what Ty said I was doing. He was probably right. I have a PhD in Overthinking. Maybe my work was so much in my head I wasn't really thinking about Ty and myself like I thought I was. I don't know... And *that* was my problem. I needed to *know*, Morgan. Surely you can understand that.

"If I went away, broke all contact, and forgot about him in no time flat, that'd say something. If I didn't care if I saw him again or not, then that meant he didn't matter.

"But it *is* different, Morgan. I just had to live my life like I did before I ever met him to see how it felt. It's just not the same. I'm an adult, and I realize there are no guarantees when it comes to love. I had to find a way to test myself to be as sure as I could be. This wasn't just for me but for *him*. It'd be better to know now rather than later when it might be too late or for the hurt to be way worse.

"I swear I have phantom feelings that he's holding my hand. When I look down, though, I see only *my* hand. And it's empty. I don't want it to be empty anymore, Morgan." Ripley wiped away the tears running down her cheeks.

Morgan was silent as she listened, understanding exactly what Ripley was saying and feeling. "I believe you, Ripley. And it makes me so happy to hear you say that you're completely miserable without him. That actually makes me happiest of all, to be honest. It's a bit selfish, but I really like knowing you're horribly miserable. Can you say it again just to make *me* feel better?"

Ripley let out a half laugh, half sob. "You're demented, you know that? Can I ask why my being so miserable makes you so blasted happy?"

Morgan turned toward the riders who were coming closer. She waved to them, and then began walking farther away from them to maintain privacy. "It's simple. You hurting tells me you truly love him. If you didn't, you wouldn't hurt at all. Isn't that what your personal experiment was all about? To see if you'd be miserable... or relieved?"

"You always were a little sneaky. But you're correct, on all accounts. I do love him, Morgan. I love him so much it frightens me because I never knew I *could* love that much. It seems like more and more every day, in spite of our being apart. Maybe it's *because* we've been apart. I'm scared that maybe I've been away too long, and he wouldn't take me back no matter what I say." Taking a deep breath, Ripley asked the one question she was scared to hear answered. "Do you think he'll take me back?"

Morgan smiled in spite of herself, saying gently, "Ripley, he never considered you gone. You're not coming back to him, not in that sense. The man is over the moon in love with you. He's just been waiting for you to come home on your own volition. That's all he wants right now. Just for you to come home and to stay."

"Okay. Can you help with something else while I've got you on the phone?"

"If it's for Ty, I'd do anything. What do you need?"

Chapter 45

Thursday, August 18

Morgan and Josh had a full house again that night for dinner. Besides themselves, they had Patrick and Annabelle, and Ty came with Channion and Raina. Of course, Joe, Lilly, and Steve came as well. Damien and Laura were also there with little Sasha and baby Jacob in tow to spend time with Josh's parents, and for Sasha to ride her favorite horse, Ivy.

Morgan said it felt like Thanksgiving in August. Steve said that was okay since retail stores bragged about Christmas in July. The others laughed as they put food on their plates.

After dinner, the men turned on the TV so they could watch sports as they played cards at the table. Damien and Laura had to leave soon after dinner to put their kids to bed. After hugs goodbye to the couple and their children, Annabelle and Lilly started the dishes. Smiling, Annabelle told Morgan to get out of her kitchen. With a grin, Morgan led Raina out onto the back patio.

"Girl talk. Leave us be!" she called out to everyone. Annabelle smiled and assured her they'd be left alone.

"Actually, let's go to the gazebo. It's screened, so there aren't any bugs in there." Morgan led Raina to the gazebo, flipping on the misting fan and sliding the light switch to low once inside. She explained, "Less bugs if the lights are low. It makes it easier to see the views too. Josh built this for me as a wedding gift. Ty, Damien, and Ryan—he's Josh's foreman—all pitched in. Isn't it wonderful?"

Raina looked around, checking out the bench seats, the fire pit, and the swing in the middle. "He was obviously serious about his love for you." They smiled at each other before Raina went on. "We have one, too, but it's not like this!" She walked over to look out the screened partitions. "Morgan, this is just so beautiful! The mountains, the views... And the stars are so bright and clear here."

In awe, Raina looked around. She could see for miles out here even in the moonlight! So different than back East with buildings, telephone poles, and trees in the way. Without turning around, she said, "You know, when I first met Ty when I was with Channion, he was so at home there. I asked him why doesn't he move back, be closer to Channion and the family, you know?

"But he said his home was here, being with you and the Center. He said he loved it where he was. Now that I'm here, I can see why." Raina smiled at Morgan as she came to stand beside her. "It's so open! I get a sense of just being, I don't know, freer? Does that make sense?"

"Yes." Morgan nodded, looking at her mountains. "And yes, I think sometimes he misses home back East. Not so much the location, but the family connections. But we have our own family out here. Sometimes the family you create is so much better than the one you're born into. In his case, he gets both."

"I understand *that* completely. My family isn't tight at all. If we call once a year, even two, then we call it good. Anymore, I'm fine with that to be honest. It's a lot less stressful, and with Channion being a cop in today's world, I have enough stress. And their family is so huge it was kinda overwhelming at first, but now I'm a *part* of it!

"It's insane sometimes when I look at how many contacts I have in my phone now. I had to label everyone in it just so I can remember who they are. I joked I needed a family tree drawn out to keep them all straight. I figured it'd be the size of a billboard by the time I got it done!" Raina smiled at Morgan as they sat down on the swing facing the mountains.

Morgan said, "Same here. When I met Josh, and then his parents? They sucked me right in! His sisters Angie and Val are terrific too. I've never looked back. All I do now is love my man like no one else can or will, and his family is just a huge bonus.

"It didn't take me long to start referring to Annabelle as 'Mom' and Patrick, well, he's been 'Pops' for even longer. Those two are so incredible. It breaks my heart to think of the time when they pass away. Josh and I can't stand even the thought... Look! I already have tears in my eyes just talking about them not being here!" Morgan's smile trembled as she wiped away the few tears that flowed over. "I think your emotional hormones have transferred to me. Shame on you."

"Sorry about that." But Raina smiled. "And I understand because Channion and I feel that way about his aunt and uncle. We're so close and spend so much time together, it's painful to imagine a day when they're gone." Raina studied her hostess for a moment. "I remember Ty once saying he thought you and I were alike coming from similar backgrounds. These must be a couple of the areas he was referring to."

Morgan smiled as her two dogs materialized out of the darkness, peeking through the screen door. Getting up, she opened the door to let them in. "Are you okay with dogs? I should've asked you first..."

"No worries. I love dogs. And I didn't really get to meet them earlier."

"They're both named Darrell. We call them The Darrells. They're brother and sister, and they're my babies. Just not by Josh, in case you and Annabelle share some chit chat later."

Raina laughed gaily at her comment as the dogs came over. They sniffed Raina's shoes and simply laid down at her feet, making her smile as she leaned over to pet them. Morgan sat back down in the swing on the opposite end of Raina, carefully stepping over Darrell G. They slowly swung for a moment, just enjoying the quiet.

Rubbing Darrell B's back with her foot, Morgan asked softly, "Did you want to talk about what happened in the barn yesterday? If you don't, it's fine. I just thought you might like to air it out, and since we're alone..."

Raina hesitated. Lulled by the darkness and the sincerity of the woman—and probably her hormones—she finally replied just as softly, "A long story very short here... About four years ago I saved a cop from being murdered in cold-blood. In the process, I almost lost my own life, but I somehow survived. I really shouldn't have.

"The two detectives assigned to my case were Channion and Ron. I was in the hospital when we met. Although I don't like to talk about it, that's how I got these scars on my face and body. Most have faded, but sometimes they seem more noticeable to me."

Morgan gasped, leaning forward. "Oh, Raina... I had no idea!"

"Ty never said anything to you?"

"No. He keeps private details of others strictly to himself."

Raina could easily see that. "Well, as it turned out, the people who tried to murder the deputy and me were part of a huge illegal weapons ring. The guy running it was wanted big time, been around forever. Law enforcement had been looking for a way to nail his hide to the wall, but he was very elusive, tricky, and he had built quite a wall around his identity."

Taking a deep, calming breath, she continued, "It wasn't long at all before he found out who I was, where I lived. Late one night my two horses were shot and killed. One was a palomino, and one was a sorrel... Exactly like Cappy. It wasn't just his coloring. It was more his piercing, soulful eyes, and his smell that triggered my memories like that, and I just..." Raina's voice trailed off.

Morgan immediately reached out, holding tightly to Raina's hand in comfort. Tears sprung to her own eyes. "Oh, I can't imagine that. I'm so, so sorry, Raina. *How* did you cope?"

"It was devastating, and it nearly sent me right over the edge. I fell apart more than once. Channion was always there for me. They were truly like my kids, and my only friends there.

"Anyway, since my case was finally closed, all's been pretty good with me. Channion, Ron, and Janet, well, they've helped me so much I can't really describe it all. I've worked through a lot of issues like living alone and driving again, not jumping at shadows. Stuff like that. The nightmares and flashbacks have pretty much gone away. I was told it's all a part of PTSD.

"But my biggest issue still is with horses. I'm better than I was, believe it or not. Channion has been helping me work through it by taking me to stables and farms. For this fundraiser, Ty wasn't sure I'd even come out. He didn't pressure me in any way to do it.

"But I thought *maybe* if I did something good for horses again, maybe *that's* what I needed to do in order to get over this whole thing. Maybe make this trip a form of therapy. I don't know. Maybe I'm just... crazy, desperate, or grasping at straws."

Raina sighed, looking over at the woman listening patiently. "I told Ty I'd do it before ever telling Channion about it. When I did, he was more than a little concerned, but he's got my back. We'd already been talking about coming out here—mainly because he really needed a vacation to recuperate. Timing is everything, right?

"He needed his rest months ago, but he made it to now. And I'll be sure he rests. I told Ty we weren't going back until I was sure Channion was ready to. I don't care how much it costs to change plane tickets. We're not leaving here until I'm satisfied he's rested and had time to just enjoy being here."

Morgan smiled. "You sound like the perfect wife for him."

"Of course I am!" Raina replied matter-of-factly, making Morgan laugh. "Anyway, in case you didn't know, Ty and Channion are plenty worried about me being here. On top of that, I'm pregnant. That scares Channion. And I admit, it does me, too, a little. But he trusts me enough to have faith in me. I *love* that man!" She smiled and sighed deeply as she looked out at the mountains. "They're watching over me like hawks even though I've assured them I can handle it. Yesterday sure made a liar out of me, though, didn't it?"

Morgan shook her head. "You did great with the other horses, though, didn't you? Dealing with a major, shocking loss is a long process, Raina. You just have to deal with your emotions as they come because there's no instant cure for tragedy. We never know what can trigger a memory, or how we might react to it.

"Emotions are a natural result of experiences, sometimes sad ones. They just happen. I, for one, don't believe they should be manipulated or controlled. Well, unless they're extreme or harmful. If they're being covered up, then they aren't being dealt with. It's good that you don't bottle them up inside."

Raina nodded. It was a minute before she could talk again. Quietly, she confessed, "It's lonely not having horses anymore, but I can hardly bear to be around them. It's like my mind is stuck in neutral or something. It won't let me move on. I probably just need *something* to happen to shove me over. I don't know..." Raina shrugged as she looked at the mountain silhouettes again.

In quiet understanding, Morgan offered, "I'll help in any way I can, Raina, if you want me to."

"Thank you." She paused, then decided to continue her story, "Anyway, after that night I was moved to a secure location and had Channion and Ron as my personal bodyguards while they worked the case. As it turned out, the next biggest shocker was that Channion and I fell in love."

Her tone went from sad to happy instantly. "Once the case was closed, we began officially dating. That love thing took us both by total surprise, by the way. Neither one of us was looking for a relationship at all... whether with each other or someone else. When we realized what was happening, then we had to make sure it was real and not just from the stress of the situation. We both knew it was very possible because we'd been thrown together in a life-or-death situation.

"On the flip side, we'd also been ourselves since we met. In dangerous situations like that, you can't fake who you are because, well, you just can't. Or shouldn't, for the safety of everyone around you.

"I still can't believe everything that happened. Later, as you know since Ty was Best Man, we got married. We married sooner than some thought we should but, luckily, we're still in love, and it's all working out. We felt life was too short to sit around and wait. Live life without regrets, I suppose.

"And now here we are, starting a family. Our own little family." She patted her belly, a soft smile on her face as she looked down at it. "I still don't believe it. I never imagined my life would go in this direction."

With a smile, Morgan said, "And now it's a grand new chapter in your lives. Of course, nothing's rosy all of the time, but you two will get through it. You and Channion will make wonderful parents. And the times you'll have with your kids will be memories for them to carry with them forever. And when you're gone, those memories will help carry them on. Make sure they're great ones, Raina.

"But please also make sure you don't have spoiled brats! It won't help them or anyone else when they need to be on their own. Make them assets to society, Raina... At least try to.

"You and I both know what it's like to not have the families we wished we had, so now it's your chance to break that cycle, you know? Make those memories the kind they'll cherish."

With tears in her eyes at the thought, Raina nodded. "My mom and I were very close. When I was in high school, she was killed by a drunk driver. The memories I have of her are still strong with me, and I'll pass them along to our kiddo. Just like we will of Channion's parents." She took a deep breath before she continued, "And in regards to making our own memories for the kiddo? We'll do our best."

"It's good you can pass on those memories of your mom. I'm very sorry to hear about your loss." After a moment, Morgan mused, "The last time Channion was out here, neither one of us were married or even dating. Now look at us. Who knew?"

They both smiled at the surprise in her voice.

They sat for a while in comfortable silence with the dogs enjoying their foot rubs when Raina suddenly blurted out, "Can I ask you for a favor?"

"Of course."

"Can you take me to your barn to see if I'm able to groom a horse? Just the two of us?"

The hopeful plea in Raina's voice nearly broke Morgan's heart. Without hesitation, she answered, "Absolutely. Let me tell the guys so they don't come looking for us, okay?"

"Yeah, that's probably a good thing to do. I'll use the bathroom before we go down."

"Good plan. Me too. We'll work this out together, Raina."

Looking at each other, the two women stood up as one.

Chapter 46

THEY WENT ARMED WITH flashlights and hope. Morgan led Raina down the lighted path to the barns with The Darrells trotting behind them.

"We'll go to Quail Run since that's where my lesson ponies are kept. Josh, Ty, and I have our own horses there too."

Raina followed Morgan through the doorway, both squinting and blinking when Morgan turned on the bright lights and turned off the alarm system. After unlocking the tack room, Morgan led Raina to the halters and lead ropes. She grabbed a caddy already filled with grooming supplies and motioned Raina to the doorway.

Stepping out into the aisle, Morgan looked at Raina. "I'm just going to ask, okay? Did you want to try Cappy? I don't think Ripley would mind us brushing him. If he's the one that triggers you, it could go either way on whether or not to use him. It's your decision."

Raina hesitated. "Let me work my way up to him, okay? It might be better to start with someone else, someone less emotional for me."

Morgan nodded, silently agreeing. "Okay. Type of horse... Tall? Short? Dark? Gray? Male or female?"

"Let's go with any size. Bay. Male. Who'd that be?" Raina asked, her nerves beginning to show.

Keeping it light, Morgan announced cheerily, "Well, you obviously chose the most common model of horse, and we happen to have a nice selection of them here at Harmony Hills. As a matter of fact, we can use my own horse. His name is Bombay. Let's go get him."

Morgan noticed Raina's face showed a tad of sweat already and inwardly wondered if they should be doing this. But she had to trust Raina to know if it was too much, and when to stop.

Encouraging her, Morgan said, "Baby steps, Raina. We're taking baby steps here, okay?"

"Well, I *am* pregnant."

They grinned at each other as the two dogs watched them curiously. Morgan noticed their looks and said, "No ride, guys. You can just relax this time." She signaled for them to lay down which they did immediately.

The two women walked down the aisle side by side, but before they reached Bombay's stall, Raina happened to look over and came to a dead stop. Morgan glanced back. When she realized she'd stopped at Monte's stall, understanding came in a flash. One of her own horses, she'd said, had been a palomino.

Raina took a step closer, and Monte walked over and poked his muzzle through the bars. Raina couldn't get herself to touch him though. She was frozen.

Morgan came to her side, encouraged her. "Monte is Ty's horse. Friendly as they come."

Raina heard her and forced herself to reach through the bars, pet the white stripe on the golden horse's face. Her hand shook, but she made herself stand her ground.

She'd faced down murderers... *Surely* she could pet a horse! she told herself.

Monte moved so she was now touching his neck. She ran her hand down the sleek coat a couple of times, her range limited by the bars.

When she withdrew her hand, Morgan said, "It's a start, Raina. You're doing wonderful. Horses are the best therapists in the entire world."

Raina nodded. She'd always said the same thing. But what does one do when both of your therapists get murdered, she wondered to herself, because you weren't there to protect them?

When they reached Bombay's stall, Morgan handed the halter and leap rope to Raina. "You're up, slugger."

Her stalls all had doorways that led to an outside pen for each horse. Bombay, recognizing Morgan and curious about the lights being on, came back inside and headed right over to the stall door. Morgan quietly encouraged her. "You can do this, Raina, but if you want to stop, you can. No pressure at all, understand?"

After a moment, Raina steeled herself, prepped the halter and opened the door. Bombay pushed his large head into her chest, lightly bumping it. The stall light wasn't on, but she could still tell he was huge.

"Holy cow! What is he?" Raina asked when she realized he was way bigger than she was expecting. "Is he a Dutch Warmblood?"

"Nope. He's a moose." Morgan teased her to keep it light. She was rewarded when Raina flashed a grin. "He's a pure Thoroughbred. He's a calm one, not one of the hot ones. If you want someone shorter, we can—"

Raina interrupted her, "No. No way. I wouldn't want to hurt his feelings. He's probably just a gentle giant. All the big guys are really babies. Right, big fella?"

With a natural ease, Raina slipped on the halter. She opened the door the rest of the way, making sure the latch was slid out of the way before she led out the tall horse. Now that Bombay was beside her, she stared at him. "He's taller than I am. What is he... Seventeen hands?"

"Nearly. Sixteen three." Morgan automatically scratched her horse's favorite spot right behind his ears when he lowered his large head in her direction. "He was no good on the track, so he was put up for sale. We met, we clicked, and he's solid. Now he's my jumper and trail horse who also participates in the occasional parade.

"Most people out here don't know what to make of a horse that isn't a Quarter horse or a grade. He's nearly twice as big as most!" She chuckled as she ran his forelock through her hands. She kissed the white star on his forehead.

They walked down the aisle to a set of cross-ties. Besides the sweat, Raina was doing good so far. She took her time, first making herself run her hands all over the dark brown horse with the big white star and the two white socks. She ran her hand over his coarse black mane. She spoke to Morgan as she did so, partly to share with her new friend and partly because she didn't want the silence.

"The therapist back home said I should maybe retrace a typical day with one of my horses to bring it all home, so to speak. Make a connection... Whatever they say when they don't know what else to say."

Morgan nodded, silently encouraging her.

Raina blew out a breath and took another. She made herself touch the horse again. The slick coat felt like an old memory as her mind absorbed the fact she was touching a horse again. Leaning forward, she could smell the clean, familiar scent of a horse. How she'd missed that smell!

As she slid her hands down Bombay's long, sleek neck, she began speaking, describing in detail what it was like to be home again from the hospital that first night, and how she'd missed her horses who she saw as her kids. She described how it felt seeing them again, hugging them, smelling the scent that was their own. The feeling she had of just *being* in her little barn, and how it was the best place in the world.

Morgan listened, her heart aching for the woman brushing her horse. She knew this was an optimal form of therapy, and she was most willing to help Raina any way she could. And it was hard for her, too, as she'd used horses as therapy herself when her own life had crashed many years before. While Morgan couldn't share any of her past, she *could* share her horses.

Raina stopped talking for a little while as she brushed all around Bombay's large frame. She didn't seem to notice how big a horse he was anymore. Her mind was taking her back to another time, another place. Time went by as Raina tried to purge her mind and her heart of these memories that kept her from moving on.

When she described how Channion had found them dead, she stopped grooming and stared at the brush in her shaking hands. The memories came at her so quickly now. Dropping the brush, she just broke down and sobbed.

Morgan quickly went to her, wrapping her arms around her shaking body. She let her own tears out, knowing she would've felt the same guilt. Knowing how loved they were, they would've most likely trusted whoever walked into their barn, not suspecting a thing. Or did they sense the evil intent? She shuddered herself at the thoughts racing through her own mind.

Morgan lowered Raina to the floor, her arms wrapped around her shoulders, as Raina cried her heart out. Morgan never said a word, just kept her arms around her in support. She felt awful for Raina, trying to imagine the guilt she carried inside.

She'd understood at the end: It wasn't just a shattered heart she suffered from. Raina was still suffering from survivor's guilt. She felt responsible for their deaths because she wasn't there. They died instead of her.

When Raina finally stopped crying and the sniffles began, Morgan was there to comfort her. She finally removed her arms from around the woman, letting her have some personal space to get her composure back. She didn't know what to say as she knew probably everything had already been said to her at one time or another.

What could *she* do to help this grieving woman she'd just met? What would *she* need if she were Raina? She didn't think it was sympathy—That probably just reinforced her own guilty feelings of not being there. Thoughts raced through her mind on how to break through Raina's guilt, but before she could say a word, someone else did.

A soft but firm voice from down the aisle reached them. "It wasn't your fault."

Morgan knew that voice and quickly looked over.

Ripley had returned!

Morgan's big smile was joined with new tears. Tears of sorrow for Raina and tears of joy for Ty now mingled together. Her heart squeezed tight, almost painfully, in both mourning and in excitement.

At Ripley's questioning look, Morgan motioned her over.

Ripley looked at Raina and knelt down on her other side. Taking hold of her shaking hand and holding it firmly, Ripley said again in a stern voice, "It wasn't your fault they died, Raina. It's hard to do, but you need to accept that as fact. Come to terms with it to start moving forward. You didn't call them into their stalls. You didn't pull the trigger. You weren't even there."

Raina quickly cried out, "I *know* I wasn't there... That's *why* they died! That *makes* it all my fault! Can't you see that? *They died! They* died... And *I* didn't... It was supposed to be *me*... I started all of this... It's my fault..."

Ripley let go of her hand and took her face firmly in her hands. She noticed Raina had just spoken in the present tense in those last sentences. Her mind was stuck somewhere in the past and the present.

Ripley looked right into her eyes and said with mean conviction, "Bullshit, Raina Stewart-Scott. You stop feeling sorry for yourself right now! It wasn't your fault, so it's high time you moved on! It's over. There's nothing you can do about it now except move on. Your duty to your horses was to give them a loving home. Did you *love* your horses, Raina?"

"Of course. With all my heart!"

"Your duty was to feed and water them. Shelter them. Did you do that—daily?"

"Of course!"

"Did you clean their stalls, make them comfortable in all types of weather?"

Ripley's voice was as firm and hard as Morgan had ever heard in anybody. She was impressed. And more than a little surprised.

Raina said hotly, "I took *excellent* care of my kids!"

Ripley asked sternly, "Did you make sure they had care from vets and farriers when needed?"

"Always! I always did my best." Raina jerked her face from Ripley's hands.

"And did you show them how much you loved them every damn chance you got?" Ripley demanded, grabbing her face again.

"Every day!" Hot, scalding tears poured from Raina's eyes again.

"Don't you *dare* lie to me, Raina! *Did you?*" Ripley yelled at her. She was pushing the woman past her emotional safe-zone, pushing her to break through it, for her mind to stop tormenting her. No more gentle understanding and sympathy. She'd had enough of both.

"I'm *not* lying, you crazy psycho! I loved them to death!" Raina yelled back.

"You sure did! So if you loved them so damn much, then why'd you pull the damn trigger that killed them? It's *your* fault they're dead since *you* pulled the trigger! It's *all* your fault. *You* did it! All of it is your fault!" Ripley yelled.

Defensively, Raina shouted back at her, "No, it's not! I *didn't!* I didn't pull the trigger! It *wasn't* me! I wasn't there, so *I* didn't kill th..." Raina stopped in mid yell. Her look was one of both deep confusion and boiling hot anger. But then the confusion and the anger began to fade as the truth began to slowly seep in. Something finally broke free inside her mind.

Ripley nodded to herself when she saw it happen in Raina's twisted facial expression. With her voice still firm and her voice only a shade softer, she said, "Damn right you didn't. It *wasn't* your fault. You can't hold yourself responsible for every situation, every outcome in life, Raina. You can't control everything. *None* of us can. Control is just an illusion.

"Sometimes bad and horrible things just happen, so get over yourself. And welcome back to the real world where we all make mistakes, and sometimes life really hurts. It can often be tragic and heartbreaking. And other times, it's absolutely beautiful. We can only do so much. You need to move on. Focus on all that beautiful, so you can deal better with the times when life hurts you.

"Life can still be beautiful when you accept you can't control it. When you realize—and accept—not everything is your fault. Or even in your power to even remotely control it. Stop falling on your sword, Raina."

Looking into Raina's red, swollen eyes, Ripley said again, "It wasn't your fault. They wouldn't blame you, Raina. They loved you. They *knew* you loved them with your whole being.

"No, you didn't get to tell them how very much you loved them one more time, but you didn't need to. They *already* knew that on a daily basis. Raina, they already *knew*. That closure you've been looking for was already done. You've had it all along."

Ripley nodded firmly at Raina's questioning gaze. "You've held this deep and horrible hurt locked deep inside of you long enough. It's past time you let it go. I can't even imagine what you've gone through, and I'm not going to insult you by saying I do.

"You've already faced the devil down. And *you* sent him back home with his tail between his legs. But he was still rude enough to leave one of his little demons behind to live in your soul. You know what? I think we just chased his little scrawny red ass back home too.

"It'll still take some time, Raina, but you're going to be all right. You just need to forgive yourself because I'm positive your horses already did." At Raina's semi-shocked look, and the glimmer of realization coming through, Ripley nodded. Firmly, she repeated herself, "*You need to forgive yourself.*"

She ran her hands over Raina's hair before she cupped the shaking woman's face gently now in her hands, looking directly into her eyes. Tears still spilled over and were running down Raina's face... but not like before. The hot tears were being replaced by cool, healing ones.

Ripley advised her, "It's okay to keep on living. It's okay to enjoy life. You *aren't* betraying them by moving on... Even to loving another horse someday when you're ready. It wasn't your fault. Do you take all the credit when things go perfectly? When things are going right?"

Raina shook her head.

Ripley asked, "Then why do you take the credit when things go wrong? Just because you weren't there? You can't take the credit for everything, Raina. That's just greedy of you."

Morgan wiped away the tears from her own eyes as she sat there on the hard, concrete floor beside a visibly shaking Raina. She could sense the change in the woman already, but she knew it wasn't completely over either.

Ripley gave Raina an order. "Say it... *It wasn't my fault.*" She waited until Raina repeated it. "Again, stronger." Raina did. "Now tell yourself that you're forgiving yourself. You're letting yourself off the hook. You *keep* telling yourself this because it's the truth. In time, you'll be able to fully forgive yourself. You'll be healthier and even stronger when you do."

She looked deep into Raina's eyes, making sure she was looking into hers, paying attention. "Forgiving yourself *doesn't* mean you're forgetting them, Raina. You don't need to mentally berate yourself anymore to keep them alive in your heart.

"You've fallen on your sword far too long and far too many times. As of right now, that sword is broken in half, and we've thrown it down a deep well. You can never retrieve it again.

"'Forgive and forget' is the worst phrase because rarely can anyone ever actually do both. It's a phrase I never use, and this is a prime example of why. One may be able to forgive, but rarely do they ever forget.

"You don't *need* to forget in order to move on. I do think you need to forgive yourself of all the things that were simply out of your control. But you're going to be all right. I know it."

Ripley gave Raina another firm squeeze on her chin and a hard look before she let go and sat down beside her. Weary from driving all day and into the night, she asked gently, "Did you know some species of animals have been seen mourning?"

Morgan wasn't sure who Ripley was talking to, so she kept quiet. She wasn't sure if Ripley's spontaneous form of therapy was over or not. From the corner of her eye, she saw Ripley nudge Raina with her elbow and smiled to herself.

Her voice scratchy, Raina answered, "Yes."

"Did you know horses were one of them?"

Raina's voice was thick with tears when she answered, "Yeah, I've heard that."

Hoping she'd overheard enough to say what she was going to, Ripley quizzed softly, "And if Channion hadn't rushed you to the ER, and you two were killed first that night... Do you think they would've left your horses alive?"

Knowing there was more than what she'd said earlier, Raina finally nodded her head, whispering, "Yes."

Ripley continued, "I agree. Now, who would've had the highest chance of suffering, of mourning? You or them? You know in your head you weren't at fault, but it's your heart that's leading you right now. You need to connect the two.

"From what I heard, Raina, you were not only in the hospital, but in the ER. How exactly were you yourself supposed to have saved them? Even if you *were* at home, you were basically useless. Even if you *were* in the barn with them... What would've you done to the killers... Talk them out of it?"

Morgan silently agreed.

Ripley went on, "If your horses had lived, what were the odds they'd end up in a home as loving as yours? In my vast personal experience, I'd say it was slim. Possible, sure! But still slim. Worse yet, they would've been separated most likely.

"So now, they've lost you—Their loving, doting mom. And they're confused and scared because they no longer had their home and familiar routine. And now your kids are being separated... and sent to only God knows where. Maybe to Mexico."

Raina sniffled and wiped her nose with her hands. She was silent as she thought it all out, allowing the healing to come.

Ripley wasn't done. She stated firmly, "So... You died. They lived. But who knows how long and in what conditions? On the other hand, they died—and apparently quickly. No suffering, Raina. They didn't suffer.

"And you know what? You still came out the winner. You not only lived, but you got the guy. You found love, Raina. Your love has just been transferred, that's all." Ripley saw Raina slightly nod her head. She smiled as she reached over for her hand and held it in hers. It was cold and shaking. She held it tighter.

"You lived *and* found love. If you had died, where'd Channion be right now? If not dead beside you from trying to protect you, he'd be alone, Raina. Would you want him to be alone... And full of guilt for not saving you? For not taking you to the ER when he knew he maybe should've? For failing in his sworn duty to protect and defend you? You were Channion's priority, weren't you?"

Raina nodded and used her shirt to wipe at her tears.

Ripley continued on, "If you lived because he died for you, how would you feel then? I can't imagine it myself. As rough and as painful as it was, I think if this situation had to have happened at all, it happened the best possible way. They died quickly, you and Channion didn't, and you and Channion found love. I know without a doubt you loved your horses. If you didn't, you wouldn't be going through this right now.

"But you still came out the winner in all of this, Raina. And don't feel guilty about it. You found love with a man who loves you back. Someday, maybe, you guys can start a family together. You couldn't have done that with your horses, now could you?

"I know they were your family, but now you can have another one. You don't need to forget them though. You'll just have different kids, if that's what life holds for you.

"And you know what else? One day, when you're ready, you can add to your life another deserving horse... or two or three. They're just waiting for you. There are so many out there needing someone like you. They're waiting for someone just like you to love them forever.

"Don't give up, Raina. Don't give up on them. They *need* someone like you. You're exactly the kind of person I'm looking for when I rescue a horse."

Ripley figured she was done. She was emotionally played out. She let go of Raina's hand, closed her eyes before resting her head against the wall. She sighed. Man, she was tired!

There was complete silence for a few moments. It was almost deafening compared to before. Ripley heard Raina actually laugh before she said, tears thick in her voice, "I'm pregnant right now."

"That was fast," Ripley managed, hearing Morgan's chuckle. She added, "Then I'm sorry I yelled at you."

"I'm sorry I called you a crazy bitch."

"You didn't. You called me a crazy psycho."

"Same thing."

"I forgive you—this time." Looking at her, Ripley then said seriously, "But don't ever call me a bitch in real life even in jest. I won't put up with that, not from anybody. Any friendship we may have at that point would be scrapped immediately. I won't be disrespected like that. Understand?"

Raina nodded and said, "Yes. Same here."

Raina's respect for this woman of Ty's went up another notch. Ripley was a strong and confident woman. She respected and stood up for herself. Just as she would and, she imagined, Morgan would too. Ty needed a woman like that beside him.

After a moment, grasping for normal again, Raina asked, "How'd you know my name was Stewart and not just Scott?"

Ripley had closed her eyes again. Not bothering to open them, she answered, "It was on your website."

"Oh."

Morgan snorted at Raina's short response, trying not to laugh.

"I'm Ripley Capilano, by the way."

"I figured that out as you were yelling at me. It must've been Ty's loving description of you that tipped me off."

"Yeah? He did that?" Ripley's voice had a tinge of glow in it.

"No."

Morgan did laugh then.

Ripley peeked out of one eye and took a look at Raina. She was smiling at her. Ripley smiled back and closed her eye again and sighed. "Are you really pregnant?"

"Yes."

"Boy or girl?"

"Gee, I hope so!"

Morgan lost it. Her laugh was contagious, and it got Raina going. As tired as she was, Ripley couldn't help but join in.

It felt good, laughing again. Really good.

Chapter 47

He was done waiting. The three women remained on the cold concrete, not even talking, until Bombay decided he'd stood there long enough for no good reason. He'd stood as still as he could while the women raised their voices at each other. And in his horse-sense way, he figured the coast was now clear to remind them *he* was supposed to be the center of their attention.

"I know, Bombay... I'm coming, my darling. You're such a good boy!" Morgan sighed. "What time is it anyway? I'm glad I closed the trail rides tomorrow so we had more time for the fundraiser. We can sleep in, maybe."

Morgan finally inched her way up the wall, dusting off the butt of her jeans with her hands, then wiping the drying tears from her cheeks with her shirt. She needed to blow her nose. She checked her watch, saying, "Oh, it's not really that late at all. It just feels like it. The guys at the house have got to be wondering what happened to us though!"

The Darrells decided to chance walking to the women, stopping at Morgan's side. She reached down and ran her hands down their heads and backs a few times to reassure them everything was fine. Standing up straight again, a thought came to her.

"Um, Ripley? Ty's up at my house with Josh and Channion. If you don't want to see him just yet, for the reasons we previously discussed, we need to hide your RV and get you gone."

Ripley quickly looked up at her. "Crap! I figured he'd be at his house when I headed over here. I should've known better, but I just figured he had guests and would be there at night. Of course, now that we're settling down in here, *she's* here"—she tilted her head at Raina—"so it makes sense *he* would be too. Figures.

"Well, all my lights are off, so he shouldn't see me anyway. Once you guys go back up, I'll decide what to do." She closed her eyes to rest them. And to think.

Morgan nodded. "Okay."

Raina looked at her, surprised and more than a little concerned. "Why don't you want to see Ty? You don't miss him?"

Ripley looked at her. "I *do* want to see him. Just not yet. And yes, I've missed him like crazy."

Raina replied, "Okay... Well... It's not my place to pry into your personal business... as much as I'd love to." The other two women grinned at her honesty. "The important thing is that you're here now, and that's what he was waiting for."

Ripley looked at them. "What? Does *everyone* know?"

They both nodded while Morgan replied cheerfully, "Pretty much!"

Ripley groaned and leaned her head against the wall and closed her eyes.

Morgan held out her hand for Raina, pulling her up and giving her a long, impromptu hug. She felt Raina lean into her, hugging her back. Pulling back, she asked, "Are you okay now?"

"Yes... I think so. With any luck, maybe I'm cured. Seriously, this has been... a long time coming. Perhaps it's the beginning of the end as well as the start of a new beginning. Thank you both for being there for me. Things like that go a long way with me, and I won't forget it. And I *really* won't forget Ripley yelling at a pregnant woman she didn't even know! Talk about first impressions."

Ripley opened her eyes, saw both women standing over her grinning. "Yeah, well, I didn't *know* you were pregnant at the time. And I've found that I have a genuine knack for making incredible first impressions here. Ty and Josh are prime examples of that."

Morgan smiled, knowing what Ripley was referring to.

"Would you have still yelled at me had you known?" Raina inquired.

"Absolutely," Ripley immediately replied.

"Thank you."

"You're welcome." Grinning, Ripley closed her eyes again and just listened as Morgan gathered up the brushes and headed back to the tack room. She heard her come back and talk softly to her horse, probably petting him before she led him away. She figured she'd get up once she heard Bombay's stall door get closed and latched, so she just remained where she was.

Suddenly, Ripley opened her eyes and stated, "Your therapy session isn't over, little missy." Both of the women were staring down at her, so she said, "You need that final piece of closure. Morgan, go get her some peppermint candies. Raina, you feed them. Be sure Monte gets some."

Morgan understood. Raina stood there, wiping her face with still shaky hands. Morgan handed Raina some paper towels first so she could wipe her eyes and blow her nose. She then handed her the wrapped candy.

All the horses knew that unique sound of that specific crinkly plastic wrapper. Suddenly, there were horse muzzles poking out of nearly every stall around them. A few nickers accompanied the sound of the candy being unwrapped. All three women smiled.

Raina took a breath before she went to Monte's stall. She opened it half-way, stepping closer to feed the golden horse a peppermint. A few tears rolled down her cheeks, and she fed him another and another. Smelling the mint, hearing the crunches, feeling the soft lips gently removing them from her hand made more tears flow, but Raina felt something odd happening.

It felt like her life was coming back to her in a full circle, like she was waking up from a long sleep. It honestly felt like her life was buffering after a reset, and she could see the circle in her mind's eye showing it was nearly complete. The memories simply didn't hurt as much now.

She ran her hand down Monte's head, over and over. She leaned her head against his neck, smelling the calming scent of horse. Morgan slipped a few more candies in her hand to encourage her. She unwrapped them and fed them all to the horse that reminded her so much of one of her own. Her Aspen Glow.

Morgan went back to the tack room and got more mints. She began feeding them to the other horses as Ripley just watched Raina. A contented smile formed on Ripley's face as she still leaned against the wall on the hard concrete floor. Raina was beginning to relax, she noticed.

When she saw Raina whispering to the horse and smile, she knew her job was done here. It gave her great pleasure to think, to hope, she was helping this courageous but broken woman heal even more. It was a small part she played in it, but she hoped it was enough to propel her forward. The rest was up to her.

Raina stepped back and showed Monte her hands, just as she'd done with Rodeo and Aspen. "Blackjack hands," she'd called it. It was the only way her horses would accept she had no more candy. Monte sniffed both of her hands, then he, too, accepted it, and began to turn away. Raina's heart broke free even more, and a mist of tears blurred her eyes.

"Goodbye, Aspen. I'll love you forever," she whispered as Monte walked out to his pen. His golden coat faded into the dark of the night.

Raina finally closed and latched the stall door, and when Morgan was done, they both came back over to Ripley. "Thank you, Ripley. And you, Morgan. You two just might be what the doctor ordered and charged a mint for... No pun intended there. Who would've thunk it?"

Morgan and Ripley both grinned. Morgan looped her arm over Raina's shoulders. "It was our pleasure. We're both here if you need us, Raina. I'll listen to you, and she'll yell at you. That's what friends are for."

They all smiled at each other.

"I'm feeling a little chilled. I guess from the emotional roller coaster I just rode." She rubbed her hands over her arms. "And I guess we should head back up soon, huh? But not yet. I bet I look horrible because I'm not a pretty crier at all. I don't want Channion to see me like this. He'll worry. I don't want him or Ty to worry about me."

Concerned and understanding, Morgan said, "We'll run to the restroom here in the barn in a minute. You can wash your face and pull yourself together, okay?"

Raina nodded. "Wow... This has been a long but incredible day. It seems like flying out here was a lifetime ago! I'm for sure sleeping in as long as I can again before rehearsals tomorrow. I'm betting Channion will too. He really needs some R and R. He's on vacation, y'know. He's out here to chill and regroup because he really needs to, and I intend for that to happen."

Ripley looked up at her in admiration. "You're a tough cookie, Mrs. Scott. Just don't overdue yourself all right? If anything happened to your kiddo or to you..."

Raina smiled at her. "I slept really good last night and probably will again tonight. I should be fine, but I'll be sure to rest when I can. It's pretty sweet of you to be concerned."

"Well, I do have my moments," she replied with a quirky smile before closing her eyes again. The Darrells came over and happily lay down beside her. Feeling them, her hands automatically began to pet them.

Noticing how comfortable the woman actually looked there on the floor, Raina asked, "Are you planning on sleeping there, Ripley?"

"It wouldn't be the first time she's slept in one of my barns!" Morgan teased as she walked over to Bombay, unclipping him from the cross-ties. She motioned to Raina to put him away. "If she sleeps in here, she'll have just one more barn to go before she's slept in all of them!"

Ripley chuckled but kept her eyes closed. "Not true. I haven't slept in Red Rock."

Morgan laughed. "And that's the most comfortable one. Save the best for last then, Rip. Maybe you two can have a real roll in the hay!"

Ripley smiled and shook her head.

After returning Bombay to his stall, Raina returned to Ripley's side. "Are you going to get up?"

"Eventually. I'm just resting my eyes until you two are ready to go."

Raina said, "Oh, okay." She paused for a moment before asking, "Where *are* you staying tonight?"

"No clue, but I have a few options to choose from."

Gently, Raina asked, "Not to pry or anything... But is staying with Ty one of them?"

With no hesitation at all, Ripley replied, "No. He doesn't know I'm here anyway."

Where *should* she stay for the night? she wondered to herself. She could hook up the RV in the dark and worry about snakes, scorpions, and tarantulas... Or better yet, just use it the way it was for the night and then hook it up in the morning. She could also drive it to that rest stop that wasn't too far from here so Ty wouldn't see that she was back. Maybe she could crash in one of Morgan's rooms.

She didn't feel like meeting up with her relatives yet, so no hotel room visit. Tomorrow was soon enough. She knew if she went over there, they'd be up all night joking and laughing. And she was just too bushed right now.

She had so much on her mind. Returning here brought so many feelings rushing back, and she needed to settle herself first.

She'd driven here simply because she knew she could park her RV here. She'd also wanted to see Cappy and the others, but she'd figured the barns were all closed down. She certainly didn't want to set off the alarms.

Ripley felt the dogs leave her side as she heard slight movement in the aisle. She assumed it was the two women cleaning up and patiently waited for them to finish.

Morgan asked, "Ripley?"

Her eyes still closed, Ripley asked, "Yeah?"

"Do you really love Ty? I mean, really, really?"

Ripley smiled because she couldn't stop it in time. With her eyes still closed, she replied, "Yes. Really, really."

"Say it."

"Why?"

"Because I want to hear it from you myself."

Ripley gasped and jolted at the sound of Ty's voice right in front of her. She jumped so hard, she smacked her head on the hard wall behind her and saw stars.

"*Crap! Owwww!*" She howled in pain as she held her sore head. When the stars cleared from her vision, she looked up into his face. She could tell he was trying to hold back his smile. Curse those sexy laugh lines.

Feeling like a complete idiot, she saw Josh with Morgan and Raina with a handsome man she pegged as Channion. And everyone was looking right at her, all smiling. She gave a direct, accusing look at Morgan, who just scrunched her face in sincere apology and shrugged. Ripley dropped her hand from her sore head, realizing it was now or never.

Transferring her gaze back to Ty, still squatting down in front of her, she let out a long breath. She was so happy to see him, it took all her willpower to not jump into his arms. The pull between them was incredible. And yet both held back as the air practically hummed between them.

"Hola, mi amor. Te he echado de menos," he whispered to her. *Hello, my love. I missed you.*

She sighed, not completely understanding him in words, but she did from his soft tone and the tender look in his eyes. And she felt her heart just melt at hearing his softly spoken words in the language she loved to hear him speak. She knew *mi amor,* and that's all she needed to understand.

He raised an eyebrow and waited. And then he smiled. In English, he said just as softly, "We need to stop meeting this way, Sugar. People will talk."

She whispered, "You're ruining my surprise."

He whispered back, "And what would you call this?"

She just smiled.

With a straight face now, he added still in a whisper, "I'd think with all the money you have, you could afford a nice bed. Do you need a loan?"

Her smile got bigger as his humor was one of the things she loved most about him.

Channion groaned. "C'mon, you two... *Speak up!* It's just too hard to eavesdrop when you're whispering, for Pete's sake!"

Everybody laughed.

"Say it, Ripley. Just let-'er-Rip!" Ty teased her.

"Oh no! You've been spending time with Steve!" She moaned good-naturedly. It was a risk she had to take sending him here before she got here to defend herself from his stories.

Ty laughed and nodded. "Well?"

She smiled, and feeling the moment *was* right, said softly, "Te amo, mi amor. I love you, Ty Stanton. Forever and ever until my dying breath."

His entire being settled at finally hearing her say it. He was amazed at how he felt just because she'd said those words to him at long last. And in two languages to boot.

"I told you so, Sugar!" He smiled broadly. Hauling her up in his arms, he kissed her soundly. "I love you, too, until my dying breath." He kissed her again.

Their friends cheered. Channion was leaning against the wall, acting all worn out from the wait.

Ripley laughed and wrapped her arms tightly around Ty's neck and just held on. "I missed you, Ty. So, so much!" she whispered in his ear.

"And I missed you. Don't you *ever* put me through that again. Got it?" he whispered in hers.

"Got it."

"Didn't I tell you long ago that you loved me?"

"Yes, you told me." She smiled as she let go of him and stepped away. "And I never denied it. I just didn't confirm it."

Channion came over and rested his hands on her shoulders. He said with emotion, "I've waited a long time to meet you, Ripley. Ty means the world to me, so you're going to treat him right from now on, aren't you? You've got his heart. Do you have his back? Forever? No matter what?"

Touched by his words, Ripley nodded and confirmed with a soft but firm, "Yes. I promise."

He smiled before he said, "Good. If not, I'll sic my wife and Morgan on you!" She laughed. Channion gripped her shoulders tightly for a second before saying a little softer, "And if you just helped cure my wife of her survivor's guilt, I'll *never* be able to thank you enough."

"You guys were here for all of that?" Ripley asked, astonished.

Channion glanced at Ty, knowing all three men were beyond happy when they'd figured out Ripley was back, and then stunned when she began yelling and swearing at Raina. Standing outside the doorway, they'd decided to let it all play out, figuring Raina could stand up to Ripley if needed. And there was always Morgan. If Ripley went too far, she'd step in.

Still, Channion was worried about his pregnant wife and wanted to interfere. But Ty had silently motioned for him to just wait, to see what happened.

When their women got quiet, they still held back, not knowing if they were done. They were right to wait. Peeking around the corner, they saw Morgan giving Raina mints, instructing her to feed them to Monte.

Ty had motioned for them to still wait. "Let them calm down. They might not be done yet. This may be exactly what she needs, Channion. She's okay," he'd whispered to his cousin.

Not knowing exactly what they were all talking about, Josh figured to follow Ty's lead.

They'd finally decided it was time to make their presence known. The Darrells had happily got up to greet them when they walked through the wide doorway. Morgan and Raina stood there like deer caught in the headlights of an oncoming car. Neither said a word in warning to Ripley when Ty motioned to them to stay quiet.

Now, Channion decided to just say, "Yeah, we were here. Coming from you as it did, maybe that's what she's needed all along. Nothing else seemed to work."

Ripley replied, "I'm sorry I yelled at her, but I sensed she needed to break through a mental wall. She needed a big push. It's not my usual greeting to people I've never met. It was yet another original first impression I made here... For you both! I got in a two-for-one deal, didn't I?" She offered a small smile when Channion grinned. "Now, well, I guess only time will tell."

Channion squeezed her shoulders before saying sincerely, "Maybe you don't rescue only horses. Maybe you rescue people too."

Ripley's eyes filled with tears at his sweet words before he thanked her again and went back to his wife.

Josh came over next. With a twinkle in his eyes, he asked, "If I may hug you?" He wrapped her in a long hug after she smiled and nodded. "It's so good to see you back, Rip! We all really missed you. We missed Riptide!"

"Same here!" She hugged him again, happy to be back where she finally felt she belonged.

Morgan came over and gave Ripley a long, considering look. Then with a grin, she hugged her and whispered, "Welcome back home, Ripley. I think you're really going to enjoy it here!"

She felt Ripley squeeze her back and whisper with feeling, "Thank you for everything, Morgan."

Ty broke them apart, bringing Ripley back to his side. She looped her arm around his waist, keeping him close.

Ripley asked, "Is Steve here? My aunt and uncle?"

Ty replied, "Your relatives left a while ago. That's how we saw you come in. We saw the vehicle lights and wondered who it was. I hoped it was you because it looked like an RV and a car on the back, but I also didn't want to get my hopes smashed again. You didn't stop where you were before, so I wasn't sure. Since the lights stopped at the barns, we got curious and figured to check on Morgan and Raina while we were down here."

Happy that things were looking bright again, Morgan said cheerfully, "Okay, well, I think we need to let Prego over here get some rest. And Channion too. Besides being on vacation, he also needs his energy built back up so we can have a kickboxing match while he's here. I don't want to share the mat with a wimp." Channion laughed at her as she playfully punched his arm. "How about we get this place closed down?"

Raina said, "Sounds like a plan. But first, we need to figure out what to do with our little runaway here. Suggestions? Rope, chains, or handcuffs?"

"I vote for handcuffs!" Ty piped up, his arm around her shoulders.

Ripley laughed as she and her new friends headed toward the door, the dogs trailing behind with their happy dog grins and wagging tails. She couldn't think of the words that truly described how she felt right then.

But the best word she could come up with was *home*.

Chapter 48

SHE HAD AN EPIPHANY. It wasn't until later that night as she was stepping out of the shower that Morgan replayed her conversation with Raina in her mind. As she dried off with her towel, her mind was more relaxed than it had been in weeks simply because Ripley had returned.

For no other reason than it simply popping into her head, she heard in her mind again some of the words Raina had shared with her in the gazebo.

"About four years ago, I saved a sheriff's deputy from being murdered... In the process, I almost lost my own life... The detectives assigned to my case, as well as to my personal protection later on, were Channion and Ron. That was how we all met... The people who tried to murder the deputy and me were part of a huge illegal weapons ring. The guy running it was wanted big time, been around forever... He was very elusive... He found out who I was, where I lived..."

Stunned, Morgan stood there for long minutes replaying the entire conversation in her mind, and then what Raina had said in the barn. Her conclusion was the same. Tears misted her eyes as the enormity of the situation hit so very close to home. Placing her hands on the counter, she leaned forward, closing her eyes as memories took her back to four years ago.

Remembering back to when Ty was in Illinois for his annual family reunion, staying as usual with Channion. And Ty calling her the very day his plane was to return him home. After making sure she was alone and could talk on her cell, Ty explained briefly that he needed to stay indefinitely longer to help Channion and Ron on a special case they were deeply involved in. He knew he could help them out, but he wasn't sure how long it'd take.

They'd used their code so she knew he was going back into the Agency. She'd been scared spitless for him until he contacted her weeks later, letting her know he was fine.

Not too much longer after he'd returned, Ty had come up to the house one evening where he and Morgan had total privacy, used their code, and broke the news to her. *"Sweetheart, it's over. The man who headed the weapons ring, the man who ordered Shane killed... He's dead. It's been confirmed. The man who carried out the hit is gone, and now the one who ordered it is too. We have the closure we both needed. You should be safe now. There are still some more out there, but we got the two main ones."* In a softer voice, he'd said as he held her tightly, *"Shane has finally received justice, and so have you, Natasha."*

She'd nodded, and crying silent tears, had leaned against Ty's solid body as they comforted each other. Using her real name gave her more closure, which is why Ty had used it. Only Ty and Josh knew her real identity, but neither ever used her name or any details from her past. In this case, knowing they were alone, Ty had.

Later when Josh had come home, she'd told him. He was as relieved for her as Ty had been.

Wondering what was taking his wife so long, Josh walked into their bathroom and saw Morgan crying over the counter.

"Sweetheart! What's wrong?" He quickly went to her, cupping her face, searching her eyes.

"Polar bears love to slide on snow," Morgan said quietly as she tried to control her tears. She used their private code for something serious they needed to discuss.

Without a word, he wrapped her towel around her more securely, took her hand and led her to the most private place in their bedroom. After locking their bedroom door in case his parents wanted to talk to them again before turning in themselves, he turned her toward the only place he knew of that was secure. With no vents to carry sounds and voices, and no rooms beside them for anyone to hear through the walls, he led her into their large walk-in closet.

"Sweetheart, what is it?" he asked as he wiped the tears from her cheeks.

"It was Raina... I'm *sure* of it, Josh. It seems impossible, but there's just no other conclusion that makes sense to me!" She held tighter to his hands as she repeated, "It was *Raina!*"

"What was Raina? What about her?" he asked, confused.

She recounted her earlier conversation with Channion's wife to her husband, who stood there in stunned silence long after she was finished. He leaned against the wall, processing what his wife explained to him.

She finally asked softly, "Am I wrong? I can't be. But it'd be too much of a coincidence, wouldn't it? It seems utterly impossible! But based on the talks between Ty and me around that time, it all fits. And remember *I* was called *at home* after Shane was gone? Raina said they found out where *she* lived... That's another link that it was the same guy, right?

"Or am I just wrong? Am I for some reason looking for something that isn't even there, for whatever reason? You were with me at the trial, so you know what I know. Maybe I'm just... I don't know..."

Josh shook his head, looking his wife straight in her eyes. "No, I don't see how you could be wrong. This is too much... No wonder Ty raves about her. Not only did she save a police officer, she stumbled onto the same man who changed your life forever. And then she ends up marrying the cousin of the man sent to protect you... Could our world really be that small?"

They stared at each other in shock.

Finally, Morgan said, "We can never tell her, you know. Or even Channion. Although I could probably trust them, we just can't say a word. They can't know about *me*... The knowledge we have will have to be enough."

Josh pulled her close and hugged her. After a moment, he whispered, "You realize what this also means, right?"

"What?"

"If my gut is right, Channion must know about Ty. They grew up together, and he's been Ty's sole confidant until you. Maybe not, but my bet is he does. I don't know if they would've told her though."

After considering his words, Morgan nodded. "I think you're right. But I can't risk my life—or yours now—just to tell either of them thank you. And it'd probably be best to not let Ty know we know it was Raina... at least for now.

"We can confirm it later after everything else has calmed down. This is his time with Ripley, and I don't want to ruin it. This isn't about me. It's about them. I'd rather celebrate their happiness than closure that I already got."

Josh kissed her wet hair and still held her close. "I understand," he replied.

Long minutes passed before Josh brushed her wet hair back as he cupped her face to look into her vibrant eyes. "Sweetheart?"

"What?"

"Polar bears love to slide on snow."

"Frisky little fellas!" Morgan smiled at her husband, seeing his lighter expression. "Okay, tell me. What do they want this time?"

He loosened her towel, and let it drop to the closet floor.

Her muffled laughter was soon cut off when, with a wide grin, he lowered his head to kiss her.

Chapter 49

Friday, August 19

Her aim had improved over the years because she hit her alarm on the first try. Feeling groggy and a little disoriented, Ripley opened her eyes and just lay there for a few minutes, staring at her wall.

With a suddenly clear mind and a light heart, she remembered last night. After they'd left Quail Run, she'd said she had to make a quick trip to see Cappy, so everyone tagged along to Grand View too. Cappy immediately recognized her and walked eagerly to the door when she called his name. Ripley was overjoyed he remembered her. Ty wasn't surprised at all.

Slipping into the stall, Ripley hugged the horse and kissed his nose. He happily soaked in the attention from her. He nibbled at her long hair and blew his warm breath on her neck and face as she ran her hands over his head.

Ripley looked over at Raina outside the stall, held out her hand to her in invitation. Softly, but firmly, she said, "You can do this."

Raina fought to come to terms with the feelings coursing through her this particular horse ignited. After an encouraging back rub from Channion, she finally stepped inside the stall. Standing beside the horse opposite Ripley, she stroked the horse's warm neck and back.

She smiled at Ripley in happiness as the need to break down again seemed manageable. Tears came to her eyes, but neither woman was sure if it was from relief or residual emotions.

"Congratulations, Raina!" Ripley whispered to her over the horse's back.

Raina smiled at her as she felt herself breaking free even more than earlier. Baby steps, or giant strides, had been taken tonight.

Those watching all smiled, with Channion being the most relieved. Maybe his wife was now healed completely from her ordeal? He was immensely thankful they'd come out to visit Ty simply for this accomplishment. He wondered if they should've come out long ago? But maybe it was in the timing. And that timing was Ripley.

After leaving the barns last night, her friends insisted on hooking up her RV with the use of flashlights and moonlight. It took a considerable amount of Ripley's willpower to tell Ty to go home. And the rest of it to not go with him. After she'd kissed Ty goodnight—three times—and sent them all on their way, she'd taken a shower, ate a snack, and crashed into her bed. She'd been worried she'd toss and turn all night. Instead, she'd slept like a rock.

She was up, dressed, and checking voicemails as she drank one of her nutrition shakes when she heard knocking on her door. Opening it, she smiled at Morgan. "Good morning! Come on in."

Morgan climbed inside her RV, fascinated again at how incredibly homey it was. She wondered if she could live in one like Ripley did. "So... First off, I'm sorry about last night. The three of them just turned the corner and walked right in. I couldn't warn you at all. And there was no way you could've run and hid. As they said later, they'd been there for quite a while so it wouldn't have mattered anyway."

"Yeah, I figured that's what happened. It's okay. With the exception of the bump on the back of my head, *I'm* okay." She saw the look of concern on Morgan's face. "Nah. Nothing major. I took a few aspirin. Don't worry. I won't sue you. I can't. I signed your waiver, remember?"

Morgan chuckled as Ripley confided, "His appearance and the subsequent events just took some of the... surprise value... out of my plans. But I still want to do the rest of it. Do you think I should?"

"Rip, I'd *love* to see you do it! And Ty would be floored. I think every great love should have a grand gesture, something you've never done before. It'll make such a memory. It's a brave thing to do too. If the song fits, and it sure does, it'll be your song forever. Or at least one of them. I say go for it!" Morgan encouraged Ripley to stay strong.

Ripley blew out a breath and put her hand to her stomach. "I'm feeling sick to my stomach. Remind me to never get pregnant so I can miss throwing up every morning!"

Morgan laughed and sat down on her couch. "Are you about ready?"

"Almost. Let me shoot off a couple of texts and emails here so I don't leave these people hanging. They know I'm off for a while, but I'd still like to take care of it while I can. It's easy stuff. Help yourself to something to drink or snack on while I do this. It shouldn't take more than ten, fifteen minutes tops." She pointed to a cabinet. "Food is up there. Drinks are in the fridge."

With a smirk, Morgan chided her, "I know you're really just stalling." She walked around Ripley's home on wheels eating a granola bar she got from her cabinet as Ripley got a little work in. She got a 7-Up from her fridge to wash it down.

When Ripley was finished, she put her shaker bottle to soak in the sink, grabbed her things, and followed Morgan out the door. She made sure it was locked before they got into her truck.

Morgan drove along the highway and waited for Ripley to comment on where they were. It wasn't long in coming. "Wait, whoa the truck. Why are we heading to Ty's?"

"What? 'Whoa the truck'?" Morgan laughed. At Ripley's look, she explained with a smile, "To pick up Raina. She wanted to come. She called me earlier and asked what I was doing this morning, so I told her.

"If she got to come along, it'd let Ty and Channion have some time alone, she said. She knows they'd like some time with just the two of them. This was a perfect way to do it because they didn't have to ask her for it. She's pretty cool to know that about those two."

"Hey, doesn't that mean she called outside of your office hours?" Ripley teased.

"She barely fit her call in, but I still gave her a verbal warning," Morgan joked back.

"I thought she wanted to sleep in?"

"She apparently couldn't. When she called me, she said she was too excited to sleep away her morning." Morgan smiled. "She's plucky, isn't she?"

"Yeah. After last night, I'm not sure what to expect this morning. It's great to hear it sounds like she's better than ever."

After driving another mile or so, Morgan asked, "Do you know anything about her? Ty ever tell you?"

"No. I just heard her talking last night. I don't know how much I missed, but I got the gist pretty quickly. To me, it sounded like she was in a seriously bad situation, and Channion was there to protect her. And I assume that's how they met?"

Morgan nodded before Ripley explained further, "I saw the lights on, so I was curious. I listened for a while and decided she needed strength and force, not sympathy and understanding. She had survivor's guilt. Her self-blaming was just going to keep eating her alive. She needed a breakthrough, and she wasn't going to get it unless shoved over the edge."

Morgan nodded. "I agree. I was trying to figure out how best to do it when you walked in the door. She's been through hell. She'd told me some more before we went to the barn. It's not my place to share her confidence, but let's say she's a remarkable woman.

"As much as you heard, she probably wouldn't mind you knowing the rest, but that's not my call. If she doesn't want you to know, I don't want to break her trust, you know? I can feel her out, ask her. Or heck, you could ask her yourself. Your first impression has already been made, so what do you have to lose?" she teased.

Ripley grimaced.

Morgan continued as she drove along, "She's a pretty direct and straightforward person, but this is pretty private and traumatic. She has a strong personality, it's right there to see, but she's really nice too. She has a cool sense of humor from what I can tell so far.

"And she seems perfect for Channion. They're a great couple from what I can tell from the short time we've all been together. I sometimes wondered what kind of woman he'd choose, or if he'd stay single. He always struck me as a family man though. It takes a strong, stable woman to marry a cop if she's serious about making the marriage work. I'd say they both are."

Morgan slowed down for the truck and stock trailer in front of them to turn left. "Going to the barn last night was at her request. It was a last-minute decision on her part, and I wanted to see if I could help her. Thanks for coming in and taking over. That was a side of you I'd never seen before, minus that night of the wreck when you yelled at that guy blocking us. You can be a fiery little thing, can't you?"

Ripley blew out a breath. "I have a temper at times."

"It wasn't temper last night, Ripley. It was caring and compassion. It was tough love, tempered love," Morgan explained. "And it seemed like it was exactly what the doctor called for."

Ripley ventured, "I think it worked. At the very least, it's maybe a springboard for her to finish healing. Hopefully."

Morgan nodded. "I think you're right."

After a moment, Ripley confided, "It did occur to me later that I could've made it worse because, I admit, I didn't know all the story. But what I *did* hear, well, it was so clear what was happening inside of her. And I have no idea if some professional shrink would rip me a new one with how I handled it. It actually scared me a little thinking about it this morning."

Morgan shrugged. "Well, the shrinks and doctors she's already seen apparently haven't been able to help her with *their* methods, so who can say? She seemed fine with it last night, and she seems fine this morning. I'd say she took a sharp turn toward relief, with a good dose of enlightenment.

"Now that we know the guys were there, I'm sure Channion would've jumped in to protect her if you were really that far off base."

Ripley sighed. "Well, I guess we'll see, won't we? I'm a little nervous to meet either of them now in the morning light, you know? What if they hate me?"

"You'll just have to suck it up." At her wide-eyed look, Morgan grinned and reassured her, "I don't see that happening, Rip. Have some faith in them... and yourself."

Arriving in good time, Morgan turned into Ty's driveway. She debated whether to honk the horn or go to the door. "Duck down, Ripley. If Ty sees you, we'll never leave!"

Grinning, Ripley laid down on the seat before sliding onto the floor.

Morgan laughed at her and got out of the truck to get Raina. She knocked on the door. It was opened almost immediately by Raina. With a wink and a grin, she said softly, "Shh... The guys are still sleeping. Here, help me carry this stuff, will you?"

Morgan noticed the alarm was on and quickly turned it off. "*Whoa!* That was a *close* one!"

Slapping her hand to her forehead, her eyes wide, Raina exclaimed, "He told us right before we went to bed it was on. In my excitement at seeing you, it slipped my mind. I can't believe I *did* that as we have an alarm at home too. It's a good thing you know his code because I don't. I'd be trapped in his house unless I crawled out a window!"

Morgan shook her head. "They're all connected."

"Ours are too," Raina admitted a bit sheepishly.

They grinned at each other.

As quietly as possible, they gathered her things and slipped out the door after Morgan reset the alarm. Raina had left a note on the upstairs bathroom mirror letting the guys know where she was.

After Raina put some things in the back seat of the truck, she opened the front truck door, stopping in surprise when she saw Ripley on the floor. "What in the *world,* Ripley?"

Laughing, Ripley said, "Quick. Get in."

Morgan tossed Raina's things in the back seat, grinning at her. "Move it, Prego!"

Raina climbed in over Ripley, both of them laughing.

Morgan slid behind the wheel. "Wait until I tell you, Rip. I don't trust those two." Once she'd pulled out of the drive and got down the road a bit, she said, "Okay. Get up here, and get your seatbelt on."

"Good morning, Ripley. I see you found a place to stay last night," Raina joked as Ripley crawled onto the seat beside her and fastened her seatbelt.

Ripley and Morgan grinned at her.

Driving into town to The Neon Moon, Raina decided to share her story with the two women about the gum incident between herself and Channion. The two women laughed and agreed to keep her method of gaining an apology, and acknowledgment of one being needed, in mind for future reference.

Morgan grinned and asked, "So who actually ended up buying the flowers anyway?"

With a big smile, Raina answered, "He did. We have copies of our credit cards in our safe. I just opened up that sucker and filled out the online form."

They all laughed again, strengthening their new bond.

But Raina wasn't done with her humorous take on being married to a cop. "Oh, here's another story that you two will like! Okay, first off to kinda set the scene in case Ripley doesn't know, Channion is a homicide detective, and I'm a private music teacher as well as a singer. Good?"

Ripley smiled and nodded.

Smiling in remembrance, Raina said, "This happened just a few weeks ago. I was sitting on the couch one night watching some true crime show. I'm a bit addicted to them, but I generally only watch them when he's not home because I figure he needs a break from work. If he comes home and it's on, I'll normally give him the remote to let him pick the channel.

"Channion got home at a reasonable hour that night, like the first night in *ages*. So, I'm watching this show about this wife who murdered her husband, and how it was a really tough case for the police to solve. Y'know, the typical scenario.

"Chan comes in with a drink and a sandwich, sits in his recliner, gets comfy. I toss him the remote, but then he begins watching it. Maybe he was trying to solve it himself... I don't know."

Morgan and Ripley laughed.

Raina continued, "They were saying how there's no perfect crime, but they were really struggling for evidence against her.

"For some reason, I got distracted thinking about a new student I was working with. I picked up my notebook that was beside me and started writing notes to myself about stuff I wanted to go over with her. Then I'd watch the show again, think of something else about her, write it down. You get the picture?"

Morgan and Ripley both nodded.

"Suddenly, Channion practically yells my name. It startled me... I'm thinking something happened like the place caught on fire or something. So I naturally asked, 'What? What's wrong?'" She started laughing so hard she couldn't finish her story.

Her laugh was contagious, making Morgan and Ripley laugh too.

Finally, Raina got control of herself, wiping the tears from her cheeks. "He asked me, oh my gosh... The *look* on his face! He asks me, 'Are you taking *notes?*'"

The women laughed so hard they had tears in their eyes.

Morgan wiped away her tears. Her voice full of humor, she said, "Poor Channion! He thought you were planning his demise? He really *does* need a vacation!"

Smiling, Ripley asked, "What'd you say?"

Raina shook her head. "I don't think I ever answered him. I was laughing so hard I nearly fell off the couch!"

Raina was regaling them with another story when Morgan pulled to a stop at The Neon Moon.

WHEN THE THREE RETURNED to Harmony Hills hours later, Morgan drove straight to where the stage was. They discussed that night's schedule again before getting out of the truck.

"We may have to bumble along, so we all need to be prepared to adjust our plans at the last minute, okay? Be flexible!" Morgan warned.

Ripley grinned at them. "Perfect! That's how Ty and I roll. We bumble along. We decided long ago it was just our style."

Raina said, "Wonderful. That's a good sign then! I'll keep an eye open for your signal, Morgan, and stop at the end of whatever song I'm singing, get the band off the stage, and give the mic to Ripley. I'll turn it off as I put it on her, and then turn it back on right when she's ready to walk up. As long as her recorded music is set up and ready, I don't see this being too hard to do. The rest is up to Ripley here."

"Look! I'm so nervous, my hands are shaking!" Ripley whined.

Raina, not worried at all, shared her secret with her new friends. "Morgan, give her some of the rum and Pepsi we just bought. You know, a Captain Morgan, before she goes up. It'll help loosen her up and make her fearless. She's pretty nervous, so better make it a tall one. Give it to her a bit before she goes up so it has time to take effect.

"Until I got in the family way, it's what I did every time before I went on stage. They said caffeine is bad for expectant mothers, so now I just drink the rum," she added with a straight face as they opened the truck doors.

The other two women laughed as they headed toward the stage for rehearsal.

Lilly saw them and came over, enveloping her niece in a long hug. "Oh, darling girl! Here you are! I saw your RV and went down earlier, but you obviously weren't there. This is going to be so much fun!

"And you look amazing... I adore the glow you have now. And I can see why you tripped all *over* that man of yours. He's an absolute first-rate choice for you! I approve of him, and Joe and Steve do too. Excellent choice of men, Ripley, dear. Your parents will be so happy to meet him too."

Smiling, Ripley asked her aunt, "Is everything good to go? Or do I even need to ask?"

"We have everything set up." As she led the way to the stage, she included the other two women in the conversation. "This is so exciting, isn't it? Morgan, you've done a fabulous job! Maya and her husband, Tony?"

"Toby."

"That's it. Those two have been on the phone non-stop. I was wondering if maybe we could turn this into a two-day event to allow more to come?"

She stopped when the other three did. Her sharp glance went from one to the other, explaining, "I don't see why not. We're all scheduled to be here another few days, anyway, right? Everything is set up. People are still calling, and we don't want to turn away anybody. This is a wonderful opportunity, and I think we should take full advantage of it!"

Morgan, being a businesswoman foremost, thought about it. "Well, if people are still calling for tickets, we aren't going to be playing to an empty seating area. I'm good with it. I do have trail rides set up though."

She ran options through her head. "We can run our normal schedule with our trail rides. They're fairly out of the way at Sunset Ridge. We can maybe even just skip the last one or two rides, reschedule them if there's anyone on them now. We can get chores done just before the fundraiser would begin. Assuming my staff is available after hours. I'll need to check with them."

Turning to Raina and Ripley, she asked, "Did you two have plans already set up for tomorrow or tomorrow night with the guys? Do you want to do a second night?"

Both also being businesswomen, Ripley and Raina saw the business opportunity as well. Ripley nodded. "Good for me. I'm off, and it might be nice to have the second night so I can enjoy it without being a nervous wreck!"

Bewildered, Lilly asked, "Why on earth would you be a nervous wreck? You've done this before."

Ripley grinned. "Not like this, Lilly!"

Her aunt studied her. Seeing that she was nervous, Lilly said with excitement in her voice, "Ohhh... Let-'er-Rip is up to *somethin'!*" She grinned. "My, oh my. This is gonna be somethin' all right. I don't even want to know! I mean... I do, but I don't. This time, surprise me!"

Raina smiled, shrugged. "Well, if Let-'er-Rip can do it, I can too! I do back-to-back performances all the time like this, so a two-night performance is no big deal for me. All I do is sing anyway.

"Channion may have plans, so I need to make sure. Let me text him right now. He should be awake although he may not have his phone on him. But I say go for it because I need to make as much money as I can while I can. We have to build a secure fence around our pond now, so this could help."

She looked at Morgan as she pulled out her phone to text her husband. "Is this considered overtime pay or just another night's?"

Grinning, Ripley said, "Well, crap. I forgot we'd have to pay her for a second night. Oh well. Why not? She's family."

Morgan joked, "At least in the family way!"

The four women smiled just as Josh's parents walked up. His dad, Pops, smiled. "My goodness! All these lovely ladies in one place!"

Morgan loved that her parents-in-law still held hands. Annabelle smiled at her as she said, "Josh had to go into town for a while. The renters in his old house called with a minor issue. He said he'll be back in a few hours, tops."

"Okay. Thanks for letting me know. Have you met Ripley? This is Ty's..." She trailed off, not knowing exactly how to label her.

Ripley stepped in smoothly, holding out her hand. "Ripley Capilano with Just One More. And Ty and I are—"

Pops interrupted with a big grin, "A pretty hot item, I hear. We've been looking forward to meeting the woman who stole that good man's heart!" Looking at the attractive woman in front of him, he nodded. "I was told you were as beautiful as our Morgan here. If you're as great on the inside as the outside, Ty's a very lucky man!"

Dryly, Ripley inquired, "Who told you I was beautiful like Morgan? Was it Josh, by any chance?"

"It was. Why?"

Morgan and Ripley laughed before Morgan explained, "Your son once said he was okay with Ty dating Ripley because she was pretty. Apparently, that's the only stipulation he required."

Josh's parents laughed. With a twinkle in his eyes, Pops replied, "Well, it worked for him, so I don't see as how he's wrong!"

Ripley answered, "That's *exactly* what he said too. Oh, and that I took out the trash!"

Annabelle smiled at them all, shaking her head. "I tried with that boy. I really did."

They all laughed again.

Looking at Raina, he said, "And you are as beautiful as ever, young lady! You have that glow I remember my Annabelle having when she was pregnant with our first."

Raina smiled. "Thank you."

Lilly clapped her hands together once. "So. Are we extending it another night? Adding more seating, food? I'll need to check with the caterer too. We may have to adjust the dinner menu.

"And I need to let Maya and Toby know right away. We're booked up for tonight, so we can begin overflow calls for tomorrow night once you're sure. Do you want to check with your men first, or just go with it? I'll ask the staff."

Ripley, Raina, and Morgan all nodded in agreement.

Morgan said, "Since I haven't heard a word about any plans for tomorrow night, I doubt there are any. Extend it. Same time. We'll text the guys so they know in case they're planning something."

Raina glanced at her phone and didn't see a reply text from Channion. She figured he'd just leave it up to her anyway, so she agreed.

Annabelle asked, "We're doing an extra night now?"

Lilly nodded. "Calls are coming in like a broken spout pours water! We can't turn away people who want to come in with heavy pockets and leave with lighter ones, can we? We just never know when a dry spell will come, so we need to line the coffers when we can. Our horses depend on us!"

Pops nodded. "Smart. It won't really cost you too much more, so why not? Does the band know?"

Raina slapped her hand over her mouth. "Oh! I forgot they aren't my band... I guess we *should* ask them. My gosh, I *never* forget things like this, and that's all I'm doing lately. Is this baby brain?"

Lilly patted her shoulder. "Probably. But don't worry, dear. It'll go away." And then she was off and running, waving her hand in the air, calling back, "I got it! Leave it all to me!"

They shook their heads in amused wonder as she flew across the grounds to the office. Ripley smiled when she answered the unspoken question, "Yes, she's been like that since I can remember. Her energy is endless!"

Morgan looked at her in-laws. "Just like you two are! Kids at heart still. So, Mom and Pops, what are your plans for today?"

Annabelle replied, "Well, we wanted to go on a ride soon... Just one of the trail ones, not a personalized one. Maya said it was no problem when we asked her. After that, we'll hang out at the house to make lunch for everyone unless you need us for anything at all, and then it's fundraiser time!"

Morgan replied, "Sounds like a plan. We need to go down now and rehearse a few things. If we need you, trust me, you'll know!" She looked over at Raina and Ripley. "C'mon, you two. We can't let Lilly show us up!"

Chapter 50

THE FUNDRAISER CROWD WAS large and buzzing. Pops, Annabelle, Kat, Mel, Drew, and Toby were out in the parking lots to help with parking and greeting people. They instructed them to the seating area or to the barn to see the eleven rescues prior to the dinner, speeches, and the concert.

Alexis, Rory, Eric, and Kim were also greeting the guests and handing out programs, complete with envelopes for possible extra donations separate from the cost of the admission and catered dinner ticket. A locked donation box was also set up near the office, with Bo and an off-duty officer monitoring it for security purposes.

Ty, Dell, Steve, and Joe were in Grand View, showing the horses to people and answering their questions. Even Deputy Matt Harvey was there, mainly for security, but also to answer questions since he did work the scene that long ago night. Although they weren't really expecting anything to happen, they never knew with large crowds, and Harmony Hills was a very popular place around there. And people were there with money to spend. Morgan had asked if she could have a couple of officers looking for some extra money to work the evening and three had volunteered to help out.

The catering company had their tables and food set up, and a few workers were already serving light fare from a buffet table. The main course would be coming out soon.

Josh, Lilly, and Maya were manning the phones in the office, still setting up for the following night. Morgan had called the TV and the radio stations, asking them to make an announcement about the extended night. As hoped, and expected, the calls just kept coming in. She also put an update on her website, and Lilly did the same for Just One More's. Raina went ahead and put an extended notice on her site too.

Morgan roamed the grounds, greeting people, answering questions and represented not only Harmony Hills, but also Just One More and the work they did.

Morgan was pleased when she saw Dr. Shamis arrive with his wife and daughter. He smiled at her surprise. "You don't think I'd miss *this*, do you?" he asked after he introduced his family to her.

She smiled. "I guess I figured you might be busy." Turning to his family, she said, "I can't say enough about the wonderful job he did for these horses!"

They spoke for a while before she ushered them off to the buffet tables.

For now, Channion was with Raina, resting up at the house before the dinner started. Like Morgan, Ripley roamed the grounds. She mingled with the crowd, happily running into Dr. Shamis herself.

When she saw a large group of people coming toward her, she clapped her hands together and smiled as she made her way to them. Julia and her husband, Cory, had arrived—along with about thirty more of her business friends.

She hugged Julia, saying, "Oh! I'm *so* glad you're here." She smiled at the others. "And you guys... I didn't know you *all* were coming!"

Eric smiled, saying, "Are you kidding, Ripley? Julia here said we all had to come or else. We even have a few corporate people here. They should be arriving any minute. She didn't mind threatening them, either, I might add."

Ron smiled. "He's kidding, y'know. We wouldn't miss this event for you and your horses, Ripley. Even though we just parked our cars and walked in, this looks to be the biggest fundraiser you've ever had for your place. It looks impressive, and it hasn't even begun yet!"

"It'll be an incredible event, I just know it!" Zahra put her arm around her friend's shoulders, asking, "Now where is that gorgeous man of yours? He *is* here, isn't he?"

Ripley laughed. "Yes, of course, he is! Ty's in Grand View with the horses. It's that big barn over there..." She pointed to it. "Go say hi, and don't tell him anything bad about me, okay?"

Zahra laughed. "No promises!"

Jenny said, "Wow. This place *is* crazy cool, Ripley, just like you said it was. And the views out here! Jack and I arrived yesterday and have toured around. You know, I can see how you fell in love with the area. You can see for miles every way you look. It's a big change from New Hampshire, that's for sure."

Ripley smiled warmly at her friend. "As great as the views are, Jenny, the people here on site are even better. If you see someone with a *Harmony Hills* pin on, that's a staff member. Talk to them, and you'll see what I mean. Morgan, the owner, is particular about who she hires, and it shows in the best of ways. She's around here somewhere. You'll know it's her because of her green eyes!"

Julia took her aside, asking her, "You're still good to go, right? You're not chickening out? I'm still to do what you want me to do with Ty?"

"No, I'm not chickening out. But I shake like a leaf when I think about it!" she admitted. "I hope I don't mess this up and make a fool out of myself, Jules!"

"Sweetie, when it's for love, we're all fools."

"That's not *really* what I was hoping to hear from you."

Her best friend laughed. "You just go up there, and do your thing!"

"I'll give it my best shot. Thank you, Julia, for being there for me through all of this. I really appreciate it."

"That's what friends are for. Remember what I told you about him. He's the end of your rainbow. Now, go mingle. We're going to go raid the buffet line, and go see a bunch of pretty horses."

"Enjoy both!" Ripley smiled as her friends walked away.

Chapter 51

From the sidelines, Ripley watched as the first portion of the evening was getting started. The catered meal looked and smelled delicious. She wished she could've eaten it, but her nerves had her uptight. She needed to grab some, though, so she'd have enough strength to finish the night since she hadn't really eaten throughout the day either. Most guests were already seated, mingling with others seated near them.

She watched her friends and was so thankful they were there. On the other hand, knowing they *were* all there added some more stress to not screw up. None of them except Julia knew of her plans for later on in the evening. Anxious to get it over with, her nerves were on edge, making her jumpy.

She just took deep breaths and tried to focus on her fundraiser. She and Morgan walked around, checking in with staff or guests, giving personal attention to those who were gracious enough to come and support the horses. The caterer seemed to be a hit since everyone was cleaning their plates.

She and Morgan were ready to speak when Ty and Josh got prepared to bring up the horses when they were called.

Alexis, Kat, and Mel were tasked with making sure the horses were groomed to perfection and ready to be handed to Drew, Toby, and Dell, who would run them back and forth from Grand View to Ty and Josh. Joe was there in case he was needed for anything at all. He would also go on stage before Ripley to talk about Just One More's mission. Steve, as the resident vet, would also go on and talk briefly about the health and care aspect of the horses. Ripley's job after that was to ask people to dig into their pockets for a good cause.

Maya and Lilly were done with the phones and could just enjoy the fundraiser now. They were seated at a table, finishing off their dinner. Channion and Raina were also at the tables for family and staff with the band members a couple of tables away. They'd all eaten the catered meal and currently were just spectators, drinking, and talking with each other as they waited.

Eating at their little table, Bo and the policeman continued keeping an eye on the donation box. Both were pleased that many also were donating via apps on their phone in lieu of cash or checks. Morgan had come by already and taken the donations in the box up to that point to put into the safe, just in case.

Every now and then, Ripley heard The Darrells bark from the large kennel Morgan put them in when big events like this were held.

When Morgan walked on stage, she turned on the mic and greeted everyone and asked them to take their seats and prepared to give the introduction. Rory and Kim sat by the laptop in case the clicker in the speaker's hands wouldn't work.

After the guests took their seats and it got quiet, Morgan launched into the story of the night the call came in from the police dispatcher, calling for her help. Courtesy of the local news station, the footage they took was shown from their archived video collection on a large projection screen. The live feed video from that night added more impact as the lights swirled, and the energy could be felt as the anchorwoman, Brenda Michaels, described it all.

After it played, slides showed the wreck that night in still form: The emergency vehicles everywhere, First Responders helping wherever they could, and the veterinarians with the injured horses. There were even a couple of photos of Ripley and Maya holding the horses off to the side. Ripley had no clue photos were even taken.

She was surprised to see one of her as she was gazing sadly into the eyes of one of the rescues. With her caring heart clearly on her face, that photo depicted a lot of emotion.

As Morgan continued the story, the slides showed it in graphic form. And they didn't shy away from showing a few slides showing the horses that died at the scene. This was their reality.

As Ripley watched and listened, to her it seemed like a lifetime ago. Had it only been barely over a year? So much had happened in that amount of time!

Moving along, Morgan began to describe the reality of what many abandoned, dumped, and abused horses, and other animals, lived through unless they were rescued, rehabbed, and re-homed. Annabelle had given her photos of some of the horses she'd rescued over the decades as well, so there was no shortage of material. Morgan slid smoothly into the condition of the horses they were able to save and rescue that night. That was the cue for her workers to be ready.

One by one, either Josh or Ty would walk the actual horse around the audience as Morgan described its condition when it came in. Photos taken during their time there at Harmony Hills were on the large screen as that horse was discussed. From wounds healing, weight gain, being wormed, hoof care, and simple grooming, to being ridden, loading and unloading in the trailers, and given ground work, each horse's history was described in detail. They added in candids of the horse relaxing in the sunshine or being fed treats. They also played some video that pertained to each horse so people could really see it all in action.

Morgan also described each horse's individual personality. She knew if people could see them as furry people and not just objects or creatures, they were apt to give more in support. And also remember them when they left and returned to their own lives.

Ripley was impressed with Morgan once again. The woman was a natural speaker. And because her love for horses was so great and real, her passion came across in her words and body language. It wasn't long before Ripley was about ready to donate herself.

The last horse to be brought up would be Cappy. He was their shining star after all.

His story was told in video form before he was brought out. Ripley thought Morgan was the best to tell his story as she was the one who had to go in that night and get him out of the trailer. In the video, including still shots from the wreck again, she narrated his story. His injuries made people gasp while his hatred of men had them shaking their heads. They had video of his behaviors and most people couldn't believe the horse could be anything but what he was: Mean and unpredictable. Dangerous.

And then Morgan had the new Cappy presented in photos and video. Filled out, glowing from being groomed and exercised. And finally... Being worked with by men. Ty, Josh, and Toby, then later with Joe and Steve. The crowd loved it, clapped, and cheered. Ripley beamed with pride.

There was even a shot of the day Ripley and Ty had taken Cappy for that walk in the desert. Ripley hadn't even known there *was* a picture of that day! One of Morgan's staff must've taken a candid as she could tell the quality wasn't the same as the professional pictures taken by the police department and the Humane Society.

It showed Ripley and Ty walking side by side, looking at each other, hand-walking the alert, tall sorrel horse under saddle toward the trails. It was a beautiful photo with the mountains as their backdrop.

Ripley actually blushed when she heard whistles and cheers at that picture, knowing it was coming from her friends. Morgan laughed, paused, and said there was a lot more to *this* story too. More cheers and whistles. The rest of the crowd joined in that time.

Ripley couldn't help but smile. She wondered what Ty thought. She knew he could see and hear everything going on from where he waited with Cappy. Wanting to keep her planned surprise a real surprise, she hadn't seen him all day. It took a bit of tricky scheduling to manage that feat. Ripley took another bite of the food she'd finally snagged, happy in how the night was going so far.

Once the video and slideshow about Cappy were finished, Morgan smiled. And then she changed the script.

She said the sole reason they were able to transform the broken-spirited gelding was through the instant bond, love, and understanding from one woman. Knowing she wasn't to go up until after Joe, Ripley was chewing her food when she heard Morgan call her name and tell her to come on stage. She about choked.

Hurriedly, she swallowed the food, took a quick drink of punch and headed quickly to the stage. Smoothing back her hair as she climbed the steps, she walked onstage with a smile.

Morgan's eyes twinkled, knowing she'd put her friend on the spot.

Once she was onstage, Morgan introduced her as the woman who had a natural ability to bond with horses. And the one person there that this vicious, terrified, abused horse had immediately bonded with. Trying to keep a straight face, Morgan announced her name and her position with Just One More. She handed her the wireless mic as the audience welcomed her.

Graciously, Ripley thanked her. She also wanted to get in a gentle dig at her friend for putting her on the spot. Ripley smiled at the large audience. "As we all know, the key to creating and maintaining a relationship is common courtesy. You wouldn't want to pull a horse away from its feed before it was done... Just as you shouldn't pull a friend from *her* first meal in endless hours!"

The crowd laughed when Morgan shrugged her shoulders and laughed. She walked off the stage, sitting down beside it, letting Ripley take over.

Feeling her way now since they went off script, Ripley told of how she founded Just One More years ago, beginning with just an acquaintance's horse, then a couple of neglected horses she'd come across. Over time, she'd get more calls from concerned strangers asking for help.

As the need for more space was apparent, she'd located an old deserted ranch in New Mexico and breathed new life into it as well as the horses she was keeping there. Photos were on the big screen of Just One More from the very beginning to the present to show the growth and need for facilities like this.

Having to work on her own business, Ripley explained how she'd hired her trusted relatives to run her new project. Needing the capital to build it, she simply worked more to avoid going into major debt. Then they began to have fundraisers to raise the much-needed money to care for the horses properly.

Her younger cousin was also ideal to hire as he was already in veterinarian school. With a smile, she said, "As soon as I heard he graduated with Honors, I just *knew* he was going to ask for a raise... which he immediately did. How could I say no?"

The crowd cheered.

"I had no idea of the impact I was going to be making in the lives of so many horses needing a new, forever home. And not only the horses, but the people who love horses enough to take one in and promise to care for it no matter what. Horses change our lives as much as we have the ability to change theirs. They are just more unconditional than we are.

"If I had never begun Just One More, I'd not be where I am today. And where would all those innocent horses be now? Especially a horse who needed unconditional and unlimited love, understanding and patience, like our last horse this evening needed?"

Ripley paused, a catch in her throat as she remembered the first time she saw Cappy. She took a moment to gather herself together and began her tale of how "This horse fell in love with me, head-over-heels in love, which," she said, "was a dangerous thing when there were four feet instead of the normal two!"

The crowd laughed.

She described how she had to sleep in the sand that first night. How this abused, scared horse had bonded with her and refused to let her leave his line of sight. "How does a horse pick its human? It may be one of those mysteries we may never fully understand.

"But, for whatever reason, this horse chose me. And it was an honor, it still is, to know I'm his human. He's my horse simply because he chose me first, and I'd not want to break that bond, that trust, he has in me."

Figuring it was a good lead-in for her surprise later, she even told how she was awakened in the morning by the horse. "He was trying to tear through his stall simply because there was a man present. He was trying his best to warn me of impending danger.

"This is when it became apparent he hated men. I don't mean he *disliked* them, I mean *hated* them. He practically tore through his stall trying to get to any man that he saw or heard. Just *seeing* one, he'd break out into a sweat, his skin shivering, the whites of his eyes showing his true distress. I'd like to throw eternal shame on the men in his past that turned a loving, innocent animal into a terrified, tormented, hateful one!

"That morning when he woke me, he felt *I* was in danger," Ripley explained honestly. "After all, to him, men represented a loss of safety, identity, of self, of freedom, of the basic right to live as God had created him to do. Like an abused human, his distrust became his all-consuming thought. And distrust often breeds hate out of that fear, which can breed violent acts.

"Sometimes these acts are purely *defensive* ones after a wrong or an abuse has been committed. But in other cases, they are *offensive* in the animal's—or the human's—natural instinct of self-preservation.

"That morning, just *seeing* a man near me, this horse's only thought was to warn me, to protect me. Horses can be very protective of their people. And I have no doubt that if he'd broken through that stall, he would've attacked in order to do it. Horses are really no different than humans. They feel. They learn. They mourn. And most of all, they *remember*.

"When I awoke that first morning, I realized almost immediately the reason for his sudden distress. He was quiet as a lamb when it was just me, but that changed when a single man happened to come in the barn. He'd been looking down at me sleeping in the sand on an old horse blanket with two dogs by my side."

She heard the *oohs* and *awws* and smiled.

"Yeah, that was my exact same response, too, once my head cleared from whacking it on the wall after he startled me awake."

The crowd laughed and clapped.

"As it turned out, three things just never really worked out there in the beginning: Me, sleep, and that man! And I mean that in a purely professional way!"

The crowd erupted in whistles, laughter, and cheers. She saw Morgan laughing on the side of the stage and grinned back.

"Yes, every time I wanted to sleep, there he was... Knocking on my door waking me up!" She smiled at the laughter. "But, you know, I always respected the fact that Morgan and Josh Wright, and Ty Stanton, all from here at Harmony Hills, never once were too proud to come and get me when they needed assistance with this particular horse.

"They never once hesitated to swallow their pride and come ask a woman to help them with an abused horse who'd bonded with her. Rather than twitching this horse or fighting with him, or even drugging him, they... or rather *he*... would come knockin' on my door, waking me up, requesting my help.

"And I honestly never thought of not coming. For, you see, it wasn't about me and my needs, but about the *horse* and *his* needs." She waited for the clapping to die down. "Thank you."

With sincere passion, she explained, "When it came time to handle this particular horse, my role was simple. I was there for his safety, for his support. I was there to keep him calm and focused. Telling him it'd be all right, that no harm would come to him while I was at his side. And that we'd get through it, together.

"That no matter what his past had been like, we were making a new beginning then and there. All he had to do was trust me, believe in me. I wouldn't leave his side, and I wouldn't leave him alone."

She waited a while for the clapping to die down. She then deadpanned, "So once I got that *man* calmed down, *then* I went to go get the horse!"

She got a standing ovation for that joke and laughed along with the audience. Morgan was nearly doubled over in her laughter, Ripley saw.

Once the audience was seated again, Ripley explained, "It took time, skill, and patience working with this horse. Sometimes males are just harder to work with, but we women understand this. Right, ladies?" She smiled at the laughter. "Yes, I'm just kidding, men. Well, to a point." She grinned at the laughter. "It really goes both ways, I know."

She paused, thinking. "I remember something Ty Stanton, that handsome man in the picture..." She looked at Rory and Kim, asking, "Can you pull up that picture of us walking Cappy toward the trail? Thank you," she said once it was up on the large screen behind her. "You know what? Could I have a copy of this? That really is a great shot!" She smiled at the laughter from the crowd.

"Back to the handsome man there." She smiled at the whistles. "Yeah, I know. Trust me... *I know.*" More laughter, cheers, and whistles.

Ripley stood there quietly for a few seconds before she shook her head and admitted, "As usual, that man has stolen my concentration. I forgot where I was going with this whole thing!"

The crowd loved it, and their laughter and whistles gave her time to recall what she'd meant to say.

"We love you, Ripley!" she heard some people yell out. Recognizing their voices as her work friends, she grinned and quipped, "Yeah? Open up your checkbooks and prove it!"

The audience laughed.

When she remembered where she was going earlier, she laughed and held up her hands, a signal she had her wits back.

"Thank you. I've never done that before!" She smiled at the cheers. "Anyway, he told me right after he woke me up that first morning as he was, I found out soon after, taking me to breakfast..."—laughter and smiles from the enthralled crowd—"...that the mind is a powerful thing. And that it can latch on tightly to things, creating an invisible bond that can be nearly impossible to break. But that even the strongest cable has to have some give to it.

"And that is so true. And that bond can be negative or positive. In this case, the horse's bond with me was, thankfully, positive. The only negative thing we had going was when he couldn't see me, he'd bang on his door. It was a true worry to all of us, but we finally worked through that.

"It took weeks and weeks of patience with this last horse. It took understanding from *everybody* that it wasn't his fault he was like this. He wasn't *born* being mean and hating all men. He wasn't even born by choice.

"Can't you just picture this horse as a baby? Being frisky and happy in a sunny pasture? An adorable foal nursing from his mom? He probably loved to have someone pet him, brush him, and talk to him. He wasn't born expecting a life of abuse, torture, and starvation. He wasn't born just to be unhappy and miserable until it was his time to die.

"Uncle Joe once referred to him as Black Beauty. And Joe? That is really an apt description. If any of you haven't read *Black Beauty* by Anna Sewell, you need to right away. It's not just a book for kids. It's for everyone of any age. It's timeless.

"In this case, after much work and speculation, and yes, some progress, we narrowed his behavior down to a simple thing as him needing dental work. Imagine that! He just needed to have his *teeth* worked on, and that was really the next turning point in his attitude.

"He'd been living in terrible pain, and his behaviors were simply signs of his very real distress. He was just trying to tell people what was wrong. He just needed a dentist!

"But instead of the people previously in his life trying to figure out what was *causing* his actions, they beat him instead. That mistreatment then caused his behaviors. It's all cause and effect. It's a vicious cycle that must end!"

She paused, trying to control her temper she felt bubbling up at the thought of what Cappy and countless other horses had gone through. "Let me tell you all something right now—You cannot beat a severe toothache out of any living animal any more than you can a human. As many horse whisperers have agreed upon, 'People don't have horse problems, horses have people problems.'"

Clapping and nodding of heads.

"And I really want to stress something else here. Morgan Wright has graciously given me the credit for this horse's turnaround. She's right, of course." She smiled at the laughter. "I had to say that because I'd never want to tell her she was wrong." More laughter. "But she *was* right, but only to an extent. Yes, I was here to calm the horse, for him to have someone there he trusted, to show him these people, these *men*, weren't there to hurt him, but to help heal him.

"But so was she and the other women here. I would have to say it's more accurate in saying I, and later the other women, were more like liaisons between him and men. A channel for open communication.

"He just needed a change of environment and of heart. To be given the basics of love, healthcare, of simple understanding, and the opportunity. To have just one more chance to live as we all want to. That we all have the *right* to. I think we can all learn from this horse, don't you?"

More clapping.

"Although I was the horse's... stabilizer, the ones who *truly* deserve the credit for this horse's turnaround are the *real* men who had the faith, and the *guts*, to get in with this horse to begin re-training him for a new life.

"Let me tell you, that video seems mild to what he was like in real life! We took precautions so it was safe for both man and horse. But it still took a strong, real man to be willing to risk injury to go inside a round pen with an animal that weighs about twelve hundred pounds, who he knew didn't respect him on sight. Ty and Josh are real men. They know it takes care and reciprocated respect when you truly love an animal, especially one who needs help."

Ripley paused before saying, "Real men never abuse an animal. Real men take the time and effort to understand, to be patient. This applies to women, too, of course."

Ripley paused and briefly debated with herself before saying with true feeling, "Force and abuse have absolutely no place with a horse... or any animal. If you can't love and respect an animal unconditionally, then you have no business having it. If you can't love and respect an animal for being what and who they are, then *why* should they respect you? It's a two-way street.

"Just because we're the humans, it does *not* make us automatic masters, or make us better than they are. I once had a couple of people who'd been close to me admonish me by quoting the Bible, saying we have 'dominion over all the animals, per God.' They said it was their right to basically do whatever they wanted to any animal.

"My reply to that horrendous mindset is that having dominion over an innocent, trusting animal doesn't give anybody the right to abuse, torture, or neglect it. If that's your God or your religion, I'll look for another, more compassionate one. He made my heart, and apparently yours, too, a caring one toward animals. If God didn't want us to care for and love animals, then why *can* we?

"We *all* deserve love, compassion, care, respect. Be responsible, and give that animal to someone who does. You don't dump animals either. You find a safe place to take them to."

A standing ovation with approving nods from the audience gave her hope that her message was being heard. Would they carry it out for her and for so many others who cared? she wondered.

After the audience sat down again, Ripley went on, "I could've probably easily trained this horse to do tricks, but that wasn't what he needed. He's not a circus act. He needed a man to work with him, not a woman. So I can honestly only take so much of the credit. I just made it safer for both man and horse to learn to work together, to be able to open that line of communication between them.

"That being said, I want you all to give a huge round of applause to Ty Stanton and Josh Wright for being willing to work with Cappy to improve his future. To even having one. And to Toby, Bo, and Drew for helping out!"

She smiled and clapped along as the audience showed their appreciation for the work the men did, and many in the crowd even stood back up.

"Also, I want to thank Morgan Wright for her remarkable facility here, her flat-out passion and love for every single horse she encounters, and her incredible hospitality and openness. We met by complete accident one day... By that, I mean she hit me." She smiled at the laughter. "Okay, I'm joking about that. But we *did* meet in an opportune moment and somehow through the twists of fate, here we are.

"She's one of the best humans I've ever met, with a humble, generous spirit, a quick wit, and a sense of humor. Her compassion and loyalty are traits that I greatly admire. Please give a huge round of thanks to Morgan Wright, owner of Harmony Hills Equestrian Center!" Ripley motioned for her to come up.

When Morgan came back on stage, she waved and bowed to the cheering crowd. Ripley motioned for her to stay with her.

"I'd also like to thank from the bottom of my heart everyone else involved with Just One More, including my relatives Joe, Lilly, and Dr. Steve Ceravolo who are all here this evening, and to those here at Harmony Hills who did their best in caring for all the horses we rescued late that night.

"Pretty much anybody here you speak with was involved in rescuing these horses, especially Maya, Toby, and Bo who were with Morgan and I with the trailers that night at the site. But Alexis, Mel, Kat, Rory, Kim, and Drew were also here to care for them.

"Also, Laura Hinton helped the staff here prepare for their arrival. And the two veterinarians, Dr. Shamis and Dr. Sanders, also stayed here until two o'clock that morning to help them. Dr. Shamis, would you please stand up? Let's give this man some love, everybody!"

The audience clapped as the vet smiled and waved before sitting back down.

"You'll be hearing from Joe and Dr. Steve Ceravolo from Just One More in just a few minutes but first I wanted to say something else before I forget..."

Smiling, Ripley waited for the cheering to die down before she said, "I bet you thought I was going to talk about that handsome man again, didn't you?" She smiled at the laughter before she said, "Not this time. I wanted to thank *you* for coming out, to donating your hard-earned money for such an important and life-changing cause.

"Just One More, as any facility that relies solely on donations and most often volunteers, sincerely appreciates every single penny, nickel, and dime that's given to us so we can help horses have a better life. It costs a lot to care for horses, from feed, vet and blacksmith care, to taxes on the land, insurance, to payroll, to repairs and maintenance of buildings, tractors, and fences. Please believe me when I say every penny, every nickel, and every dime, *does* help us!

"For those who wish to donate more to help us be able to help the horses in our care now, and for future residents, there's a secured donation box placed behind the seating area by the office that you can use, or if you prefer, you can give directly through our website or via phone apps, which are all listed in your program. Donations can also be given via the websites of Just One More, Harmony Hills as well as our featured Guest Entertainer this evening, Raina Stewart-Scott.

"I humbly ask you all to spread the word of our mission, to allow us to continue changing the lives of horses, and the caring humans who are looking for a forever companion."

She waited for the clapping to die down before she signaled she was ready for Cappy to be brought out.

"Okay, so I'd now like to bring out the last horse we rescued that long ago night. He was the last one out of the wrecked semi-trailer. He's a prime example of what we can do to save abused and neglected horses when we have the funding to do so, of what they can become again—free, trusting, and loving.

"He was nicknamed Cappy, but like all the horses who don't have names at Just One More, we give them a new name for a new life. Having a nickname me and a certain other person were given many months ago, I've decided to give that same name to this horse. Seeing as he's really a part of both of us, two people who came together in this amazing journey to heal one troubled horse. I'd say we've *all* been rescued.

"So here he is, our own proof of what love and understanding can do... *Riptide!*"

Chapter 52

AFTER ALL OF THE speeches were over and the band and Raina were getting ready to go on stage, Lilly and Annabelle caught up with Ripley and Morgan.

Lilly exclaimed, "Ripley Capilano... That was the *best* presentation I've *ever* seen you do! And your humor made it all so earthy..." She smiled and hugged her niece tightly. "Oh, I just love your surprises!"

Ripley and Morgan both looked at her before Ripley said, "Oh, but *that* wasn't the surprise at all, Lilly. Unless you count Morgan calling me up early while my mouth was full of food!"

Morgan laughed. "How was I to know that? Besides, you pulled it off with ease. You were a complete natural up there. And Joe was so eloquent. It's hard to imagine Steve being so real and serious since he's always joking around, but his knowledge and passion clearly showed through. I bet he and Doc Shamis would love to get together. I'll be sure to introduce them to each other. This whole fundraiser is looking to be a fantastic thing all around!"

Annabelle nodded. "I agree. It's been an impressive event so far! What's the surprise then?"

Morgan shook her head, smiling. "Nope. No special privileges. You'll have to wait like everyone else!"

Morgan happened to glance over Annabelle's shoulder and saw Ty and Josh heading toward them. "Oh! We gotta run! Now. Mom, Lilly, keep those two men from following us, but be natural about it! Julia should be coming around any time, so look for her. You remember meeting her earlier, right?"

Both older women nodded, both wondering what the younger women were up to as Morgan rushed out, "Great! You all need to get back down to the stage area because Raina is starting soon... And take those two guys with you!"

Lilly started saying, "But I think Ty wanted to tell you—"

Morgan began pushing Ripley away, interrupting her, “Sorry! No time right now. Later!”

Laughing, Ripley and Morgan took off as quickly and as naturally as they could.

IN THE LIVING ROOM area of Ripley’s RV, Morgan smiled at her. “You’re a vision, Ripley! He’ll fall out of his chair for sure.”

Ripley laughed, smoothing her hands down her gown. “That’d make my night. The two of us would both look like fools together.” She gave a nervous smile before confirming again, “You’re *sure* wearing cowboy boots with this gown doesn’t look stupid?”

“Are you kidding me? Who’s gonna be lookin’ at your *feet?*” Morgan smiled again, encouraging her friend. “Anyway, it’s better to be safe!” She handed her a tall glass. “Here. Drink up.”

Ripley gratefully took the rum and Pepsi from her hand and drank it.

Slipping her light trench coat on to cover up her gown so she wouldn’t attract too much attention, she said, “All righty then. I’m ready to go out there and grovel for my man for all the world to see!”

“*That’s* the spirit!” Following her out the door, Morgan added cheerfully, “Maybe people will be so overcome with emotion, and the joining of Harmony Hills and Just One More, they’ll give even more!”

“Or they could ask for a refund,” Ripley retorted.

“We don’t give those. It says that in writing.” Morgan smiled at her friend’s chuckle.

Ripley carefully turned around to lock her door, slipping the key into her coat pocket.

They discreetly made their way to the back of the stage, listening as Raina belted out another song.

Ripley said, “Man! She *is* terrific! Her voice is clear and has such a quality to it. Ty told me once the first time he heard her sing he couldn’t believe it was coming from her. I see what he meant. I thought rehearsals were impressive, but she saves it all for her shows, doesn’t she? And she’s pregnant on top of that!”

Morgan nodded. “Yeah. Now don’t you feel bad about yelling at her the other night?” They both chuckled. “I’m glad we hired her. And that she’s singing here and not at The Neon Moon on karaoke night. I’d hate to sing with her around…” She clapped her hand over her mouth. “Oh! That came out so wrong and is so ill-timed! I’m sorry, Ripley.”

Ripley had to smile at the stricken look on her friend's face. "It's okay, Morgan. I'm in no way going to compete with Mrs. Scott out there. If I survive it, awesome. If he loves it, even better. If I choke up and die, perfect! Make sure all posthumous donations in my honor go to my place, okay?"

Morgan wrapped her arm around Ripley's waist in encouragement. "Ripley, your voice is beautiful too. We rehearsed this song, you know it by heart, and you look absolutely ravishing.

"And what's even better is that song seriously fits you two! The words literally fit your situation. It's like it was written for you guys. He'll get it!" She handed Ripley another tall glass of liquid she took from a cooler by the corner of the stage, ordering, "Drink this. All of it."

"What is it?"

"Raina's special concoction, she said. It's probably basically another Captain Morgan. She made it before she went up. She said it'll help with your nerves, remember?"

"But I already had one in my RV after your shot of Irish Whisky, remember?"

"Of course I do. I'm not the one drinking. You are. Have another!" Morgan grinned, raising Ripley's hand holding the drink to her face.

Ripley took a cautious, tasting sip. "Go make sure he's there. It won't do any good if he's not even out there. And I'm *not* doing this a second time!" Ripley shoved at Morgan. "Go look."

Ripley took deep breaths to calm her nerves before drinking the rum and Pepsi. How long would it take for it to kick in, she wondered? After she was done? She smiled at the thought. But she had to admit, she *was* feeling somewhat more relaxed already.

Morgan walked out, casually looking around. It was hard to see around all the dancers and the big crowd even when she knew where she was supposed to be looking.

But between them dancing in the open area just for that purpose or at their appointed seats and tables beside each other, she spotted Julia, Ty, Josh, Channion, Damien and Laura with their two children, Annabelle, Pops, Joe, Lilly, Steve,... and *oh!* Ty's parents were there too!

She wasn't told they were coming! How did she not see them earlier when she walked around? Since she didn't eat dinner at the table, she simply didn't see them at all. Almost in a panic, Morgan didn't know if she should tell Ripley or not. It might freak her out either way. What should she do? She wondered if Ripley would know his parents by sight.

Debating with herself, she decided to not say a word. Ripley seemed confident right now. Morgan didn't want to put even a dent in her armor at the very last minute.

From the stage, Raina made eye contact with her and Morgan smiled and nodded. Raina gave their signal for confirmation. Morgan nodded again as Raina never missed a beat of her singing which impressed Morgan. Morgan then looked over at the Sound Guy, as she called him. He saw the nods between Raina and Morgan, so he was ready himself. He nodded at Morgan. She nodded back.

Heading backstage, Morgan smiled, hoping her own nerves weren't coming through. She was suddenly as nervous as Ripley now.

"He's where he's supposed to be?" Ripley asked.

"Yep."

They soon heard the song end on stage. Once all of the whistling and cheering died down, they heard Raina asking everybody to take a seat for a special event.

Taking the drink from her hand, Morgan took off Ripley's coat. She straightened out the gown and her hair. She gave her back the tall glass of rum and Pepsi, nodding in approval once Ripley had drank it all.

"Good girl! I feel like I'm your Matron of Honor before you walk down the aisle."

Ripley groaned. "Oh, *that* just sent me in a tailspin, Morgan! Why'd you say that?"

"I'm sorry... I'm sorry! But at least it's a happy event where no one boos!"

"But they *can* object!" Ripley forced out a smile, held out her hand. "I'm shaking, Morgan!"

Gripping her shoulders, Morgan said, "I can't yell at you like you yelled at Raina because people would hear. All I can say is the world is a beautiful place as are you and your voice, and your love for my best friend. If Cappy was able to overcome his fears, so can you. Go get him, tiger!"

Raina was ending her little introduction, just summing it up by saying it was a special, requested performance for a certain somebody who did so much for this person. Raina then walked off the stage toward Ripley, slipping the cordless mic onto her now and giving Sound Guy time to put in the CD with the song's instrumentals.

They didn't speak even though they all knew the mic was off as Raina had whispered that news to them. Ripley tried to smile as Raina squeezed her elbow in encouragement before she pointed to the mic with a raised eyebrow. When Ripley nodded, Raina reached up and turned it back on.

Ripley took a deep, deep breath, and then slowly released it.

Once the portable stage lights lowered as they had requested earlier as a signal Sound Guy was ready, Ripley took another breath. With Raina and Morgan encouraging her with a touch of their hands, she stepped onto the few steps that led up to the stage.

Chapter 53

THERE WAS A HUSHED silence as the audience waited in anticipation for the lights to come on to see who the surprise performer would be.

In the darkness highlighted with the Arizona moon and stars, they could make out a walking silhouette coming onto the stage, coming to a stop near the center. At the small cue given by the silhouette, the lights slowly came up, not with the usual white-hot glare but just a gentle, soft blue spotlight.

As the performer's features became recognizable, the audience cheered loudly. Amid the clapping and the whistles, those who knew him and Ripley took a quick look at Ty. The controlled surprise on his face was there for them to see even in the dim light.

Ty's parents, Phil and Lois, knew Ripley just from her time on stage that night during the speeches. They were captivated by her beauty, humor, her passion, and professionalism. They hadn't yet met her because she could never be found. They both stared in wonder at the woman on stage in the beautiful gown.

Raina and Morgan quickly ran around to be there to watch in person and to be a support. They stood to the side, praying she did it as flawlessly as she did when they practiced earlier at The Neon Moon. They even did a mini rehearsal that very afternoon when they heard the guys went into town on a little errand.

It just hit Morgan what that errand was—Picking up Ty's parents! Who was going to be surprised now? she thought, humor finding its way through her nervousness for Ripley.

Ty felt Julia take his hand and felt her squeeze it. His heart was kicking so fast and hard in his chest, he wondered if anyone noticed it trying to leap out.

Was he dreaming this was happening? He knew how much she *hated* to sing in public, so he knew she was doing this solely for *him*.

He couldn't tear his eyes away from a Ripley he had yet to see. She wore a long, flowing dress, the bodice molded to her curves. The material hugging her torso was a deep blue. As it flowed down, it shaded into a lighter and lighter blue until the very bottom of the gown was pure white. The design was simple but stunning. Around her throat was a matching choker.

Perhaps because she knew he preferred it that way, Ripley had let her hair remain loose and long, with the soft, curled waves raining down her back with the sides twisted up and secured with decorative combs. The soft lighting lit upon her small smile and the tears in her eyes as she looked at Ty. She couldn't stop herself from looking at him.

She blinked back the tears hovering in her eyes as the music of the song "I Told You So" began. Every line in this song perfectly fit their lives, their relationship. When she'd heard Randy Travis singing it on the radio as she was driving over a month ago, she was stunned at how perfectly it fit them. That's when this idea began. She then also found Carrie Underwood's version. She loved both of them.

Ripley tried to block out all but the words of the song. She was hoping no one could see her legs shaking. She suspected they would, so she'd chosen a long dress to cover them.

She was looking directly at Ty as she began to sing in her clear voice. Passion and emotion made the song even more powerful than it already was.

The cheers from the crowd began loudly when the music first started and slowly dimmed to a hushed quiet as she began singing. Ripley drew upon what she felt inside for the man who changed her life. She sang with everything she had in her for Ty, and for what she felt for him, as the chorus began.

By the time she got to the next verse, she was so focused on the song, her nerves were gone. She locked eyes with him as she sang. She used her hands and facial expressions to express even more of the song all the way to the sweet end.

As the music slowly died away, the lights went down. The cheers of the crowd were loud and heartfelt as everybody was on their feet as Ripley left the stage. Morgan and Raina were both crying like probably every woman present. Even some of the men had misty eyes, including the men who knew Ripley or Ty.

Even the stoic Ty himself had a sheen of tears. He knew what it took for her to do this for him. And although she'd picked the perfect song, her effort alone told him all he needed to know.

Amid all the cheers and wiping of tears, Julia squeezed Ty's hand again to get his attention. She wasn't sure if his eyes were also misty, or if it was just her own making it seem like his were. She tried to quit crying, but she was such a romantic at heart, she couldn't help it. And Ripley was her best friend on top of that.

Josh handed her some napkins so she could wipe away her tears. She thanked him with a trembling smile.

Blowing out a breath in an attempt to get her emotions under control, Julia leaned close and said in Ty's ear, "Never doubt her love for you, Ty. She's the one for you, and I believe you're the one for her. If I were you, I'd go back there right now, grab her tight, and never let her go!"

He nodded, not being able to speak.

His beaming parents, along with Ripley's relatives and the bulk of the crowd, watched him as he looked around and pulled himself together. Damien and Laura both smiled at him, both very touched by Ripley's gesture of love for their friend. Laura was still wiping her eyes with her hands as the tears fell over.

Both Channion and Josh smiled widely, nodding their heads at him in their silent signs of encouragement, acceptance, and approval of his choice of woman.

Annabelle, holding a sleeping Jacob in her arms, and Pops, with Sasha on his lap, smiled at him.

Tilting his head toward the stage, Pops asked, "Ty, whatcha waitin' for? You sit there much longer, and she's bound to get the wrong idea, get embarrassed, and disappear on you!"

Ty's parents smiled and nodded in quick agreement. His mom was looking awestruck at her son. "Yes, my dear! He's right. She's wondering why you aren't there already, maybe wondering if she made a mistake... That took *courage* for her to do for you!"

"No, Mom. She knows better than to think that was a mistake. If she wasn't already sure of my love for her, she never would've done what she just did for me. Trust me on that." He smiled at those around him and said, "Excuse me."

They all smiled as he scooted his chair back.

Channion stood up with Ty and walked a few feet away with him, saying with emotion so only he heard, "You got yourself a winner, Ty. I'm so proud and happy for you. Ripley can make you as happy as I am with Raina. I think she's the next best chapter in your life like Raina has been for mine."

"Thanks, Channion. I hope you're right... I'm actually pretty sure you are," Ty said with a slight tremor in his voice as he was still overcome with emotion. With a smile, he then turned to walk toward his future.

THE RELIEF SHE FELT now that it was over made her dizzy. Or maybe it was from the potent concoctions her friends had made her drink. Ripley immediately went backstage with Morgan and Raina coming around the corner right behind her.

Morgan turned off the mic first thing since she got to her before Raina and wrapped her up in a rocking hug. "Well done, Ripley! *Well done!* It was a gorgeous performance we'll never forget!"

Ripley wiped away her own tears of relief as she held onto her friend.

Pulling back a step, Morgan asked, "You okay?"

Ripley could only nod at that point. She was slightly shaking in a post-adrenaline rush.

Raina gave her a strong hug next, wiping her own face with some paper towels before she headed back onstage with the band. She noticed they were all still quite touched by Ripley's performance, clapping and cheering with the rest of the audience.

Raina held Ripley's hands and squeezed them. "You did a beautiful, *beautiful* job, Ripley! You have every soul out there in tears. I'm not sure how I'm supposed to go out there now. How am I supposed to top *that* performance? Get my unborn kid to sing?"

Ripley smiled broadly, saying with a shaky voice, "Raina, you're amazing. I don't think you'll have any problem there. And thank you for your pointers earlier... And all the rum and Pepsi. Really. It was a sure cure."

"Works every time!" Raina agreed with a wide grin.

Ripley blew out a breath. "And I'm *so* glad that's over! He'd better have enjoyed it immensely as I don't intend to do anything like that *ever* again."

Morgan and Raina laughed.

Ripley shook her head, saying firmly, "I *mean* it. I'm *done* singing in public!"

Her two companions just laughed again.

"And I'm probably gonna have to go pee soon since you made me drink so much on an empty stomach..."

Morgan and Raina laughed at her again before they heard the roar of the crowd, their cheers and whistles starting up again. The women decided Ty must've stood up and was now making his way to the back of the stage. What else could he do?

Morgan said gently, "He's coming for *you*, Ripley. Now you treat him with great care, you hear me? He's one of the best men to ever walk this planet." After another quick hug, Morgan smiled again at her.

Looking at Raina now, Morgan said, "Get back out there, girl! Break's over. I'm paying you to sing, not cry." She smiled and winked at Raina as she began to quickly walk away. "Don't forget to turn on your mic!"

With a smile at Morgan as she walked away, Raina gathered herself together as much as her hormones would allow and squeezed Ripley's hands again. "Now you go and get that amazingly awesome man and make him your own. Treat him the way he *deserves* to be treated, Ripley, and I bet he'll treat you like a queen."

Raina then turned around to head toward the band members waiting for her. They all walked up the steps and back onto the stage together.

Ty came around the far corner of the stage and ran into Morgan first. She'd left Ripley so she could pull herself together and to give them the privacy she was sure they'd want when she ran into him. She automatically wrapped him up in a bear hug. She held on tightly and tried to speak, but her throat was closed up from trying not to cry. She gave Ty a watery smile instead until she could find her voice.

After a moment, Ty found his own voice. It was shaky when he asked his best friend, "You in on this?"

"Sorta, yeah... We just had to keep you away from her, but then make sure you were here tonight. Everything else, the entire idea, was all Ripley's." In a stronger voice she said, "She really and truly loves you, Ty. She was willing to bare her soul in public for you with the perfect song. It took a lot of courage for her to do that. I think she's *still* shaking."

Morgan also communicated with Ty with her green eyes shining even more brightly because of her sheen of tears. She rubbed her hands up and down his arms before she said, "Since Josh found me, you've been alone. You've been by my side for over a decade now, and it's time you made a bigger life for yourself. This is it.

"You two love each other like Josh and I do, like Channion and Raina, Damien and Laura, like your parents and Josh's. We all want the same thing for you both. It takes some work, but we all want you to have that happiness we feel. And Ripley is the one to feel, and share, it with. *She* just needed to know it for herself. She does now... with no reservations."

She took a deep breath and pleaded, with just a touch of humor, "Just don't forget about me, okay? And don't forget I love you too."

Ty listened to her words, knowing in his heart she was the best friend beside his cousin Channion that he could ever have found. His heart thudded in his chest when he looked over and saw Ripley standing there in her stunning gown, watching them.

He leaned down, kissed Morgan on her cheek, and said, "I'll always love you, too, Morg. And I'll always still be here for you, and you're still my best friend. That part of our relationship won't change. Ripley is good with that too. She's just my other best friend now like Josh is yours."

She nodded, tears rolling down her cheeks. "I know. And I'm passing the baton." She patted his cheek, kissed it quickly, and then walked away.

Ty then made his way to the love of his life.

Raina came back onstage with her band, still wiping her face with her hands.

Once she was sure her mic was back on and working, she said with a voice shaky with emotion, "Wow. I seriously don't know how to follow up with Ripley's performance! This is what y'all should be waiting for, you know? True love.

"Set your standards high, and don't lower them. Be true to yourself, and have faith the rest will come along. It happened for me, and now it's happened for Ty and Ripley. And it can always happen to you too!"

The cheers from the crowd made her smile and gave her time to collect herself. When the cheers quieted down, she said, "Are there any other romantics out here under this gorgeous Arizona sky besides me?" The crowd responded loudly. "Good! Well, let's crank up this party again and give those two backstage something to come back out here for!"

She laughed as the crowd shouted and cheered their approval as the band began to play.

As Ty walked away to go to Ripley, his parents sat there, more than a little stunned and more than pleased.

Lilly smiled, wiping her eyes. "Yes, indeed! That's what happens when we say *Let-'er-Rip!* That young woman has more class, style, and heart than most anyone I know."

She looked at Phil and Lois. "If your Ty is even half as great as I think he is already, those two are going to have a fantastic adventure ahead of them! I think they have a great chance of staying together, don't you? I don't think they'll fizzle out. I think she's finally found her man."

Phil smiled in genuine pleasure. "I'd say he is. Thank you, Lilly. He's made us proud parents many times over. And your niece, Ripley? I don't know *what* to say! I'm blown away... She seems to be excellent at everything she does. And even better, she appears to be very down-to-earth as she does it!"

Lois nodded, having wiped away her own tears with a napkin. "We've always hoped he'd find someone he could love and grow old with, to share life with. Someone he could trust unconditionally. He's been on his own for so long.

"Ripley is incredible! I can't wait to actually meet her. She seems strong, confident, passionate. He needs a woman like that. And her sense of humor keeps it all wonderfully balanced. Like you, Lilly, I think they've got what it takes. If not, I give up!"

Joe smiled. "She's always been strong. Once she found her way in the world, she took off. It took a lot of work, grit, determination, and guts to get where she is now. She's earned everything she's accomplished. She gets ideas, sets goals, and then works at them.

"We love her like she's our own daughter, and we couldn't be any prouder of her if she were. It's a shame her parents weren't here to witness this! I'm sure somebody recorded it, though, right? They'd be so proud of her tonight!"

Morgan came around to their tables and just sat down in Josh's lap with barely any warning. His strong arms came around her waist to pull her close. "Hey, sweetheart." He placed a soft kiss to her bare shoulder before he asked gently, "They okay?"

"More than, I imagine. I thought they might want some privacy." She wiped the tears from her face and tried not to cry any more of them.

"You?" he asked, just as softly.

Leave it to her sensitive husband to know how her heart was both joyful and sad in sharing her longtime best friend. Josh had never been jealous of her strong friendship with Ty even though he knew it ran deeply. Even before he knew why.

They both were also aware this was another step in her friendship with Ty, but this one was separating them just a little bit more like when Josh had married her. Morgan knew Ripley was to be first in Ty's heart and thoughts now, just like Josh was in hers.

Morgan truly wanted Ty to be happy, and that was only one of the two reasons she could bear it. The other was because her love for Josh was genuine, strong, and soul-deep. And she never doubted his love for her was the same.

Her mouth trembled, but she gamely smiled. "Yeah. It's all good, sweetheart. She's his, and he's hers. Just like you're all mine, and I'm all yours. I ran into him first and told him I was passing the baton."

He understood what his wife was saying.

She leaned down and kissed him sweetly. "You know how much I love you, right, Josh?"

"As much as I love you?" He smiled at her.

"Something like that," she said before she kissed him again, and then held him in a hug for a moment. She wiped the last tears from her cheeks and blew out a breath. Still leaning against him, she said, "I think Raina's hormones have transferred to me. I usually only cry at goodbyes."

He nodded. "It *was* a goodbye in one sense, but I think your tears are happy ones."

She blew out another breath, realizing he hit the nail on the head.

Josh kept his strong arms around her, anchoring her to him. One of the things he loved about his wife was she never cared if their friends or family were around. If she wanted to show him she loved him, she did. And he did the same. Since his parents were the same way, he figured that made them both feel more comfortable themselves.

Morgan looked over at Ty's parents, smiled warmly at them. "Phil, Lois! Welcome back. It's so good to see you two again! I had no idea you were coming.

"Here we were planning on surprising Ty when he turned the tables and surprised us with you two! I came out earlier to make sure Ty was over here, saw you and nearly died of a panic attack. I didn't tell Ripley you were here. It'll be up to Ty to break the news to her now!"

Ty's elderly parents genuinely smiled at her. Just like everyone else, they never understood how this beautiful woman and their handsome son didn't get together. Lois just assumed they would after they'd first met her about eight or so years ago, but it simply never materialized. She could sense their chemistry; she just couldn't grasp what kept them apart.

Then they'd heard that Morgan married this man named Josh, who they really liked and had to admit seemed perfect for her. They'd met him during one of their visits to see Ty. Both admitted Josh and Morgan were a strong, very well-suited couple.

Then when Lois first met Raina Stewart at their huge family reunion years ago, she had hopes for her and her son, but then Raina ended up with Channion. They made a wonderful couple, and now were starting a family of their own.

Happily, Lois nodded. "It's wonderful to see you again, too, Morgan! Ty called us a few weeks back, saying he wanted us out for a visit. He didn't tell us about his girlfriend until we arrived this afternoon, so to say we're in a little state of shock is an understatement.

"First, we learn he *has* one, then we see her onstage, hear her giving speeches, then she sings only to him... Nothing has ever been easy with that boy!"

Channion laughed at his aunt's words. When he and Ty had picked them up at the airport earlier and told them about Ripley, they'd been very pleased and surprised. And relieved. They didn't want their grown son to be alone. Their humor about it now was icing on the cake.

Smiling, Annabelle said, "You know what, Lois? Josh did that *same* thing to us in regards to Morgan. He never mention her at all until well after our plane landed, and we were halfway here! It was enough to give Patrick and I a heart attack from shocked happiness. There must be something in the water out here!"

They all looked at Josh and Morgan, and both of them laughed over the memory of that long-ago day.

Phil grinned and added, "We should've known *something* was up with Ty though. He was pretty insistent we be here. And I don't think that young lady even took note of anyone at this table except our son. And that makes me love her already."

Steve smiled as he looked at who he assumed would be future members of his family. "If you think you love her now, just wait until you meet her!"

Chapter 54

Ty walked through the shadows of the night toward her, a vision in blue and white under the Arizona moon and stars.

She walked straight to him, right into his open arms until their bodies were tight together, their arms locked around the other. They didn't speak because they didn't need to. They just held onto each other.

When he finally pulled back, his arms still wrapped around her, he said, "I didn't know I could love you even more than I did. You took my breath away, Ripley. I thought my heart was going to jump right out of my chest. I was sure everyone could hear it pounding.

"And knowing how you hate to sing in public, but you did it anyway... Just for me." He kissed her forehead.

She cupped his face in her hands and smiled. Her heart was beating furiously in her chest. "I'd do anything for you, my love. Even risk being shot down and looking like a complete fool. And even worse, singing in public!"

Smiling, he leaned down and captured her mouth with his. Their kiss began as sweet and tender, but then their love and passion deepened it. It was a long while before they ended the kiss and even heard the music and Raina's amazing voice belting out the words to a rowdy, foot-stomping country song.

Both fought to catch their breath, working to control their desires. There in the mountain valley, under the clear sky and the glow of the moon and stars, they knew this was what they'd both been waiting for their entire lives.

"I love you, Ty Stanton."

"And I love you, Ripley Capilano."

Ripley saw the love shining from his eyes. "Morgan said she was glad Riptide was back in town when she helped me get dressed. She's good with us. She told me so. I may not completely understand your friendship, but I want you to know that I completely trust you. And that I believe in you to love me forever. And I will do the same for you."

"There's nothing to worry about there, Sugar. She'll always be one of my best friends, and I'll always be there for her and her for me. She knows *you're* first in my heart now just like Josh is in hers and has been since they got together.

"Between our ups and downs, always remember I'm here for *you*. You belong to me like I belong to you."

She gazed into his dark eyes for a moment before she said, "Lilly told me a while back something that I loved. She said that great relationships aren't great because there are never any problems. They're great because two people love each other enough to be willing to work through them. You can't give up, but sometimes you do have to give in. She and Joe are prime examples of that.

"I want us to be like them when we're old, Ty. Still true friends. Still living life. Still in love. I want you to know I'm willing to work through those tough times with you. That I'm not one to throw in the towel at the first sign of trouble."

He nodded. "It's the same with my parents and Josh's. And my Uncle Ron and Aunt Janet. We can do it, too, Ripley. It'll just take work, patience, and compromise. And we can't take the other for granted either. We can't get lazy. We both know so many others who let it all go, and now they're alone. But I say we can work through whatever comes our way."

She smiled, nodded, and kissed him sweetly on his lips. She toyed with his hair, running her fingers through it. "So where do we go from here?" She looped her arms around his neck and waited.

"Nowhere at all. I'd say we're home, wouldn't you?" He kissed her forehead, letting his lips stay a second longer before pulling back. "Are you ready to park your RV? Are you willing, ready, to stay here with me now?"

"I meant the next step in our relationship," she explained although she had a feeling he knew what she was really referring to.

He smiled, knowing what she was asking. "I asked first. I need to know, Ripley... Are you willing to stay here, in one spot, with me? To make a home here?"

Ripley decided this was their first major compromise. "Yes. I'll just work from home, *our* home, here. I'll still need to take trips to events, trainings, and the like. Some will be short trips, others longer, but I'll live here with you. This, and you, are my home base. Can you handle that?"

"Yes." He smiled at her, kissed her cheek. "*That* was the next step in our relationship... You staying."

She waited, but he still didn't ask what she wanted to hear. Finally, she inquired, "Well?"

"If I ask again, are you going to cry again?"

"Most likely."

"Will you answer me this time?"

"Only one way to find out."

Ty decided to make her wait a little bit. Instead of asking what she wanted him to, he commented sincerely, "I loved your speech. I was holding... Riptide... and you about made me tear up. Then I had to walk out there, leading that horse, while everyone knew you were talking about me. That whole speech was one of the best I've heard, Sugar. I loved it.

"And I knew you were talking to me. The part about never leaving my side, forgetting the past, to believe in you, to trust you, and we'd make it together. That was for me, wasn't it?"

She smiled. "One of the things I love about you is your intelligence. I knew you were listening and would get it. I bared my soul in words and in song in public for you because I love you. And I sincerely hope you enjoyed it, babe. Just so you know, that's as extravagant as I'm going to get for you. Don't be counting on me doing that ever again! I'm *done* singing in public."

He flashed his grin at her. "We'll see!"

She suddenly figured out who he reminded her of and smiled broadly. Black hair, dark eyes, those facial features, his height, his physique, riding horses. How could she have missed it all this time?

Ty saw her smile bloom. "What?"

"Clint Walker." Ripley laughed. "It took me a year to realize you remind me of Clint Walker!"

"The Western movie star?"

"The one and the same."

Ty laughed, pleased with the comparison. He loved old Westerns as much as Ripley, so he was quite familiar with him. "That's quite a compliment, Sugar!"

Ripley tilted her head as she studied him. "You're not *exactly* like him, but there's enough for me to see it. It's been driving me crazy practically since the day I met you."

"I thought that's what *I* did to you!" he teased.

She laughed. "You did and still do!"

They stood there quietly, Ripley just resting her head on his chest, their arms around the other.

Ty finally broke their silence. "Oh, I have a surprise for you too. I tried to let you know, but you kept disappearing on me."

She laughed again. "As big a place as this joint is, it was actually hard to stay hidden from you. Morgan and I had a heck of a time running the other direction all day long!"

"Yeah, I got that. Josh and I were wondering what you two were up to. I was about to wring both of your necks. I still might." He grinned when she snorted.

He said, "I like Cappy's new name, by the way. He may still be known affectionately as Cappy though. But you're right that it's a perfect name for him—half you, half me. He brought us together, so it was only fitting to name him that. He's like our adopted son!"

"Funny you should say that because I've thought the same thing!" She paused before she asked, "Like him, we've been transformed, haven't we? The three of us are rescues. We all got a new life that started right here, didn't we?"

"Yes, we did. We rescued each other."

She waited, knowing he was stalling on more than one subject. Ripley decided to help him along. "All right then, what's *your* surprise?"

"My parents are here. Out there. They came here to meet you."

She froze in his arms. "No, they're not! *Are* they? Did they really..." She sputtered, her poise unraveling at the thought.

He laughed before kissing her again and hugging her. "It'll be okay, Sugar!"

"Will they like me? Seriously?"

"I think they fell in love with you. From speech to song."

She shuddered just thinking about his parents watching her sing her heart out to their son. She didn't know why she felt shy about it, but she did.

"Ty." Her tone had a slight warning in it.

"Ripley." He tried to hold back his grin as he mimicked her.

"Ask me. *Now*, dang it."

He grinned, leaned down, and kissed her cheek. Cupping her face, he asked tenderly, "Ripley Capilano, will you marry me?"

Her heart beat like a caged bird's wings before it simply got loose and flew free. With tears in her eyes, she whispered, "Yes... A most definite yes!"

She smiled, pulling his head down to hers to kiss him, letting her love flow into it. He did the same for her. It was a long, tender kiss that made them both want more. They finally pulled apart but didn't let go of the other.

Fighting back the tears, she asked, "What about a ring?"

"I don't have one on me. This wasn't my plan. It was yours, remember?" Ty teased her.

"Well, what am I supposed to show your parents? Out there?" she asked, grinning.

"Let's keep it just between us, at least for right now. They'll be here for a few days. One surprise at a time for them. Got it?"

"Got it."

Looking into her eyes, he asked, "Since it's just us right now, I want to ask you... Where do you want to stay? Did you want to stay with me while they're here or in your RV? I don't want to make you uncomfortable so you do what *you* feel, okay? My house will be a full house, but I have room for you—if you stay in mine," he added with a tender smile.

"They won't care if we share a room, Sugar. We're grown adults after all. And Channion and Raina are more than happy to have you there. They're here for about another week... or until Raina says he's clear to go back to work." He smiled, loving Raina for having Channion's back.

She considered. "I don't know. It's your parents, Ty. Channion and Raina, sure, but your parents?"

He smiled at her as she thought about it.

"Let me acclimate slowly here, okay? I'll stay in my place for at least a day or two, then we'll go from there. Let me get through this fundraiser, get settled in again. Meeting your cousins is enough for me right now, to feel relaxed.

"Obviously, I can come over, we can all go out, whatever, but let me still have my space right now. I still need my space." She cupped his cheek with her hand. "All right?"

"Sure. I understand. There's still no rush with us, Ripley. It's going to be an adjustment for both of us having you here all the time now. Neither one of us are going to rush it, right?"

"Right."

They stood there under the moonlight, listening to the music. It was now a slow song, and Ty led her into a slow dance. It was just the two of them, dancing in the Arizona sand. Ripley rested her head against his chest and sighed.

"So you had your parents come out to meet me. What if I didn't show up for the fundraiser? What would you have done then?" she asked, amused.

"Left," he said bluntly.

She laughed. "And where were you planning to go?"

"Wherever you were," he replied tenderly.

She pulled back a bit to look up at him. "Excellent answer," she replied softly.

Resting his hands on her hips, Ty said, "But I had faith in you. I trusted you to be here for something so important. And not only for Just One More, Harmony Hills, your friends... But for the horses. You wouldn't let *them* down, not after everything you did to save them. But I also had faith in *us*. I still do. And you didn't disappoint me."

"I'm sorry it took me so long, Ty. But I just needed to know you were different from the others. And that what we had was worth it. Worth the work to make it a lifetime trip. Thank you for allowing me the space I asked from you.

"It must've been so hard on you, and I *am* sorry about that. If it was as hard on you as it was me, I can never apologize enough. I'll do my best to not do that again."

"You'd better not. It *was* hard on me, but I was relying on what we had going to see you through it all. God knows, I missed you like crazy." He kissed her softly before saying, "You were worth it to me, Ripley."

She smiled at him and turned toward the stage, then back to him. She raised her eyebrows in a silent question.

"You ready?" he asked, understanding her look.

"No. You?"

"No, but we have to do it at some point. We might as well get it over with." Ty stroked her cheek with his knuckles before saying with a grin, "Maybe your heartfelt, romantic performance will double the donations!"

"After that? They'd better triple!" She hesitated a moment as she looked up into his eyes. "Julia told me you were the end of my rainbow. Truer words have never been spoken. I just thought you might like to know that."

Deeply touched, he just looked at her. "I don't know what to say, Ripley. *You're* the end of the rainbow I didn't really know I was even looking for... And never really thought I'd find if I did."

She wiped away the tears that plopped over and ran down her cheek. Swallowing hard, she said, "Okay. Enough of this romantic stuff for a while. We're getting way too mushy!"

He kissed her before he took hold of her hand, their fingers lacing together unerringly.

When they walked around the edge of the stage, they were immediately noticed, and the crowd began clapping and cheering. They made their way toward the tables where his parents and their friends who weren't currently dancing were waiting for them.

Channion walked up to them first. Hugging Ripley, he said just loud enough for her to hear over the music, "I sure hope you said yes this time!"

She pulled back and looked into his warm, welcoming eyes. Without a word, she confirmed it with a smile, a wink, and a finger to her lips.

He smiled back in understanding and nodded. "Welcome to our huge family, Ripley. If you need pointers, Raina will help you," he joked. "And you did a marvelous performance, by the way. It was extremely touching, and it hit Ty right smack in the heart. And I'm certain also everybody else's."

"Thank you, Channion. It'd *better* have touched him because it's not ever happening again!" She smiled when the two cousins laughed.

Ty led her to his parents, who couldn't be any happier to finally meet her. Ty and Channion smiled as Phil and Lois each hugged Ripley before asking her questions as they were pulling her into a seat next to them.

As they later danced to Raina and the band, Ty said, "I have to say, you did an excellent job at your idea of a date, Sugar. It's truly original in every way, I must admit. This is the best fundraising event I've ever been to. Definitely the first time I ever got engaged at one!" he teased.

Ripley laughed. "It'd better be your *last* time too! But just wait until tomorrow night."

He looked at her. "There's a tomorrow?"

"Sweetheart, there's always a tomorrow!" As the song ended, and she looked out over the crowd that was still gathered, she asked, "Do you know what I see most out of all of this?"

"What?" He looped his arm around her waist as Raina began another song and pulled her closer.

"Hope. Hope from these people to give hope to the horses still out there. It's what I see when I work my business, Ty. To me, my purpose is simply the same thing whatever it is I'm doing. Resurrecting hope in people and in horses.

"So many give it up, or they forget that hope even exists. Do you know how many more people and horses I still have to reach out there?"

"Yes. As a matter of fact, I do, Sugar. Just one more."

With a loving smile, he leaned down and kissed her.

Epilogue

THE TWO MEN WATCHED as Ty and Ripley danced to Raina's music.

Feeling contentment at what he was seeing, Jerrod turned to his friend. "She's passed all of your tests with flying colors. She's proved herself to be a woman of her word. She 'walks the talk,' as Nick says. She used her wealth and her compassion to return the horses here where they were safe and loved.

"And she seems to have his back as much as she had theirs. She's given hope back to them all." He paused as he watched them dancing. "They look really happy, don't they?"

Storm nodded, satisfied in the outcomes of his private tests. "I felt I owed it to him to have his back. He's had mine all these years without even knowing it, so I could do no less for him.

"I just needed to be certain she was the real thing and that she was trustworthy. And to know that she was *safe* for him. She's checked out on paper, but I needed to see it myself to be sure. I needed to see what she was made of. They deserve this happiness."

His friend said softly, "You do too. You can still find your own happiness."

Storm shook his head slightly. "My mission is still unfinished. And I *do* have some happiness. It's just that my happiness is bittersweet. Keeping an eye on her gives me enough to know this is how it all should be. She's safe and happy right now, and that's the most important thing to me."

Understanding who he was now referring to, Jerrod turned to watch the dancing couple again for a moment. "Well, we need to be back by morning. We came. We saw. We donated. We had our hearts yanked on. We ate and drank, and we had fun. You ready to go now?"

With a smile at his friend's quick and accurate summary of their night, Storm nodded. Using the table and a chair to steady himself as he stood up, he took a moment to make sure his bad leg would support him before walking. He glanced over to where the lady named Morgan was now dancing with Ty while Ripley now danced with Josh. He watched them for another minute, not knowing when—or even if—he'd ever see her again. The ache in his heart still hit deep, but it also had settled into a kind of acceptance. And he could only accept it because she was safe and happy herself.

As Jerrod and Storm made their way toward the parking lot, Morgan just happened to turn her head in their direction and saw them. With an inexplicable pull on her heart, she watched as the two men disappeared into the dark.

Review Request

Thank you for reading *The Rescues.*
I truly hope you enjoyed the journey of Ripley and Ty...and Cappy.
If so, could I humbly ask you to write an honest online review for me? What did you like best? How did it make you feel? Did it make you laugh, cry, etc.? Please give me the good stuff so I know what made you like/love it! Be honest.

If you didn't like it, please be tactful. (Surely there was *something* you liked?)

Thank you so much in advance!
Stay tuned for future releases.

Happy trails,
Jordan

About Jordan Standridge

An avid reader and writer since childhood, Award-Winning and Best-Selling Author Jordan Standridge is joyfully and happily expanding her literary sphere. Influenced by Walter Farley and Louis L'Amour growing up, and later Julie Garwood, Jordan now creates her own stories. Weaving many of her real-life experiences with her imagination, she infuses them with her humor, love for animals, life lessons, values, and romance. And then she'll probably add a dash of mystery and suspense because she can. A frequent traveler and mover, Jordan currently lives near Lexington, Kentucky.

Need More?

Thank you for reading my story!

Here's where you need to go now for some extra tidbits:

www.JordanStandridge.com

For a direct link, scan my QR code above.

Be sure to sign up for my newsletter:

"Join the Family"

www.JordanStandridge.com/newsletter/

For a direct link, scan my QR code above.

For signing up, you'll be sent a FREE character backstory—

"Where It All Began"

My FREE e-newsletter showcases upcoming cover reveals, book launches, trivia, background stories, promos, & more.

I hope to see you there! ~Jordan

Additional Resources

<u>PLEASE spay or neuter your pets to help curb the number of animals already in need.</u>

- NEVER leave your pets in your car. EVER. *(Leaving the windows cracked 1" or even 6" is <u>nothing</u> especially in the summer. Even in cooler temps, cars get hot and stuffy very quickly. Try sitting in one with all windows up yourself to see. Running ACs generally automatically turn OFF after a certain amount of idling time.)*

- NEVER make your pets walk on hot pavement or leave them in truck beds with no protection for their paws from hot metal. *(Touch the pavement or metal yourself. If it burns you, it'll burn them. Let them walk in the grass. Carry water and water bowls with you for their walks. Let them rest-especially little dogs with short legs. They tire so quickly. And clean up after them.)*

- NEVER yank and swing little leashed dogs by the neck so they "catch up" to you. *(Carry them if they get tired. Or stop and let them rest and cool off.)*

- NEVER leave your pets chained or tied up. *(This is cruel. Especially with no, or inadequate, shelter from the various elements, and/or with no food or fresh water. Animals need to run and play for their health. What if it got attacked? Or a fire, flood, tornado came? How could it defend itself?)*

<u>Continued on next page</u>

- NEVER leave your pets constantly caged, stalled, or penned. *(Be sure they have something soft to lay on and to protect their feet when they are. This applies even to animals raised for meat. Be humane!)*

- NEVER breed animals for fun or extra income. *(These are not inanimate toys. They are living, breathing creatures who feel and need care and love. There are millions—read that again— of unwanted animals already out there. Do not add to the problem. Irresponsible/backyard breeders are a huge part of the problem. Even responsible breeders can be too.)*

- NEVER dump or abandon your pets anywhere. *(Not in the middle of nowhere. Not on a street. Not when you move. Just don't.)*

- NEVER EVER throw an innocent, trusting animal from moving cars or do any other cowardly, despicable act. *(There's nothing more to say on this one.)*

- NEVER abuse them in any way. *(Physical abuse is unacceptable as much as verbal. Pets should never cower in your presence.)*

- DON'T yell at or hit your dog when it barks to let you know someone is there. *(They're only trying to protect and warn you. Say something positive like, "Thanks for letting me know. I hear them." instead. It's better than verbally or physically hitting your own dog for doing what most people get a dog for!)*

- NEVER use them for fighting for so-called entertainment. Ever.

- YES to vet care, being spayed/neutered, getting shots, nail trims, etc.!

If you don't, or can't, love them unconditionally, then find someone who will.
(Because they're already doing that for you.)

Remember they may just be a part of your world, but to them, you ARE their world.

Book Club Discussion Material

"The Rescues"

Book 3: The Women of Strength, Courage, and Hope Series

Also available for FREE downloading at www.JordanStandridge.com

1. When Morgan and Ripley meet by chance, Morgan says things happen for a reason. Do you agree/disagree?

2. Cappy and Ripley have an invisible bond that happened immediately. Why do you think Cappy chose her as his human? How was Ripley open to it?

3. Discuss the issue of sending animals to slaughter. Are there valid reasons for it? Or no excuse? Only if humane? Or not at all?

4. In Chapter 14, Ty surprises both Ripley and himself by driving to Phoenix to take her out. Discuss the courage, vulnerability, and nerve it (traditionally) takes for a man to ask out a woman?

5. In Chapter 15, Ty and Ripley set some basic ground rules for their new relationship, both wanting more than a "simple fling." Do you agree ground rules and talking out the basics are essential, or is it just easier or better to "wing it"? If one of you decides to break your rules, what happens then?

6. Also in Chapter 15 (this is a good chapter!), Ripley lays down her rule/beliefs for why she won't have sex with Ty. When he surprisingly agrees with her, she automatically thanks him—then gets immediately angry that she did. Discuss her reaction, and why she even had it. Do you agree/disagree with her viewpoint?

7. Discuss the parallels of Ripley and Cappy bonding with Ty—and his trusting them.

8. In Chapter 20, Ty and Ripley discuss the shortfalls of Americans learning another language. Do you agree/disagree?

9. Also in Chapter 20, you may have learned ASL (American Sign Language) is the 3rd most-used language in the USA [after English and Spanish]. What are your thoughts on this?

10. Still in Chapter 20, Ty relates a story about a male customer ignoring Morgan (a woman) to speak to Ty (a man). He discusses misogyny, and how he hates it. Discuss the type of man it takes to condemn ignorance like that.

11. Morgan senses, even hopes, there's a romance brewing between her best friend and Ripley. Discuss why she feels this way even as she knows it could take Ty away from her.

12. In Chapter 21, Josh speaks about the relationship/deep friendship between himself, Morgan, Ty, Damien, and Laura. Nowadays, it seems more like luck to find people who have this kind of bond and maturity. Do you agree/disagree? What should we all do to have this for ourselves? Is it possible anymore?

13. Also in Chapter 21, we learn that if something were to happen to Damien and Laura that Josh and Morgan get full custody of their child/children. Damien and Laura were smart enough to plan ahead. Give the reasons why they chose Josh and Morgan. Do you have something like this in place for yourself? Do you have end-of-life measures in place (POAs, DNRs, wills, etc.)?

14. We learn early on that Ripley lives in an RV and travels the country for work and adventures. Is this something you'd like to do? How hard/easy would it really be?

15. In Chapters 22, the gang is at The Neon Moon. We learn Laura is pregnant and a bit scared due to her past miscarriages. How do you support a woman (and father) who has experienced this? What is the right/wrong/best thing to say?

16. Also in Chapters 22-23, Ripley stresses she does not want to sing karaoke, but she's basically coerced into doing it. Later she resents being pushed into doing it, but she also admits to herself it was harmless and to pick her battles. Do you

agree/disagree with her sentiments about this situation?

17. In Chapter 23, Ripley is astonished when she realizes her new friends had automatically stopped drinking alcohol in order to later drive home safely. What do you think about that happening? She also reveals her personal thoughts about groups of people going out, and why she avoids doing it herself. Do you agree/disagree with her viewpoint?

18. Ripley makes note that she can tell a lot about a person in regards to how they treat not only other people but animals. Do you agree/disagree? Why?

19. In Chapter 25 especially, different methods of "controlling" a horse are mentioned by Ty and Ripley. Ripley also realizes what problem *may* be to blame that started Cappy's behavioral issues that possibly resulted in those awful methods being used on him. Have *you* ever thought to take the time to figure out *why* an animal behaves the way it does, or do you just assume the worst, and that's how it is? Do you try to take the time to understand? Is it the same with people?

20. In Chapter 25, it's also revealed that Ripley has a successful career in the oft-condemned network marketing business. How do you feel about this industry? Is it really a "scam" as so many people claim? Why does it work for many thousands of others all around the world if it's a "scam"? What is a *true* "pyramid scheme"?

21. In Chapter 28, Morgan and Ty discuss having a "void" inside of them, and how they believed one can be filled. Do you understand what they're referring to? Can you relate?

22. In Chapter 30, the rescues are ordered to be sold at auction. Discuss the issue of animal auctions. Do you ever consider these events from the animals' point of view? How stressful and scary do you think these places are to an innocent animal?

23. Ripley makes it a point to not tell Ty how wealthy she is. Do you agree/disagree with her reasons?

24. In Chapter 32, Ripley finally admits to Ty she's wealthy. Discuss Ty's feelings and thoughts about it, and her concerns. Do you think it's a credible issue

between men and women?

25. In Chapter 36, Ripley's internal thoughts cover stories of how men disrespect and treat women in regards to help/dating/sexual favors. Can you relate to these instances? If it happened to you, how did you react/respond?

26. After Ty and Ripley make love, she soon tells him she needs to temporarily break all contact with him and everyone else at Harmony Hills—but to trust her and not lose hope. She explains her reasons for it to Morgan in Chapter 44. Do you agree/disagree with her doing so?

27. Ripley had a little issue with Ty and Morgan's friendship, but she soon accepted it. Ty later learns that one of her own best friends was a man. He questions whether she saw the irony. Do you think she did?

28. After Ripley leaves Harmony Hills, months go by without her and Ty seeing each other. They both feel this actually benefits their relationship in some ways. What are your feelings on long-distance relationships?

29. In Chapter 39, when Raina tells Ty she's pregnant, he immediately places his hands on her belly. She responds by saying her belly isn't "community property," but she didn't mind so much because it was Ty. Have you experienced strangers/people doing this to you or someone you know? How did that make you feel? Did you say anything to them?

30. In Chapter 51, during the fundraiser Ripley gives an impassioned speech about the treatment of innocent animals and others that need help. And about the responsibility of humans in regards to them. Do you agree/disagree? Do you help support animal rescue centers/rehab centers/charities?

31. For the overall story itself, did you catch foreshadowing? Easter eggs? Hints? Throwbacks? Did you like the pace? The story? The ending? The humor? The values? The tone?

Sneak Peek

COMING 2026

Book Four

The Women of Strength, Courage, and Hope Series

The stories continue. The mystery is not yet solved.

More mystery, suspense, and true love are on the way from your favorite characters and some new ones!

Coming in 2026

For updates, sign up now at www.JordanStandridge.com/newsletter/

www.ingramcontent.com/pod-product-compliance
Lightning Source LLC
LaVergne TN
LVHW041056080826
845145LV00007B/1592

* 9 7 8 1 9 6 7 4 5 7 1 1 3 *